CU00429479

**First Edition**

**Copyright ©Gareth J. Reilly 2015 - Published in the U.K.**

G. J. Reilly has asserted his right to be known as the author of this work, in accordance with the Copyright, Designs and Patents Act 1998.

# Thanks

To Kath, whose confidence in this series means world to me.
And to David and Ju for their patience and enthusiasm.


Find out more at:

**www.gjreilly.co.uk**

# Piper

## The book of Jerrick
## Part 2

# Chapter One:
# Song Of The Unwanted

The gargoyles of the old Masonic temple glared out into the dimly lit street. It was one of the coldest nights on record and even their stone seemed to shiver. Mist swirled around them giving the air a greasy texture and hiding the stars.

At night, the alleyway that led to the temple's door was almost forgotten by the residents of the city. The only sounds to be heard there were the scurrying and scuttling of rodents and other scavengers, including the two-legged kind. They were the unwanted and the un-cared for people, the people nobody would miss. People that haven't really existed in any real sense for so long that nobody remembers them.

The heavy temple door opened, billowing warmth into the frozen alleyway. Slowly, bundles of cloth and newspaper stirred from their places against walls, other nearby doorways and from piles of discarded items that most people regard as refuse. They formed an orderly queue near the newly opened entrance as the heavenly scent of steaming soup wafted into the dark thoroughfare. A trolley appeared just outside the doorway, heavy with vats of hot food, empty disposable bowls, plastic cutlery and baskets of the most delicious looking bread. It was being served by ordinary people in ordinary clothes. The homeless were grateful. They were hungry. They were icy cold in the chill of the night, but they were grateful.

As the feeding continued, the line didn't appear to grow any shorter. More and more shambling mounds joined the back of the queue from the cover of the mist. There was barely any noise, save for the scraping of the ladle in the metal vats and the muffled, embarrassed thanks of the recipients. It had been this way for a long time. Even during the summer months the door had opened under the cover of darkness and food had been served without question of payment, as though someone did actually care after all. Without warning, a series of alarms began to sound, shattering the peace.

'They're coming!' yelled a voice from deep within the building.

The trolley was hurled into the wall opposite and the temple door slammed shut with a series of metallic clanks. This left the hungry to clamour and elbow each other out of the way in an attempt to salvage the last of the food.

At either end of the alleyway, beyond the choking mists, clumps of darkness began to mass, their long shadows hurled into the confusion of bodies by the streetlights beyond. Sensing the imminent danger, the unwanted turned in disbelief, some with bread half to mouth, some with hot soup dripping from bedraggled beards or unkempt hair. Then it began.

An enormous pressure crept in from both sides, causing the mist to ripple and condense into a thick, foggy blanket that wrapped itself around the helpless homeless. They began to panic like cattle corralled before the slaughter, trampling each other in an effort to escape their invisible cage.

'Don't struggle, it's not you that we want!' came a deep, resonant voice from one end of the alley, half drowned out by the mixture of alarm bells and cries. But the warning went unheard as the wall of force slammed up against the crowd from all directions.

Terror-stricken, panic turned to violence. Clothing and hair were torn, fingernails raked against skin and the jarring, snapping sound of bones could be heard over the howls of the immobile stampede. Blood mingled with the sludge of food, detritus and moisture of this grim place.

The shadows advanced into the gloom as unseen hands tossed the struggling homeless into the air and held them there. The pressure shattered the temple door into splinters and, leaving two of their number behind, the shadows forced their way inside.

Cautious and deliberate, they pressed on along the parquet floor of the entrance corridor and into the main hall. The windows had been blacked out with paint and the crunching of light-bulbs under foot gave the aged building a sinister feel.

'Eyes!' hissed the deep voice above the alarms.

Something clattered in the blackness before bursting with a loud bang and bathing the room in a magnificent glare. In the new light, the shadows became robes that covered the faces of their wearers. Startled, they suddenly came face to face with a group of assailants looking strangely identical to themselves.

Across the width of the hall, a row of wooden ramps butted against crudely framed mirrors that were connected by hinges. This meant that they could be easily be pulled like a curtain along runners set into the floor. Belongings discarded in haste lay strewn here and there, indicating that an evacuation had taken place. In the confusion of the fading artificial light, a low rumbling made itself present over the din of the ringing bells.

Soon the rumbling became an insistent, vibrating hum, causing cracks to spider-web on the highly polished glass of the mirrors. The panic in the air was obvious as the intruders realised what was about to befall them.

'Everybody down!'

One by one, the mirrors exploded outwards. Razor-edged shards of shrapnel shredded the air as the volley passed along the line, drawing screams from the Inquisitors. Fleeing the hall, they returned to the alleyway in terror, only to find that the guards at the door had released their captives and deserted.

The alarms ceased as abruptly as they had started. Only the pained groans of the injured and dying were left to mingle with the blind sounds of the city.

Minutes passed like hours before some were able to crawl out from the mass of twisted limbs. In the true spirit of the street, they gave themselves over to helping their comrades, knowing that no help would come from the world outside the alleyway. It came as a shock then, that in that desperate moment, the groans eased and the crying ceased. Even the ever-present heartbeat of the city faded, replaced by strains so beautiful that there was no choice but to listen.

The gentle music promised so much – comfort, warmth, food aplenty and love. All the listener was required to do was follow the pipe and patchwork coat and it could all be theirs. As well as the woolly calm of their minds, the injured found their bodies soothed by the melody. Within seconds the line reformed, and the Inquisitors joined them as they began to shamble towards the mouth of the alley, into the care of the Piper.

*** 

In the in-between of the mirrors, Michael, Anna and Lefrick were gaining ground on the line of evacuees led by Jerrick. It had been more than two years since Michael had been smuggled from the Inquisition's training programme to the safety of the Elder Council by his aunt. Though life was treating him well given the circumstances, he still missed his family at home and his friends at Braxton Academy – especially Tamara. But she was another problem entirely.

Leaving the academy had meant Michael's death, literally. And as far as most people were concerned, Michael was still deceased. Only his sister, Alice, knew different. She was still keeping in contact with him from time to time when Michael could get the odd message to her.

It wasn't often that he would, but on this occasion, Michael gave Alice her due credit for keeping his secret. When they had last spoken face to face, Michael had promised that he would try to keep in touch. He'd also promised her that he would try to set things straight so that he could go home. It was proving to be a lot harder than he'd expected.

There aren't many fourteen-year-olds who cope well with being chased by a society of upper-class megalomaniacs with psychic powers, such as the Inquisition. But life with the nomadic sorcerers of the Elder Council had its perks. The Council had believed that he was destined to become the next Grand Inquisitor, which is why they tried so hard to 'rescue' him from the academy. This left Tamara with the dubious honour of leading the Inquisition in their ancient struggle for dominion over mankind. Now that he was free of them, Michael had learned so much more than he had dreamed possible. And he had witnessed so many wonders - like the one he was witnessing at this point in time.

The London branch of the Council had left its temporary home at the old Masonic temple when their spotters had seen the Inquisition's scouting party approaching. Thankfully, the scouts had been so eager to please their masters that they hadn't waited for backup. It had given the Council enough warning to evacuate through the mirror portals, which led to the wonderland they now occupied.

The twilight grey of the sub-dimension between the mirrors was not a place to stop and admire the view, in spite of the vast sea of stars that lay on the horizon on all sides. Michael could already feel the presence of something more; something sinister and hungry that was heading for their ragtag group of refugees.

In this place, Michael's whisper might as well have been a shout. 'Anna, there's something out there!'

His aunt turned her head to check behind them. 'Just keep moving, Michael. The portals look farther than they are, especially when you know *they're* out there.'

Michael let his gaze follow the dim blue glow beneath his feet that indicated their path. Ahead of them, their comrades were nearing a hazy anomaly in the air. Standing out against the emptiness that surrounded it, he could make out a twisted, writhing obelisk that reflected the space beyond - like looking at a room through a goldfish bowl.

Jerrick stood to one side and began assisting the evacuees through the portal one by one, golden eyes sparkling like the stars around them. Each time someone passed back into the world, the crackle of static filled the air.

Michael, Anna and Lefrick weren't far behind them at all now, but the hunted feeling grew in Michael's bones. By the time they reached the clutch that was queuing for their freedom, the hairs on the back of his neck were standing on end. A cry from somewhere near the centre of the column set Michael's teeth on edge:

'Flayers!'

On command, a small band of individuals broke away from the main group, forming a protective semi-circle around the dwindling line, absorbing Anna, Lefrick and Michael into their number.

'Remember,' Anna called out to them, 'any power you use here is reduced tenfold. Put everything you can into your incantations, but for god's sake don't target them directly. I don't want anything on fire either. If it runs into the group, it could blow the portal!'

Sickeningly white against the backdrop and a few hundred yards to the right of them, the small pack of Flayers slowed their sprint to a prowl and surveyed their prey. Humanoid and starved in appearance, running on all fours with an awkward, lolloping gait, Flayers were the hyenas of the sub-dimensional plains. Half dead and hunting in packs, Flayers craved the energy of life, feeding on it greedily whenever they could, especially if the victim was fluent in the art of magic. A sorcerer's control over the natural energies of the world was to them as blood is to sharks – they could smell a meal from miles away. Sniffing at the air, the leader cocked its head upwards to let out a banshee-like wail.

'What are they waiting for?' Andy, the huge former doorman of the Masonic temple asked in bewilderment. 'They usually just charge!'

'That ...!' Michael responded, his finger shaking in the direction of a spectacle none of them would have thought possible, even in their wildest nightmares.

From behind the leading pack, as many as a thousand Flayers charged. Any normal, fit adult stood no chance of surviving a one-on-one Flayer attack. Sorcery afforded only an equal chance. But with these numbers, the fleeing group's options were limited to one.

'Jerrick, get them moving, now!' yelled Anna.

'They are working on it as fast as they can!' Jerrick yelled back in his diluted Middle Eastern accent.

As if answering all their prayers, another shimmering portals appeared beside the first. The column shifted automatically, pushing and shoving their way to freedom as the Flayers closed on them.

'We're almost there, Anna. Can you purchase just another minute?' cried Jerrick above the frantic commotion of the evacuees.

'Are you kidding me? Do you have any idea how many of them there are?'

Raising an eyebrow in his aunt's direction, Michael said, 'Wouldn't a barrier work?'

'They'd eat right through the energy.' Anna replied shaking her head.

'Not if we make it small enough to just surround us. They wouldn't all be able to hit the barrier at the same time, would they? It'd be like causing a traffic jam. Besides, how much can one of those things eat?'

'There's no time to argue with the boy, Anna. Here they come.' said Andy the doorman clamping his hand onto the shoulder of the person next to him.

One by one, arms went out to the shoulders of the guards to form a chain, until Anna was framed at the centre of the half circle. Palms upward, she muttered her incantation as the others chanted another song in unison beside her. In front of them, an almost liquid trail formed at chest height, throbbing with a glowing green light. It spread out to form a bubble all around the panicking crowd.

The super pack of Flayers struck the barrier hard, yelping in pain. Then their ranks splintered, enabling more to feed on the abundant energy. The sights and sounds of their gorging were sickening to the mind, worse so when Michael realised with horror that he'd been wrong.

The Flayers jammed behind the feeding line began to climb onto the backs of their leaders, engulfing the dome of the barrier. Through their concentration, the protection detail could see pointed fangs bearing down on them, dripping with a sticky ooze of saliva as the unspeakable horrors ate their fill. With each inhalation, the strength of the shield began to waver, crackling as it weakened.

'Okay, you're almost clear behind,' Jerrick warned. 'Time to get out!'

On cue, the sorcerers at either end of the chain broke their link, stepping backwards through the portals. Immediately, the strain of the loss was felt by the others. Outside the dome, Flayers changed places, replaced by hungrier mouths. Again the circle shrank as another two protectors dropped away to safety. This time, it caused the remaining group to stagger under the weight of the bodies against their mental efforts.

Just then, above the snarling gulps, a clanging, jarring sound rang out. The frenzied feeding stopped as the Flayers appeared to recognise the tune. Michael's eyes caught the faces of the ghouls closest to him and saw the hunger in them become a seething anger. From behind the shield of energy, every note sounded cracked and tuneless, as though a child were blowing a tin whistle in the street. The pyramid of Flayers began to collapse from the top down, and those at the rear of the pack lolled to one side.

'What is that racket?' Michael asked, breaking his contribution to the group spell.

Lowering her hands, Anna let the shield drop. 'I don't know, but it sounds close ...'

Her voice trailed as the dome evaporated and her eyes glazed over. The discordant din had become so rich and soulful that the remaining protectors stopped to take it in. It promised so much to them that they were drawn to it, feeling compelled to follow wherever it led. Not even the baying of the Flayers could drown out the sweet melody. The pack turned and broke into a fresh charge away from the portal, towards a new quarry.

Following in their wake, Michael's feet began to carry him to who-knew-where, his head not resisting the pull of the melody. He barely noticed the rough hands at the collar of his shirt but struggled to get free as they dragged him backwards. His eyes blurred, his ears vaguely registered a pop, and he barely felt the rush of air against his skin. Scrunching his eyelids closed, the lullaby had become discordant again, drowned by the familiar *whump* of glass shattering in reverse as the portals closed.

'Wha ...?' he managed, coming to his senses.

'No time to explain ...' said Jerrick, hauling Michael to his feet like a rag-doll and steering him into the familiar arms of Mrs Davis. 'Margaret, sweet tea for the nerves and a quiet place for them to lie down, I think.'

'Very well, sir,' the former academy housekeeper replied.

Pallid and shaken, Lefrick turned to his old friend, the palm of one hand wrapped around the side of his face and skull as he tried to steady himself.

'What was that, Jerrick?' he stammered, struggling with the words.

The genie already had his hand against the glass of the

mirrors again and turned with a grimace.

'It was the song of the unwanted!' he said and was gone before another word could be uttered.

***

Far away from the turmoil in the backstreets of London, cocooned in the comforts of the thirtieth Braxton Foundation Academy, Emily Parker clutched at her platinum blonde head as others looked on.

'I can't see them!' she said, sagging in her chair.

The room was dimly lit, the way it should be for a practiced seer to concentrate on the task at hand. Around the rim of the room, black cloaked figures sat, some with pads and pens, frantically taking notes. There were a number of robes with fur trimmed hoods amongst the onlookers, the lavish adornment signifying their rank within the Inquisition. But one, in particular, was set apart from the rest. His hood was down about his shoulders, revealing a face scarred over its right-hand side. Otherwise devoid of colour, the eyeball and pupil beneath the deep rent were still clearly visible.

'Can this be verified?' said the man's voice in measured tones.

'Yes, sir,' said another of the robes. 'I saw the same. One minute they were lying on the floor bleeding, the next there was this terrible music and they were gone.'

'Gone where?'

'I don't know, Mr Catchpole,' said Emily. 'It was like the sound was causing interference in my vision.'

'I want the assault team leader on the phone as soon as they get back to the staging area! When I find out who caused this foul up, I'll have their guts for garters!' Catchpole growled to a nearby scribe.

'Yessir,' nodded the scribe as he backed away to the door.

A smaller figure in a black robe trimmed with white fur strode to the centre of the room and placed a hand on Emily's shoulder.

'That's all for tonight,' it said with a vague wave of its other hand. 'We'll have a full report on the situation in the morning. In the meantime, there's nothing else we can do.'

The remainder of the crowd filed out, leaving just five Inquisitors alone in the room. Free to relax, hoods were dropped to reveal their faces. Lithe and athletic, with hair the colour of midnight, Tamara Bloodgood, Grand Inquisitor of the British Isles stared at the floor in deep thought.

'Why would they be feeding the homeless?' she asked of no-one in particular.

'Human shields?' said a newly uncovered face. He sported close-cropped black hair. The physique beneath his robe suggested a muscular, strong, yet lean body.

'I don't think they'd be that cruel, Rupert,' said Tamara.

'Well, this is the Elder Council we're talking about,' said Rupert. 'Since when have the things they've done been anything but selfish?'

'I know, but they're not desperate,' said Tamara. 'They had no idea we were raiding tonight, so there's no way they would have planned to use the homeless as shields. I think it's probably just coincidence.'

'I agree,' said a satin voice from one corner of the room. 'It's more likely that they were keeping the homeless around as witnesses. I don't think they were expecting us to attack with so many normals present.'

Catchpole rubbed his chin. 'I'm not so sure Clarissa. The Council have been more guarded than usual since ... the trials. They must have known we were coming for them, or how else would they have evacuated so quickly?'

Clarissa Cunningham, House Mistress of Solaris and trusted personal counsellor to the Grand Inquisitor, walked casually towards the centre of the room. Her mousey mane was as impeccable now as it had been before the hood had covered it.

'What I want to know is,' she said, 'how did they get out of there without anyone seeing them? We had guards at the back of the building as well, but nobody saw them leave.'

'When I was tracking the scout group,' said Emily, 'I could have sworn I saw myself in the light of the flare like I was looking in a mirror ... or more like a whole wall of mirrors. Then there was that piercing hum and everything went dark again until that racket started up.'

'Hmm, the same way they broke into the academy,' Catchpole snorted.

'What's that?' said Tamara.

'I'm sorry, milady, I was just thinking out loud. Modern Lore has a section on mirrors as portals, but until recently I was sure that it was just a myth.'

'Yes, I think I remember it,' said Miss Cunningham.

'But in all of the stories I've come across, I've only ever heard about individuals using them, never a group of that size all at once.'

The corners of Tamara's mouth turned into a wry smile as she recalled something from happier times. 'There's a grain of truth in every story.'

'That's what Michael used to say,' said Emily, raising her eyes to look at her friend and leader. 'Strange how it's sometimes the smallest things we remember about him.'

'I don't want to talk about it,' Tamara shot back. 'Mr Catchpole, have someone look into it would you? I'm tired and I think I should get some rest.' Turning, she marched out of the room. Leaving the door open behind her, she rested her back against the wall and sighed, unable to help overhearing the last of the conversation.

'Was it something I said?' asked Emily.

'I wouldn't worry about it, Em,' said Rupert. 'She's been like that since Michael's funeral. I don't think she ever really got over his death.'

'Nevertheless,' said Catchpole with an air of sarcasm, 'I must do as the Grand Inquisitor commands. I suppose I'd better get started. No rest for the wicked, eh!'

***

In her room, Tamara sat alone in the black leather executive chair behind her desk. For two years, she had been advised and counselled. Those people who had once been her closest friends were now her only friends. Despite being the figurehead of the Inquisition in her country, she

15

still didn't feel like she really led them. Though the final decisions were hers, Catchpole still seemed to be calling the shots. He'd explained his motives – that she was still only fourteen and that she needed guidance. But really, Tamara thought, he enjoyed his role as her mentor a little too much.

She pulled back the sleeve of her robe and played with the silver charm bracelet around her wrist. Tonight had been difficult in more ways than one. The High Marshalls would want to know how she had lost a scouting party and, more importantly, why there weren't at least three members of the Elder Council in custody. Catchpole would blame her inexperience as usual, but she knew there was nothing that could have been done to prevent the incident. She hadn't wanted to go along with her mentor's suggestion in the first place. But Catchpole had insisted that the time had been right and wouldn't take no for an answer.

'Michael wouldn't have let himself be pushed around like this!' she told herself. 'He would have stood up to Catchpole and done the right thing, I'm sure of it.'

She turned to the desk and picked up a small, framed photo she'd been given as a remembrance gift by Michael's parents. In the picture, Michael and Tamara were wrapped tightly in each other's arms. Mrs Ware had taken it from the back of a cafe they had been at together, just before Michael's birthday a few years back.

'Oh, pull yourself together, girl,' she said, dabbing at her eyes with the black sleeve of her robe of office. 'He wouldn't want to see you like this.'

She replaced the frame on the desk and turned out the

lamp, wishing there was someone she could talk to about Michael. Even though she had forgiven Emily and Rupert, she hadn't forgotten the part that they had played in events that had led to Michael's death. But worst of all, the emptiness that had consumed her for so long since the day of the trials had been replaced by a boundless, rational hatred of the Elder Council. Catchpole had discovered that they had drugged Michael's water, causing him to be incapable of defending himself during his duel with Tamara. It had ultimately led to him being smashed against the wall of the training hall and killed.

As she got herself ready for bed, something Catchpole had said piqued her curiosity. Reaching out with one hand, she mentally ran her fingers over the covers of the many books on their shelf in the study. In the two years since her inauguration as Grand Inquisitor, she had been encouraged to read as much as possible, until the bindings of the many tomes in her possession had become familiar to her senses. She felt, more than saw what she was looking for and, extending her will, she brought her copy of *Modern Lore* to her waiting fingertips.

The pages of the book began to flutter and turn, as if they had a mind of their own, coming to rest at a chapter titled *Musicians, Music and Magical Instruments*. Casting her eyes along each page, Tamara scanned the text to find a description matching Emily's vision:

## Der Rattenfänger von Hameln (The Pied Piper of Hamelin) and The Flute of Shattered Dreams

*... 1284, in the town of Hameln, legend tells ... man in pied (or motley) clothing came to rid the townsfolk of a rat infestation ... Robert Browning supports the traditional account ... Piper cheated out of his payment by the town's council ... vengeance through the abduction of the town's children.*

*... What is apparent, is that the Piper's flute (called the Flute of Shattered Dreams in some accounts) ... qualities far in excess of any instrument explored in the pages of this manuscript.*

*During his investigation, Browning interviewed descendants of the surviving child known only as Wilhelm ... music of the sweetest kind that appealed to the child's very soul and nature ... Other known survivors say ... a clanging din that sickens the mind and body ... requiring time to recover ... leads us to conclude that the Piper's melody cannot be heard by those possessing negative power ... though other exceptions may also apply.*

The book snapped shut under Tamara's guidance. It occurred to her that in all the furore of the night's events, she had missed something she really ought not to have missed. Everybody else had been curious about the mirror portals. Everyone else had wondered about the ghastly music that Emily had described. Everybody except Catchpole. Tamara picked up the receiver of the phone on her bedside table and dialled.

'Mr Catchpole? Yes ... No, I'm alright. Sorry to call you so late, but I think I have a few questions that need answers. I want you to tell me what happened tonight. I know ... yes, I'm sure there's a lot to discuss. Why? Because, Mr Catchpole, I'm the Grand Inquisitor.'

# Chapter Two:
# Underground Railroad

The small hours of the morning were uncomfortable for Michael. He'd suffered from nightmares for a long time. Originally they'd been about the history of a strange book that had belonged to Jerrick, which he still wasn't allowed to read. Then, after the trials to determine who would be the next Grand Inquisitor, he'd had nightmares about almost killing Tamara with a blast of fire; although, he was in control of his pyromancy these days.

That night, his nightmares were filled with the inhuman faces of the Flayers and the skin that sagged over their bony bodies. But it wasn't just the razor sharp fangs, or the way they were drawn to life with a furious hunger that bothered him, there was something else about this dream that he couldn't place.

He woke in a cold sweat, on an unfamiliar bunk, in a room that wasn't his. It wasn't the first time that he'd woken up that way. Just a few years ago he would have gone looking for Anna for comfort. These days, he logged the nightmares in his mind so that he could discuss them with his aunt later.

The smell of breakfast cooking was enough to convince him to swing his legs out of bed and go looking for its source. Before long he found himself in a brightly lit, pillared hall. It had magnolia coloured, plasterboard walls and had been set with tables and chairs. At the back of the hall, a wide hatch opened into a vast kitchen. There, his best friend's mother, Mrs Lucas and Andy the doorman were busy helping a number of other men and women to cook. The aromas of bacon, eggs, sausages and Mrs Lucas's most amazing vegetarian loaf were too tempting to resist. Scanning the room for a breakfast companion, Michael was stunned to see a face that he hadn't seen since his last days with the Inquisition. Striding across the hall, he came to a stop next to a very neatly dressed man in an impeccably well-pressed suit and black bow tie.

He cleared his throat, indicating to an empty chair. 'Is this seat taken?'

The well-dressed man looked up from his newspaper and practically threw his floral china teacup across the room. In one swift motion, he kicked his chair back to give himself space before throwing his arms around Michael's neck.

'Michael. Good to see you!' He let Michael go and stood back. 'Let me look at you. My good lord, you've grown into quite the young man!'

'Thanks, Mr Davis,' Michael gasped, trying to recover from the bear-hug. 'You're looking well, too.'

Davis's cheeks flushed as he cast his eyes to the floor. 'I … I … I didn't get a chance to tell you how sorry I was for poisoning your water at the trials. I thought I was doing the right thing by you. Can you ever forgive me?'

'There's nothing to forgive, honestly,' said Michael laying his hand on his friend's shoulder. 'Now come on, let's forget about that.' He motioned to the empty chairs again and took one for himself. 'I thought you were supposed to be coming to the temple after the trials. Every time I asked about you and Mrs Davis, nobody was willing to answer me. Where've you been?'

'Lying low,' the butler replied. 'After we cleared out of the academy, Jerrick thought it might be best if we didn't come back to London in case we were seen. Margaret and I were in service at the academy for years, as you know. It was agreed that there might be too many people in the city that might recognise us and start asking awkward questions. We didn't want them following us back to the temple, as you can imagine. So we went into hiding.'

'You've been here all this time?'

'Goodness no,' the butler gasped, and then seemed to gather his wits. 'No. Look, I don't know how much I'm allowed to tell you, Michael, but this place is relatively new. You must believe me when I say that if we'd been anywhere safe, I would have sent word. We only arrived here last week ourselves.'

'Speaking of here,' said Michael, 'where are we?'

'On the top of a mountain in the Brecon Beacons, far away from London,' said Anna pulling up a chair and looking as tired as Michael felt. 'Hello, Roger. How are you?'

The butler bowed his head in respect. 'Fine thank you, Anna. Michael and I were just catching up.'

'I'll take you outside later, Michael, so you can see exactly where we are,' said Anna. 'But for now, I want you to promise me that you won't go out without an escort.'

'But ...' Michael protested.

'I know you can look after yourself,' Anna sighed. 'Just trust me for now, okay? After last night, I'm not sure what's safe and what isn't at the moment. Nobody's going out of here alone, so it's pairs minimum until we get the all clear, understood?'

'Understood,' Michael confirmed in almost military fashion.

'So ...' Davis interrupted. 'You know what I've been doing. What about you, Michael? What mischief have you been getting into since we broke you out?'

'Same old, same old,' Michael replied trying to be as evasive as he could.

For the last two years, Michael's life had been anything but normal. At the academy he, like so many others, had been taught to develop his mental abilities. Of course, the Inquisition had had to drug him to produce those abilities in the first place. Then he'd learned that his best friend Sam's father was a part of the Elder Council, along with his supposedly missing aunt Anna.

Since his apparent death and subsequent kidnap, Michael had been living in an abandoned Masonic temple in the backstreets of London, with a group of people he'd previously been told were trying to take over the world. Less believable was that he and Sam were now being taught the ancient arts of sorcery by a former genie. The idea was, that when the Inquisition came looking for them, they would be able to defend themselves and hopefully live to tell the tale.

Up until a few days ago, Michael had been aware of only a few other Elder Council safe houses in operation in Britain. But the number of people that he'd seen coming and going from the dining hall suggested that there were more members than he could have possibly imagined. It convinced him that up to this point, his life with the Council had been sheltered. Understandably, their location in one of the busiest hubs of the Inquisition had made it dangerous to go out during the day and even more so at night.

What had Michael been doing for the last two years? He had been training to hurt, kill and heal. And he had become very good at them. He'd even earned a special place on Anna's team of Guardians. While he couldn't match Sam's thirst for knowledge when it came to research, even Master Lefrick had been in awe of Michael's natural talent for the arts - magical and psychic. He had become the youngest dual ability member of the Elder Council since Jerrick - a fact that, for the moment, Master Lefrick and the other Council leaders were anxious to keep very, very quiet.

In addition, he had been teaching Inquisition lore at the temple. Having been one of only a handful of people to have experienced their training first hand, Michael was the obvious choice for the job. Whilst he'd been willing to learn the history of the Inquisition from the point of view of the Elder Council, he'd enjoyed telling his new family about the propaganda spread by the other side as well. It had caused quite a stir among some of the Council members.

Then there was Tamara. For two years, Michael had been hardening himself against the idea that he might be able to get the word out to her, to let her know that he was alive and that he still cared for her. But now that they were on opposite sides, how could she still care for him? Because of that, Michael had decided early on in those two years, that it was better for Tamara that he was dead. That way she could move on, even if it still made him sick with envy to think about it. He sighed as he thought about his exile from any hope of a normal life.

'Yeah, same old, same old,' Michael repeated. 'But now we're here, I'm sure that's going to change. Especially after last night.' His usual smile slipped back across his lips.

'What happened exactly? I've heard of Flayer attacks, of course, but never an attack of that magnitude,' Davis asked.

'I'm not sure,' Anna replied. 'Maybe it was the number of us travelling the same path at the same time that drew them. I thought we were pushing our luck taking so many at once. The weight of all those people and their belongings in the portal pushed the exit so far away from us. I think the amount of power we used to keep it open drew the Flayers in.'

Michael shivered at the memory. 'There must have been a thousand of them.'

'That's curious,' said the butler. 'I always knew there were a few hundred of them, but I didn't think they bred.'

'They don't,' said Anna, 'according to the lore books, at least.'

'Why were there so many of them?' Michael asked.

'Perhaps we should ask Jerrick ... if he's back yet,' said Anna.

'Back?' asked Davis.

'Yes,' said Anna. 'He went after whoever was playing that awful music last night and hadn't come back by the time I went to bed.'

'Margaret didn't say anything about music. What music?' the Butler pressed.

'Lefrick said it was something about the unwanted – a song or a tune or something,' said Anna. 'It sounded like someone strangling a yak when we first heard it. But then it turned so sweet that I really had to follow it. The next thing I remember, I was sitting in here with a hot cup of tea, and a hangover I haven't had since Jerrick gave me a bottle of his bathtub vodka.'

Davis winced. 'Hmm, that bad, eh? Still, I don't think I've ever heard of music giving anyone a hangover before. Of course, you've got your magic harps like in Jack and the Beanstalk, and pipes, like the ... oh hell ...'

Anna seemed to catch Davis's meaning the instant his curse had left his lips. 'But it can't be, can it? It can't be Nahar.'

'What's a Nahar?' Michael asked beginning to get frustrated with being left out of the conversation.

'Nahar isn't a thing,' said Anna, 'he's a person and a very dangerous one at that. If you thought some of the Inquisitors you met were bad, you need to think again.'

'Great,' said Michael. 'That really helped, Anna. Thanks for filling me in!'

'Don't get snarky,' Anna shot back. 'It's been a long night for both of us. I know as much about Nahar as you do, except that ... he was the Pied Piper.' She struggled to her feet. 'Michael, get some breakfast down you and get your coat, we're going to the library.' Turning on her heel, she strode away beneath a thundercloud of concern, with

26

Michael and Davis watching her until she was out of sight.

'Why is everything around here always so complicated?' Michael mused.

'You ain't seen nothing yet,' Davis huffed.

'What do you mean?

'Turn around,' said Davis indicating over his young friend's shoulder.

Michael turned to look at the breakfast queue and where the butler had been pointing. He scanned the faces of the waiting crowd and was relieved to see Sam safe and well, and hungry as usual. He was speaking to a girl of about the same age. But it wasn't until they both turned to look for a table together that Michael realised who she was. He turned open-mouthed to look at Davis.

'But she's ... I mean, you said ...'

'Miss King is with us now,' said Davis. 'I thought it would be best if she came along, given the circumstances.'

'But she tried to kill me at the academy!' Michael blurted.

'You know as well as I do that it was an accident! Besides, you brought her to me, remember?' said Davis.

'Yes, but I brought her to you because I thought you were going to hand her in to the authorities, not make her a part of the Elder Council!'

'When you left us, Harriet and I spoke at length about her circumstances. It appeared that she had been all but abandoned at the academy by her father. I offered her an alternative, just like the Council did for you and many of the other people you see around you ... including Sam Lucas and his family. We've been doing it for years now,' said Davis.

Michael's brow furrowed. 'What do you mean?'

'We've stayed out of the Inquisition's way for a long time,' said the butler. 'But recently we've noticed that more and more of them were starting to find life under their leaders unbearable. Eventually, one of them came to us and asked if he could hide in the Council, so we set him up with a new life with us. In return, he provided us with the names of others who might be willing to turn if we could keep them safe. So Jerrick set up the Railroad and we've been smuggling people out of the Inquisition ever since.'

'The Railroad?' said Michael.

Davis chuckled. 'I don't suppose you will have heard of it before now. It pays homage to what happened in America from the late seventeen hundreds onwards. The Underground Railroad was set up to help smuggle slaves to freedom. Free men and women alike worked the Railroad to help free as many as they could. So now we use the same idea to get people out of the Inquisition.'

'But that would mean that there are more people inside the Inquisition helping you to get them out, wouldn't it?'

'A few,' Davis nodded. 'But not as many as we'd like.'

'And how do you know you can trust them? I mean, it's like Harriet King. How do you know you can trust her? She could have been set up to come here so that she can spy on us,' Michael said beginning to get agitated.

'Like you?' Davis replied. 'How did we know we could trust you? You were meant to be the next Grand Inquisitor, but we allowed you to come here, didn't we?'

'That's different!' Michael snapped.

'Is it?' Davis shot back. 'How is it different, Michael? She needed our help. And she spent enough time being evaluated before being brought here, which is more than I can say about you. All we knew about you was that you didn't like what the Inquisition was telling you. Neither did you particularly like the idea of them killing Tamara if you'd won your duel.'

Michael blushed. 'I suppose. I'm sorry. It's just that it's hard seeing her again. The last time I saw her, I didn't trust her one bit. Now you're telling me she's one of us. It's a lot to get my head around.'

'That's what a lot of people said about you, even Andy,' said Davis. 'But look at you now. I suggest you reserve judgement until you speak to Miss King. I think you'll find her a very different person. For now, though, I think you ought to get your coat. If you're not ready to go by the time your aunt gets back, she'll be on you like a pack of wolves.'

*** 

Michael had never been to the library before; not this one at least. There were several reasons why, but mostly it was because its location was a closely guarded secret. Few normals were allowed there, and those lucky enough to have access had some very special connections. It was a haven site, neutral territory, where the Slingers of the Elder Council and the Inquisition's Psychs could go to study in peace.

'When we get there, speak to nobody but me!' Anna

warned as she put her hand on the frame of the great mirror.

'No problem,' said Michael. 'But do we really have to go by portal? Last night gave me the screaming willies to be honest … all those teeth.'

'We'll be fine. It's a short trip to the library, so I don't think we'll have any bother from the Flayers. Besides, I thought you could look after yourself?'

'I can with anything human,' said Michael. 'And there were so many of them.'

'That's part of the reason we're going,' said Anna. 'Ready?'

'Come on then,' Michael sighed. It wasn't that he didn't like the portals. When the rules were followed, they were usually quite safe. But last night had unsettled him.

The laws on travelling by portal were simple. Firstly: the greater the weight of the individuals travelling, the further the distance between the destinations. This was why it had taken so long to travel between the Masonic temple and their new hiding place in the mountains of South Wales. Normally, travelling between portals took next to no time at all, even between continents. In the short time he had been in Anna's company, Michael had learned that the dim blue path beneath them, as they walked in the sub-dimension, was something the Council used to stop its members from getting lost in the vast emptiness.

Secondly: only mirrors could be used to travel, and then only if they were large enough to enter. Something the size of the rearview mirror of a car was great for seeing but was far too small to squeeze anything but the smallest of hands through. Likewise, glass windows were good for spying on people, but the reflections in them weren't nearly strong enough for travelling.

Lastly: intentionally trapping any living creature between portals was forbidden, and always had been. Nothing grew in the sub-dimension and no water flowed there. The only lifeforms, if you could call them that, were the Flayers, and Michael dreaded what fate awaited anything alive that was caught by them.

There was nothing to fear this time, and soon they were standing in a luxuriantly decorated room of rosewood panels and red velvet chairs. Behind them, the most beautiful mirror Michael had ever seen was set into a large frame. On closer inspection, there were figures carved into the wood: a wolf, a girl in a hooded cloak, a boy with an axe and many others, intertwined with the branches and leaves of a plant that made up the border. There was an archway that led into another room beyond and as they passed beneath it, Michael could see that it was some sort of locker room. The floor was inlaid with foot square black and white tiles. At the centre of the room, a lady with round features and thick spectacles sat behind an impressive wooden reception desk. As they approached, Michael felt strangely tired, as though his store of power were being emptied out of him against his will. He gave a start, but Anna squeezed his forearm gently, to reassure him that everything was alright.

'Just two today?' the receptionist asked with a welcoming smile.

'Yeah, just two please, Eunice,' said Anna.

'Twenty and twenty-one. Enjoy your visit,' the receptionist beamed again as she handed over two small keys with brass tags.

Placing a hand in the small of Michael's back, Anna ushered him to the correct lockers. Then opening her own, she removed her coat and placed it inside before taking out and unfolding a green robe. Michael did the same, slipping the gown over his shoulders and pulling up the hood. He wasn't surprised when the thickly meshed silk veil slipped over his face, guessing that it was to keep the identities of the library's patrons hidden from one another.

A buzzer sounded behind them. Then, what appeared to be just another panel in the wall swung inwards to reveal part of the wall on the other side. They sandwiched a thick metal door between them and reminded Michael of the door of a bank vault. He skirted around the reception desk where Eunice had gone back to filling out paperwork and took his first steps into the library, followed closely by his aunt.

Even the grandest libraries of the world only have a few floors, vast though they may be. They usually also have huge windows that carefully control the light so that the books aren't damaged. This library had none. But Michael's first glimpse took his breath away. From the doorway, he could see that the aisles of books stretched away into a dimly lit distance on either side. Rows of ornate wooden tables inlaid with polished, semi-precious stones poured out in front of him. The vaulted ceiling was far, far above him, covered in geometric symbols of blues and gold, and staircases led to each of at least seven mezzanine floors that overlooked the study area. In Michael's opinion, it was one of the most beautiful buildings he had ever been inside, in spite of the absence of windows. But the grand chandelier that hung down deep into the room more than made up for it.

'There must be a million books in here!' he whispered.

'If not more, I dare say,' said Anna. 'But you won't find any novels here. This is a research library. As many events as it's been possible to collect have been recorded and stored here. It's even been said that some of the world's greatest writers received their inspiration from this place.'

'I didn't think normals were allowed down here.'

'Not many,' Anna shrugged, 'just a special few.'

'It's fantastic,' Michael huffed with a hint of disappointment.

'But ...'

'Well ... I suppose I half expected the books to be floating by, or a hum of power or something.'

'There's plenty of magic here if you know where to look for it,' said Anna.

'Actually, I meant to ask you about that,' said Michael. 'What happened in the reception hall? When we left, I felt like I could have taken on an army. Now I feel like that army just marched all over me.'

'It's a haven site, right?' said Anna. 'That means there's no fighting in here. Which means that they drain your power on the way in and give it back on the way out. Now come on, enough with the lessons for now, we've got books to find.'

'Would it help if I knew what we were looking for?'

said Michael.

Anna heaved a sigh. 'You're right, I'm sorry. I'm just a little on edge at the moment because of Jerrick. It's really not like him to run off like that unless it's something really important. Even then, he usually takes someone with him for backup.'

'It's okay, I understand,' said Michael. 'Now let's get looking shall we?'

'Right,' said Anna, shaking herself off. 'We're looking for events that reference sightings of anyone in motley clothes, who enchants living creatures to follow them. I'm going to look for references to Nahar specifically.'

'No problem,' said Michael. 'So where do I start?'

'I swear you've been away from real life for far too long. It's a library, they have index cards,' said Anna pointing to the wall opposite. You do remember how to use a library don't you?'

'Uh ... yeah, I think so.  Where are you going?'

'I'm going to start with some of the older scrolls on this floor. They're catalogued, but they couldn't scan them because of the damage it would have caused. Remember, any problems and you come and find me.' She stalked away between long rows of shelves, disappearing into the half-light.

The building was quite crowded considering it was a library. Michael noticed that all of the other patrons were wearing the same coloured robes, but that the library employees, who bustled back and forth with cartloads of books, were all dressed in normal attire.

'Excuse me, are you lost?' came a voice from one of the

rows to Michael's right.

'No, no I'm fine,' said Michael. 'I was just wondering where your computers were.'

A woman stepped out from the shadow of the bookcase. She was young, perhaps in her late teens, with the look of a student about her. Her baggy knitted sweater and tight black jeans complemented her Middle Eastern complexion. Her swept back hair was held in place with a velvet scrunchie and, although it was as black as deepest midnight, it glinted almost blue as she passed under the lights. She held out a hand and beamed.

'I'm Sher,' she purred with enthusiasm. 'C'mon, I'll help you find what you're looking for. The computers in here are great for surfing the internet, but terrible for finding books in the collection.'

'Aren't the computers supposed to tell you where the books are?' Michael asked.

'Usually,' Sher shrugged. 'But there are so many people in and out all day, that it's likely what you're looking for is on a cart, not on the shelves. That's where I come in.'

'I don't follow,' said Michael.

She tapped her temple with a finger. 'Photographic memory. It's one of my many curses. Now, what are we looking for?'

'The um ... pumpf hrmfmph ...' Michael muttered.

'Sorry, I didn't quite catch that,' said Sher. 'For a second there, I thought you said "The Pied Piper".'

'I did.'

'Well, there's nothing to be embarrassed about,' Sher giggled. 'Around here, that's a perfectly normal request.'

'It is?'

'Of course it is! Come to think of it, he's quite popular today.'

'There are other people looking for the same thing?' Michael gasped.

'Yep,' Sher nodded. 'And I know just where to find what you're looking for. Follow me, Kisses.'

She set off at a canter that Michael wasn't expecting given her petite size, almost floating across the floor to one of the many staircases and leaving Michael to jog behind in her wake. Trotting up the steep flight of steps, she sped away again around the gallery and up to another floor. Eventually, she came to a stop next to a trolley full of leather bound volumes.

'Thought so ...' she said, picking a few of the books from the pile and handing them to her panting charge. 'Seventy-four, Ninety-six and Thirteen were all looking at these. But ...' she hesitated, looking around, 'I think you'd be more interested in the one Ninety-six has out at the moment.'

'Is that one better?' Michael asked.

'It is for what *you're* looking for,' said Sher.

There was a hand on Michael's shoulder that made him jump.

'And how would you know what he's looking for when he doesn't know himself?' said Anna. 'You're supposed to be impartial, Sher. That's why this place is safe for us.'

'Okay, so I faked it,' the librarian hissed, lowering her voice to little more than a conspiratorial whisper. 'I know who you are. Jacob said you'd be by sometime.'

'Jacob?' said Michael.

'She means Jacob Grimm,' said Anna. 'I hate it when he gets insightful.'

'Look,' said Sher, 'I don't know who Ninety-six is exactly, but I wouldn't go above the third floor if you know what I mean.'

'Point taken,' said Anna. 'Can you get that book down to us?'

'As soon he's done with it, I can.'

'Thanks, Sher. We'll be right there,' said Anna pointing down at the reading tables on the ground floor.

'Okay, I'll be as quick as I can. See you soon, Kisses.' She winked at Michael as she slipped back into character and trotted away.

'You,' Anna rasped, not looking in her nephew's direction, 'downstairs, now!'

Michael wound his way back to the bottom floor, practically throwing himself into a waiting chair behind the reading desk Anna had indicated.

'I suppose I'm in for another lecture?' he said.

'No, I'm not going to lecture you again,' Anna sighed leaning against the table. 'Look, Michael, I'm sorry I'm not a very good parent, but you really have to start listening to me.' When Michael made an attempt to break in, she held up a hand and kept her voice low. 'I already know what you're going to say. You keep reminding me that you can take care of yourself. But last night's got me spooked. I thought the Guardians could handle almost anything. After all, we managed to keep a thousand Flayers at bay. But when I came out of that trance, Michael, I realised that I couldn't have kept myself safe at that moment in time, let alone you as well.'

When Anna hung her head, Michael guessed that she was ashamed, or that she was feeling like she had let him down. His mood gave way a little and he stretched out a comforting hand.

'I'm sorry too. I suppose I just felt like I could take care of myself so that you wouldn't have to. I knew what I was getting into when I agreed to be a Guardian, and I guess I just wanted to make you proud.'

She turned her head slightly in his direction. 'You know, for someone who's only fifteen, you're doing just fine. I'll try to remember to stay off your case.'

'Fourteen,' said Michael. 'For someone who's only fourteen.'

'Sorry,' said Anna.

'And if it helps, I think you would have been a great mum … because, well … you've been a wonderful aunt,' said Michael tracing the outline of some of the inlaid stones with his finger.

'Thanks …' said Anna blushing a bright scarlet.

'Too much?'

She cleared her throat. 'Yeah, just a bit.'

They sat in silence for a few minutes, each contemplating what the other had said. Finally, the fog seemed to clear from the air and Anna took Michael's hand, pulling him up from his chair.

'Come on, how about I show you the most spectacular part of the building while we're waiting for Sher to come back?'

'Okay,' Michael agreed, allowing himself to be led to a set of stairs. 'So, um …. Tell me about her.'

'She's pretty, isn't she?' said Anna.

'I suppose,' said Michael. 'I'm not really interested. There's something odd about her. Anyway, I was going to ask why she kept calling me Kisses.'

'Oh,' Anna laughed. 'It's the number sewn onto the shoulder of the robe. They're Roman numerals – XX is twenty, which is the number of the locker you're using. It helps the librarians keep track of who's where and which exit they should be leaving from.'

'Kisses!' Michael gagged.

'Why else do you think she referred to the other patrons as "Ninety-six" and whatnot?'

'I didn't really think about it,' Michael confessed.

'Well, never mind that now.' She manoeuvred Michael into a spot next to the railing above the door they had come in from. 'Hush. Listen!'

He cocked his head and did as he was told. The air was filled with the whispers of conversations. Each time he turned, he could catch snippets of discussions from all over the building.

'They call it the Whisper Gallery,' said Anna. 'This is the magic I promised you, Michael. Oh sure, the stories and all the events are magical. But there's no *power* in this place, except here.'

'How does it work?'

'I asked Lefrick the same thing the first time he brought me here,' said Anna. 'He said it has something to do with how the building's constructed. "An acoustic sweet spot", that's what he called it. It's like all the sounds of the library are reflected to this spot and nowhere else.'

'That would mean that anyone could have heard our conversation down there, or worse, our conversation with Sher! '

'That's why I came after you. Sher's nice and all, but nobody knows which side she's really on.' Anna warned.

'I thought the librarians were supposed to be neutral?' said Michael.

'They usually are,' said Anna. 'They're only in it to collect events for the library. The things we do aren't usually recorded by the normals, except in trashy tabloid papers and stupid paranormal magazines. But things are changing. Master Lefrick noticed it a few years ago when we were at the Grand Council meeting. He wouldn't show it in public, but he's really worried because there wasn't a meeting last year. Now there's talk that there won't be one this year either.'

'Is it that important?' Michael asked.

'Yes,' said Anna. 'No meeting means no information, no consensus. If the Elders aren't deciding together what the branches of the Council are doing, it may as well be a dictatorship. It may as well be … the Inquisition.' She somehow managed to look uncomfortable beneath the layers of green cloth. 'This isn't the place to talk about it. Besides, it's not something you need to worry too much about. Lefrick and I will see to that when the time comes.'

Across the gallery, Michael could see Sher waving at them, a ledger-sized book in her other hand.

'Look,' he said pointing. 'She's got it for us.'

They headed back towards the table and arrived just in time to meet the librarian. Strangely, Sher just winked and flashed a smile at them as she placed the tome on top of the other books and headed away.

'What was that about?' Michael whispered, more cautiously now, knowing what he knew about the acoustics of the building. Anna said nothing. Instead, she pointed her thumb over her shoulder to the Whisper Gallery.

Michael had been right to worry about their conversation. In the gallery, staring with absolute intent in their direction was a tall figure. The embroidered, golden XCVI on the shoulders of his robes declared him to be Ninety-six. Anna reached into the pocket of her robe and extracted a small pad of paper and pencil, hastily scribbling the words: *No speak, he's listening! Arrived just after we came down!* To which Michael nodded his understanding.

Anna motioned to the chairs and they sat together. Michael took the pad from his aunt and wrote: *I think we should just try to look busy. Is that okay with you?*

*His aunt* nodded her agreement as she took the ledger sized book from the top of the pile, turning it spine on to read the title and author. Showing it to Michael, he understood why Sher had thought this book was so important. It had been written by Jacob Grimm himself.

Michael began leafing through the first of the books he had brought down. He was surprised to find that, alongside the usual story of the vengeful Piper of Hamelin, there were stories from as far afield as Syria and Africa. All gave roughly the same account of a man in unusual dress, who promised to rid a town or city of an infestation. All ended with dire consequences. Where the stories differed, however, was in their description of the musician and the instrument he played. There wasn't a single definite lead as to who they should be looking for. After his sixth telling of the story, Michael began to see the Piper more as a cautionary tale and, if it hadn't been for his aunt's insistence that he was real, Michael doubted that he would have believed in his existence at all.

With every turn of the page, he could feel the eyes of the watcher from the gallery tunnelling into the back of his head, making him feel uncomfortable. He risked a glance over his shoulder and, sure enough, Ninety-six was still there. Beneath the veil, he closed his eyes, trying to feel his way around the room with his mind. But the drain on the way into the library had left him with no way to perform even the simplest of tasks. Heaving a sigh, Michael searched his mind for a way to identify the intruder without having to use any energy.

It came to him like a storm. In his training for the trials at the academy, Michael had been taught to read auras. It was a talent that he'd almost forgotten about because he hadn't needed to use it in the years since. It was also one of the only talents in the arsenal of both sides that didn't require any energy to perform. Even a special few normals could do it well enough to make a living out of it.

Michael made a show of turning in his chair to look at the watcher and let his eyes unfocus, the way people do when they look at those three-dimensional posters that were all the rage. The thing about auras is that they reflect the personality of the person they belong to. They are almost impossible to fake or hide and don't require anything but life to sustain them. The watcher was no exception. His aura began to come into focus against the dimly lit background of the Whisper Gallery. The glow that came from the robe was dark, almost black. Had Michael's eyes been closed, Ninety-six's aura would have been deeper than black, so black that darkness shied away from it, and he knew to his soul that he had seen that kind of darkness before.

Michael's heart sank to his boots as he turned back to the table and scribbled furiously on the pad: *Need to get out of here now!* Sliding the pad in front of his aunt, he motioned surreptitiously to the gallery.

'What's wrong?' Anna whispered, turning to look.

Michael shot a glance over his shoulder, but the listener was gone. 'Ninety-six ... Ninety-six was Catchpole!'

'Okay, so the Inquisition is after the same thing. That's nothing new,' said Anna.

'But what if he knows it was me?' Michael urged as a shadow descended over the table, causing his heart to beat so fast he thought the rest of the world could hear it.

'It's alright, Mr Ware,' said the tall figure of Jacob Grimm pulling up a chair opposite them. 'He's gone. And I don't think he's any the wiser about you.'

'You can't be sure of that,' said Michael.

'You're right,' said Grimm tweaking his green tweed tie. 'Who knows what Mr Catchpole can do, with or without his power? He isn't what you'd call a typical Inquisitor.'

'You can say that again,' Michael snorted. 'How do you know for sure it was him?'

'I check the logs,' Grimm replied. 'I like to know who's in my library. I must admit, had I known you were coming here today, I would have had Eunice turn you away at the reception desk. No offence.'

'None taken, Jacob,' said Anna. 'It must be hard to keep somewhere like this neutral.'

'About that,' said Grimm. 'I came to warn you.'

'Warn us, about what?' said Michael.

'The gathering storm,' said Grimm, flipping to a passage in the ledger sized book that Sher had brought. 'I'd almost forgotten until today.'

When he turned the book back to face Anna, Michael recognised the last part of the passage immediately:

*...and in the gathering storm,*
*Once every one hundred years,*
*The Grand will meet in conclave, riding out*
*To do their duty until the score is settled.*

'It says here that the Piper's appearance seems to coincide with some sort of meeting of the Grand Inquisitors,' said Anna.

Grimm's face darkened. 'The conclave's no ordinary meeting, Anna. They meet to decide their strategy for dealing with the Council.'

'What happened the last time there was a conclave?' she asked.

'Hundreds died. Men, women and ... children,' said Grimm. A tear rolled along the bridge of his nose and collected in the rim of his spectacles. 'The Grand Council had forbidden the training of children, believing that if they couldn't fight, the Inquisition would ignore them. They were wrong.'

'How long?' said Michael.

'I don't know. It could be weeks, or months before they meet again,' said Grimm.

'But why don't they just keep going until they finish the job?' said Anna.

'Last time, the cull took a heavy toll on the Inquisition as well. They lost too many of their Grands to continue the fighting. We think they were trying to force the war on too many fronts at the same time,' Grimm replied.

'But what has any of this got to do with the Piper?' Michael cut in.

'That's just it. It's why I remembered about that passage,' said Grimm. 'We've noticed that before the conclave there are always a lot of disappearances. The two appear to be linked, so we did some research. It seems that the Piper only ever shows up for a few months once every hundred years or so before vanishing again.'

'And because the Piper's neutral, you want our help to deal with him?' asked Anna.

'I know I have no right to ask,' said Grimm, 'especially with the cull so close behind. But you owe me for that favour I did you. Sleeping draughts aren't cheap you know, and *Near Death*'s an absolute bitch to get the ingredients for these days. Don't even get me started on the antidote!'

Anna held up her hand. 'Alright, alright I'll see what Lefrick has to say about it.'

'Lefrick, what about Jerrick? Wouldn't he be better

given his history with ...' Grimm broke off his sentence as his blush reached almost to the crown of his bald head.

'Jerrick hasn't been too forthcoming about that part of his life,' said Anna. 'What can you tell us?'

'Oh no, I made him a promise,' said Grimm. 'You're not getting any more out of me than I've given you already. Besides, I owe him a favour as well. He said I'd know when the time to pay up would be. It isn't now!'

'Well your luck's in, he hasn't been seen since ... Ow!' said Michael rubbing his shin. 'What did you kick me for?'

'Hasn't been seen since when?' asked Grimm.

'Since last night,' said Anna. 'Which was why we were looking for information on the Piper. He said something about the song of the unwanted. Look, Jacob, we're really worried about him. Isn't there anything you can tell us?'

Grimm stood and began to jot on Anna's notepad, saying, 'I've already said too much. I've no doubt that my time with you has drawn some very much unwanted attention. Now take this to Eunice at the reception desk and wait there.'

'But ...' Michael tried to argue.

'It's the only thing I can do for you,' said Grimm as he collected the books from the table and strode away.

'It's okay,' said Anna. 'I think we got what we came for.'

'But we didn't have time to look at anything.'

'All good things come to those who wait,' she smiled.

Anna did as she was told and handed the notepad to Eunice at reception. In the minutes that passed while they waited, Michael could feel the power beginning to return to him in a small stream that felt as though it was coming through the floor. Eventually, a panel in the wall slid sideways and Sher appeared pushing a book trolley.

'Well, Kisses, aren't you the lucky one,' she frothed.

'Am I?' said Michael cocking an eyebrow.

She handed him the ledger-sized book. 'It's not every day Jacob lets someone take a book home. You must have done something right.'

'Gee, thanks,' said Michael. Hefting the tome under one arm, he followed Anna into the mirror room.

'Take good care of it. I don't want to have to fine you for damage to library property,' Sher called.

'I won't let it out of my sight, Sher,' Anna called back in her best impersonation of the younger woman, before dragging Michael into the portal.

# Chapter Three:
# The Bargain

At other public schools, there are dormitories, and pupils are assigned to teams that they call houses. The Braxton Foundation felt different. At the academies, the houses are just that – houses. Big ones. At the thirtieth academy they were modelled on the original house, each set in its own unique environment on the vast grounds of the estate. At Braxton academies, each house serves a purpose, almost like the management structure of a company. But the Inquisition was a company its employees only left feet first.

To continue the metaphor, most companies have silent partners, but that was not the case with the Braxton Foundation. The foundation encouraged its members to be vocal, placing them in high visibility positions, such as Police Commissioner or Secretary of Defence. But they never took positions that were too public, such as Prime Minister or President. Indeed, it used to be said that behind every great man, there had to be a great woman. However, since the last conclave of Grand Inquisitors (under the guidance of the High Marshalls) the phrase had changed. Now, behind every great man (or woman) there was an army of tireless individuals working to secure the dominance of the Inquisition. Not that the general public ever knew that.

It was a fact that fourteen-year-old Tamara Bloodgood, Grand Inquisitor was trying to come to terms with. And as she sat on a bench overlooking the lake that surrounded House Solaris, it bothered her. Solaris was the seat of the Braxton Foundation's true power. It trained those with latent mental abilities to become soldiers in the age-long struggle against the ancient enemy - the Elder Council.

Tamara considered this too. From what she had read and what she had been taught, she knew that the war had been raging since a king named Jeshamon imprisoned the leader of a tribe of nomads in a lamp for poisoning his city with their magic. She also knew that Jeshamon had trained the first Inquisitors to harness the power of their minds, to hunt the nomads down.

*It all seems so complicated, and so long ago,* she thought as she watched the wind pick ripples into waves on the lake.

Since becoming Grand Inquisitor, she hadn't had a great deal of time to herself. Catchpole always seemed to be on her back about something. But if he was the devil on one shoulder, then Clarissa Cunningham was the angel on the other. Tamara valued her counsel. It was always calm, measured and non-judgemental. Catchpole continuously pushed and goaded, manipulating Tamara into situations she wasn't sure she wanted. Miss Cunningham discussed and appraised, forcing Tamara to think before acting.

Taking some torn up bread from a paper bag, she threw it at passing duck that was used to being assaulted with food by now. It wasn't that Tamara was cruel; it was just that she was too deep in thought to consider the feelings of the duck. She'd been that way since ... then.

*Don't start that again!* She chided herself. *It's no use beating yourself up about it every day. It's time you started acting like a*

*Grand Inquisitor. And that means giving orders, not taking them.*

But she couldn't help herself. She wondered how Michael would look today if he had lived. Would he have grown his blonde hair out, or worn it short? Would his grey eyes still have that steely dazzle when he was excited and would they still darken when he was angry or upset? How would he have coped with Catchpole's "guidance"?

Had she known that Michael was still out there, his frame broader, but looking very much the same as he had done then – short blonde hair, lively grey eyes – things might have been very different.

*But how can I hate them and not hate the Inquisition? Aren't we two sides of the same coin after all?* She pelted the duck again. It quacked gratefully for the offering. *No,* she concluded, *we're not the same! The Inquisition doesn't control, it guides. We put people on the path that's right for them. The Council wants to control. They want to treat the normals like children, punishing them when they do wrong, little treats when they do right. Training them like puppies to be obedient to their masters.*

'Deep in thought again?' Miss Cunningham said sliding onto the bench next to Tamara.

'Hmm?' said Tamara, her latest projectile catching the duck square between the eyes.

Miss Cunningham laughed. 'You're going to give that poor creature brain damage if you're not careful!'

'Oh,' Tamara blushed as she watching the duck shake itself off. She stared into the abyss of the paper bag, not really seeing the bread. 'I was wondering what it was all for, the war I mean. Are we doing the right thing?'

'I honestly couldn't say, milady,' Miss Cunningham

replied.

'It's okay, it wasn't a test,' said Tamara. 'And drop the "milady" out here, there's no one around.'

Miss Cunningham heaved a sigh, her mousy ponytail struggling against the breeze. 'All I can tell you, is that there are hundreds of people working hard to do what you tell them is right. But can we ever justify killing?'

'The Council seems to manage it,' Tamara responded harder than she'd intended.

'So you're going with the eye for an eye defence, are you?' Miss Cunningham snapped back.

'But it's not about them or us, is it? It's about the millions of normal people going about their daily lives unaware of what's hanging over them!'

'Trust me,' Miss Cunningham snorted, 'the normals find enough reasons to kill each other as it is, without dragging them into this as well.'

'So you're saying that by waging a war and leaving countless dead on both sides, we're really just protecting the innocent?'

Miss Cunningham shook her head. 'No, please don't misunderstand me. I'm not saying that killing is ever right. But giving your life for another, especially someone who can't defend themselves against their aggressor, that's got to be a worthy cause, hasn't it?'

'I suppose so,' said Tamara.

'Look at it this way: if there was a peaceful solution to all this, don't you think the Marshalls would have found it by now?'

'Would they? I don't know,' said Tamara. 'Everywhere

I turn, present company excepted, people are baying for blood, just as they did in the past.'

There was an awkward pause before Miss Cunningham spoke again. 'I have a confession to make. Do you remember what you said in your acceptance speech?'

'Yes, I do,' said Tamara. 'It was something along the lines of: "Get those thieving, poisonous bastards out of my country once and for all!" But I was very angry then, and I don't think I actually meant that I wanted them all dead. Or did I? I don't know anymore.'

'That's what I wanted to confess,' said Miss Cunningham. 'The moment those words left your lips, I thought it was going to be like it was under Grand Inquisitor Renfrew.'

'Was he that bad?' asked Tamara.

'I was at the academy myself when he died,' said Miss Cunningham. 'But I remember the announcements whenever he'd gained a victory over the Council. And trust me, there were a lot of announcements. It wasn't until much, much later that I understood what that meant.'

'That victory for him meant that someone else had died?' Tamara suggested.

'Exactly! But it wasn't just the enemy that was dying. Renfrew had a reputation for losing Inquisitors that went into battle with him. It got so bad near the end, that he had to order people to go with him, or face the consequences for disobeying.'

'You mean people were afraid that if they went with him, they wouldn't come back?' said Tamara. 'Did you think that was going to happen to me?'

'The way you were talking in the early days of your appointment, yes.'

'Huh, even if people had followed me, they would have been Catchpole's orders,' Tamara chuckled. 'But that's going to change, I promise. I'm going to be the one calling the shots from now on.'

There was a crunching on the footpath behind them, and the two friends turned to look as a messenger approached. Like all good messengers, he waited some distance away until he was waved over before making his announcement.

'Milady, there is ... um ... a visitor to see you,' he said fidgeting with his hands.

'I don't have anything scheduled for today, do I?' Tamara asked Miss Cunningham.

'Not that I'm aware of, no.'

'Very well,' she sighed. 'Send them to my study. I'll be along shortly.'

'Er ... that's just it, milady,' the messenger quaked. 'The visitor is already in your study, and has requested that you attend at your earliest convenience, or sooner ... if you'll pardon my impertinence.'

'Fine!' Tamara snapped waving the messenger away. She waited until he was out of earshot before she spoke again. 'It's one thing being pushed around by Catchpole, but I'm not taking it from a perfect stranger.'

'It can't be an Inquisitor, or they would have followed the protocols,' said Miss Cunningham. 'I wonder who it could be. Do you want me to come with you?'

'Please. Oh, and could you have Emily and Rupert

come down too? It couldn't hurt to have a full detail there, just in case.'

By the time they got to Tamara's study, Rupert and Emily were already waiting outside the door for them, both looking very concerned.

'Where's Catchpole?' Miss Cunningham asked. 'Doesn't he usually make an appearance around about now?'

Stifling a laugh, Rupert said, 'He left early this morning. Said he had something important to do in London. I don't think he'll be back until late tonight.'

'It's just us then. What information do we have?' Tamara asked.

'No idea,' said Emily. 'Whoever it is, I can't get a read on them. So I'd suggest a full on defensive strategy.'

'Agreed,' said Rupert. A look of concentration crossed his face. 'Ready?'

The group nodded their confirmation and Tamara pushed the door inwards with as much confidence as she could muster, believing in her bones this time that it was her study, and she wasn't about to be pushed around by anyone else.

The sight that greeted them was most unexpected. Sitting not behind, but on the Grand Inquisitor's desk, and looking out across the gardens was a figure in a patchwork coat. When it noticed them, it raised a flute to its lips and began to play. It was about the most awful racket the four Inquisitors had ever had the misfortune to hear.

Tamara cleared her throat. 'If you're looking for the orchestral auditions, the music department is in the main building. I would recommend you, but I'm afraid I don't have any authority in that area.' It was a blatant lie. Tamara had more authority at the academy than almost anyone else, but she didn't want to hurt the visitor's feelings.

The musician stopped mid-phrase, dropping the flute to its side. Tamara couldn't make out any features beneath the deep hood, but she had a sense that its wearer was confounded by something. It was as if something were profoundly wrong with the situation. She found it unsettling and, judging by the expressions on the faces of the others, so did they.

The visitor tapped the flute against the table, then spun it around and turned it into the light, looking down its shaft. Several moments passed in silence whilst the flute was dismantled and reassembled.

'How is that possible? Your kind has no magic,' it said.

'I don't understand,' Tamara responded. 'However, isn't it usually considered polite to introduce one's self *before* asking questions? And while we're on the subject of social etiquette, isn't it usually polite to be invited into another person's private chambers?'

The intruder hesitated, apparently considering Tamara's rebuke.

'I apologise,' was all it said as the hood was taken back to reveal the long, tousled, sandy hair, blue eyes and ivory skin of a young woman. 'In this country they call me the Piper.'

'Oh, surely you don't mean the Pied Piper?' said Emily. The girl nodded.

'But that was over seven hundred years ago,' Tamara

55

gawked.

'That is correct,' said the Piper. 'The magic of the flute keeps me young.'

'According to the stories ... like ... all of the stories, the Piper was also a man,' Tamara challenged.

'Stories can be wrong,' said the Piper. 'But tell me, how is it that the flute doesn't work in this place?'

'We all have our secrets,' Miss Cunningham answered before Rupert gave himself away.

'Very well,' said the Piper. 'I may not be able to influence your decision, but I still have a proposition for you - a ... deal, as you say in your language.'

'And what could you possibly have to offer us?' Tamara asked trying to brim with confidence. Now that the situation was upon her, she was adamant to prove that she could handle it.

'I have it on good authority that you have an infestation. I would like to offer to rid you of it,' said the Piper.

'Rats?' Miss Cunningham laughed. 'We don't have any rats at the academy. Even if we did, we have ways of dealing with them for ourselves thank you very much.'

'You misunderstand,' said the Piper. 'I am not talking about rats or mice. I am talking about vermin of another kind. The kind with two legs.'

'Ah, you mean the Elder Council,' said Tamara.

'I do.'

'Then let's say you manage to do what the Inquisition hasn't been able to. What is it you expect in return?' Tamara asked remembering that things didn't end well for those who make deals with devils.

'All I want is them. All of them. Nothing more,' the Piper replied.

'So ...' said Rupert, 'just the souls of the damned then?'

'Yes,' said the Piper.

'What do you want them for?' Tamara asked not certain that she had really heard the Piper's reply properly.

'What I want them for is my own business. Do we have an agreement?'

'Wait,' said Miss Cunningham. 'What assurances do we have that you're not just wasting our time?'

The Piper raised the flute again and paused. 'May I?'

'Be my guest,' said Tamara.

She began to play again. This time, although the music was just as awful, to the assembly's surprise the door behind them opened and four black-robed Inquisitors sloped into the room, their faces as blank and unresponsive as zombies. As soon as the music stopped, their expressions changed to looks of confusion. Tamara immediately recognised them as the part of the assault team who had invaded the Masonic temple without permission.

'A gesture of good faith,' the Piper smiled. 'I didn't realise when I took them that they belonged to you. I thought they were unwanted. I apologise for any inconvenience this may have caused you.'

'Thank you,' said Tamara. 'But I'm curious. What did you mean by unwanted?'

The Piper's face blanked again. 'I only take those whom nobody will miss. The unwanted. The creatures others call vermin. They are of use to me in my work.'

'I thought you drowned the rats of Hamelin?' Emily interjected. 'Forgive me for saying so, but isn't that why the town council refused to pay you the price they agreed?'

'I have learned since Hameln,' said the girl.

There was something in the way that she said it – "Hameln" – like she was fond of the place or even missed it. There was an accent too - a hint of German that had been diluted through lack of practice. Tamara turned her back on the Piper and mouthed something to Emily, to which Miss Cunningham nodded her approval. Emily stepped forward, leaving the confines of Rupert's protective bubble, brushing past the Piper on her way to the window.

'The deal?' the Piper insisted.

'Let me get this straight,' said Tamara, trying to keep control over the conversation. 'In return for ridding us of the Elder Council, all you want is to be able to keep the bodies?'

'In a manner of speaking, yes.'

'It sounds fair to me,' said Tamara, glancing at Miss Cunningham for approval. 'But there is one thing I would like to add. I want proof with my own eyes that they're gone.'

'That is acceptable,' said the Piper. 'I will notify you of a time and place to attend and you shall have your proof.'

'Agreed,' said Tamara. 'We'll stay out of your way until you say otherwise.'

The Piper bowed her head before replacing the patchwork hood. Extending a hand to seal the deal with Tamara, she left. As the latch of the door clicked into place, the four hostages came to their senses, confused with the reality of their new surroundings.

Miss Cunningham turned her attention towards them, her face like thunder. 'You lot, debriefing room now, and for your sakes I hope you remember something worth telling Catchpole. Our resident Magister isn't too pleased that you blew the raid!'

'I don't think he'll be too impressed that we made a deal without him either,' said Tamara once the room was clear. 'Emily, what did you get from the Piper?'

'Nothing,' said Emily. 'In fact, it's really beginning to bother me that I couldn't get anything. It's like she didn't really exist or wasn't even here.'

'Whether she was here or not,' said Rupert, 'at least we know that flute doesn't work on blanks. Strange that she didn't though, don't you think? Still, I wouldn't like to be those guys when Catchpole gets back.'

'I don't really want to be us when Catchpole gets back either,' Tamara sniffed. 'I don't really want to have to face a session with one of our own interrogators, even if he is supposed to be on our side.'

'It won't come to that,' said Emily. 'Under the circumstances, I think the deal was good for us. If the Piper wants to put herself in harm's way, that's fine by me. We can always deal with her later. It gives us a good chance to see what she can do, and how the Council will react to it.'

'Two birds with one stone,' said Rupert.

Tamara shook her head. 'I don't know if I'd go that far. I mean, if Emily can't read her, and she can come and go from here without anyone challenging her, how are we supposed to keep an eye on her? No, Catchpole's not going to like this one bit.'

\*\*\*

Far away from prying eyes, in the cathedral cave under what was known as Koppelberg hill, a golden portal closed. This was a portal unlike any other. As it closed, instead of becoming the usual shiny glass, it separated like golden mercury into small circles embedded in the rock. On closer inspection, one might have noticed that the coins had been struck with the name of Hamelin town, and there were fifty of them.

Trailing down from the unusual mosaic, stone steps led to a path through the heart of the cavern. There was a strange breeze, as though the air were being dragged into this place from somewhere else. It was enough to keep the few sconce-mounted torches alight. Their dim light cast dancing shadows on the walls, adding their yellow to a strange blue glow that came from several contraptions on the cave's floor. It gave the whole cave an eerie green tinge.

Her eyes growing accustomed to the light, the Piper descended into the gloom, coat billowing behind her. As she considered the success of her visit to the academy, she began to hum a merry little tune and went about her chores.

There was a disjointed crunching noise from the other side of the cave and an ancient man tottered into view, supported on two carved, wooden walking sticks. In spite of his great age and frailty, he was still broad shouldered.

Had he been otherwise, he would doubtless have been wheelchair bound.

'Ah, I thought I heard you singing, Katja. How did it go?' he rasped.

The Piper cast a smile over her shoulder at the old man. 'Very well actually, father,' she said as she twirled and swayed in time with her own music. 'They've agreed to let us handle the Elder Council and they're going to stay out of our way.'

'Good,' the old man cheered. 'That'll make our job much easier. However, you know they'll be watching from now on, don't you? You'll have to be extra careful now. They have eyes everywhere.'

'On me, yes.' the girl beamed. 'But not on *us*. Look, father, they're almost a quarter full,' she said tapping on the side of a thick glass tank. It looked like a giant fish bowl with a copper and brass hose fitted to it. There were ninety-nine more just like it lining the walls of the room, some empty and some containing an amount of blue liquid.

'I can see,' her father replied. 'But it seems to be taking more and more every time. It's as if there's no life in people these days.' He eased himself onto a stool behind the tank, stroking something in the darkness. 'What has the world done to you my friend, to leave you so lifeless and desperate?'

'It's not their fault, father,' said Katja. 'It's just that hope isn't what it used to be, I suppose.'

'What's that?' said the old man as he fiddled with some small brass taps placed at intervals along a copper pipe where he sat. 'Oh, hope … No, hope isn't what it used to be. I remember helping the Caliph of Bagdad out of a fix once. Now there was a city full of hope! Even the lowliest street urchin had dreams of becoming a sultan. Half their number could have filled our bottles tenfold, not like these poor wretches. All they hope for is that they'll see the next day.'

'It wasn't like that with us either, was it?' said Katja joining her father by the copper tube.

'No,' the old man agreed. 'But then you were only children.' He turned a release valve carefully, but nothing happened, except for a faint groaning. 'See; empty! You really shouldn't have let those Inquisitors go. They would have made a considerable difference.'

Katja rolled her eyes at him. 'But rules are rules, father. Nobody that anyone will miss, remember? Unwanted people. Besides, you'll have enough unwanted to keep you going for a thousand years before long.'

'I'm really not that bothered, as long as *he's* one of them,' said the old man. He struggled to his feet, his sticks wobbling beneath him. 'Now come on, it'll be dark in a few hours. Take the empties out and get some rest.'

Katja leaned over and kissed him on the forehead. 'I will. You get some rest too. It won't be long before we're ready.'

She watched as her father tottered away into the shadows at the back of the cave. Then she drew the black cloth away from where he had been fiddling. Beneath was a mess of hair and flesh, bound to an X-shaped metal table by heavy leather straps. The victim, much cleaner than he had been a few nights ago, lay face down in a man shaped groove in the table. Needles protruding from the skin over each of its vertebra connected to plastic tubing that fed into a copper junction box on the floor. In turn, a canvas band linked a flywheel on the top of the box to a small, brass clockwork pump. It both drew fluid from the victim and pumped it up to a distillation vat where it was processed. Finally, the vat dripped its glowing blue contents through another copper pipe to the glass tank.

It took some time for Katja to disconnect the twenty-five bodies from their respective machines, but when she had finished she heaved a sigh and drew the hood of her coat up over her head again.

'The Piper thanks you for your service,' she said, as though it was a rule in some macabre ritual that had to be followed to the letter. She raised the flute to her lips and began to play, watching the faces of her victims until the song of the unwanted took its hold over them. Turning, she led the empties away along the path to the portal and piped them through into the space between mirrors, sighing with regret as she closed the golden gate behind them.

Returning to the tanks, she made her way to the back wall. Following a corridor to an ante-chamber, she came to a stop at the rows of metal bars that had been dug into the thick stone of the floor and ceiling to form a huge cage.

'Bath time,' she trilled.

\*\*\*

'You did WHAT?' Catchpole yelled, his usually pallid

face purple with rage.

'I made a decision because the opportunity presented itself, and you weren't on hand to give any advice,' said Tamara.

'I was busy doing research,' Catchpole snapped.

'And did you find anything?'

'Yes, as a matter of fact I did.'

Tamara raised an eyebrow, trying to press Catchpole into offering more, but he seemed to ignore her.

'I need to know the exact contents of this deal,' he said.

'Well,' Tamara began, but Catchpole silenced her immediately.

'Miss Parker, in here if you please,' he shouted towards the entrance of the study.

Emily's face appeared around the door. 'Yes, Mr Catchpole?'

'Come in, please. I need to know the details of your meeting today. From what I've read, the Piper's renowned for sticking quite rigidly to the small print. Any misinterpretations on our part could be catastrophic.'

'And how can I help you with that, sir?' Emily quizzed. 'I'm sure the Grand Inquisitor would be better at telling you the details than I would.'

'I'm sure she would,' Catchpole pressed. 'But I don't want to hear what happened second hand. I want to be there myself.'

'And how do you propose to do that?' said Tamara.

'Like this,' Catchpole grinned. 'Miss Parker, take a seat and relax. Let me do all the work,' he said motioning to a comfortable armchair at the far end of the study. Once

Emily was sitting, he drew a footstool beneath himself and placed his hands on Emily's temples.

When Emily closed her eyes, Tamara could see that she was struggling to breathe easily, as though she were fighting against some invisible force. Finally, her prolonged wince drew ragged lines on her forehead.

'Stay still, girl,' Catchpole warned as his fingers explored Emily's skull.

Emily tensed again. 'You're hurting me.'

'Just hold still will you, I don't want to have to strap you down,' Catchpole barked.

'You'll do no such thing!' said Tamara losing her cool with his disregard for her friend.

'Almost,' said Catchpole. 'Almost got it.'

Emily gave a yelp of pain mixed with fright. 'Stop, sir. Please, you have to stop!' Lashing out with her foot, she caught the Magister heavily in the groin.

'Nnnnn …' he groaned as he continued with his task.

Emily's eyes rolled. Their lids fluttered like paper in a breeze and the whites showed whiter than her porcelain skin. A humming started in her throat, building to a groan. The groan became a wail and quickly evolved, becoming a piercing scream that rattled the windows of the room. The cry brought the household guard running from their posts.

'Enough!' Tamara yelled.

Her fists clenched with anger. She channelled her will into them and braced herself. Raising her arms, Tamara lifted her former mentor from his footstool and suspended him some eight feet above the floor, his nose pressed firmly against the ceiling.

'You will not do that again!' she growled.

'I understand,' Catchpole replied, struggling for breath. 'But there's something you ought to know.'

'What?' Tamara spat.

'The girl you made the deal with today … she's not the Piper.'

Tamara lowered him closer to the floor, turning his face towards her. 'What do you mean? If she's not the Piper, then how did she get into my study? And what was she doing with four of our assault team in tow?'

'I don't know,' Catchpole panted. 'But I'm guessing she knows where the real Piper is.'

Releasing her mental grip on the Magister, Tamara dismissed the bewildered guard. She crossed the floor and stroked Emily's hair, hoping that her outward compassion would make up for her lack of internal feeling.

'Next time, I'd appreciate it if you just asked,' Emily groaned as she seemed to come around from her ordeal.

'I got a lot more that way, believe me,' Catchpole crowed. 'For instance, I now know that you couldn't read her, either from inside or outside the room. I also know that I haven't felt that kind of energy before, which means she's not a blank. In fact, she's not anything. She's a normal, without being normal.'

'How can you be normal without being normal?' said Emily.

'No idea,' Catchpole shrugged. 'But I'd be willing to bet it had something to do with that flute. I also got the impression that she's not what she appears to be. Her eyes tell me she's older than we think she is.'

'So she looks good for her age, so what? Lots of girls do,' said Tamara.

Catchpole shook his head. 'No, it's more than that. *She's* more than that. She feels like she doesn't belong. As for how she got into your study, Tamara, I think it was by mirror.'

'Why is it that everybody else does it with mirrors and we're the only ones that have to go by car?' Tamara asked beginning to feel angry. 'If she can do it, it makes her no better than the Council. When she's done her job, I want her gone.'

'Gone as in out of the country, or gone as in *under* the country?' Catchpole asked.

'Dead, Mr Catchpole. I want her dead,' said Tamara.

'But she's just a girl,' said Emily.

'She's not one of us,' Tamara replied. 'And if she's not one of us, she's one of them. She's already proved that she can do too much to allow her to continue.'

'After you've used her to do your job for you,' Emily mumbled. Suddenly her cheek flushed as her face whipped sideways. 'Ouch! What was that for?'

'Insubordination,' Tamara snapped.

Emily rose from the chair, tears giving the fresh welt on her face a diamond twinkle. 'You're starting to sound like him!' she said shooting Catchpole a glance. 'Michael would never have …'

'We'll never know what he would have done, will we?' Tamara snapped again, cutting Emily off.

'Can you hear yourself?' Emily sobbed. 'You've been on some two-year-long temper tantrum since he died. Let it go will you?'

Tamara watched as Emily stormed out of the room clutching her cheek. Flopping into the chair her friend had occupied, she buried her face in her hands and counted to ten under her breath before speaking.

'She's right, isn't she?'

'I disagree,' said Catchpole. 'You're doing your job. However, I'd be happier if you could consult with me before making any deals that concern all of us.'

'But that is my job,' Tamara sighed, 'to make decisions that could affect us all. I just wish Michael were here to help me make them, that's all.'

'Now, now,' said Catchpole, perching himself on the arm of the chair next to her. 'Don't go thinking like that. You're doing just fine with the advisors you have. Even I forget that you're still young sometimes. Don't go making the same mistake.' He put a hand under Tamara's chin and lifted her face so that he could look into her eyes. 'Why don't we leave the question of what to do with the Piper until after she's done? You never know, the Council might get there first and we'll be back to square one.'

'I guess,' Tamara replied. 'Yes, let's leave it for now. Besides, I'd better go and talk to Emily, before she decides that she can't advise me anymore.'

'Run along then,' said Catchpole, his usual half-smirk returning.

Tamara got up from the chair and started her way back to the apartments.

*Run along,* she thought. *Who does he think he is? He's just dismissed me from my own study. And I let him! One day, Mister*

*Catchpole, you and I are going to dance. I promise you'll regret ever thinking you could use me as your little puppet.*

Her footsteps echoed through the corridor as she climbed the stairs to the rooms set aside for the Grand Inquisitor and advisory staff, known as the apartments. The usual rooms at the academy were on the more opulent side of luxurious. With their lavish fittings, separate study and bedroom with en-suite bathroom for each student and a balcony that looked out over the grounds, they were the envy of other public schools. But the apartments were different.

They were a series of suites all of their own, with a lounge, study, several bedrooms and a private dining room in each. They had been designed with the intention of entertaining dignitaries, or housing the upper echelons of the Inquisition when they came to visit. Dripping with crystal chandeliers, expensive works of art, silk tapestries, antique furniture and marble floors, they put some palaces to shame.

Tamara stopped outside the door to Emily's apartment. She could hear her talking with Rupert inside, sounding upset but not angry. When she thought about it, Tamara couldn't ever remember a time when Emily had been openly angry with her. She rapped on the door. There was no reply.

'Em, it's me. Can I come in?' She called, trying her best to sound apologetic.

The door opened a crack and Rupert's eye and nose appeared in the gap. 'Is it you, you, or evil twin you?' he asked.

Tamara blushed and looked at the floor. 'It's me – good me. I owe you both an apology. Please let me in.'

Rupert stepped aside, pulling the door with him. 'Go easy with her. She thinks you're trying to pull rank or something.'

'I can speak for myself, thank you,' said Emily from behind him.

'Can we sit down?' said Tamara. 'I need to talk to you both. I think I need help.'

They sat and talked for what felt like hours. Being a weekend, there were no tutors to distract them with unnecessary lessons. Tamara confessed that since the trials she had felt empty, and that the weight of her role as Grand Inquisitor had been an added worry. Emily was quick to add that both she and Rupert had been feeling like Tamara still blamed them for their part in Michael's mishap, but that they both understood that it would take time before Tamara could forgive them properly.

'It's not that I haven't forgiven you,' Tamara insisted. 'You didn't do anything that needed to be forgiven. It's not like you had a choice.'

'Then why did you lash out at me today, if you're not still angry with me?' Emily pressed.

'It's … him,' Tamara replied, meaning Catchpole. 'He brings out the worst in me every time. I was trying to show him that I could make the important decisions, that I'm ready to take command without him looking over my shoulder all the time.'

'So you slapped me for stating the obvious just to impress that creep?' said Emily.

'It sounds so stupid when you put it that way, but yes,' Tamara confessed.

'I think it's time you told her, Em,' said Rupert.

Tamara glanced from one face to the other. 'Told me what?'

'It's Catchpole,' said Emily. 'He's up to something, and knowing him it's sinister.'

'Up to what?'

'I don't know for sure,' said Emily. 'But when he was poking around in my head, I saw something that was almost familiar. It was like a screwed up version of déjà vu.'

'I don't follow,' said Tamara, an expression of confusion crossing her face.

'Do you remember when I had that vision just before the trials? You know, the one where I saw Michael standing over you with fire in his hands?' Emily continued.

'Yes, but that can't come true now, can it?' said Tamara. 'Michael's dead. Unless someone's going to take his place.'

'That's what I wanted to tell you,' said Emily. 'I sort of recognised the building where it happens. It's the library that Catchpole was at this morning, only it was a wreck the first time I saw it.'

'But it's not going to happen because Michael's dead, and the library's not a wreck.' Tamara insisted.

'There's something else,' said Rupert. 'But before Emily says anything ...' He hesitated, looking sheepish. 'You have to promise not to go nuts.'

'What could possibly be so ...'

'Promise, Tam,' said Rupert.

Tamara held up her hands. 'Okay, okay, I promise I won't go nuts!'

'I think that Catchpole's holding something back about Michael,' said Emily.

'That's not news,' Tamara said, visibly relieved that it wasn't anything bad. 'Miss Cunningham said that she spoke to him after the investigation and that he felt guilty for not stopping the trial when he had the chance.'

'No,' said Emily, 'that's not what I meant. Look, all I know is, when he was rummaging around in my head, I suddenly had one thought. One thought that definitely wasn't mine. Which means it was his.'

'And ...' said Tamara, suddenly anxious again. 'What was it?'

Emily took a deep breath. 'I think I heard him think ... Well ... I think I heard him think the words: "They must have taken him". Michael's alive!'

'How can that be?' Tamara gasped. 'We saw him lying there. You saw it as well as I did. Davis said he was dead!'

'I know,' said Rupert. 'I was just as gobsmacked as you are when Emily told me just now.'

'That's what I heard,' said Emily. 'I saw the library in my head from Catchpole's point of view. He was looking down from somewhere at a set of tables listening to some people. Then I saw one of the people he was looking at turn around and there was a feeling, like a jolt of excitement. And that's when he thought it. What's worse is, the tables he was looking at are where the marble altar-thingy I saw in my vision was two years ago.'

Suddenly, Tamara flung her arms around her friend.

72

'I don't know what to say,' she said, a glow of hysteria replacing the numbness inside her. 'He's alive. Michael's alive!'

## Chapter Four:
# Smoke and Ashes

'I promised you yesterday that I'd take you outside the compound. So let's go,' said Anna over breakfast the next day.

'Sure,' Michael beamed. 'But I thought you'd want to go over those books that Grimm lent us.'

'That can wait, there's something special I want to show you first.'

'Let's go,' said Michael, cramming the last of his sausage and egg muffin into his mouth.

As they wandered back through the hall, Michael sensed a smugness in his aunt's demeanour that meant that she was proud of something. He also noticed that the whole place was quieter than usual, as though most of the other residents were still in bed, or in hiding.

'It's a bit quiet isn't it?' he ventured.

'That's what I wanted to show you,' said Anna, leading him through a set of corridors and up a ramp that came out at a corrugated metal barn.

'I really miss living in the open,' Michael sighed as they crossed the hay-strewn floor. 'Not that I'm complaining. I prefer being alive, don't get me wrong. But when you have to be careful everywhere you go, it can be a real pain in the … Hello, what's all this then?'

The sight that greeted them as they left the shelter of the barn was, in the truest sense of the word, awesome. It was like standing on the top of the world. Except for the scattered buildings of the farm, all that Michael could see for miles around were mountain tops. Though the grass wasn't the lush green of the lowlands, there was plenty to see. Heathers and thistles dotted the landscape in blues and purples. The sun pushed its way through the clouds in shafts, lighting the coats of grazing sheep with winter gold. There was a wind here that shook, rather than swayed the tops of the small, dense patches of fir trees. In his head, Michael finally knew what Macbeth's blasted heath was. However, this blasted heath came with sorcerers, not witches, and there were more than three of them. Many, many more.

'You're about to see something that hasn't been done in Wales since the time of the druids,' Anna smiled.

Michael gawked at the crowd that had amassed outside the barn. It was more like looking at an audience of festival-goers than looking at the people he knew.

'Where did they all come from?'

'Here and there,' said Anna. 'There hasn't been a lot of word from the Grand Council for a long time, as you know. The last orders that were issued were to train people to fight. Lefrick thought it would be best to bring everyone in our branch of the network together after the temple raid, so that's what he did. They've been arriving in dribs and drabs for a while now.'

'How come I haven't seen them all before?' Michael asked.

'They're back and forth,' said Anna. 'I can't say too much just yet, but some of them are more like refugees now that ...' She hesitated and drew a deep breath. 'Let's just say that it's not good to keep all your eggs in one basket, so a few camps have been set up same as this one. The difference is, we're going to be working as a much closer group now, which is why we have so many at the moment. They've come here to be trained before they go back to their own bunkers to train the others. I suppose one day they'll merge them all. That'll be a sight to see I'm sure.'

There were tones of anxiety in her voice as if she thought it was wrong, or disagreed with what was going on. Michael had seen that look on her face before, whenever she'd let slip about her feelings towards the Grand Council and its recent silence.

'Is the farmer one of us?' said Michael.

'In a manner of speaking,' Anna replied. 'Actually, he and his family are all normals that Lefrick has known for years. They'll be putting up with us for a while in exchange for a few favours.'

'What kind of favours?'

'Oh, food or work, that sort of thing,' said Anna.

The members of the crowd seemed to reach a mutual consensus and split into two groups. The larger group turned away from one another and began to pace in all of the directions of the compass, each carrying a small, white bag made of sackcloth tied at their waists. At the appointed distance, Michael could see them take handfuls of light brown grain from the bags and scatter them evenly about the place. Meanwhile, the smaller group walked in lines, up and down sections of bare earth, again scattering grains from the cloth pouches at their sides.

'What are they doing?' Harriet King whispered over Michael's shoulder.

'Beats me?' said Michael. 'How's tricks, Harriet? Been keeping out of trouble?'

'As much as I can in a place like this,' said Harriet. 'I met a friend of yours yesterday - Sam.'

'I know,' said Michael. 'I saw you both at breakfast. Listen, Harriet, I'm sorry you got mixed up in all this.'

'I'm not,' Harriet laughed. 'Michael, the things I've seen since Railroad took me away. I'd never have believed them in a million years if I hadn't seen them for myself!'

Michael turned to look at her. 'What about your family? Surely you miss them, don't you?'

'Sometimes,' Harriet replied. 'I still miss Max too. I don't suppose I'll ever see him again, not now.'

The sadness in her voice reminded Michael of his own whenever he thought of Tamara. However, he couldn't understand how anyone could feel like that about Maxwell Bennett. Bennett had been a bully and a thug during his brief few weeks at the academy. One day, Michael had even had to physically defend Rupert from him. Not that Michael had ever regretted it, but it had cost him a trial in the peer court, and sadly the life of one of his housemates. But while Michael hated Max Bennett for what he was, he was still unable to forget Harriet's part in it. Strangely, Michael felt a pang of sympathy for her. He knew what it was like to miss someone you could never have.

'Okay you two, they're ready. You can catch up in a minute. You really need to see this,' said Anna.

Michael turned to watch as both of the groups reunited

to form a vast circle, hands outstretched and fingertips touching, around the farm. They turned their faces skywards as the chanting began low and slow. At first there was a warm sensation that cut through the bitter bite of the breeze. It was a feeling that was familiar to most of the onlookers that had gathered to witness the spectacle. It was the warmth of the earth, the tingle of the air, the excitement of fire tempered by the calm of water. It was the tingle of magic being unleashed on the world.

Sorcery is just that. It's the taking of energy from a source – usually from nature – the ground and plants and suchlike, even other people occasionally. At least, that's what Michael's tutors had taught him. Because these sources are usually warm (because they are alive), the magic that comes from them is warm.

Sorcery is not the sacrificing of life for the benefit of magical work, although some living materials are used in the process, like leaves or berries. And it's generally accepted that the sorcerer will only take what is needed, and never so much that the donor will suffer or perish. Michael had found the concept difficult to accept when he'd first arrived at the Council.

He had been used to drawing energy from his environment as an Inquisitor, but only as much as he could store or borrow from others. Sorcerers didn't store energy that way. When it was necessary, they took it directly from their surroundings and gave any unspent energy back to the world when they were done. There were even some sorcerers that considered themselves to be vegetarians of a sort. They only ever took energy from plants, or the elements, believing that the energy of animals is a sacred thing.

Michael watched in fascination as the tingle in the air built with the chanting of the voices. It was musical, almost Gregorian, like the monks of old. He was used to the whispered chanting of incantations, but this was new and wasn't only because the Council was alone on the mountain. There seemed to be a new kind of freedom in the voices of his colleagues.

Beneath the song, a rustling joined the chorus and the ground began to quake. Harriet reached out and grasped Michael's hand as the rustling became a groaning, but he barely noticed. Neither had he noticed that fronds of green had pushed up from the earth, nor that they began to sprout first into saplings, then into juvenile trees. The sound of it all was earth shattering, as if someone had brought every creaking door from every horror movie ever made to this spot at the same time. The chanting picked up speed now, growing louder and louder. The juveniles kept pace until they became towering evergreen giants.

The circle turned inwards and continued their incantation, focussing their efforts into the carefully sown lines of soil. Faster this time, the shoots sprouted and grew. Their shapes changed to produce succulent berries, carrot tops, cabbages, potatoes and even a small crop of wheat. If this had been a market garden, it would have been the envy of competitive growers everywhere. The food was ripe and abundant. The aroma of it filled the air with a sticky, sweet perfume, as the chanting stopped and the incantors stood back to admire their work.

Harriet heaved a sigh. 'They could have put up a few flowers.'

Freeing his hand from hers, Michael rubbed his palms together, closed his eyes and whispered a chant of his own. Slowly, he began to widen his arms, drawing his hands apart until everyone could see the green stem beginning to form. With an effort of concentration, he continued, sweat beading on his furrowed brow, as leaves and scarlet petals began to form. When he was done, he took it gently by the base of the stem and gave it to Harriet.

'It's a rose,' he said. 'Sorry, it's not scented. I don't know how.'

'It's beautiful, Michael. Thank you,' replied Harriet. 'Does this mean you forgive me?'

Staring at the floor, Michael shuffled his feet in the grass. 'I … Let's say it's a start. After all, we're both in the same er … boat.'

'Are you trying to be funny?'

'No,' Michael replied. 'I'm just trying to say that I understand how it must be for you to be away from your family and missing Max.'

'You should give this to Tamara next time you see her,' Harriet ventured as she held the rose back out to him.

'That's okay. It won't last long. It's not *really* real,' he smiled.

'How can it not be real? It feels real,' said Harriet.

'It's too … perfect,' said Michael. 'It stands out too much. If you were to put it next to another rose, you'd see.'

'But those trees don't look any different, or the food,' said Harriet, squinting to see the difference.

'That's because they were encouraged to grow from the seeds they planted,' Michael explained. 'The rose was conjured out of thin air. It looks like how I imagined it should look, not how it would have decided to look if it had had its own pattern to follow.'

'Well done,' said Anna. 'That was the best explanation I've heard in a while for the difference between true nature and conjuration. You're really getting the hang of it now, Michael.'

They stood admiring the grove for a while as birds began to settle in the treetops. The tingle of magic was so fresh in the air, that the yellowing bracken lining the rough driveway sprang to life again. It was as if Mother Nature was in a hurry to kick-start a second spring. A commotion behind them broke the spell.

'Anna,' Lefrick shouted. His face was full of horror. 'It's Jerrick. Come quickly and bring Michael, he's asking for him.'

'Asking for me?' Michael gasped.

'No time for questions, Michael,' Lefrick chided. 'Do as you're told now and come inside. Harriet, I'm sorry, but this is private. I'll have him back as soon as I can.'

'It's okay,' Harriet called to their retreating backs. 'I'll just um ... stay here and admire the view some more.'

They ran through the barn and down through the corridor. Michael hadn't noticed the difference on the way out, but it was warmer down here and the air was stale. So many bodies together in one place, not that it was particularly cramped, generated a sweaty stickiness. The temple had been cool, sometimes even cold. As people parted to let them through, it filled Michael with a strange twofold homesickness. As well as the academy, with its grotesque amounts of space per head, he longed for the temple, where too many blankets to keep out the cold was preferable to this stifling, airless dungeon.

Heads turned as they passed, their faces a mixture of confusion, dread and panic. As the trio sped through the refectory, Michael could see Mrs Lucas passing a pan of boiling water to Mrs Davis, and Andy the doorman was tearing sheets into rags like they were tissue paper. They followed Lefrick out into the bunk rooms, stopping at a gaggle of onlookers.

'Come on now,' Lefrick berated, shooing people out of the way. 'This isn't the opera. Make way, make way.'

Once Michael had squeezed past the press of bodies, the scene hit him like a rock. Jerrick was laid out on the covers of his bed. Deep rents in his arms and legs oozed scarlet. His usual neatly plaited beard was ragged, and Michael gagged when he saw the flash of ivory as the man turned his head, exposing the bone of his chin when the flap of skin flopped sideways.

'What happened?' Anna gasped.

'Flayer attack, I think,' said Lefrick. 'Judging by the state of him, he ran out of magic trying to get home and they jumped on him.'

'I thought they just sucked the life out of you?' asked Michael.

'They do,' Lefrick confirmed. 'Sometimes, when there are so many of them trying to get to the same food source, a fight breaks out and they end up destroying the prey in the melee.'

'Why hasn't anyone done anything?' Anna barked, rolling up her sleeves and kneeling by the bedside. She placed her hands over a particularly nasty gash on Jerrick's forehead and began to chant.

'We've tried that, it doesn't work,' said Lefrick. He pinched the bridge of his nose. Michael had seen him that way when they'd been talking about plans and discussing tactics.

Mrs Davis bustled into the room with the pan of water and the rags Andy had been preparing. Dousing each to sterilize them, she wrapped them around Jerrick's wounds, trying to stem the flow of the bleeding.

'What about your ointment, Mrs D, would that help?' said Michael trying to be of some use.

'Not for this kind of wound,' said the housekeeper. She plunged her hand into the pan of water, wincing as the heat scalded her skin. When she pulled it out again, she was clutching a reel of cotton with a needle threaded onto it.

Jerrick's eyes flickered to her and he shook his head. 'No,' he said, his Middle Eastern accent heavier than Michael had ever heard it. 'It's alright, Margret, there's no need for that.'

'We have to stop the bleeding,' said Anna choking back her tears.

The genie's mouth turned up into a painful smile. 'It's too late for that, Habibi. I need to speak to Michael, is he here?'

'I'm right here,' said Michael pressing his way to his mentor's bedside.

'Ah, good. Forgive me everyone, but I need to speak with the boy alone. Lefrick, take them out my friend, and be so kind as to close the door, would you?'

'Of course, Jerrick. Whatever you say,' Lefrick replied ushering the others out into the corridor, the latch of the door clicking behind him.

Jerrick heaved a ragged sigh, his eyes half closed. 'Now then,' he breathed. 'Do you know why I brought you here?'

'Because I was supposed to be the next Grand Inquisitor. You brought me here to stop them from gaining strength too quickly,' said Michael.

The genie croaked a laugh. 'No. And yes. You are the Grand Inquisitor. Well, half of him. Renfrew's power resides in you as much as it does Tamara.'

'Does that mean you should have taken Tamara as well?'

'No,' Jerrick replied. 'My plan was always to leave her there. You and she are the same side of the same coin.'

Michael's brow furrowed. 'Don't you mean ...'

'I mean you are the same side of the same coin,' said Jerrick waving a hand. 'But that's not why I brought you here. I brought you because you have the potential to do what I could not.'

'How can that be?' said Michael. 'You're far more powerful than I could ever hope to be.'

'Not so,' Jerrick spluttered. 'You have learned their art and now you will learn ours. I have wasted my time, squandered it in the noblest of ways.'

'I wouldn't call trying to bridge the gap between the Inquisition and the Council a waste of time,' said Michael.

'You've always taught me that peace is worth the price we pay for it.'

'But not any price.' Jerrick coughed, blood bubbling at his lips. 'You must finish what I started, Michael. The Grand Council of Elders has turned its back on me, but I was too arrogant to accept it. Once they wanted only peace, but they have turned their backs on that also, choosing to coerce the normals to fight for their cause.'

Michael dabbed at his mentor's lips with a sodden rag. 'I don't understand!'

Jerrick put a blood-stained hand on his pupil's arm. 'They too are looking for the Piper. It's my fault, Michael. It's my fault.'

'Master, you need to rest. We can talk about this when you're stronger.'

Jerrick shook his head and whispered, 'There will be time enough for that. You will become the master of my house. I leave it all to you. Lefrick knows my will and he will help you. You must get to the Piper before the others. When you find him, you must tell him that his revenge ends with me ...'

The genie's chest sank and didn't rise again, his eyes still fixed on Michael's.

Michael passed his hands over his mentor's eyelids to close them. Jerrick's fingers were still locked around his other arm. But try as he might, he couldn't prise them open.

'A little help in here,' he called over his shoulder.

At once the door burst open and Lefrick, Anna and the Davises clambered into the room. To their surprise, their approach was halted by a translucent glow, as a shimmering haze came into being an inch above Jerrick's body. Michael tried to pull away, but the hand at his arm gripped more tightly than it had when its owner had been alive. Only now it began to smoke, along with the rest of what remained of Jerrick's flesh.

Billowing clouds began to fill the room behind the glowing wall, obscuring Michael and the corpse from sight. He could hear Anna chanting, trying to break whatever spell Jerrick might have thrown up accidentally with his dying will, but it was no use. By the time she began to throw her whole body against the bubble, Michael was struggling to breathe.

He knew that it had happened to Anna once before – on the night she had lost her husband. Their home had been invaded by a Grand Inquisitor named Renfrew, on New Year's Eve - the night Michael had been born. Trying to even the odds a little, Anna had barrelled Renfrew's bodyguard through the downstairs front window of their house, to get him out of play. The blank must have known what was coming because he'd turned tail and ran from her. But when she'd tried to jump through the window to get back into the fight, she'd been repelled by a wall of translucent green magic and been rendered unconscious. By the time she had come to, both her husband and Renfrew were dead.

'Michael, get out of there,' his aunt yelled as she pounded her fists against the wall.

Michael turned, dragging the still clinging Jerrick in the direction of her voice. The smoke had filled almost the entire space now. Choking, he slumped onto all fours, trying to get under the suffocating fumes, his head butting up against the glow. The fist of his free hand clenched, he hammered as hard as he could against the barrier until his aunt's face appeared twisted and distorted, on the other side.

'Help me,' Michael mouthed, unable to scream.

Anna pawed at the other side of the magic glass, her face streaked with tears and red with fury. Suddenly there was a terrific bang that shook the room like an earthquake, bouncing Michael like a rubber ball against the barrier and back into the smog. The cloud turned in on itself with a noise like a pressure release valve, hissing and sputtering. Anna and the others barely recovered in time to watch, as the vapour subsided like the steam from a kettle in reverse into Michael's open mouth, nose and eyes.

'NOOOOOOOO!!!' Anna yelled at the top of her lungs.

The barrier fell. Hurling herself to the floor beside her nephew, she cradled his head in her lap, feeling at his neck for a pulse.

'Don't you dare, Michael. Don't you dare do this to me again!' she sobbed.

Michael gasped for air, his eyes fluttering open. 'Are you an angel?' he croaked, before passing out.

***

'I swear that boy's going to be the death of me,' said Davis, trying to catch his breath.

'I hope not,' Lefrick snorted with his back to the others.

'What is that?' asked Anna still nursing Michael's head as she squinted to see what her colleague was busy with.

'It's what's left of a good friend,' Lefrick replied. He took a small copper oil lamp from a shelf. Taking off the lid, he returned to a neat pile of ashes and carefully swept them into the lamp with a piece of folded paper from his pocket. When he was done, he replaced the lid and stuffed the end of the spout with one of the rags that Mrs Davis had brought with her. 'I'll keep this safe. How's Michael doing?'

'He'll be alright,' said Mrs Davis. 'The boy's taken harder knocks and *we all* know it.'

'What about the smoke?' Anna asked. 'What the hell was that about?'

'The end of an era,' said Lefrick.

***

'This is the latest incident in a long line of disasters to hit public sites, following a fire at a museum in Berlin in two thousand and eleven. However, a spokesperson for the Archives of Paris, speaking on French national television today, has insisted that a warning was received by the curator shortly before the fire broke out. We cross now to Andrew Finchley, who is live at the Archives of Paris, with the report.'

'Thank you, John. As you can see, I'm standing some way from the archive building, having been warned by the

French fire services that the building could collapse at any moment. The fire started at around five-thirty local time this morning and thankfully, it appears that only two people were injured.'

'What about the claims that the curator received a warning before the incident, Andrew? Is there any truth to them?'

'Yes, John,' said Finchley, nodding his head. 'French reports say that the letter is under investigation by the French authorities and that a group calling themselves "The Council" is claiming responsibility for the fire.'

'If that is the case,' John, the news anchor chimed in, 'surely that would be a step up from an arson attack to something more serious.'

'That's right. It's not clear whether the French government is treating this as a terrorist attack, or whether it's simply a group of individuals with a grudge. I'll let you know more as the story unfolds. For now, it's back to you both at the studio.'

'Andrew Finchley there, with what could be an attack on the French government. Coming up later in the programme ...'

Tamara clicked the off button on her remote control and stared at Catchpole. 'Why would they attack the Paris Archives?'

'Like the library, it was a haven site,' said Catchpole. 'It was somewhere where both sides could go to do research, etcetera.'

'Isn't that like cutting off your own nose to spite your face?' Tamara pressed.

Catchpole raised an eyebrow. 'Yes, I suppose. But who knows what goes on in the heads of those animals. I can only think that perhaps they did it because the French Inquisitors were getting too close to something.'

'Perhaps. But I still don't understand why they would burn it to the ground.'

'Simple,' said Catchpole. 'There's no other way to protect their interests in a place like that. It's not as if you can blast off a few bolts once you're passed reception, is it?'

Tamara's face brightened with understanding. 'So the fastest way to hide something is to make sure it doesn't exist anymore?'

'Right!' Catchpole confirmed. 'But don't worry, if I know Grimm and his bunch, there are bound to be other copies of whatever it was they were trying to hide.'

'What's to stop them going after the other haven sites as well?'

'That's all been taken care of,' Catchpole grinned. 'The Home Secretary will be issuing a statement tomorrow to confirm that the fire was indeed an act of terrorism and that the United Kingdom will also be on alert.'

Tamara looked dismayed. 'The Home Secretary's an Inquisitor?'

Catchpole nodded with a smug wink. 'One of ours.'

'Good grief,' Tamara sighed. 'But how do you know for certain that the Council was involved?'

'Because the High Marshals say it was. Besides, it's the perfect opportunity for us to turn the tide of public opinion against them.'

'So you're saying that you don't know it was the

Council for sure,' said Tamara. 'But we're going to tell people it was so we can go after them?'

'Something like that,' said Catchpole. 'Look, we can't very well go around telling people that a group of sorcerers calling themselves the Elder Council exists, can we? Worse still, imagine telling them that they're trying to free mankind from the "tyranny and oppression" of the government they elect. They'd think we were insane. No, the only way to convince them that we have their best interests at heart is to build a strategy.'

'I see,' said Tamara wearing her doubt on her sleeve. 'So what? You'd rather tell them that the Council are a bunch of terrorists and have the government set up a body called "The Inquisition" to stop them?'

'I hadn't really thought past branding them all terrorists myself,' said Catchpole. 'It could work.'

'Do you really want the Inquisition to be public knowledge?' Tamara sputtered.

'That's the beauty of it,' said Catchpole rubbing his hands. 'We've been a part of society for so long that people already know we exist. We're nothing new to them, except for the psychic stuff. We've guided them, taught them and led them for so long that it would be second nature. It would be like setting up a new police force. A few new policies through parliament and it's as good as done.'

'There would be objections,' Tamara countered. 'Civil liberty is a big thing right now, especially since the riots. I'm not so sure the public would go for another police force as such. It would be just another system of control to them.'

'Then we dress it up as something else,' said Catchpole.

'You know, milady, I do like the way you think sometimes. It sends shivers down my spine!' With that, he left the study and a stunned Tamara behind him.

'Not half as much as you send shivers down mine, *Mister Catchpole*,' she whispered.

*That lunatic's going to get us all killed!* She thought. *He keeps talking about the High Marshalls like they're all in his pocket. Huh, knowing him they probably are. He wants to dress up some phoney policy to try and squeeze the Council out of hiding. I don't know whether to stop him or let him. They've probably got Michael locked up somewhere, trying to get what they can out of him.*

She rubbed at her eyelids with the backs of her hands and sighed.

*I've got to get to Michael before Catchpole puts his idea to work. I know the others would be willing to help me, even Miss Cunningham; But how? Even if I could find it, it's not as though I could just waltz into wherever they're hiding him and ask for my boyfriend back.* She laughed quietly to herself.

*No, it's going to be harder than that, it always is. If he's alive, he might have found some way to get the word out to someone; but who? His parents? Sam? No, it would have to be someone he could trust to get the news to the Inquisition. Someone Catchpole would allow into the school without too many questions.*

She lifted the receiver of the phone and dialled. After several rings, there was a voice at the other end of the line.

'Hello?'

Tamara took a deep breath before launching headlong into her request. 'Hello, Mrs Ware, it's Tamara; Tamara Bloodgood? You probably don't remember me, but I was at school with Michael. May I speak to Alice, please?'

There was a tense silence before Michael's mother answered.

'Hello, Tamara. What an unexpected surprise, love. I'm afraid that Alice is away at Oxford. Can I ask what you're calling about and perhaps we can get her to call you?'

Tamara hadn't prepared herself for this. She'd been hoping that Alice was there, certain that if Michael had been able to get a message to anyone, he would have chosen her. On the other hand, if he hadn't, it would have been easier to have broken the news to her that her brother was alive, rather than having to put Michael's parents through the whole ordeal again. She wasn't even sure that Alice would have taken the news any better, but it was a good place to start.

'It's nothing really,' Tamara lied. 'I was hoping that she might have some old photographs of Michael that she wouldn't mind lending me. I didn't want to trouble you with it.'

'It's no bother,' said Mrs Ware. 'I'm sure she'd be happy to help. Let me give you her number.'

Tamara scribbled the number down and thanked Mrs Ware for her time before hanging up the receiver. She folded the paper carefully and put it into her pocket, a smile flitting across her face. There was no way that she could let Catchpole know what she was planning. Even letting him know that she knew about Michael could put a lot of lives in jeopardy, including her own. She was certain that her calls from the study were being monitored. There was always an intermittent clicking in the background she'd never heard from any phone outside the academy.

As she left the study, the guards on either side of the door bowed their heads respectfully, as they always did. Sometimes she felt like a celebrity with her protection detail. They didn't follow her around the grounds of the school, as a rule, but when she went outside the academy they were always there.

The apartments and study were at the back of the main academy building. Miss Cunningham had explained to her that it was for convenience. It allowed the Grand Inquisitor access to the main library and to any of the school's masters at any time, day or night. Rather inconveniently, it meant that Tamara, Rupert and Emily had to travel to House Solaris for mental training or to see their friends.

Guessing that Rupert and Emily would be visiting at one of Solaris's three common rooms, Tamara crossed the quadrant, rounded the fountain at its centre and passed beneath the archway at the far end. The gardens were in hibernation at this time of year, but the air was fresh and clear. Usually, she would have walked to her old house, especially on a day like today. But there was something she needed to do urgently and in person. At weekends, there were always trolleys to take students back and forth to the gates that led into the nearby village of Hambley. And it wasn't long before Tamara's taxi was trundling its way along the path through the trees. As it went, her mind was filled with old conversations and laughter, with the night Michael had held her hand and, in that awkward way of his, asked her to be his girlfriend. In the past, she would have shut any such thoughts out of her mind, but today was different. Michael was alive, and for the first time in what seemed like an eternity, Tamara felt alive too.

When the trees parted and the trolley crossed the stone bridge to Solaris Island, Tamara's heart began to pound in her chest. It wasn't the first time that she had done something without Catchpole's permission or knowledge, but Tamara knew that it had to be done without him.

When she arrived at the house, she took the familiar double staircase two stairs at a time, hurtled along the corridor and flung herself through the door of the second floor common room. Ignoring the other students, who had stood to attention on the arrival of their superior, she headed for the far corner of the room, to where Rupert and Emily were talking to a dark haired young man whom she recognised immediately.

'Adam,' she yelped as she approached them. 'What on earth are you doing here?'

'Grand Inquisitor Bloodgood,' said Adam Dakin, former head boy of Solaris. He stood and bowed until he couldn't keep a straight face any longer. Then he opened his arms wide and received Tamara into the biggest hug. When he finally let go, they slumped onto the sofa together.

'I'm so glad you're here,' Tamara panted. 'There's something I wanted to talk to you about.'

'I know,' said Emily. 'You want to ask us to go to Oxford with you, to talk to Michael's sister, Alice.'

'Damn it, Em!' Tamara replied, caught completely off her guard. 'How long have you known?'

'About seven minutes,' said Adam. 'I was just telling them that I had a vision about the three of you visiting with me at the university, so I came to you instead.'

'But I was looking forward to going on a trip,' said Tamara. Feigning disappointment, she poked out her bottom lip

'Now, now,' said Rupert, 'just listen to what Adam's got to say. I think you'd approve.'

'Alright,' Tamara sighed.

'Alice and I are already on pretty good terms,' said Adam. 'I don't remember how it happened, but some friends and I were talking about where we were at school over a drink one day. She must have heard me talking about the academy because of what she asked me. She wanted to know if I knew about a boy that had died on the school grounds. Naturally, I assumed that she'd meant poor old Craig Hathaway because they'd kept Michael's death out of the press.

'The mouthful she gave me was enough to make a barman blush until she mentioned Michael by name. Long story short, I apologised and said that of course I knew Michael and that I was very sorry for her loss. It was a bit strange. Every time she saw me, she would poke around for information about the academy, asking questions like: "So, what really goes on there behind closed doors?" and "Isn't it strange how a lot of really powerful people started out at the Braxton Academies". I didn't know what to think at first.'

'You haven't told her anything you shouldn't, have you?' Tamara asked.

Adam looked shocked. 'Of course not. However, I think I remember her looking up the Elder Council on the internet one time. I was going to report it, but I honestly thought that it was just a coincidence. I only put two and two together when I had that vision of you at Oxford.'

'So what is it you're proposing?' Tamara asked, her impatience getting the better of her.

Adam grinned. 'We're in the same town, and we go to the same college, don't we? It wouldn't be difficult to get myself invited to a party at her place and do some digging around. It'll keep Catchpole off your back, and you'll arouse less suspicion if I do it for you.'

'You just want to say that you got your orders directly from the Grand Inquisitor!' Tamara ribbed him.

'Of course!' Adam laughed.

'Okay, but you need to do it quickly. And don't tell her anything about our lot. We don't know that we can trust her,' said Tamara.

'Agreed,' said Adam. 'The last thing we want is her finding out about the Inquisition and its purpose. It's likely to end up in the press, and then where would we be? Nobody wants to involve the normals in an all-out civil war. This has to stay between them and us, or things could really get out of hand.'

Tamara's heart sank. 'Things are starting to get out of hand already. If Catchpole gets his way, every man and his dog could be hunting the Council by tomorrow evening.'

'How do you mean?' asked Emily.

'I can't go into it right now,' said Tamara, flicking her eyes at the rest of the room. 'I think I might have put an idea in his head without meaning to. But between Catchpole, the Piper and the rest of the Inquisition, things are about to get rough for the Council. Very rough indeed.'

## Chapter Five:
# The River

It was dark as Katja descended the steps to the riverbank and crossed the muddy sand, leaving no footprints. When she reached the concrete base beneath one of the arches, she hunkered down and drew her coat around her against the cold.

In the dim light of the fire, she could see the shapes of other people around her, rubbing their hands and chatting idly about everything and nothing.

'Bitter, ain't it?' said a man in a shabby, woollen overcoat to her right, as he held out a bottle of something clear.

Katja ignored him.

'Go on, take a snort. It'll keep the cold out,' said the old man.

She continued to ignore him.

'Suit yerself, missy. Girl like you shouldn't be out on yer own on a night like this, though. I bet you haven't even stuffed, have you?'

'Stuffed?' she asked, curiosity getting the better of her. 'If that's some strange euphemism, I don't think it's appropriate.'

'Now, now, you can get a body into trouble thinking thoughts like that,' said the old man. 'What I meant was: taking old newspaper an' stuffing 'em into your clothes. Keeps you warm ...'

'Oh,' said Katja. 'Then no, I have not stuffed.'

They passed a few minutes in silence. A police river cruiser shone its light on them once or twice, just to make sure that nothing untoward was going on. Eventually, it lost interest and motored on like a baritone bee with asthma.

'Scraps,' said the man.

It took a moment for Katja to realise that he no longer had the bottle in his hand and that he was attempting to introduce himself. She took it in the same way that one picks up a damp napkin and shook it as briefly as Scraps' calloused hand would allow.

'Katie,' said Katja.

'Huh,' Scraps huffed. 'You ain't been on the streets long then. Most people avoid using their real names out here, on account that they're either runnin' or hidin'.'

'Who said Katie was my real name?' Katja countered.

'You got me there,' Scraps laughed breaking into a hoarse cough that filled the air with the stench of alcohol. Reaching into the pocket of his coat for a pouch of rolling tobacco and some papers, he expertly skinned an even, supermodel thin cigarette. He lit it and puffed hard to keep it going. 'I would offer you one, but somethin' tells me you wouldn't accept.'

'I've never tried it,' said Katja. 'But it smells foul. So thank you, but no.'

Scraps laughed again. 'Tell me then, what is it that's keeping young Katie out on a night like this?' he asked, his voice taking on a more serious tone.

Katja sighed hard and turned to look at him. 'I've done something terrible ...'

'Hmm,' the old man mused, 'haven't we all?'

'Not like this,' said Katja, shaking her head.

'I'm sure it's nothin' that can't be forgiven,' said Scraps.

'Not this time,' said Katja. 'It's not something I think anyone can forgive.'

The old man scratched his straggly beard. 'They all think that. You think yer the first youngster I've seen on the streets, missy? Sooner or later, they remember that somebody loves 'em. Ain't nothin' so bad it can't be forgiven, believe you me. Not everyone's as honest as me or as harmless neither. Streets are no place for someone yer age.'

'How old do you think I am?' she asked.

Scraps sparked his lighter again and held it up, squinting at her face. 'About fifteen, if I had to guess.'

'Not bad,' Katja smiled, 'but, at the same time, so far off it's flattering. I've been fifteen years old eight times now.'

'You youngsters and yer flights of fancy,' Scraps chuckled.

'It's true!' Katja snapped. 'I could prove it to you ...'

'Alright,' said Scraps. 'Let's say I believe you. What's the secret? Are you some sort o' ghost, or one o' them vampires or somethin'?'

Katja took a deep breath and let it out slowly before she spoke. 'Nothing quite so romantic I'm afraid. I'm just the silly little girl I used to be. At least my father thinks so.'

'An' what do you think?'

'I've been around for so long, I'm not sure anymore,' said Katja. 'I've seen wars - even started some of them. I've seen famine and drought in some of the farthest reaches of the world. I've seen sunsets over Table Mountain, fresh snows falling near the North Pole, knights in gleaming armour riding valiantly to the aid of the helpless. I speak almost every language there is, and even some that no longer exist. But after seven lifetimes, I've only ever done what *he's* wanted me to do. That's what I think.'

'You still ain't answered the question, though,' said Scraps, taking a deep pull on his bottle. 'What's the secret?'

'It's complicated.' Katja blushed with shame in the darkness. 'After my mother died, my father travelled the world looking for a way to bring her back. He's never found it. Along the way, he learned from a monk in a temple in the East how to share life with others. But mostly he just uses the secret to keep us both going until his work is finished.'

'And what's that, taking over the world?' Scraps snorted.

'No, he's not interested in that,' Katja replied in what she hoped was her most lofty tone. 'He's ... in pest control and recycling.'

The old man burst into a huge, belly rolling laugh. 'Pest control? You have the secret to eternal life, and you choose pest control?'

'Stop it!' said Katja, slapping him on the arm.

Scraps dried his eyes with a filthy sleeve. 'I'm sorry, I couldn't help it. He must really love his job.'

'That's just it,' Katja sighed. 'He despises it. There's a contract he couldn't finish. That's what's keeping him going. I've asked him so many times why he can't just let it go, but he keeps saying that they paid him in advance and the contract must be settled. It's the lore, and it won't let him rest until the job is done.'

'But if it's his job, where do you fit in?'

Katja half closed her eyes, straining to see the past. 'I used to remember, but now it's sort of like a dream. We moved from town to town. He would take work while he was trying to finish that one job. I remember him saying that he wanted me to take over the family business when he was done, but the rest is all a bit of a blur, it's been so long. I don't think he expected it to go on like this.'

The water lapped on the bank of the river. It was quiet below the level of the street, as though the sound were too afraid to venture into the darkness, clinging to the life that was going on all around the city. The police cruiser chugged by again, a biting breeze following in its wake. Katja looked up, studying the clouds in the night sky far above them.

'I don't know how people can stand to live here,' she said in a faraway voice. 'Even when the skies are clear, you can't really see the stars.'

'My little girl used to love to look at the stars,' said Scraps. 'She used to go out into the garden and just stare up at them for hours. My wife would make hot chocolate in the hope that she could lure her back inside, but she wouldn't come until she'd seen at least one shooting star.'

'What happened to her?' Katja pried.

Scraps cleared his throat. 'I used to work shifts back then, at a factory that probably ain't even there anymore. Anyway, I went to work one afternoon an' came home to find the police at my door. There'd been an accident, they said. They were both killed walking home from the school by a truck that had swerved to avoid some ol' biddy that had stepped into the road without lookin'.'

'How awful,' Katja sympathised. 'Is that why you're here now?'

He nodded. 'I just couldn't live without 'em, not really, so I got lost in the bottom of a bottle till I lost my job. Eventually, they took my house and I ended up on the streets, too drunk to work and too ashamed to ask for help. But o' course that was more than forty years ago now.'

'Weren't you scared, you know with the cold, or the other people out here? You could have been murdered, or frozen to death.'

'Nah,' said Scraps. 'After a while, you get to know where there's food an' shelter of a night. Usually, you do something that'll get you tossed in the cells, or cut yerself bad enough for the doctors to let you stay in the hospital. But I'm passed carin' now, 'cause I ain't got long left anyway.'

'What do you mean?'

'I'm an ol' codger who drinks an' smokes too much,' said Scraps. 'It don't take a lot to figure that you're on yer way out when you can't breathe for coughin' of a morning.'

'I should get you to a hospital right away,' Katja blurted. 'Get you to someone who can take care of you.'

'And let 'em take me away from the only home I've got left? No thank you,' said Scraps. 'Besides, there's no one to miss me. Who knows, perhaps those nice officers off that boat will find me an' put me somewhere nice after I'm gone.'

104

'And after that?'

'I don't understand the question,' said Scraps.

'Where do you think you'll ... go, you know ... after?' said Katja.

'I haven't really thought about it,' the old man replied. 'I don't know if there's anywhere *to* go for people like me, is there?'

Katja nodded. 'Of course there is. And when you get there, your family will be there waiting for you, I promise.'

'That's sweet of you to say, missy, but don't go promising things you can't give. I can't be fillin' my head with nonsense at my age,' said Scraps.

'What if I could show you,' Katja retaliated. 'Would you believe me then?'

She reached into her coat and produced the flute from its folds. Putting it to her lips, she piped the sweetest, most heartfelt melody. But it wasn't her usual refrain. There were no empty promises, lures or enticements, only a calm serenity that soothed his eyes into closing under the weight of their lids.

Sharing in his dream, Katja felt Scraps lose himself in the notes of that wonderful air until they found themselves floating in a white mist. Minutes passed like seconds until they reached rolling green fields, dotted with gold and amber leafed trees. The grass caressed their naked toes as they ambled in warm sunlight towards the sounds of laughter. There was a playful splashing from the silver–blue lake just beyond, and a red and white picnic blanket on the ground. Rubbing his hands through his hair, Scraps laughed, proffering his palms to show her that his calluses were gone. His face was fresh, clean and beardless. Instead of his ragged and torn garb, he wore a clean, short-sleeved white shirt and trousers of the softest linen. And he was young.

As they approached the lake, they could see the shapes of swimmers in the shimmering haze on the water, and Katja knew that Scraps recognised them immediately. She watched as he tried to call out to them, but the words stuck in his throat. The mists were engulfing them again, the cold bite of the Thames breeze chilling their bones as it had done before. The sounds of the city came back to them in a rush, and Scraps' eyes fluttered open, filled with tears.

'I don't know whether to thank you or curse you,' he whispered.

'I'm sorry,' said Katja getting to her feet. 'I shouldn't have done that.'

'Done what, given an old man some hope?' Scraps smiled.

Katja slipped the flute back into its resting place and pulled the hood of the coat deeper over her head.

'I'm sorry,' she said again. Then she turned, and ran as hard as she could towards the steps.

***

Michael looked out through eyes that weren't his at the icy sea beneath the bow of a wooden ship. As it creaked and rolled on the waves towards the frozen shore, he was very much aware of himself.

*You're dreaming again,* he thought.

***You're not dreaming, Michael,*** said another voice in his head. ***You're remembering.***

'Now I'm dreaming strange voices, telling me that I'm remembering,' said Michael.

There was a tingling sensation beside him and he became aware of a presence that was both familiar and unnerving. But he dared not turn to look because he didn't want to confirm his suspicions.

'There's no use ignoring me, Michael. In this place, I know what you're thinking, your fears and your wishes. I know everything because I am here with you.'

'Here where?' Michael asked.

'In your head,' said Jerrick.

'So, I am dreaming then because you're dead,' Michael snapped, immediately wishing he hadn't.

Jerrick laughed. 'There's no need to be bashful, you're quite correct. Well, almost correct ... sort of ...'

'I know,' said Michael. 'I can hear what you're thinking too. Listen, you're not going to do this when I'm awake are you? That could get embarrassing.'

'Don't worry,' Jerrick reassured him. 'Anything I see and hear while I'm in here will be strictly between you and me, I promise.'

'Um, that's not very comforting,' said Michael.

'Do you think this arrangement is comfortable for me?' Jerrick replied. 'I can think of better places to be stuck, you know. But it had to be you because ...'

'Because of what I inherited from Grand Inquisitor Renfrew,' Michael finished. 'You need someone who can do what you could do. That's true isn't it?'

'Yes.'

'That's why you asked for me isn't it because Lefrick, as powerful as he is, wouldn't do?'

'Yes,' said Jerrick again. 'Though that's not the only reason. I should have spent more time with you when I was um ... alive, for want of a better word. I should have prepared you while I had the chance, but there were always more important things to attend to. It's really hard being a genie.'

'Yes, it is,' said Michael. 'Always thinking you know best. And when you've lived for as long as you have, you start to feel invincible and forget that you can die. That's why the Flayers got the drop on you, isn't it? You ran off chasing Nahar, and promptly forgot that, even with your power and all your knowledge, you couldn't defend yourself against a thousand or more of them.'

'Yes, it was foolish,' said Jerrick like a child being scolded by his father.

'*You* were foolish,' Michael pressed. 'Say it, go on!'

'I was foolish,' Jerrick repeated.

'And now we're stuck without you and without any real idea of what's going on,' said Michael.

'That is not true,' Jerrick retaliated. 'Your aunt and Lefrick will help as much now as they have before, and you will let them. They must not know about us, or the Grand Council will come down on you all like a tonne of stones.'

'Bricks,' Michael corrected him. 'Like a tonne of bricks.'

'Whatever,' Jerrick dismissed. 'They have wanted me gone for some time now, and they will grasp this opportunity to make their move.'

108

'But you let those Flayers get to you,' said Michael. 'I can see it all in my head. You knew you couldn't beat all of them on your own. You let them tear you apart, just so that you could do ... this.'

'That is true,' said Jerrick. 'You are getting really good at this!'

'And that's not all while we're at it. You're such a lying sod,' Michael continued. 'People thought you were some all-powerful genie, like in the movies. But you're not. You're just like them.'

'Oh no,' Jerrick cut in. 'I'm not like them, not like them at all. Have you ever noticed how people never used the words "I wish" around me? The rules of Jeshamon's curse - the fine print, as you say - states that I must grant every wish asked of me by whomsoever possesses the lamp. What the rules definitely do not say is how I must fulfil that wish. I did what I did for Al'Hadin because he was a nice guy. But the others who possessed the lamp before him were driven by greed and avarice of the worst kind. They all wanted to be Midas or live unnaturally long lives with power, fortune and glory. All I gave them was what they wished for.'

'You made people, who wished for fame, infamous, by turning them into killers,' Michael ranted. 'You made people who wished for fortune so rich that they were robbed blind by con men, or murdered for their wealth. When people asked for long lives, they lost their friends and families until they were alone, and still you wouldn't let them die!'

'Is it my fault that they were short-sighted?' Jerrick

retorted. 'Is it my fault that they hadn't fully considered the implications of what they were asking? I gave them what they asked for.'

'Without compassion!'

'I was angry,' Jerrick shouted. 'You try being shut up in a lamp for a century or two, then you'll know how it feels!'

'I know how it feels because you're remembering it right now. You were angry because you let the others down. You thought it was your fault that they were being hunted. You gave up your leadership because of the lamp. And that was a mistake as well because you couldn't stop the Council from going to war,' said Michael beginning to feel hoarse.

'They wouldn't listen to me,' said Jerrick. 'They were sick of being hunted. And I don't blame them. But where the Council was trained to heal, Jeshamon's Inquisitors were trained to fight. The Council used me as a weapon to teach them how to twist my sorcery to kill instead of serve, and all by the rub of a lamp.

'Al'Hadin was like you,' he continued. 'He was level-headed and resourceful. When he took the lamp, he had no idea who he had stolen it from. The Council was in disarray. They were cruel, twisted and hell-bent on open war, no matter the cost. What was done to me was no longer a part of their anger. They had lost so many friends and family over decades of hunting. Then the cull was invented, and the great empires were forged from the blood of both sides. Where do you think the Sumerians went, or the Egyptians, the Persians, Assyrians? They conquered each other to near extinction, each side

110

determined to erase the other from existence.

'When Al'Hadin stole me back from that forgotten cache of treasures, I taught him to see what the Council was, and shared with him the original plan for my people's magic. He understood it. He took the lamp to the ends of the earth, to where no one had heard of the Council. He brought it here.'

Jerrick pointed to the shore, where long huts of wood had been built into a community. Boats were beached and fisherman worked on nets, whilst women gutted and prepared the day's catch, drying it over wooden racks near a fire.

'Why are you remembering this?' asked Michael, confused by what he was seeing. There was an awkward silence while guilty thoughts invaded his mind from somewhere beyond his control.

'I see,' he said at last. 'You think that what happened in Hamelin was your fault - when Nahar took those children?'

'If I hadn't been so arrogant as to think I could solve their problems, it would never have happened. None of it would have,' said Jerrick.

When the ship they'd been travelling on came to ground, Michael felt compelled to step off. When he did, the scene changed. There was a battle raging on the beach, as the villagers tried to defend themselves from a band of marauders. One of the longhouses was heavily aflame, and a number of bodies lay bloodied and strewn around the clearing near the fire. Despite the efforts of the defenders, a number of the marauders had broken through and had raided the village food stores, carrying their plunder away with them.

Somewhere in the midst of the carnage, Michael could see the darker skins of Council members that had arrived on the boat with Jerrick. They gestured wildly as they spun magic in the air, trying to aid their hosts in the battle. Under his hands, Michael could feel the hot, sticky blood of a man, as he tried to stem the flow from a deep shoulder wound.

'It's not stopping,' he yelped in panic.

'It will,' said Jerrick. 'This is Nahar before he went by that name. He was Agnar Bjornson then. His wife, Sigrun, is behind us in the water. She's risking hypothermia to protect their unborn child from the raiders. It takes time for even sorcery to heal a wound that severe. Even then, we must hope that the patient doesn't bleed to death beforehand. You are feeling the same panic I felt when I thought I would not be able to save him.'

'But you've done this hundreds of times, haven't you?'

'Frankly no, not like this,' said Jerrick. 'It may be difficult to believe, Michael, but I had never really been in a battle like this. Usually, weapons are not a threat to us because of our sorcery. That's why the Inquisitors developed their mental abilities.'

'Well, by the look of him, Nahar wasn't a great fighter either,' said Michael looking down at the mass of blonde hair matted with blood.

'He wasn't,' Jerrick replied. 'He was a fisherman and soon to be a father. Look at him, he's so young.'

'Why were you here anyway? This isn't the sort of place I would have imagined the Council hiding out.'

The scenery shifted again. Agnar Bjornson was no longer lying on the ground bleeding. He was sitting in muted conversation with other villagers and members of the Council. They were discussing the food shortage and the coming winter. The raids had been frequent and costly. Michael was sitting a little way off from the group, pieces of crudely carved bone in his lap and a whittling knife in his hand.

'They slot together to make a flute,' said Jerrick.

'You used to make them for the children at the oasis. Your father taught you how,' said Michael snorting in disbelief as he recalled memories that weren't his. 'You'd never made one from bone before, just wooden ones. You enchanted it for him didn't you, while you carved it? It's going to charm the fish to come to the nets so that the villagers can land enough to see them through the winter.'

'He was badly injured in that attack,' Jerrick explained. 'He couldn't haul the nets like he used to, and he was afraid that his family would starve. Sigrun was due to give birth soon and was in no state to fish in his stead. I wasn't there to see it, but I am told that when he played, the boats were almost carried back to shore by the hundreds of fish that swam beneath them. Of course, they only took what they needed and were grateful for it. It was the same with the deer and hares. They took enough to feed the village and let the rest go free. Each time he played, the animals would flow to him like the waters of a river. That is why I named him Nahar.'

'So what happened to him? How did he come to take those kids from Hamelin?' Michael asked.

'One night, he took his boat out with Sigrun. He said that she wanted to look at the full moon from the water, like they always did. When I went to the village to trade the next day, they were not there. I wanted to check on Sigrun, to make sure that mother and baby were doing okay ...' Jerrick's voice began to crack. 'I was so proud that she had asked me to assist them with the birth. By mid afternoon I was concerned, so I persuaded some of the other villagers to take me out to search for Nahar's boat. When we found it, he was lying in the bottom, his face covered with blood from a wound in his head. Sigrun was gone.'

'Raiders?' said Michael, the memories of that day coming to his mind.

The scenery shifted again.

'No,' said Jerrick. 'That's what I thought at first, but the raiders never came by water there. It was worse. The Inquisition had tracked us to this place. When Nahar refused to help them find us, they took Sigrun and gave him an ultimatum.'

'His wife, for the Council,' said Michael.

'Yes. With the permission of the others, I told Nahar to bring them to a small clearing, where we had set up a crude camp that was meant to be a diversion. Some of us would stay to meet the Inquisitors while the others fled. We were going to meet up again if we managed to escape.'

'They brought Sigrun with them,' said Michael. He sounded horrified as he described what happened next. 'When Nahar brought them to you, you didn't know that the Inquisition had added the lamp to the bargain, did you? So while you were busy defending yourself, he was looting

114

the camp looking for it. He took the lamp and ran.'

'Yes. He took the lamp and ran back to the shore, where the Inquisition was waiting for it. He couldn't have known that we were close behind. When we got there, I realised that the Inquisitors had anticipated our plan but hadn't accounted for our close relationship with the villagers.'

'They defended you long enough to get to the boats, and you watched as Nahar held out the lamp to trade for his wife.'

Jerrick sighed. 'The Grand Inquisitor that had come with them was displeased by the village's show of defiance, and cut Sigrun's throat there and then.'

'And Nahar cursed you for not saving her, vowing never to rest until he saw you dead at his feet.'

'Not vowing,' Jerrick corrected, 'wishing. He *wished* that he could live long enough to see me dead, and because of the lore of the lamp, it was granted. It took them all by surprise when I pulled the lamp from his hands and willed it back to me.'

'The Grand was furious,' Michael smirked.

'Furious enough to cut Nahar down where he stood. But the spell was already made. His wound healed without so much as a drop of blood touching the floor.'

'That Grand must have crapped in his loincloth.' Michael laughed out loud. 'First a genie, then some fisherman that wouldn't die.'

'Quite the contrary,' Jerrick replied. 'He took his revenge by ordering the execution of every man in the village. Nahar was the only male left alive after the slaughter. He would have been burned at the stake if the raiders hadn't chosen that day to attack. Nahar was clever, he had already realised that his wish had come true. In his fury and despair, he took up a blade and ran himself through with it, lying in the mud until the raid was over.'

'How do you know?' Michael quizzed. 'Wouldn't you have been too far away by then to have seen it?'

Jerrick nodded as a dusky mountain top came into focus. Michael was standing face to face with a figure in a long patchwork coat. When the figure drew back the hood and the thick mane of yellow hair shed about its shoulders, it was plain that Nahar had become the Piper of legend.

'It comes to this,' Nahar said, in old, broken English. 'I am grateful that I should be the one to break my own curse, yet sad that it must be through bloodshed.'

'Why did you take the children?' Michael asked with Jerrick's voice.

'To teach them a lesson,' Nahar replied. 'They are safe in Carpathia, not dead. I am not so cruel as to murder children.'

'Not murder, no,' said Michael. 'But what you've done is worse. You've robbed them of their lives to keep yourself young. How long will it be before those children are dead, five, ten, fifteen years?'

'Long enough to have children of their own and care for them,' Nahar retaliated.

'You've stolen their futures to feed your past!' Michael shouted.

'Do you know what curse I have on me?' said Nahar. 'I cannot die, but that does not mean that I do not age. I

116

grow old and decrepit until my bones ache and my lungs spit blood, and still I cannot rest. Their youth is my salvation. I take a little from each, and am young again for another lifetime.'

'That doesn't make it right,' Jerrick spat through Michael. 'You have no right. It was your own wish that damned you. It's not their fault.'

'I was owed,' Nahar barked. 'I played for them, drove away their plague in exchange for the gold I needed. But in their greed, the townsfolk refused my price. I took the children to teach them a lesson ...'

'You took them to satisfy your own agenda,' Jerrick/Michael cut across him. 'You're no better than they are. What need have you for gold anyway?'

'It was to buy enchantments from the wise men of the East,' said Nahar. 'How else would a man kill a genie?'

'It's easier than you think,' Jerrick admitted. 'Tell me, are they so wise that they need gold to part with their wisdom or have they played you like the pipe you cling to?'

Nahar's fingers sparked with tongues of green fire.

'I have learned the craft of sorcery from them,' he crowed. 'I tried to follow your ship once the marauders had defiled the wives of the dead and finished their looting. Decades it took me to track you by the stories you left in your wake. When I came to the East, I learned what I needed from anyone willing to teach it, in exchange for the services of the pipe. Sorcery is highly prized in the courts of the emperors. The Inquisition has no jurisdiction there.'

'Not yet,' Michael replied, knowing from his time at the academy that sorcerers had been hunted as much in the Far

East as they had been in Europe. Witch hunting it seemed had been a global pastime.

'I know what lies between the mirrors,' Nahar continued. 'There is nowhere that you can go where I cannot follow.'

A foggy emptiness descended again, fading into a deep black.

'What happened? I want to see the next part,' Michael blurted.

The genie was silent.

'Jerrick?'

There was yowl in the void that knotted Michael's intestines and churned his stomach. A dull, golden glow shimmered into life a small distance ahead of him, and the sound of cracked notes and twisted melodies rang in his ears.

'It's the pipe, isn't it? I heard it when we were running from the temple.'

*Yes*, said Jerrick's voice, like a child frightened into speaking. It was coming from inside Michael's head again. In the distance, the yowl sounded again. The glow shimmered as shadows began to pass through the portal into the space between mirrors.

'Why are our portals so bright compared to that? Is it a different kind of magic?'

*Yes. Whoever is opening that portal isn't using a mirror. I haven't seen a portal that dim since before the days of silver and glass. It's what happens when you use something that doesn't reflect properly, like unpolished metal.*

'It's gold,' Michael ventured. 'But it can't be a plate or a cup because they're too small. I've never heard of a gold mirror that size; copper maybe, but not gold.'

*They're coins,* said Jerrick. *Fifty golden guilders. It was his price for taking the rats from Hamelin. The mayor himself left them at the mouth of a cave, on the hill where the children disappeared. He hoped that Nahar would bring them back in return for his payment. He didn't.*

'Well he obviously didn't kill you when you fought him,' said Michael. 'So what did happen?'

*The same as happened after this,* Jerrick whispered. *I had followed the music here, the night we evacuated the temple. I didn't recognise the portal, or the place where it springs from, but it felt familiar somehow. The air here feels cold and damp when the portal is open. I watched as Nahar piped those poor people through the portal. They looked so tired, so worn that they could barely stand. Then he left them in the daze of the pipe and closed the portal behind him.*

'I hate to correct you,' said Michael. 'But that wasn't Nahar with the pipe. Can you look at that memory again?'

It was like watching a video tape in fast reverse. The portal opened and the Piper stepped through backwards, skipping back to where the line of drained homeless people had been discarded.

'There,' said Michael. 'From what you showed me of Nahar just now, that's not him. Whoever that is, it's too small to be a man, look. The shoulders are too narrow and she even walks like a woman.'

*Two Pipers?* said Jerrick. Michael could feel his confusion. *I only made one pipe. And the spell contained in it is of my own making. It could be replicated I suppose, but it would take a very competent sorcerer indeed. And I doubt Nahar would part with his lightly.*

'Even the music's the same. It's the song of the unwanted, you said.'

*Yes, the same song that Nahar used to charm the plagues from towns and cities. The song he played to the children of Hamelin was different. It has to be Nahar. Perhaps he's older now or has been unable to get what he needs to stay youthful.*

'And has suddenly decided to sway his hips every time he walks?' Michael chided. 'No, I'm betting it's someone else. Can we get closer?'

*No!* Jerrick snapped. *I only saw it from here because of ...*

The scene began to play again, only this time, the yowl had become a baying. In the distance, the pack of Flayers had gathered and had already begun to charge. They tore into the frightened huddle of vagrants like a hammer on glass, dragging individuals this way and that before being joined by their pack mates. Michael felt sick as he watched them suck on the flesh of their victims.

'There's no blood,' he whispered, desperate not to be heard by the Flayers for some reason, even though he knew that it was only a memory.

*Flayers don't eat the way we do. They suck the energy right out of you. I don't know how, nobody has*

120

*ever managed to catch one to find out. But that's not the interesting part, watch what happens next.*

Michael watched with morbid fascination as the Flayers drained their prey. When they withdrew, he could see the deep rents and bites where their teeth had pierced their skin to the bone.

'Why didn't you do something to stop them?'

Even as Michael said it, he instantly regretted it. He unwillingly began to edge closer and closer to the fallen. Spreading his arms wide and chanting a barrier spell, he drove the attacking Flayers backwards. Then he spun on his heel and saw that the barrier was in place in a wide circle around the bodies of the dying, but it was too late. So many Flayers had been in the pack that nearly every body showed signs of at least ten attackers. Whatever had stemmed the flow of blood began to fail, and soon their wounds were so severe that Michael couldn't tell the difference between one bite and the next.

'They're going to bleed to death,' he gasped.

He felt the genie's power, pity and rage well up inside him as he rounded on the baying pack. When Michael had guarded the fleeing Council members, he had felt his own energy drain quickly. He'd always been taught to double his efforts when performing magic here because of the effects of the void. But even with the immense amounts of will that Jerrick was expending, Michael still felt as though he could take on an army of Inquisitors. That was until it hit him.

There was a sharp pain in his shoulder and his head whipped sideways like an owl, trying to see what it was that

121

had attacked him. Then panic set in as he realised that it had drawn his attention from his incantation. The barrier had dropped. Another sharp pain in his calf drew his attention downwards. In his efforts to prepare to drive away the pack of attacking Flayers, he hadn't noticed that the corpses at his feet were rising again, devoid of blood and skin sagging like wet tissue paper.

'They're zombies?' said Michael gawping at them.

*No,* Jerrick replied. ***They are still alive. Think of it like a sort of cross between a vampire's kiss and a werewolf bite.***

'But they don't exist!'

*Okay,* Jerrick complained. ***Then think of it like a sort of cross between a vampire's kiss and a werewolf bite ... in theory! Look, I'm about to get eaten again, and I'd really like not to relive the experience.***

'Agreed. Show me how you got out.'

With his magical defences down, Jerrick had no option but to resort to the traditional approach. Michael's legs kicked wildly, dislodging the newborn Flayer at his feet as he began to run.

The space between mirrors has its own rules. Michael was aware that the time it took to travel between two portals relied on complex calculations of weight and distance. Usually, portals were opened between two points - departure and destination, or where you are and where you want to be. But he had never encountered a situation where there was no destination portal. When Jerrick had come back into the void to chase down the Piper, Master Lefrick had closed the portal behind him. According to the rules of the Council on searching for missing travellers in the sub-dimension, Lefrick would only open it again for one minute in every ten.

Michael knew that you could open many portals to the same location at the same time, but that it would cause the distance between the entrance and the exit portals to expand - like putting a lot of weight on the end of a spring. But with no portals open, it was impossible to see any way out, only the twinkling stars of possibility on the vast horizon. When Lefrick opened the portal, it flashed like a lighthouse beacon and had given Jerrick some sense of direction.

The pack was at his heels and Michael could feel every step becoming more laboured as Jerrick's blood leached from his wounds. The portal closed again, but at least there was the hope that he would reach it in time for the next opening. The newborns began to tear at their clothing with their long nails, trying to shed weight and gain ground on the chasing pack. It occurred to Michael that it was the clothes that had bothered him the first time he'd seen the Flayers. It had given them the look of real people in inhuman form. The obviousness of clothing, however, had escaped him in the same way that one would expect wolves to be furry.

The blood on his shoes made them so slick that Michael could feel their grip give way on the ethereal landscape of the sub-dimension. Nevertheless, when he reached the spot where he knew the portal would appear again, he turned to try to shield himself from the attack. His feet and body were in disagreement and he hit the floor with a thump that knocked the wind out of him. Looking up into the empty sky, Michael tried to take stock of what was going on. He could feel Jerrick's panic growing inside his head. Between the running, falling and chasing, he had lost count of how long it must have been since the portal had closed.

The first of the pursuing Flayers had reached him, and in his clamour to get back to his feet, Jerrick had misjudged the attack. The razor sharp claws tore into his jaw and scrapped against the bone, gouging the flesh into a ragged flap. The rest of the pack arrived almost immediately after, trying to displace the leader in an effort to feed. In the confusion, they began to turn on each other, biting, snarling and lashing out with hands and feet.

Michael could feel Jerrick trying to raise his power to focus on an incantation, but the blood loss had left him confused and unable to concentrate. He tried to dodge out of the way of flailing limbs and managed quite well until another misjudgement left a deep gash in his arm, spinning him violently. When rough hands grabbed at him, he knew his time was up. They dragged him backwards until there was the sound of shattering glass in the air.

The scene of the memory went black.

'Lefrick was right,' Michael sighed, relieved that it was over. 'You couldn't have raised enough power to have defended yourself any more than you did.'

'No,' said Jerrick from beside him. 'That is not the end of the story either. I could feel the blood draining from me, and there was very little that could be done. Had I begun to change, I would have faded into nothing. The Flayers cannot exist outside the mirrors. It is that place that keeps them alive. So I took the only course of action I knew - I tried to return to the lamp.'

'That's what you did after you fought with Nahar, wasn't it? He beat you so badly that you were going to die.'

Jerrick nodded. 'It is not as hard as you might think to kill a genie. If he had simply wished me dead that night when the lamp was in his possession, I would have died. As it was, the lamp was my greatest strength. It allowed my body to heal. But like all wounds, it takes time.'

'Is that why the lamp was in Berlin when the Inquisition tried to steal it?'

'No, that's a different story,' Jerrick sighed. 'One that I'm afraid you will have to discuss with your aunt and Master Lefrick.'

There was a long pause as Michael considered what he had seen. He could understand why so few people knew about Nahar. Jerrick had held himself responsible for the children of Hamelin for nearly eight centuries. He had also been beaten. And who would want a genie that isn't all-powerful?

'At risk of sounding impolite,' Michael hazarded, 'how long are you going to be staying?'

Jerrick's usual, raucous belly laugh echoed around Michael's head, making him feel more than a little nervous.

'That's the best part,' the genie chortled. 'I have no idea. I suppose it will be until this mess is sorted out once and for all.'

'Great,' said Michael. 'You're going to ask me to go after Nahar aren't you?'

'Yes,' said Jerrick. 'I'm also going to teach you a few things along the way. There are hard times coming, Michael, when the Grand Council will use my absence as an excuse to go against our traditions. Someone must be there to help Master Lefrick finish what we started the night you were born.'

'Don't tell me,' said Michael changing his voice to impersonate Jerrick's, '*it is my destiny!*'

The genie looked a little hurt. 'No. As the new leader of the Elder Council, it is your solemn duty. It is time to stop warring in the name of ancient sects and realise that we all came from the same beginnings.'

'Tell that to the Inquisition,' said Michael trying to feel brave.

'I can't,' Jerrick replied. 'I'm dead ... ish. That's why I need you!'

## Chapter Six:
# Old friends

Grimm slumped into his chair behind the counter of the bookstore. At this time of the day, the door to the alleyway between London's Jermyn Street and Piccadilly would usually have been wide open. But not today.

There were never many customers in any case. Grimm's was a bookstore for the more discerning reader. There weren't any novels on the shelves, no books on cookery or gardening. Titles such as "The Fall of Gigantem Civilitatem" and "Why Broomsticks Don't Fly and Dragons Don't Breathe Fire" languished on the shelves, next to a number of dusty volumes on German grammar and stacks of the many editions of "Modern Lore". Not that Jacob Grimm minded the quiet. He preferred it that way and he'd never enjoyed letting his books go to just anybody. In fact, he had been known to refuse to sell the odd book to a customer, believing that they wouldn't appreciate it the way he did.

It had been the same way with the library to begin with. Grimm had refused to let readers from the Inquisition attend at the same time as those from the Council, on the basis that the books might be damaged in the crossfire. That was until someone had come up with the idea of having orbs embedded at the entrances. The orbs were responsible for the drain of energy on arrival at the library and had saved a lot of trouble in the long run.

Though looking small from the outside – squeezed into

a hole in the wall between the neighbouring buildings - the shop was one of the largest premises in the area. Above it were a number of rooms belonging to Grimm, which sometimes, if seldom, played host to a very select few of his friends. Beneath the bookstore was the library itself, and it was his pride and joy.

He pulled open the bottom drawer of the counter and stared into it. There were several odds and ends in its depths, including a silver brooch in the shape of a wolf's head howling at the full moon it was set on. But he didn't reach in. He just stared.

'It's not going to open itself, Jake,' said Sher from the doorframe she was leaning on.

'How long have you been watching me?' Grimm asked, not looking up.

'Come on Jacob, it's what we do - watch the world go by unnoticed. That's why there are so many books down there.'

Grimm snorted. 'Have you ever heard the expression "teaching your grandmother to suck eggs"?'

'Yes, I think so. Except that I'm old enough to be your ...' she looked at her hands, '... I don't have enough fingers to count how many greats there should be, not that it matters. Now, are you going to open that bottle or not?'

Grimm continued to stare into the abyss of the drawer and shook his head. 'Not sure this was the right time it was intended for.'

'I don't think your brother had a specific time in mind,' said Sher. 'I just think Wilhelm wanted you to open it when you thought fit.'

'You're right. Of course you are,' Grimm sighed pulling a bottle of brandy and two glasses from the desk and wiping them carefully with a cloth. He poured two generous measures and stoppered the bottle again before passing a glass to his companion.

'To Wilhelm,' Sher toasted, her glass held out to chink.

Grimm touched his glass to hers and sipped from it. The raisin tang of the brandy warmed his mouth and nose before the trickling heat soothed his stomach and began to wash his worries away. Grimm didn't drink, as a rule, except on very special occasions. But even if this didn't count as one of them, the occasion certainly warranted marking in some way.

'I suppose it's too much to hope that this will pass us by?'

'Yes,' said Sher. 'The same as it was in thirty-eight.'

'Hmm, you know how I feel about that,' said Grimm. 'Let's not go into that just now.'

'So what is it that's bothering you? I've never known you to close the library in the considerable time we've been friends.'

'I've never needed to before now,' the old man conceded. 'I'm worried, Sher. I'm worried that they'll come for us soon, if not next.'

'No, they wouldn't dare. Besides, my contacts at the other archives tell me that the Elder Council aren't exactly innocent either.'

'Oh, don't be so naive, girl. You know damned well who was behind the attack at the Archives de Paris! And it's more than just a rumour that they've taken hostages. I haven't heard from them since the place burned to the ground.'

'Now you're just being paranoid,' Sher retorted. 'It's not uncommon for us to not hear from them, is it?'

'Normally, no. But under the circumstances, I would have expected them to have reported in, especially following an incident like this.'

'The Home Secretary called it terrorism,' said Sher. 'It was obvious to those in the know that, when he said "a group calling themselves The Council", he meant *our* Council.'

Grimm's eyes snapped upwards, fiery with passion. 'And you believed it? You're even more naive than I thought.'

Sher thumped her glass onto the table. 'Careful, old man! I thought you knew me well enough to know that even I have lines that shouldn't be crossed.'

'Then stop being so blind and think about what's happening,' said Grimm. His tone mellowed again. 'This isn't just a game you know. The cull is almost here.'

'I know that. I just don't see what it has to do with us - or any of the other haven sites for that matter.'

'Then you're missing the bigger picture,' said Grimm.

'The Inquisition just wants an excuse to start an old fashioned witch hunt,' said Sher. 'They've given themselves licence to come out of the shadows, that's all. It has nothing to do with us. We're not the ones they're after. And the Elder Council aren't exactly blameless in all this. I mean, just look at what they did in Berlin.'

'That *was* an accident,' Grimm defended. 'I happen to

know that they were looking for something when the Inquisitors arrived. It was the fight that started that fire, not the Council.'

Sher shook her head. 'If it's not one of them, it's the other, it always is. It's not our place to get involved.'

'Just like in thirty-eight?' said Grimm.

'I thought you didn't want to talk about that,' said Sher.

'I don't. I was just reminding you of what happened the last time we decided not to get involved.'

'You couldn't have helped then any more than you can help now,' said Sher. 'If we get into the middle of their war, they won't thank us for it. It'll only make us a target.'

'What if they start taking prisoners? Those people are our friends. You can't just sit back and watch this time, Sher.' Grimm stood and walked to the window. He wasn't sure what he would find on the blank wall opposite, but it was helping him to organise his thoughts.

'How can we choose sides when you're not even certain which side has taken them hostage?' Sher insisted.

'I'm not suggesting that we choose sides,' said Grimm. 'That would go against every principle the archives were founded upon. No, no sides.'

'Then what do you suggest, Jacob?'

Grimm rubbed his stubbly chin and pondered. He'd been asking himself that question all day. Time and again the only answer he could come up with was:

'Honestly, I think we should have our own side.'

Sher coughed, sputtering brandy everywhere. She pulled a tissue from her sleeve and began to mop up the mess.

'Now I know you're off your rocker. We can't go up against either of them. It would be like trying to stop a nuclear missile with a peashooter. We don't have either the power or the numbers for it!'

'Not yet,' replied Grimm, still transfixed by the grey of the wall. 'But stranger things have happened. Now that the Inquisition is out, I dread to think what sort of place this little island will become. And it won't stop with the Elder Council either; that I guarantee you, my girl. Why else do you think they want the Piper? Imagine what sort of power they'll have at their disposal.'

'Is that why you let those books go to that boy and his mother? You want the Council to intervene before the Inquisitors can get their hands on the flute?' Sher grinned.

'It wasn't his mother, it was his aunt. It's a long story. And no, I gave them those books for safe keeping.'

Grimm returned to the counter with a new twinkle in his eyes, something that he had never shown before. It was mischievous and a little dangerous, as though he were plotting something.

'Don't the other archives have copies of those books?' Sher asked.

'Not *those* books,' said Grimm with a renewed vigour. 'I think that's part of why they've been targeted.' He rooted through the pile of paperwork on his desk, pulling a green paper file from near the bottom of the mound. 'Ha! Yes, I thought so,' he exclaimed, slapping the file open on the desk in front of his companion before taking a ledger from the shelf behind him. 'They're going after the unique collections, the books there are no other copies of. Every
132

archive has them.' He thrust the ledger under her nose, tapping a column of index numbers.

'But all of the books were burned in the fire,' said Sher. 'How could you possibly tell that anything was missing?'

Grimm was hopping from one foot to the other like an excited schoolboy. 'Look at the photographs from the Paris fire. The regular stacks all have mounds of ash mixed in with the rubble and other wreckage.'

'I see that,' said Sher sifting through the photos in the file.

'Now look at the photographs from the special collections cage and tell me what you see,' said Grimm.

Sher examined the indicated pictures, her forehead wrinkling as she concentrated. 'I see the same, except the ash seems to be patchier, more spread out.'

'Meaning ...?'

Shoulders sagging, she compared the locations of the ash with the index numbers of the ledger. 'Meaning there are books missing. And if they're anything like us, they wouldn't normally let books from the special collections leave the archive.'

'If I'm right,' said Grimm holding up a finger, 'whoever burned the Paris archive was looking for something particular, something they didn't want the other side to have. They set the fire to cover up the theft.'

'But which one of them was it, and how can we prove it?'

'Right now it doesn't matter. If my theory's correct, we are indeed a target.' Grimm pulled the wolf's head pin from the drawer. 'I can't explain it all to you now, but that boy and his aunt may be about the only people we can trust. That's why I gave them those books on the Piper.'

'What about Jerrick? You can trust him, can't you?'

Grimm shook his head. 'You know as well as I do, Jerrick's only as trustworthy as the person who controls the lamp. Besides, I haven't seen him in a while, and that's never a good sign. The last time we spoke he said that the division in the Council was growing and that their leaders were no longer loyal to him.'

'I've been spending too much time in the library and not enough time out in the world,' Sher laughed. 'There was a time I would have known that for myself instead of hearing it second hand.'

'It's good to know that I still have my own sources,' Grimm teased.

'So, what do we do now? Should we move the special collections?'

Grimm paused for a few moments before saying, 'Move them to where? No. No, leave them as they are. Perhaps someday we'll find them again when all this is over.' He pulled his overcoat from the back of his chair, resting it over one arm and gave a faint smile. 'You might as well call it a day.'

Pulling the door of the shop shut behind him, and checking his pockets for his keys, he peered through the dirt of the window, watching as Sher poured herself a little more brandy. She held the glass up in a salute, before tossing its contents to the back of her throat and swallowing hard. Yesterday her insolence would have bothered him. Today, however, the situation had changed

134

and there were things to do. In the reflection in the glass, he noticed a young woman standing behind him peering into the store.

'I'm sorry, we're closed,' he said shaking himself back to reality, and deciding that he'd wasted enough time already. Without looking back, he threw his coat over his shoulders and began to stride with purpose into the world.

***

To Michael, it seemed as though the entire Council had gathered in the meeting hall come dining room. There were faces that he was familiar with, but many more were new to him. He assumed that they must have come from branches that, until recently, he hadn't known existed at all.

Lefrick and Anna flanked him as they marched steadily towards a small podium that had been placed in front of the shuttered kitchen. When they reached and mounted it, Michael could see the sea of faces spreading out before him. His stomach lurched sideways, trying to get out of the glare of so many eyes, the way it had on the day of the final trial. Lefrick cleared his throat and the assembly fell quiet.

'Thank you all for coming,' he said with an air of authority. 'I know I still haven't had the honour of meeting all of you personally, but I'm afraid that time has been against us somewhat. For those of you that don't know, I am Grand Councillor Lefrick and the lady to my right is Junior Grand Councillor Ware.

'Let me begin by saying that I am grateful to each and every one of you, not only for your patience with us but for your tireless efforts with the Railroad. In light of the Home Secretary's announcement, I know that we're in for a busy time.'

There were murmurs of nervous laughter around the room. The Home Secretary's announcement had caused ripples in the calm waters of the Elder Council, but nothing more. For most it meant business as usual, waiting for the Inquisition to make its move. For others, it meant waiting patiently to deal with the aftermath.

'However,' Lefrick continued, 'there is another matter that requires our urgent attention, and it concerns the young gentleman next to me.'

More murmurs.

'According to his will and testament, Jerrick has instructed that Michael Ware be appointed his successor in all matters within the Council. He is to be instructed in leadership, and will take Jerrick's seat at the Grand Council.'

The murmurs erupted into a loud, frantic chatter. Lefrick let them have their way for a few minutes, before calming them again and opening the floor to their questions.

Andy's voice boomed over the crowd, silencing any remaining whispers instantly.

'No offence to you, Michael, you've a good head on your shoulders. I don't think anyone would disagree that we're proud to have you as part of the Guardians. It's just that many of us still don't feel that chil ... I mean ... young people, such as yourself, should be in the firing line, let alone leading the charge.'

'Hear, hear. It sounds like something the Inquisition would do. It's diabolical, putting youngsters in harm's way,' said a stony-faced woman from the middle of the room. There were grunts of support.

'But we're already *in* harm's way,' said Harriet King. 'We're here with you by choice.'

'Tosh,' said Mr Davis from the wings. 'Irrespective of his position with the Guardians, I don't believe Michael has truly been in any real danger. Neither have you, or any of the other children.'

Lefrick seemed to consider their opinions before speaking. 'Nevertheless, it was Jerrick's wish that Michael take his place.'

'And what does the Grand Council think about it?' The stony-faced women cut across him. 'The last we heard ...'

Beginning to get frustrated that other people were deciding for him again, Michael raised his voice.

'Excuse me!'

But the argument continued around him. His anger welled up inside him. For an instant, his eyes glittered with gold as his hands flexed.

'Hey!'

The shout washed through the room like a tsunami, hushing the arguments of the throng. To their astonishment, Michael's presence seemed to fill the space almost entirely, as though they were seeing him for the first time. Even Lefrick took a double take.

'Now that I have your attention,' he said, 'there are a few things I would like to say.'

But before he could continue, the sound of glass

breaking in reverse at the back of the room drew the attention of the crowd away from him.

'I'm sure you have plenty to say, Mr Ware,' said the woman who stepped through the portal. 'But it's going to have to wait. There are far more important things to discuss than the opinions of children.'

In stark contrast to her white robe of office, she had a short bob of rust coloured hair. With the addition of the heavy, black leather armour beneath her open mantle, Michael thought that she looked like an angry matchstick. When she fixed her misty grey eyes on him, he felt small and insignificant, as though she saw him as no more than a toddler. Then he noticed that the majority of the room had bowed their heads in respect, except for Lefrick and Anna. The crowd parted like the red sea in front of her as she approached the dais. Anna took him firmly by the elbow and dragged him out of the woman's way with a look that said: "Don't mess with her". When the woman reached the platform, she took Lefrick's hand and shook it.

'Hello, Hans, you still don't look like you're getting enough sleep, poor love.'

'Mistress Maya,' Lefrick replied, his voice less than dripping with charm. 'What a pleasant surprise. What brings you to our sunny little corner of the world?'

Her face darkened. 'Cut the bull, Hans. Jerrick's gone and we have the advantage we've been waiting for.'

Ignoring the protests of her junior, she turned to address the gathering.

'The Grand Council as you know it has been dissolved,' she announced. 'Since Jerrick's passing, it has been deemed
138

to be obsolete. However, please be assured that the Council is not a dictatorship in its new form. It will be as fair and democratic as ever.'

Her audience was stunned. Even in its deepest history, since before the Inquisition had come into being, there had been a Grand Council. It was part of their heritage. It was how the tribes of the old Council were kept in balance so that no one tribe could wrest control from the others. There was strength in unity, and the unity of the Council had, until now, been its greatest strength.

'But how can that be? You can't just dissolve the Grand Council. Why weren't we informed? We should have been a part of that decision,' said Anna.

'You weren't informed because it was not your concern,' Mistress Maya answered. 'The decision was made by the Grand Elders of each of the tribes. None of the branches have been left unrepresented, I can assure you.'

'What about the other Councillors? What do they have to say about it?' Lefrick asked.

'Say? What is there to say? We are in a time of crisis. The Inquisition has openly declared war in their terrorism proclamation. There will be bills and laws setting their actions in stone soon enough. Before long they will begin hunting us in the streets. And mark my words; there will be another Salem or Pendle before they're done. The Grand Elders have exercised their ancient right to declare martial law, just as any nation would at a time like this. Surely, Hans, you better than most should know that no wrong has been committed here.'

Michael could almost feel the smugness radiating from

her smile, guessing that she must have known Lefrick had never lost his passion for academic study.

'So what you're saying is: It's for our own good?' said Anna. 'Like impatient parents persuading petulant children to take their medicine.'

'I don't see what you have to complain about,' Maya rounded on her. 'Both you and Master Lefrick will retain your authority, as will the other Councillors. The only difference is that you will take your orders directly from the Grand Elders, instead of debating every decision in committee.' She turned to the room again. 'There really isn't anything to worry about. The reason that you have been directed here, to this place, is so that you can all receive instruction on how best to defend yourselves. It's just a precaution. We have no reason to deceive you. Jerrick may be gone, but the Grand Elders will keep their word to him and continue to pursue a peaceful relationship with the Inquisition, at all costs. '

'You're turning this place into a training camp?' Andy called above the newly erupted din.

'Isn't it a training camp already?' said Maya. 'Or have you just been sitting around drinking tea and getting fat on the Council's treasury? Really, Hans, what have you been doing all this time?' She waved her hand at the rest of the room. 'I need to talk to both of you. The rest of you are dismissed, including you, Mr Ware.'

Michael followed as the others filed out of the hall whispering and gossiping about the news. He was still seething that he hadn't been allowed to have a say in his own future, not that it mattered now. It had hurt him that people who were supposed to be his friends had shown a severe lack of confidence in his ability to lead them. But amongst the feelings of annoyance was a quiet pride in Harriet for at least trying to speak in his defence.

Wandering through the windowless corridors, he was certain that he wouldn't be welcome to join in with any of the conversations because sooner or later the subject would turn to him. With the grove outside probably brimming with secret meetings, it didn't seem like it was the place to find peace and quiet. Instead, he let his feet take him back to the solitude of his new bedroom.

Although his room at the farm was more smartly decorated than his room at the temple had been, it felt impersonal, almost clinical. Michael guessed that the furniture had come from one of those generic flat-pack warehouses, where you could get the same style in a hundred colours and the shelves had funny names. The frame of the bed was made of grey lacquered steel that matched the table and chair. The desk lamp was a white affair with articulated joints and springs, and the wardrobe was a canvas covered box. Even the rough wool of the carpet was grey. The only colour in the room came from the thin green duvet and pillow cases.

The temple had been drab, furnished with things that other people had thrown away. But it had been spacious and comfortable. Best of all, it had windows. They had been blacked out with paint, but Michael had scratched a little of it from the corner of the one in his room. He'd done it so that he could look out into the street behind, or lie on his bed with the door closed, watching motes of dust dance in the narrow shaft of light.

He huffed in frustration as he looked at the luggage he should have unpacked. Heaving an old fashioned, red leather suitcase onto the bed, he unbuckled the straps and flipped the brass latches. The case hadn't been his choice. Like everything else at the temple, it had been unwanted at one time by its previous owner but had been brought out of retirement by the Council because it was useful.

Emptying its contents, Michael soon found his wardrobe crammed to creaking fullness. He hadn't arrived at the temple with anything, except for the white duelling suit and brown leather armour he had worn for the duel. Thankfully, Anna had had the foresight to smuggle a few necessities from his room - the kind of items that wouldn't be missed – when they had extracted him from the academy. Over the following years, money hadn't been particularly abundant. Nevertheless, Michael hadn't found himself wanting for much. By the Council's standards, he was relatively well-off. His only real complaint was that he would have liked Anna to have spent her money on herself sometimes, instead of always on him. That had been the main reason that Michael had wanted to join the Guardians. It was his contribution to their family and his way of earning his keep.

The ornaments were next. There weren't really many of those, just a couple of photographs and a few gifts that had meant a lot to him. Chief amongst them was the stub of a candle, which he had used to practice control of his pyromancy. It had been given to him by Tamara and had been salvaged from his bedroom at home on the night he had decided to stay with the Council.

He thought about it for a few moments. In truth, he hadn't really decided that he was going to stay with the Council. The decision had been made for him. Because he was officially deceased in the real world, going back would have meant an awful lot of trouble. Perhaps it would even have meant death – the real sort, that there was no coming back from.

Amongst his other possessions was the mirror he had taken from home. Ordinarily, those who had made a life in the Council weren't allowed to have them over a certain size. Michael hadn't understood why at the beginning. Later on, it was obvious that mirrors were for a lot more than preening. It had no frame, only a small bracket to mount it on the wall. Just the plain glass of it made him feel homesick. It had been months since he had been in contact with Alice.

Usually, he would write her a note and drop it through the mirror in her room. It was a one-way conversation, but it was better than nothing. Once, he had been surprised to find that there was a note waiting for him on the other side. Alice had written briefly to inform him that his grandmother, Laura, had fallen and was in the hospital. In his reply, Michael had thanked her for the information but warned her not to leave any more notes for him, unless it was absolutely necessary. It had seemed like a good idea at the time. After all, he wasn't supposed to have contact with anyone outside the Council. The Inquisition would undoubtedly use anyone who might know something to gain vital information on their enemy.  But it had been years, hadn't it?

*Surely they would have stopped looking for me by now,* he thought. *It's not as though I'm important to them anymore because they have Tam. And even if I'd stayed, one of us would have been taken out of the picture anyway. Would they really have killed her if I'd won the duel? Would they have killed me if I'd chosen to go back to the academy?*

They were questions that he had wrestled with since the day of the final trial. At first it had kept him awake at night. He'd gone over and over the various scenarios in his head until it ached with the number of possibilities. Later on, he had thought about them less and dreamed about them more, waking himself with his own muffled shouts of protest. Now he barely thought about it at all because it was just another fact. When those questions did resurface, it was usually at a time when Michael was upset about something else.

He stared into the mirror for a while before putting it on one of the grey metal shelves, making a mental note to find a screw or a nail somewhere, so that he could hang it properly. Then there were the few books he still owned. There was his copy of *Modern Lore* that had once belonged to Jacob Grimm, who had written and concealed the faded verse about the cull inside the back cover. There was a copy of Shakespeare's Romeo and Juliet that his aunt had lent him. It meant a lot to Michael because of the drug the friar had given Juliet. It was supposed to help her to run away with Romeo but instead had been their downfall. Michael could relate to that. Finally, in the bottom of the small trunk, was the book. *The Book*. The book that had started it all.

Since it had come to him, it had been stubborn and had resisted Michael's attempts to read it. Even now, the notion that a book could resist being read was ridiculous. It was just a book. Usually, books don't have feelings one way or another about who reads them, except this one. Strangely, as he cradled it this time, it felt unfamiliar to him. There was newness about it, a familiarity that Michael felt in his stomach rather than his fingers. He also felt an itching around his neck, where the key hung in pieces on its chain.

Gently tossing the book out in front of him, he caught it with his mind and let it hover there. His hands reached up to the dragon's head clasp and its twinkling green eyes. Pulling back the dragon's ears, its mouth opened, allowing Michael to slide the two silver barrels and the key halves from the chain.

It had been years since he had assembled it, but his fingers went to work almost as if they remembered how all by themselves. First he slotted the two slivers of the key together to make a loose "X" shape. Then he prised both of the silver barrels open with the nail of his thumb and clamped them around the two halves to make it solid.

A wave of excitement swept through him, just as it had the first time he had figured out the puzzle. Willing the book towards him, he pushed the key into the lock and turned it. With a click, the heavy metal latch of the book yielded, releasing the leather cover.

With trepidation, Michael willed the cover to turn. The first time he'd opened the book, he had done so by hand, resulting in a scream that had made him feel sick and weak.

Over the several attempts that followed, he'd learned that there was only one way to handle it, in spite of the book's resistance. The familiar golden head shimmered into life in the air above the pages, speaking in its sombre, ethereal voice.

'Much has changed since last we met,' it said, eyeballing Michael. 'Yet still I do not sense the skills in you that I require. Until you lead, others will not follow. Return when you are worthy.'

The cover snapped shut again, spitting the key back across the room.

'Nuts,' Michael sighed as he willed the book back to the bed, letting it drop with a muted thump. He dismantled the key and slumped back, resting his head against the wall. It wasn't his lucky day.

With Mistress Maya on the scene, things seemed to have gone from bad to worse. For centuries, the Grand Council had been the engine that had driven the great machine. It was the reason that they were different from the Inquisition.

Before Michael, nobody his age had taken an active role in the Council. They'd only made an exception because of his talents and training at the academy. Even so, he could understand why the others had objected to Lefrick's announcement. After all, why should they follow him? Why should they trust him to lead them the way Jerrick had? To many of them, he was still the boy from the Inquisition that shouldn't be trusted. He could see it in their faces when they looked at him. It was the same look he'd given Harriet when he'd first noticed her in the dining hall.

146

Most of the others had lost someone they cared about to the Inquisition, or at least knew someone who had. Michael was one of them, not that he'd known until relatively recently. Sometimes in the dead of night, if one of his nightmares had woken him, he thought about what Anna told him about the night his uncle, Mike, had died. He'd killed Grand Inquisitor Renfrew in a struggle for the book that now rested beside Michael, and could never have known that his namesake would inherit at least part of his assailant's power. Worse than that, Mr and Mrs Ware had been proud that their son had earned his place at the academy with his uncle's murderers, not that he'd been able to tell them any of it. Now he had a chance to set things right, perhaps even a chance to go home. There was a knock at the door that interrupted his thoughts.

'Come in,' he called, expecting it to be Anna with more news.

'Are you sure it's okay?' said Harriet, her face appearing around the door. 'I can understand if you want some time to yourself.'

'It's fine,' said Michael getting to his feet. 'All this time to myself is just making me brood. What can I do for you?'

'I was hoping you could explain a few things to me. Sam's great and everything, but he's a little bit shy for some reason.'

'That's probably because he likes you. I don't think he knows many girls.'

'Gee thanks, Michael. That makes me feel so special,' Harriet laughed.

'Sorry, that really didn't come out the way it was meant

147

to. You're um … an attractive girl, and it's not like he's spoilt for choice …'

''Cause that was much better,' said Harriet as she laughed harder.

'Sorry, I'm no good at this. Just remember, it wasn't so long ago that I thought you were trying to kill me.'

'I'll forgive you just this once,' said Harriet.

When she took a seat on the bed, Michael looked awkward and pulled his chair from under the desk rather than risk anyone bursting in and getting the wrong idea.

'So what do you wanna know?'

'Let's start with what just happened,' said Harriet. 'Who was that just now?'

'By the way Lefrick was speaking to her, I think she was a Grand Elder. I've never met them, any of them. But Anna says they can be a temperamental bunch, and judging by the way things went at the meeting, she was right.'

'She was a bit sharp,' Harriet agreed. 'What did she mean about the Grand Council being dissolved, they can't do that can they?'

'How much have the Davises told you about the Council, or about how it started?' Michael asked.

'Not much,' said Harriet.

Settling back in his seat, Michael did his best to tell it the way Anna had told him.

'It was way back before the Inquisition. There were five tribes fighting for control of an oasis deep in the desert because the waters had magical properties. Over time, the fighting became a war and a lot of people on all sides died. Eventually, the ordinary people of the tribes became angry

148

with their leaders and something spectacular happened. The people came together and united against them. However, instead of overthrowing their leaders, they made the Grand Council of tribes and elected the officials from the ordinary citizens. That way, their leaders would always be reminded that their first duty was to their people. It also meant that no war would ever happen because, for once, the people had a say in their own lives.'

'Until now,' said Harriet. 'They've stopped listening. They've forgotten that it was the little people that put them at the top ...'

'And they've gone back to the way it was,' Michael finished. 'Jerrick used to say he thought the Council had been observing the Inquisition for so long, that they were in danger of becoming them. Now they're turning their safe houses into training camps like the Inquisition did with the academies. What's next, torture?'

Harriet's voice dripped with sarcasm. 'Why not? He wanted you to take his seat on the Council, just like they did to Tamara.'

'That's different,' said Michael shaking his head. 'Jerrick wanted someone who could build a bridge between our two sides. I think he thought I was the right person because of my feelings for her. But I can't see how that's going to help now, she's probably long forgotten about me.'

'Don't kid yourself,' said Harriet. 'I still have feelings for Max and it's been just as long. Why shouldn't she still feel the same way?'

'Because I'm dead,' said Michael. 'And dead's different from just being abroad somewhere. Wouldn't you have moved on by now if Max was in my place?'

She stared at the floor. 'He may as well be for all the good it'd do me. Don't forget, I'm the one who disappeared into thin air. As far as he knows, I'm not looking for him, and there's nothing I can do about it.'

'Couldn't you write him a letter and tell him you're safe? He wouldn't need to know where you are. You could even tell someone else what to write so that he wouldn't know it was from you,' Michael suggested, knowing that Harriet would wonder why he hadn't done the same with Tamara.

'And where would I post it exactly? It's not like there's a casual postbox anywhere near here, is there?'

'Do you know where he is?' Michael pressed.

'Well, yes ... kind of. When the governors said they'd tossed him out of the academy, they'd really moved him to Germany instead. It was part of the deal his father made, in return for Max taking the blame over me.'

'So you have his address?' Michael asked.

'No, he didn't know it the last time I spoke to him. There's no guaranteeing he's still there anyway. Knowing Max, he's probably on the other side of the world by now.'

'Shame,' said Michael. 'If you knew where he was, I could have got your letter to him easily.'

Harriet raised her eyebrows. 'How's that?'

'Mirrors. If you'd had his address, I could have used mine to connect to his and dropped the letter through. As long as you're not sending anything big, the connection is practically instant. The Council uses them all the time to chat over long distances because they can't have phones or the internet.'

'Great,' Harriet laughed. She pulled Jerrick's book from under her back. 'That's something else I can't do by myself.'

'Don't worry ...' said Michael, but stopped short when Anna appeared in the doorway.

'Sorry, Michael, it's important,' she said.

'That's okay,' said Harriet. 'I was just leaving.'

'But we hadn't finished talking,' Michael protested. 'There was something else you wanted to ask me, wasn't there?'

'It can wait,' said Harriet. 'I think your aunt needs you more right now.'

'Thank you,' said Anna closing the door after her. She looked at Michael and opened her mouth to say something, but appeared to think better of it and closed it again.

'I take it things didn't go too well with Maya?' Michael asked before she changed her mind.

Anna fidgeted nervously, wringing her hands the way she had when she'd tried to broach the subject of his permanent residence with the Council.

'Michael ... I don't know how else to say this, so I'll come straight to the point. Maya and the Grand Elders know about your connection with the Inquisition. They've decided you're in a perfect position.'

'Position for what?' said Michael. He didn't like seeing his aunt this way. It was a bad sign.

'They need you to prove your loyalty to the Council before they can trust you, and us. They want Lefrick and me to put a team together to help you.'

'To do what? Some sort of trial like at the academy?' Michael asked feeling confused.

'You could call it that, yes,' said Anna.

'That's fine, I can do that. I don't know why I'd need a team, though. It's not like I haven't ...'

'We've been ordered to kill Tamara and her entourage,' said Anna.

'Oh ...' said Michael, a cold numbness creeping through his bones.

## Chapter Seven:
# Necessary Sacrifices

Tamara stalked through the shadows, certain that he was there. He was using a similar trick to the one she herself had pulled at the final trial, only far more sophisticated. This time, there were no signs of the fuzzy interference that had been present when she had done it. Squinting into the dim light from the brazier at the far end, she sent her will into every corner of the training hall, feeling for some sign of life, rather than depending on her senses.

The shuffle of a soft footstep behind a pillar to her left caught her attention. Carefully, trying not to give away any acknowledgement of it, she brought her will to the spot where she thought Catchpole was hiding and regretted it instantly. The burst of energy against her back shoved her to the ground, but she had been taught better than that. Tucking and rolling away, she bounced her will into the polished stone and sprang into the air, turning to look in the direction of the attack. Just in time, she caught the glint of the javelin tip in the firelight and halted it mid progress.

'That's dirty,' she called out in humour.

'Do you think the Council won't do the same?' Catchpole called back.

She didn't have a chance to answer him. Something cold rattled around her legs, tugging her sharply towards the floor. There was no point in directing an attack towards its source because it was sure to fail. Instead, she picked a spot on the stones beneath her and sent a sharp burst of energy out, shaping it like a cushion to break her fall. Cursing, she grabbed at the javelin that had clattered to the ground beside her and flung it backwards to where she thought Rupert would be. Luck was with her as the chain at her ankles loosened enough for her to break free, and the wooden pole of the spear shattered against the back wall.

'So it's like that is it?' she cried. 'Hello, Rupert.'

'Hi, Tam, you almost had me. It's a good job you throw like a girl!' Rupert goaded.

Eager not to be baited into the attack, Tamara ducked behind a nearby pillar and into the cover of darkness, the way she'd been taught. Un-focussing her eyes, she concentrated hard on the room. Catchpole was at one end, trying to get a glimpse of a limb or a stray piece of clothing that he could use to pull her from her hide. Meanwhile, Rupert remained at the other end of the room, prowling closer to the shadows, hunting her like a cat hunts a mouse through long grass. She thought desperately for a way out. Of course, the best thing to do in this situation would be to put Catchpole between her and Rupert. That way it would render one or the other of them ineffective.

She could try to blend into the pillar, but if Rupert got too close to her he'd see right through the disguise immediately. She could try to run for it, or take to the air again, but Catchpole would be on her like a flash. What was it he used to say right back at the beginning? "The key to avoiding any attack is not to be there when it lands". He'd already used the vanishing technique, so he'd be expecting her to follow suit. Then an idea occurred to her that she'd never tried before.

The Magister adjusted his position as Tamara stepped out from between the pillars, her arms spread wide and hands at hip height, as though she was attempting to lift him from the floor. His smile spread across his thin lips as he anchored himself to the stone. Meanwhile, Rupert stood staring at him in disbelief, head cocked to one side as though he was trying to decipher a riddle.

'Um … what are you doing, Mr Catchpole?' he said peering around the column.

'What do you think I'm doing, Mr McEvity? I'm not going to let myself get unbalanced that easily. There's not even any effort …'

By the time it occurred to him that he was defending against a phantom attack, the pressure in his shoulders had built considerably. Coupled with the down force from the anchor, it was enough to cause his knees to buckle and collapse beneath him.

Tamara grinned as she burst out from around the pillar at the far end of the hall behind him. Throwing herself to her knees, she slid across the polished stone until she reached Catchpole and took him by the throat in a mock death grip, holding him in front of her as a shield from Rupert's attacks.

'That's not going to help you,' Rupert shouted. 'He'd tan my hide if I didn't ignore the obvious threat, wouldn't you, Mr Catchpole?'

'Usually, yes,' said Catchpole. 'However, on this occasion, Rupert, I'd rather you didn't!'

'I'm sorry, Mr Catchpole,' Rupert answered. 'You've

always taught me that a potential victim will do anything to preserve their own life and that I should ignore any attempts to solicit my sympathies for their situation.'

'Very true,' Catchpole acknowledged as Tamara dragged him to his feet from the chin up. 'But this is a training exercise. '

'I thought we were supposed to treat training exercises as though they were real,' said Tamara from behind him. 'Didn't you, Rupert?'

'Oh yes,' said Rupert turning on the melodrama while he fetched a fresh javelin from a rack on the wall. 'Mr Catchpole has always insisted that we take training seriously.'

'Look,' said Catchpole, 'we both know you're not going to throw that spear, so you might as well put it down!'

Rupert glared at him, drawing his arm back until the tip of the javelin was level with his cheek.

'I'm sorry, Mr Catchpole, I can't do that. Irrespective of the victim, my first priority is the target. Them's the rules.'

From Tamara's point of view, life went into some surreal slow-motion from that point on. Rupert stepped forward, giving himself enough momentum to launch the javelin towards his mentor's shoulder. Knowing that diverting her attention towards the spear would cost her the match, Tamara pushed all of her mental energy into the palm of her free hand and loosed it into her captive's back. This left Catchpole with no choice. The speeding projectile bent sideways under what must have been a considerable effort as he barrelled towards Rupert, who was busy advancing on his target.

Taking advantage of the confusion, Tamara turned her attention to the weapons rack, hurling it across the floor into the path of the collision between the two men. Apparently, Rupert's first instinct was to leap the oncoming mess, while Catchpole's was to try to deflect the flying weapons, instead of using his energy to halt his own flight. As a result, the rack appeared to bounce into the air, causing Rupert to miss-time his jump. Snagging his feet on one of the long staves, he flipped head over heels, landing awkwardly on one shoulder, only to be sent sliding into the wall by Catchpole. Again Tamara enlisted the aid of the newly derelict rack, controlling and manipulating it until it sat like a cage over her prone and panting adversaries.

'Enough?' she said in her sweetest voice, giggling at the grunts of submission.

'You could have killed me,' Catchpole groaned, peeling himself out of the clutter.

Tamara's face darkened. 'If it had been a real fight, you'd have been dead as soon as I had my hand around your throat. A dead human shield is better than one that struggles. Isn't that what you said?'

'I don't regret anything I've taught you,' Catchpole sighed heaving Rupert to his feet. 'I know you're both responsible and mature enough to use your skills appropriately. I should hope that you wouldn't use a normal that way.'

Rupert winked at Tamara and said, 'Any port in a storm.'

'I would hope,' Tamara replied, 'that any normal caught between the Inquisition and the Council would have the good sense to run.'

'You'd think that, wouldn't you?' said Catchpole. 'Unfortunately, there have been casualties in the past. Anyway, in the final analysis of our little game, I have to say that I'm most impressed with your progress, both of you.'

'I still don't understand what you were staring at, Mr Catchpole,' said Rupert. 'We were in a great position to pin Tam down. Instead, you put yourself in a situation that could have ended you.'

Catchpole rubbed his chin as he thought. 'I can't explain it to you. Your particular gift obviously didn't allow you to see what I saw. However, I can tell you that it was one of the finest pieces of deception that I've ever seen. As a matter of fact, I've only ever heard about one person who had a particular talent for that kind of projection.'

'Who?' Rupert asked.

'Renfrew,' said Tamara. 'But I think you're exaggerating about the number of people who can project. After all, Renfrew must have inherited the ability from someone, mustn't he?'

'Yes, but it's rare at the very least, perhaps even unique,' Catchpole replied.

Tamara thought about it for a moment. 'Do you think Michael would have been able to do it … If he'd lived I mean?' She knew it was a gamble, but Catchpole didn't seem to notice.

'I couldn't say for certain, although it is unlikely. In the short time I knew Mr Ware, he displayed some interesting talents of his own, like the pyromancy for example. However, you don't seem to have developed that ability yourself. Therefore, I assume that your inheritances were individual to each of you. I would have been very interested to see what sort of Inquisitor he would have become.'

'You mean you're disappointed in who you ended up with?' Tamara jibed.

'Quite the contrary. As I said, I'm very pleased with the progress that you've made. You seem to be using the power at your disposal to the best of your abilities. You have a wonderful head for strategy, and a magnificent grasp of the situations you find yourself in. I have every confidence that when the time comes, you'll be more than ready to lead ...' he stopped mouth agape. Tamara's eyes had a thunderous look about them. 'Did I say something wrong?'

'I *thought* I was the Grand Inquisitor,' Tamara bristled. 'I don't need training wheels anymore. I'm pretty sure I demonstrated that just now.'

'With any luck, if the Piper gets her way, you won't have to do very much at all,' Catchpole countered

'That's not the point,' said Tamara. 'I need you to stop babying me, and second guessing me every time I make a decision. If something goes wrong, the buck stops with me. If the High Marshalls are going to hold me accountable for the actions of our Inquisitors, I would at least like to be able to make the decisions that get me into trouble. Because right now, I feel like I'm just the scapegoat for other people's poor judgments.'

Catchpole's face was a mixture of embarrassment and admiration. 'I didn't realise that I was being so controlling,' he murmured. 'Forgive me. I thought that any advice I had given was for the best.'

'Like the decision to send a squad to raid the Masonic temple in London, instead of a covert operation, as I suggested?' Tamara scolded. 'That didn't go down so well, did it?'

'No, I suppose not. But in my defence, we have *all* been underestimating their capabilities and, I suspect, their numbers.'

'That's all well and good,' Rupert chimed in, 'but now we have no way of knowing where they are or what they're doing. I agree with the Grand Inquisitor. A more careful approach might have given us an advantage,'

'Times are changing,' said Tamara. 'I may have inherited Renfrew's power, but I'm not him. I'm not going to have my Inquisitors too concerned for their own safety to follow me, and I refuse to adopt his gung-ho attitude to my responsibilities. I am the Grand Inquisitor, and as much as I value your opinion, we're going to do it my way.'

Catchpole bowed low at his waist. 'Very well, Grand Inquisitor. What do you suggest?'

'Firstly,' said Tamara, 'I suggest we find out where that girl with the magic pipe is. She's going after the Council, which means she's going to lead us to them.'

'We're already on that,' said Catchpole. 'She was followed to Grimm's of London. Since then, she appears to have moved on.'

'So whatever information she got there is leading her to the Council?' asked Rupert. 'If only we could keep track of her. Emily says it's like she keeps popping out of existence; like she's not really … real.'

'Hmm,' said the Magister. 'There have been several accounts of the Piper in the past, all of them puzzling.'

'In all of the accounts I've read, the Piper's not a girl at all,' Tamara interjected. 'There are hundreds of descriptions of different kinds, but it's always a man.'

'Yes,' said Catchpole.

Rupert shot a sideways glance in Tamara's direction and she furrowed her eyebrows briefly in acknowledgement. Catchpole was concealing his knowledge of the situation, which wasn't unusual. Normally it wouldn't do them any good to press him further on a subject that he was keen to avoid, mainly because he would only make some excuse to leave the room and go elsewhere. But since Tamara had won their argument about her leadership rights, she considered that she might be allowed a little latitude on this occasion.

'You think there's something fishy about her,' she said. 'I'd bet you don't think she's telling the truth about who she says she is.'

Catchpole's face was blank in his reply. 'I'm a Magister. I don't have the luxury of taking anything on face value. While I admit that I've been concerned from the beginning, my private research is only confirming my suspicions. I'll bet you my head that she's not working alone.'

'Meaning?' Rupert insisted.

'Meaning that somewhere there's a puppeteer pulling our little visitor's strings,' said Catchpole.

Tamara's will lashed out with a mind of its own, sweeping Catchpole into the air and pulling him nose to nose with her.

'You know, Mr Catchpole,' she whispered trying to control her temper, 'I'm starting to sympathise with her. Just because she's a young woman, it doesn't automatically mean that she's being manipulated.'

'Quite so,' said Catchpole. 'However, in this case, I think you'll find that it's true. You may have some sentimental notion that she's out to avenge a dead family member, or lover, or friend, but the evidence speaks otherwise. You said so yourself; all of the books describe the Piper as a man.'

'Then what is she doing with the flute, and why is she out to make the Council suffer?' said Tamara lowering him back to the floor.

'How should I know? The Inquisition has no history with the Piper, and our archives are quite limited on the subject. The only information we have is what we can get from the haven sites. It's just unfortunate that the Piper chose to appear at the same time as our actions against them. Whatever her motivation, she's made a deal she won't back out of. It's up to us take advantage of that.'

'There's a grain of truth in every story,' Tamara whispered.

'Yes, so you keep saying. Though heaven only knows why,' said Catchpole.

'I only meant that if it's true, then I think we should look at those stories again, and follow them back to where they supposedly happened.' She looked as though someone was blowing on the embers of some great idea in her head that was making her eyes light up. 'Mr Catchpole, send word to the other orders of the Inquisition asking for their assistance.'

'Certainly,' said Catchpole. 'What are they assisting us with?'

'I want them to visit the sites where these supposed stories took place. Find the grain of truth in them, and we'll find her.'

'As you wish,' said Catchpole. He bowed again and left in a hurry.

'Um … Why would you want Catchpole to find her? He'd probably only have her killed if he found her. Or worse, he'd probably try to take the pipe for himself,' said Rupert.

'That's just it,' said Tamara in what she hoped was her most sage and wise tone of voice. 'I'm not sending Catchpole out to look for her personally because I think he'd do exactly what you're suggesting.'

'Then why do you want her found? If Catchpole's right and there are more of them, it could change the game completely.'

Tamara put her arm around his shoulder. 'Trust me, Roo; I think I know what I'm doing this time.'

'I hope so,' said Rupert.

'If she finds the Council before we can get to her, she might start killing at random, or even blow the whole place sky high. That would put Michael in danger, and I don't want that, so I'm hedging my bets.'

'Won't the Piper see that as breaking the deal?' said Rupert. 'She wants the Council, and you've given it to her. She might think that Michael's part of the payment.'

'But he's not,' Tamara replied. 'Michael's a born Grand

Inquisitor. His name is on the roll here. We've got evidence that he's one of us, not one of them. As far as I'm concerned, he shouldn't count as part of our bargain.'

Rupert shook his head slowly, saying, 'I hope you're right Tam, or we're going to be up against her and god knows who else, as well as the Council. A war on two fronts could get ugly.'

She punched his arm lightly and smiled. 'I'm not bothered. I've got you to protect me haven't I?'

'Sure,' said Rupert. 'But, I don't know who's going to be protecting me.'

'Michael will, as soon as we get him back.'

\*\*\*

In the sanctuary of the cave, Nahar sat in the shadows, his fury growing. The giant cage was emptying, and there hadn't been any replacements in days. The glass jars glowed dimly, and more than half remained dry.

Brooding over the centuries since the children of Hamelin had trodden the meadow flowers into the dirt; the old man regretted his decision to keep Katja for himself. She'd been a half-starved waif, begging on the streets for scraps. When the rats had come, there hadn't been enough food for the townsfolk, so desperation had driven her into the cellars of the inn to steal. Nahar had spotted her, grey and malnourished, sneaking out of the cellar's street level door while on his way to collect payment from the mayor.

When he'd led the children away, it occurred to him that, despite her years of practice, Katja would have been alone and friendless in a distant land. He also knew that being alone in a place where you can speak the language is very different from being alone where you can't.

His hard heart softened a little when he remembered that, of all of the letters left at the site of the great disappearance each year, not one of them had been addressed with her name. Katja had been unwanted. Nahar didn't know for certain, but the city had probably been her family's home once and then turned its back on her. They had left her to die, forced her to pilfer what should have been free to a child in her situation.

When she'd passed through the golden portal and into the cave, Nahar had taken pity on her. He'd used the magic of the East to wipe away the pain of the past and give her a future. Taking her as his daughter, he had fabricated a life for her out of the one he'd imagined for his own child. Since he no longer had Sigrun, he brought the child up in the only way he'd known how - with a sense of dutiful vengeance. He had told her stories about a demon with golden eyes that had allowed her mother to die. He had also taught her to play the flute.

He seethed as he thought about the time he'd spent conditioning her to trade life with him. The arrangement had been good, until now. These days she was no more than a willful child that wanted her own way all of the time. She was a child that neglected her duty to her family. She was leaving him to suffer alone for no good reason.

The portal at the end of the hall burst into life as Katja stepped gracefully through. Nahar glowered at her as she danced and skipped between the orbs, her face a picture of simple contentment.

'Where have you been?' he snarled. 'It's close on midday and you have nothing to show for it!'

'Not to the eye, father,' she sang. 'I have something far, far better to show for my troubles than you could possibly imagine.'

'If it's one of those nasty, boiled sausages in a soggy bun, with that revolting new world mustard again, you can keep it,' he glowered.

'No, father, I know better than that. The last time I gave you a hot dog, you threw it at me. It took hours to get the mustard stains out of the coat. No, this is much better.'

'Well, what is it?'

'I've found a way in,' said Katja. 'I know how to get to the Council without them suspecting.'

Nahar leaned forward in his chair. 'And just how did you manage that, I wonder? I've been tracking them for centuries, probing them for weakness. Never once have I found a way that wasn't immediately closed to me. If you're thinking about the mirrors, I've tried that. The Council checks everyone who crosses their portals.'

'It's not the portals.' She stood behind the sallow man and massaged his shoulders. 'There's something called the Underground Railroad. They use it to smuggle turncoats from the Inquisition to safety. My source tells me that she can insinuate me into their number.'

'Really?' said Nahar. It had been a while since he'd been genuinely impressed with the girl. It took him by surprise.

Katja's hands hesitated in their motion. 'It's not going to be easy.'

166

'How do you mean?' said Nahar

'It's not like I can just march in there, kill Jerrick and lead the Council like rats to the river, is it?' said Katja.

'Why, what's stopping you?'

Katja sighed. 'I've been told that their numbers have increased. There are more of them in the same den now. That raid the Inquisition fouled caused them to flee to a single camp. It seems that they are building some kind of garrison there.'

'It's happening then. They've finally learned that facing the Inquisition is the only way. Violence, no matter how distasteful, is sometimes the only resolution to a conflict.'

'I know you don't believe that,' said Katja. 'You've always taught me that violence is never the answer. The tranquillity of the flute is its power, its lure. Granted, we can turn people against one another with it, but it's rarely successful, and only works on murderous hearts.'

'So wise all of a sudden,' Nahar growled. 'What's gotten into you, girl? Don't you want to see me free?'

'And what would you do with your freedom, father?' Katja snapped. 'Would you choose to steal lives, instead of being forced to? Or would you do the honourable thing and choose to live whatever life was left in you?'

'Insolent girl, how dare you judge me? If it wasn't for me …' the old man spat, shrugging her hands from his shoulders.

'If it wasn't for you,' said Katja, 'I'd have been at peace centuries ago, instead of being trapped here, you sour old corpse!'

He pulled his carved walking sticks towards him and

took a deep, slow breath. 'You're right. I'm sorry, daughter. I haven't given you much of a life, have I?'

'I don't know,' said Katja. 'It hasn't been all that bad. The truth is I probably would have been dead by winter if you hadn't taken me in. I owe you a great deal, father. But there must be more to life than this.'

'There was once,' Nahar mumbled, managing to stand to look at her. 'Their feeble war took that away from me. Jerrick was the cause of that. If he hadn't come to our village, I'd have had a wife and family, perhaps even grandchildren.' He paused and examined her face for any signs of a reaction, feeling relieved when she seemed to have missed his slip.

'Yet it was the Inquisition to blame for the massacre,' said Katja. 'Why didn't you take your revenge against them?'

'I did, in some small measure,' Nahar confessed. 'But I always thought that their greed would be the end of them. The blame for the whole affair lies with the Council. I don't care about the politics between them and the Inquisition, I just want Jerrick.'

There was kindness in Katja's eyes now, and her voice was soft. 'What then? You don't know what'll happen when the wish is broken, do you? It could be the end of you.'

'True,' said Nahar. 'The wish was only that I lived to see Jerrick dead. Beyond that, I don't know what will happen to me, but I have to take that chance. He has his weaknesses at least. The last time I came close to killing him, the coward crawled back into his pot to recover. It was decades before he crawled back out.'

'Can you stop him from doing it again?' asked Katja.

In all of the time he had sent Katja about his business, he'd never been willing to talk about his encounters with Jerrick.

This time, he bent a little. 'If I have learned anything in my long years, it's that even the impossible can be accomplished with time and patience. If it were as simple as possessing the lamp and wishing him dead, I could have done that an age ago. I can't deny that our last spat would have finished me had I been less than immortal, but it seems my curse is my advantage. And it's an advantage I fully intend to exploit.' He staggered his way down through the glowing jars and stopped at a particularly full one. 'I only hope that this is enough. The unwanted that remain won't give us much more than a few months between them, judging by the state of them.'

'It will be enough, father,' said Katja.

Nahar grunted in brief amusement. 'If only I shared your optimism. Come now; tell me how you plan to storm the Council.'

\*\*\*

Deep in the library, the floorboards creaked. It was long past closing. Even the night staff that restacked the shelves with pulled books had finished their duties. Unlike some old buildings that feel haunted when they're not, the library was peaceful. There was no sense of foreboding skulking between the stacks, or eerie presence prowling in the shadows, only the creaking of real, earthly feet on wood.

The footsteps came to rest at the railing of the Whisper Gallery, as Grimm breathed in the peace. He placed the small leather suitcase he was carrying on the floor. Reaching into the folds of his coat, he retrieved a hollow, square key made of brass, like the ones that are used for draining radiators. There had been no need for it since the installation of the many elaborate electric lights. Not that he had wanted the brass sconces of the gas lamps removed. They gave the place a touch of class that Grimm felt couldn't be replicated by any modern means.

'Is everything secured, Eunice?' he asked.

Eunice, who had been waiting for him in the gallery, nodded. 'Everything's just fine, sir. Only, I'm worried about *her*.'

'I know, so am I,' said Grimm. 'You know I wouldn't ask this normally, Eunice, but you're absolutely positive about what you heard, aren't you? There's no chance you could have misunderstood?'

'One hundred percent certain, sir. She did it without any threat of violence. The girl didn't even have the pipe to her lips.'

'Mmm,' murmured Grimm. 'I suspect that's why Sher gave her the information freely. That girl could have forced it out of her if she'd wanted to.'

'But she didn't have to tell her the truth,' said Eunice. 'All the girl wanted to know, was how she could find the Council. Sher could have told her to come here. She didn't need to mention the Railroad at all. Now we're all in danger if the Inquisition finds out.'

'I suspect that we've been in danger from the Inquisition since they appointed their new Grand,' said Grimm. 'Thankfully, I've been planning for this for a long time. Why do you think I had all of those copies made so cheaply? There's no need for them to be perfect when they're for show. I'm more concerned about the antiquities, I must say.'

'They've been taken care of. The night porters I selected are most trustworthy, and I made the inventory myself,' Eunice beamed. 'If it all goes to plan, they'll be back in pride of place before you know it.'

Grimm patted her arm. 'Thank you, Eunice. You don't know how much it means to me. The salary slips will be honoured, just as I promised. I don't want this unpleasantness to disturb the staff or their families.'

'That's very generous of you, sir. You will remember to let them know when the archive is operational again, won't you?'

'Of course I will,' Grimm replied. 'For now, though, I think it would be best if we kept that part to ourselves. These things always look better as they were meant to.'

'How do you mean?'

'Sorry,' said Grimm, forgetting that his head knew more than his mouth did. 'I just meant that if we appear to have jumped the gun and set up a second archive, it would look like we were expecting to be the target of a terrorist attack.' He looked down at his watch, waiting for the seconds to tick by until the thin silver hand reached the top of the hour. 'It's time to get going. So long old thing.' He caressed the railing as though he were saying goodbye to a favourite pet.

Eunice smiled at him and walked across the gallery to the stairs while Grimm removed a wooden panel from the wall, behind which was the square nut of a valve.

Pushing the key onto the valve, he gave it a smart half turn to the left, causing a gentle hiss to emanate from the old brass sconces. With the artificial stench of the gas beginning to fill the air, he took up his suitcase and followed Eunice to the ground floor reception area.

'I'm a little rusty,' said Grimm as he placed his hand on the glass of the mirror, 'but this should get you to where you're going.

'Thank you, sir,' said Eunice as the portal sparked into life. 'You will be alright, won't you?'

'I'll be right behind you,' the old man assured her. 'I'm just going to wait behind the reception desk. Once I know which side is responsible for the attacks, I'll be on my way. I hope it'll be the Inquisition, I really do.'

'Me too,' Eunice whispered, slipping through the mirror into the brief twilight.

Grimm let the portal drop and returned to the chair at reception. Of all the people he had lied to today, Eunice was the person he'd regretted lying to the most. She'd been a loyal employee for a long time and cared for the library almost as much as he did. He snorted in amusement at his own sentimentality and wondered what Sher would have said about it.

Jacob had been privy to one of the best-kept secrets of the war between the Council and the Inquisition for many years now. The library had been one of the Railroad's busiest stations. Remaining strictly neutral, Grimm had consented to its use for that purpose. He'd thought long and hard about it before agreeing to the Council's proposal. It had taken a lot of persuasion from Master Lefrick for him to agree to it at all, even though he could see the logic behind it.

It worked like this: Inquisitors would come in through the topmost entrance, where their power was stripped from them as usual. They would be issued with "special" robes with magnetic numbers, instead of sewn patches. The "passenger" would make their way to the appointed stack, sometimes accompanied by a mentor if they were particularly young. There they would meet with a decoy from the Council, who would swap robe numbers with them, and each would leave from the correct entrance. It was all managed with the utmost discretion. It was so convenient that Grimm actually admired the neatness of it.

He opened his suitcase and took a carefully wrapped sandwich from it. It had been a long day, all things considered, and there was nothing left to do now but sit and wait. While he munched idly on the maple bacon and rye bread in his hand, he wondered what could have motivated his colleague and one-time mentor to have given away the Council's location. Worse than that, she had indeed revealed information about the Underground Railroad, which had put more innocent lives at risk.

It wasn't unusual for Sher to play games with people. It was her way of trying to give history a helping hand, and hurry things along to what she felt should be the appropriate end. Grimm knew her well enough to know that she wasn't doing it to be cruel. But this time, her recklessness was almost unforgivable.

The odour of the gas was starting to creep under the door now, its unpleasantness reminding Grimm that he was there for a reason. It gave him a sense of relief that nobody had come to raid the library in the dead of night, mainly because he hadn't wanted anybody to get hurt. He also knew from experience, that the nearby shops and streets would be empty at this time of night, so there was little left to feel guilty about.

The sounds of the city clocks chiming two barely reached him in the basement, but they were enough to shake him awake from his sentimental reverie all the same. Walking with purpose to the mirror once more, he placed his hand against the ornately carved frame and crouched. There were few things he had to leave behind that he would miss more, and it would take decades to find a frame as lovingly prepared and oiled as that again. Fishing in the pocket of his waistcoat, he produced a silver lighter wrapped in a white cotton handkerchief.

His thumb rolled over the wheel of the ignition, striking the cold steel against the flint and sparking the flame into existence. Being careful not to touch the metal of the lighter, he placed it on the floor. It wouldn't be long before the stream of noxious gas reached it and it would all be over. Grimm stepped backwards through the mirror to stand vigil from the safety of the empty room beyond, his heart pounding with a mixture of regret and anticipation.

When it began, it was like the blossoming of the most

beautiful flower. As the gas hit the naked flame of the lighter, the most magnificent blue filled the room, spreading out like petals in the morning sun. In his shelter, Grimm caught the waves of oranges and reds racing away along the stream of foul air, tearing through the back wall of the reception room and out into the main atrium of the library. The mirror on Grimm's side flashed and fell silent, indicating the destruction of its counterpart, until he was left staring at his own reflection.

He turned away. Walking to the plain, half-panelled glass door of the office he now occupied, he looked out over the small warehouse below. There was a feeling in the pit of his stomach that he'd felt at the passing of another old friend – his brother. He considered it for a moment, before picking up the nearby metal wastepaper basket and throwing up into it.

# Chapter Eight:
# The Cruel Life

The first of the winter snow was falling on the ample grounds of the academy. Although it was crisp, there was no bite to the air, and only a little breeze to stir the flakes into swirling snow devils.

On the forest path, beyond the stone bridge, Catchpole wandered in a dreamy wonderment. Despite not working entirely according to his plan, things were going fairly well. The Piper (or the Piper's apprentice, at least), seemed to be doing her job seeking out the Council. With any luck, she would take a few of them with her before their Guardians ground her into the floor, leaving the Inquisitors to mop up the rest. Still, the statistics proved that there would be a number of casualties by the time they were through. It reminded Catchpole of that phrase about omelettes and eggs, which was quite handy at times like these. But he wished that there had been some news on that front in the weeks that had passed since the agreement.

Then there was *her*. He sighed and deflated a little, the fresh powder beneath his feet bearing the brunt of his frustration. Who had she thought she was, pulling him nose to nose with her and scolding him like an errant child? He could have swatted her like a bug against the windshield of a car. He should have swatted her like a bug. He shook the thought from his head. It wouldn't do to play all of his hand right away.

For Catchpole, this was a high-stakes poker

tournament. These were the opening hands, and he was watching for tells – the signs that give other players thoughts away. He was pleased with his metaphor, considering that in poker, as in real life, sometimes you bluff, sometimes you don't. But you always, always play the hand you're dealt.

Tamara's tantrum aside, she was growing into quite a fine Grand Inquisitor. She wasn't always obedient, and was getting harder to bend to his will, but Catchpole was genuinely pleased with her progress and her maturity. His only concern now was whether the High Marshalls would be able to control her. After all, since the train wreck that Renfrew's tenure as Grand Inquisitor had been, it was decided by higher authorities that future Grand Inquisitors shouldn't be granted too much freedom.

It shouldn't have been necessary for the Marshalls to restrict the Grand Inquisitor in such a way; it was almost belittling. Tamara was an exception to the usual rules because of her appointment at such an early age, and at such a crucial time. On balance, compared to Renfrew, she was positively angelic. In Catchpole's opinion, the former Grand should have been put down when the first signs of his rabid temperament began to manifest. It still stung that he, of all people, had been Grand Inquisitor in the first place. That had been a rocky affair in Catchpole's past, but at least he was better for it now.

He smirked to himself. It wasn't like him to be introspective. In fact, he liked thinking about his past about as much as he enjoyed other people's curiosity in it. Yet here in the academy's park, and the damp white flurries,

Catchpole's past was creeping up on him. The scars on his arms itched like crazy these days. In defiance of the cold, they burned with memories of past clashes with the Council and youthful scraps with rivals. Catchpole stopped stock still and thought for a moment.

'Not rivals, rival,' he said to no one in particular.

Unbuttoning the cuffs of his shirt, he spread his arms to his sides, palms upwards, letting the sleeves of his speckled robe slip up to his elbows and the gentle flakes soothe his pains.

There was movement in the brush, too subtle to frighten any of the wildlife that it shared the woods with, but loud enough to draw attention to itself. Catchpole let his sleeves drop and drew the cowl of his robe over his head. Making himself presentable, he dropped to one knee on the half covered stone path and waited.

'There's no need for that sort of formality, Rowan,' said Lady Shaw emerging from the forest. 'We are the same now, after all.'

Catchpole scowled. Not only had she had the audacity to call him by his first name, but she had thoughtlessly referred to his rank.

'Emma, even in this place there are stray ears. I would be grateful if you addressed me correctly and by my *proper* title.'

'They certainly had a sense of humour, your parents,' Lady Shaw giggled.

Catchpole stood, fists clenched. 'I'm warning you, Emma. We might be the same, but that doesn't make us equals. Even think my name again and you'll regret it, I promise!'

Lady Shaw lowered her voice. 'Now, now, Catchpole. We mustn't be seen to be disobeying a superior, must we?' She cocked her head to one side and said, 'Down you go.' But the smile disappeared from her thin, elderly lips when she saw the humanity drain from her sparring partner's face.

Catchpole let loose with a stream of will. Wrapping it around the Lady's ermine-trimmed robes, he squeezed, mentally tightening the strands around her until her arms were trapped, and she stood motionless.

'Wretched harpy,' he spat. 'Test my patience again, I dare you!' There was no point struggling, Catchpole's will was iron.

'The Marshalls will …'

'The Marshalls will what?' said Catchpole, letting her go with some reluctance. 'Do you think the Marshalls care what I do to you?' He shook his head. 'In fact, I'm certain that blowing an operative's cover is more serious than a minor disagreement between colleagues. Now, why don't you tell me what's so urgent that they sent you all the way here?'

Lady Shaw took a deep breath. 'They want to know why your Grand Inquisitor seems to be running riot.'

'She isn't running riot,' Catchpole replied. 'Tamara's training is progressing well. She seems to have found her voice and has even made a deal that could swing things in our favour long before the cull.'

'Yes,' said Lady Shaw, 'we know about the deal. That's why the Marshalls believe you've lost control. They didn't authorise anything, especially with somebody so dangerous. They feel it smacks a little of ... well, Renfrew, quite frankly.'

'It's not as though the girl's gone on a homicidal rampage,' Catchpole snorted. 'She's just finding her feet, that's all.'

'Maybe; maybe not. I still would have preferred the boy, he was more compliant. The Marshalls feel that Tamara's too willful and that the story you spun her about Michael has turned her natural dislike for the Council into a personal vendetta.'

'You know about the boy then?'

'Oh yes,' said Lady Shaw in tones too smug for Catchpole's liking. 'But you knew that already, didn't you?'

'I had my suspicions,' said Catchpole. 'I can assure you, however, that Tamara has no idea. And I would like to keep it that way.'

'I wouldn't count on her ignorance, she's a bright girl,' said Shaw. 'I doubt it'll take her long to find out the truth. If you continue to give her the freedom she enjoys at the moment, we could lose her altogether.'

'It won't come to that. She thinks she has the upper hand right now because I'm letting her,' said Catchpole. 'There's a cruelty in her that I want to foster. I'll need to build her up before I break her of course. Then I'll rebuild her to be what we need her to be.' He looked almost happy as he thought about it.

'I can tell the Marshalls that she'll be ready in time then?'

'I can tell them myself,' Catchpole answered.

'No. They want you to maintain your position here,' said Lady Shaw. 'It's best that you keep your contact with the Marshalls to a minimum for now.'

'But ...' Catchpole stammered.

'For now,' Lady Shaw confirmed. 'You'll be released from your obligation when the time is right.'

Catchpole sighed. 'I suppose you're right.' He kicked the mounting snow from the toe of his shoe. 'What do you think, Emma? Is this all beneath us? Training a Grand Inquisitor, I mean. Surely the traditional way is better, isn't it?'

'I used to believe that,' said Lady Shaw. 'But since Renfrew, I'm not so sure. Anyway, we both know that he shouldn't have been given the honour in the first place, don't we?'

Catchpole cocked an eyebrow in admiration. 'Remind me to have my files sealed when I get back,' he smiled. 'I'm just glad it wasn't you that presided over the trial.'

Lady Shaw oozed fake sincerity. 'And I'm glad that it wasn't me you were supposed to be guarding that night. Did you really think you could serve your own agenda and not be punished for it? Then again, you don't get to where we are without talent, especially at your age. If it's of any comfort, you would have been wasted as a Grand or even as a Magister.'

Catchpole puffed a single, sarcastic "ho" of laughter. 'Still, I would have liked the chance to prove it. I couldn't have done much worse than Renfrew. As for that night, I felt it was my civic duty. He was mad with power and out for blood. If I hadn't convinced the others to stay where they were and take care of things for myself, some poor no-talent looking to prove themselves would have been dead. No, Renfrew had to go, and the Marshalls knew it. Otherwise, I'd have been scrubbing latrines in Siberia by now, or worse.'

'Your report said that you ran away like a screaming girl,' said Lady Shaw.

'I did,' said Catchpole. 'It was the easiest way to ensure he died. There were two Council goons there that night, husband and wife, quite powerful too. I knew he couldn't have taken them both because Renfrew was so reliant on his backup. In truth, he was just the small child that hides behind the playground bully that is the Inquisition. By then, he was so overconfident in his own greatness that he didn't stop to think that he could die.'

'The autopsy said it was a lucky blow,' said Shaw. 'Only the tip of the glass punctured his heart. Had it been a half centimetre shorter, Renfrew would have lived.'

'And I'd most probably be dead, yes,' Catchpole acknowledged. 'I could have taken the woman with both hands tied behind my back, I suppose. But it wouldn't have given me any satisfaction at all. Not that night.'

'Well, you'll have your chance to change that soon enough. I shan't pretend that I admire what you did, but it did give me some small amusement when I read about your earlier exploits,' Lady Shaw grinned.

Catchpole pulled the cowl of his robe back to reveal his scarred eye. 'Does this give you any more amusement?'

Lady Shaw's grin widened. 'I can't pretend that it doesn't. But probably not for the reasons you think. You can't be ruthless, powerful and devastatingly handsome all at once, can you? Something had to go. I suspect it was your penance for deserting your superior.'

'Hmm,' said Catchpole nodding his head. 'I can see how some people might think that. Personally, the only lesson I believe it taught me was not to exit a room face first through plate glass. I was lucky not to lose the sight in it. As for my penance, I think it's in front of me more than behind me.'

'Still to come, you mean?' Lady Shaw probed.

'You could say that,' Catchpole replied. He drew a deep breath, chiding himself for being drawn into a conversation with someone he disliked so openly.

'What now?'

'Now?' said Catchpole trying to act casual. 'Now you're going to tell me what it is that the Marshalls want from me this time. Or did you only come for the chat?'

'Back to business then,' said Lady Shaw. 'Your orders are to allow our uninvited houseguest to find the Council. Don't worry about tracking her for yourself, they have that under control.'

'How?' said Catchpole. 'She can't be tracked. We've had our best minds on the task since her arrival.'

'I don't understand it all myself,' Lady Shaw admitted. 'It's as though she isn't really there.'

'Not really there,' Catchpole repeated.

'Sorry?'

'Something Miss Parker said when the girl paid us a visit. She tried to read the girl, but it was as if she wasn't really in the room.'

Lady Shaw nodded. 'The other Marshalls believe it has something to do with an ancient Chinese practice of sharing life. She's so old that she must have shared at least seven lives, maybe even more. But the lives she has taken have left their mark on her. Our seers are trained to fix on one source of energy, or the blank space where it should be, not on many all at once in the same place.'

'That's why it seems like she's not really there,' Catchpole mused. 'Her very essence has been diluted to the point that what she was no longer exists.'

'That makes sense,' said Lady Shaw. 'She's dead!'

'No, not dead,' Catchpole corrected her. 'She's on life support, like someone in a hospital. But instead of a machine helping her to breathe, she's stealing life from people to keep the years from taking their toll on her bones. The mind is still there, but whatever she used to be *inside* is gone. I doubt she knows how to feel anymore, except for remembering that she should.'

'I suspect that would make her cold and callous,' said Lady Shaw. 'It also means that she can be stopped if things get out of hand.'

'Oh, she's quite human in the traditional sense,' said Catchpole. 'I'd expect that she'd succumb to a heavy blow as much as anyone else. Still, it's good to know that we wouldn't require any special measures.'

'Thankfully,' Lady Shaw agreed. 'I always hated the idea of burning someone at the stake. It's so unnecessary.'

'The Inquisition has always done unnecessary very well I'm afraid, but I'm with you on that,' said Catchpole. 'I'd prefer a straight up fight myself. Who needs a ducking

**184**

stool, when you have Magisters to gather information? Besides, whenever we've publicly disposed of members of the Council, it has only led to feelings of sympathy from the normals.'

'True. It's enough to make you wonder why they're re-launching the Inquisition in the media, what with the burning of the haven sites,' said Shaw.

'Call it ... rebranding, putting a picture of a daisy on a loaded gun, if you will,' Catchpole grinned. 'It's no less dangerous, but somehow it seems friendlier. We're trying to let the normals believe that we're on their side.'

'That's going to be difficult. Grimm was well liked by the normals who knew him,' said Shaw.

Catchpole looked puzzled. 'I didn't order ...'

'We know,' said Lady Shaw. 'What we don't know is, who did and why? Rumour has it, Catchpole, that the Elders are planning some sort of offensive in an effort to wrest control over the Council.'

Catchpole smiled. 'I do love a good rebellion, so long as it's not amongst our own ranks.'

'That's as maybe,' Lady Shaw replied. 'But if they do something stupid before we're ready for them, there's a good chance it might succeed. Where would we be then?'

'Point taken,' said Catchpole. 'So as of now, we are on high alert?'

'Yes.'

'And I suspect the Marshalls would prefer fewer unexpected decisions from the Grand Inquisitor?' Catchpole asked raising an inquisitive eyebrow.

'Correct,' said Lady Shaw. 'As I mentioned, you'll be

released from your obligation when the time is right. If all goes well in the run up to the cull, I'm sure they'll see fit to reinstate you to your position.'

'Then we must hope that this Piper is as enthusiastic about the bargain as we are. Though I'd hate to miss out on all the fun.' He shrugged his shoulders in mock disappointment. 'Never mind. In that case, tell the Marshalls that Cheritton Hall is now on a state of high alert. I guarantee that the Grand Inquisitor will make no more decisions without their approval.'

Catchpole bowed and Lady Shaw returned it, although he wasn't certain how much respect there was in it.

'Always a pleasure, Mr Catchpole,' the lady cooed, leaving with no more ceremony than that - a final show for prying eyes.

'Self-righteous cow,' Catchpole muttered to himself, before heading back to his own study.

\*\*\*

A short distance from the grove, Michael, Sam and Harriet scuffed through the newly fallen drifts, relieved to have been allowed out of the musty barracks. Since Mistress Maya's visit, Michael had been feeling like the weight of the world was about to come crashing down on his shoulders, and his friends had been trying their best to lift his spirits ever since.

'Come on, mate,' said Sam trying to cheer him up. 'It's not long till your birthday. We should be planning a party.'

'And there's Christmas to look forward to between

now and then,' Harriet twittered.

Michael's face remained thoughtful and troubled.

'It's her birthday as well,' he sighed. 'Not going to be much of a present is it? What am I supposed to do, beat the door to the academy in and shout: "Hi honey, sorry it's been a few years, but I'm still alive"? Or "By the way, I'm supposed to blow a hole in your chest to show the Council Elders how loyal I am,"?'

'That's not very nice, is it?' Harriet smirked. 'You could have at least said happy birthday before blowing a hole in her chest.'

Michael glowered at her. If it hadn't been so cold already, they would have sworn that the temperature had dropped a few degrees.

'Sorry,' said Harriet. 'I didn't mean to upset you. I guess I misread what you were trying to say.'

'I'm sorry too,' said Michael, nudging her with his shoulder.

'So, it's true that they want you to go out just after New Year's, then?' Sam probed.

'No sense hiding it from you,' said Michael. 'I was hoping I could convince Lefrick to let you help with the mission tactical. Besides, it's not like you're going to let it slip to anyone who doesn't know, is it?'

'Not cooped up in there all day,' Sam huffed. 'It's a shame about Grimm's. I used to look forward to my trips to the library.'

'Seems to me that the Inquisition found something there that they didn't want us to see,' said Harriet.

'Yeah,' Sam agreed. 'It's a bit of a coincidence that you

and that old 'quis' master of yours were looking for the same thing, isn't it?'

'Knowing Catchpole, it wasn't a coincidence at all,' said Michael.

'How d'you mean?' said Sam.

'You remember that night we left the temple? I could have sworn I saw a bunch of Inquisitors through the mirror before it blew.'

'That is the reason we left,' said Sam.

'Yes,' said Michael. 'But the Inquisition doesn't usually kidnap a bunch of homeless people for information.'

'Could have fooled me,' said Sam. 'Judging by the daily news, they're taking more than you think. Either that, or there's been a severe increase in alien abductions recently.'

'I don't understand,' said Harriet.

'According to the radio, London's seen a real drop in homeless people in the last few months alone,' said Sam.

'That's good isn't it?' Harriet asked. 'Perhaps they've set up some new shelters or something.'

'It's not just London,' Sam went on. 'Liverpool, Cardiff and Glasgow have all seen their homeless all but disappear overnight.'

Michael stopped in his tracks. 'Which cities were they again?'

'London, Liverpool, Cardiff, Glasgow …'

Harriet looked hard at Michael. 'Davis took us to Glasgow before we came here. It was a dock warehouse they used to use for the shipping industry.'

'I wonder if it's got anything to do with us,' said Sam.

'I know there used to be a branch in Liverpool until

just a few weeks ago,' said Michael. 'They were evacuated not long before Mistress Maya arrived.'

'Why? Sam and Harriet chorused.

'Not sure,' said Michael shaking his head. 'Nobody seems willing to talk about it. I overheard Lefrick and Elder Carrow talking a few days ago. Carrow was saying something about the local normals turning on them.'

'That can't be true, can it?' said Harriet. 'Why would they turn on the Council? We haven't done anything to them.'

Michael shrugged his shoulders. 'Perhaps it's to do with the haven sites burning.'

'But Grimm's was after that,' said Harriet.

'I don't have all the answers,' said Michael. 'Whatever you might think, they keep me as much in the dark as they do you. Lefrick doesn't tell me very much these days, and Anna's worse.'

'Maybe they think you've got enough on your plate already,' Sam chuckled.

'If you ask me, it's more like they don't want to scare people with the truth about what's going on,' Harriet ventured. 'Propaganda can be a powerful thing. Look at the normals. The government's only got to tell them that something's true and they believe it.'

'They?' said Sam. 'You're not normal anymore then?'

'I never was,' Harriet sniffed, 'I'm an Inquisitor.' She blushed as her mistake registered in her brain. 'I mean …'

'Don't worry, Harriet, your secret's safe with us,' Sam laughed.

Up ahead, the gooselike drone of a car horn rang out,

followed by the grinding of tyres on compacted snow, and the rumbling rattle of twisting metal. Instinctively, the three friends hit the floor in an effort not to be seen.

'What the …?' Sam yelled. The last of his words were drowned out by the shattering of glass nearby.

'Sounds like a car accident,' replied Harriet. 'Come on, let's go see.' She pulled herself from the cold ground and hurried off in the direction of the noise, ignoring Michael and Sam's calls for her to wait.

By the time they had caught up with her, Harriet was standing in the road with her hands covering her mouth and tears streaming down her face. It was like a gruesome scene from a hospital drama. There was a girl lying in the road, her sandy hair matted with blood, arms strewn awkwardly as if someone had dropped her from a great height. To their left, the car that had hit her rocked on its side, the spinning front wheels not letting it come to rest. There was a man in the wreckage, but judging by the amount of red in the snow, Michael thought it unlikely that he could have survived. He was surprised to see that the airbags hadn't deployed, as they should have done in such extreme conditions, but couldn't keep the thought in his head for more than the briefest of seconds for the low moaning that was coming from Harriet.

'Sam, get Harriet out of here, and get us some help,' Michael ordered.

'W … w … what about you?' Sam stammered, wrapping an arm around Harriet's shoulders and manoeuvring her away.

'Someone's got to get her out of the road,' Michael

answered pointing at the girl. 'There's bound to be someone else along in a few minutes, and I don't want to risk blowing our cover here. Besides, she looks pretty hurt. I'm going to try to get her back to the farm at least, so they can call for an ambulance or something.'

As Sam and Harriet hurried away for help, Michael knelt in the road to check the girl's neck for a pulse, an electric shiver running through him as his fingers touched her.

*Careful, Michael,* said Jerrick's voice in his head. *There's something about this girl that's putting my teeth on edge.*

'You haven't got teeth,' Michael hissed, annoyed by the interruption. 'You haven't got a mouth either, remember?'

*Still,* Jerrick continued, *I'd be very careful if I were you. I wouldn't put something like this past the Inquisition.*

'Well you're not me,' Michael yelped as he heaved the girl out of the road. 'Now are you going to help me or not?'

*Help you? How can I help you? I don't have a body.*

'Then suggest something useful, would you?' Michael panted. He looked down at the girl's face. 'For such a thin girl, you weigh a ton.'

Once he'd managed to drag the girl to the bank, Michael carefully began checking for signs of injury other than her obvious head wound. She was pretty enough in a strange kind of way, with soft features, and skin as pale as the snow she lay in. He took a scarf from around his neck and dabbed at the gash in her scalp.

*It's not unusual for head wounds to bleed like that,* said Jerrick. *It looks worse than it is.*

'I wish I didn't have to use my scarf, though,' Michael moaned. 'Gamma Laura gave me this for my birthday, to keep me warm at the academy.'

*Some things are worth the sacrifice.*

'What were you doing out here anyway?' said Michael.

*I couldn't very well be anywhere else, could I?* Jerrick replied.

'I wasn't talking to you, I was talking to her! Look at her, no backpack or luggage. She's not even wearing the right shoes for this weather.'

*Neither are you.*

'Yes, but I'm not trekking through the outback of Wales in the snow, am I.' It wasn't a question.

Along the road, Michael could see Sam leading Anna, Lefrick and the farmer towards them. On seeing the wreck, the two Elders split from the pack to check for any signs of life, while the farmer and Sam continued on to where Michael was kneeling with the girl.

'Good lad,' he sang in his valleys accent. 'You keep the pressure on that cut, an' I'll carry 'er back to the farm. Ready? On three …'

*Michael, don't let him take the girl into the bunker. If she wakes before you get there, you're going to have to come up with some flimsy excuses.*

'What is with you?' Michael said aloud.

'Eh?' said the farmer, beginning to sound out of breath under the weight of the girl.

'Oh, nothing,' Michael lied, trying to ignore the look

192

that Sam was giving him.

*I'm telling you, there's something wrong with this girl. Don't let them take her to the bunker, Michael. Please!*

'I think it might be best if she didn't go down to the bunker with you,' said the farmer, as if reading Michael's mind. 'Not until Lefrick and Anna have a chance to check her over.'

'Good idea,' Sam nodded. 'Why didn't I think of that? It's not as if we know who she is, or why she's out here all on her own. She could be anybody.'

'She's just a girl,' said Michael, less certain now that public opinion was voicing the thoughts in his head.

*Why don't you take a closer look at her, Mr Smart Posterior,* Jerrick chided. He'd never been good at modern insults. He'd always had the tendency to get the words wrong.

Doing as he was told, Michael let his eyes slip out of focus to really *look* at the girl. For a moment, there was nothing. Then there was a queasy, lurching feeling in the pit of his stomach as his second sight tried to get to grips with what was before him.

The girl's aura swam and flitted like a paper flag in a gale, and its myriad colours collided and exploded like a psychedelic fireworks bonanza. Blues, reds, purples and yellows blended together and separated like odd socks in an endless washing machine cycle.

'Ugh …' Michael gagged trying not to vomit.

'Wassup, Mike?' asked Sam.

'I think I just trod in something nasty,' Michael covered

in haste.

'Nothin' nasty in the country, young man,' said the farmer in a sing-song accent. 'It's all nat'rul up here.'

'Must have been my imagination,' Michael replied.

***Nothing nasty?*** Jerrick sneered. ***If only he could see what we can see.***

'Where do you think she's come from?' Michael asked aloud, not remembering that all he had to do was think his conversation with his former master.

'Could be anywhere,' said Sam as they reached the farmhouse.

They were ushered indoors by the farmer's wife, to the parlour, and a comfortable looking sofa in front of an open log fire that crackled and hissed. As soon as he put her down, the farmer pulled a heavy, chequered, orange and black blanket around her, while his wife set about cleaning the gash on the side of the girl's head.

***My guess,*** Jerrick's voice echoed in Michael's head, ***is that she's not one of ours. So she must be an Inquisitor.***

'Underground Railroad?' said Michael.

The farmer's wife glared daggers at him before softening a little. 'Not so loud, we don't know for certain that she is.'

'I'm sure when Lefrick and Anna get here, they can tell us more,' said Sam.

'We are here, and we can't,' said Anna from the door. 'There's nothing in the car to suggest that she was ever in it. I think it would be best if you could call the police and let them know that a car left the road not far from here.

We'll keep everyone inside until they finish with their investigation.'

'What about the tracks and the blood?' Michael asked.

'We've taken care of it,' said Lefrick.

'And her?' said Sam pointing to the girl. 'Shouldn't she be in the hospital?'

'No,' Michael shrieked, reacting before he could think. 'No, I think she's on the Railroad.'

Lefrick smirked and shook his head. 'You can't know that for certain, Michael. She could be anybody, from anywhere.'

Jerrick's voice was insistent. *What are you doing?*

'Shut up, I know what I'm doing okay!' said Michael, his voice bursting out of him like a cannonball.

'Okay,' said Lefrick, 'we'll trust your judgment for now. But I'm warning you, the first sign of trouble, and I'll flush her out of the nearest mirror!'

'Agreed,' Michael acknowledged. 'So, help me get her to the bunker before the police show up. The last thing we want is a bunch of questions about why there are so many of us living here.'

*She's trouble and you know it!* Jerrick snapped as they followed Lefrick and Anna, with the girl between them, into the bunker.

'Yes, she is,' Michael whispered. 'You saw what I saw in her aura. It's not normal, even for an Inquisitor.'

*And have you thoughts on that?*

'Plenty, but I don't think you'd agree with me on any of them.'

*I might,* said Jerrick. His spirit felt slightly affronted.

195

'I doubt it,' Michael sighed. 'Okay, try this one. She's an experiment in trying to cross different Inquisitor talents in someone who isn't born to be a Grand.'

*That's not as wacky as I was expecting,* Jerrick mused. *That would account for the rainbow coloured aura. But it doesn't fit the feeling I got from her when you touched her.*

'You mean the feeling I got from you when I touched her.'

*Yes, yes. It was like touching someone's hatred with your bare fingers. Once we get her to a room, I need you to search her.*

'Search her, for what?'

*She's got to be carrying some clue as to her identity. Nobody walks around with nothing these days. Look at her: she appears to be a young girl, relatively well dressed, and in the middle of nowhere. Why doesn't she have one of those mobile telephones?*

'If she's on the Railroad, she wouldn't. They wouldn't let us have them at all at the academy,' said Michael feeling the need to defend himself.

*That's another thing that puzzles me about her. She looks to be about your age, yet you don't recognise her, do you? I would bet that Miss King doesn't either.*

'It's been two years, Jerrick. I've probably changed a lot myself in that time. Besides, there are more academies than Cheritton Hall in this world. She might even be from abroad.'

*If any part of your theory was true, why didn't she*

*come by portal, and where is her sponsor?*

'With Nahar in the ether, and the Flayers out there? Maybe her sponsor thought it was better not to chance it.'

'Between that and the library burning, I'm surprised she made it here at all,' said Anna over her shoulder. The surprise on Michael's face seemed enough to confirm her suspicions. 'It's okay, Sam told us about your one sided conversations when he came to fetch us.'

'From the talk and the flash of gold in your eyes when Maya was here, we've put two and two together, and hopefully got four,' said Lefrick. 'Somehow Jerrick has managed to piggyback himself onto you, hasn't he?'

**Go on, tell them,** Jerrick tutted.

Michael's cheeks flushed. 'Tell them what?'

**I'm dead Michael. They need to understand that.**

'What is he telling you?' Lefrick queried.

'He told me to tell you that he's dead,' said Michael.

Lefrick nodded as he considered the news. 'He is, after a fashion. I'm not even certain his body will repair itself this time.'

Anna looked taken aback. 'So it's happened before then?'

**Yes.**

'Yes,' Michael echoed.

'But this is different,' Lefrick continued. 'The Flayers must have taken a big bite out of his energy for his body to give out like that. What we witnessed is what would have happened if Jerrick hadn't reached his lamp in time every year.'

Michael nodded. 'He agrees with you. When he thought

he was going to die, he panicked. The spell was supposed to release him back into the lamp, but somehow he ended up in me instead.'

'You know what they say about empty vessels,' Anna giggled.

Michael wrinkled his nose. 'Can we talk about this later? He wants us to search the girl as soon as we get her inside.'

'Mrs Davis can take care of that while she's patching the girl up,' said Anna. 'I'd rather not have to search her myself, and I don't want you going anywhere near her. The fewer of us she sees, the better it'll be for all of us.'

'At least until we can verify her story,' said Lefrick.

'Whatever that is,' said Anna.

Once inside, their tracks through the straw were covered over, and the doors between the barn and barracks were sealed. It sent that choking feeling of claustrophobia through Michael, the same as he'd felt during the first few days. However, he didn't have time to dwell on it because as soon as the girl was in Mrs Davis's care, he was summoned to the training room.

He was greeted by the hulking frame of Andy, and his familiar, resonant, 'Oi, oi.'

'Hi,' said Michael. 'I take it you've been drafted for the op then?'

'Volunteered,' Andy boomed.

Michael patted him on the forearm. 'Thanks, Andy, I appreciate it. Where's everyone else?'

'It's just us,' said Anna. 'Lefrick'll be along soon. He

thought it would be best if we took a small group. This isn't a day at the park, this is a hit. We don't want to put too many people in danger now, not if what Grimm said is right.'

Michael cocked an eyebrow in her direction. 'Which part?'

Anna pulled a metal chair to the corner of the room and lurched heavily onto it. 'While you've been off gallivanting with your friends, I've had my nose buried in that book he gave us before the library burned. There are whole chapters on the history between Jerrick and Nahar, things even Lefrick didn't know.'

'I know,' said Michael. 'I saw some of it the day Jerrick um ... dropped by to visit.'
He looked sidelong at Andy, hoping his aunt would get the hint that he didn't want to discuss it. If she did, it didn't show on her face.

'Between those chapters are some on the Piper, and his connection with the culling of the Council. I won't show you those. Hell, I'll be lucky if they don't give me nightmares for a month.'

'The Piper was part of the cull?' Michael asked.

'Not directly, no. The records say that he shows up around the same time. He hangs around for anything up to a few years, until the cull happens. In the end, he takes some of the wounded and disappears until the next time. It's as though he knows it's going to happen - like an angel of death or something.' Anna's voice quivered noticeably, betraying her attempt to cover her horror.

A few heartbeats later, Andy broke the pause. 'Why

does he want the wounded?'

'No-one knows,' Anna shrugged. 'There's nothing in the books about it at any rate. What it does say, is that they seem to want to go with him, no matter what anyone's done to stop them, the way we did that night between the mirrors. It's like he's at his most powerful then. He just puts that infernal pipe to his lips and pipes them off whatever battlefield they fell on.'

'And now he's back,' said Lefrick as he strode across the room to join them. 'And according to Grimm, the cull won't be too far behind.'

'Which is why Maya wants us to go after Tamara now,' said Michael. 'If we can get to her before the cull, perhaps we can postpone it, or even avert it altogether.'

'That's the idea,' said Anna. 'But we've tried it before. And each time it's been unsuccessful.' She put her head in her hands. 'The Inquisition has been without a Grand for other reasons as well, for some culls. It still hasn't stopped them from pulling their forces together. Judging by the descriptions in Grimm's journal, those years are more vicious.'

'So we can expect them to hold a conclave soon, to decide on a plan for this coming cull,' said Michael. When the others looked blankly at him, he continued. 'It's the poem Grimm wrote in my copy of "Modern Lore". They always hold a meeting of the Grand Inquisitors before it happens.'

'So?' said Anna. 'More Grand Inquisitors in one place only makes them more dangerous.'

'I think what your nephew's trying to say, Anna,' said

Lefrick, 'is that killing Miss Bloodgood won't make a difference. The same way that it hasn't at any other time. The conclave will still go ahead and the cull will follow.'

'History repeats itself,' said Andy. 'If you're all thinking what I think you're thinking, what happens if we refuse Maya's order?'

'She and the other Elders will assume that Michael's loyalties are still with the Inquisition,' said Lefrick. 'It would also be the excuse they need to get rid of Anna and me at last.'

'I thought Maya and the Elders were going to try to sue for peace with the Inquisition?' said Andy.

'If you believe that, then you're as loopy as my aunt Fanny,' said Lefrick. 'Once the Grand Inquisitor's out of the way, they'll have the leverage they need, now that they've got us training everyone to fight. People like Maya don't want peace. They want to prove that their way is the right way.'

Andy smiled. 'I can't blame them, I'm as sick of running as they are. Wouldn't it be nice to have the normals following our rules for once?'

For the second time, Michael's eyes flashed with flecks of gold. 'No, Andy, It wouldn't be nice at all. It would just make us as bad as the Inquisition.'

There was another long pause before Anna cleared her throat. 'Well then, let's get to work. If we're going to face a Grand Inquisitor, we'd better be ready. Michael, run us through what we're up against again, I want to be absolutely clear about what to expect.'

\*\*\*

Away in the quietest corner of the compound, Mrs Davis was finishing dressing her patient's head wound. As she pinned the bandage into place, the girl's eyes fluttered as she stirred.

'Easy now, don't try to sit up,' Mrs Davis cooed. 'You've been in an accident.'

Her voice was croaky, startled and confused. 'What is this place? Did I make it? Is this the Elder Council safe house?'

'Yes, love,' Mrs Davis soothed. 'You're safe. There's no need to worry.' Her patient's shoulders seemed to relax somewhat at the news. 'What's your name?'

'Kat ... Kat ...' the girl stammered as if struggling to remember something important. 'It's Katie,' she slurred before her eyes fluttered closed again.

## Chapter Nine:
# The Trouble with Wonderland

There was a muted quiet in the grounds of the academy. Not even the birds were singing in the trees, and the snow had lost its pillow-like softness to the hard frost of the previous night. The end of term was closing in, but not even the glow from the Christmas decorations in the halls and corridors of the aged house lent comfort to the bitter, unsympathetic chill.

At the end of the long driveway, the intricate wrought-iron gates swung inwards without a sound, and a stretch limousine crunched slowly into the car park. When it came to rest and the doors opened, Alice Ware and Adam Dakin stood waiting for the driver to unload their luggage.

'There'll be a trolley along any minute,' said Adam. 'They always send someone down to the car park for new arrivals, mainly so that we can check in at reception.'

'I must admit, I'd heard this place was big, but I'd never imagined this,' said Alice, gawping in open-mouthed awe at the sight of the flags waving in the breeze from the ramparts just above the hill.

'Your brother must have told you about it sometime?' said Adam.

'Not really,' said Alice. 'He always said he wasn't allowed.' She pulled her grey woollen coat tighter around her against the cold. 'Why all this interest in Michael anyway? You haven't stopped asking about him.'

'What do you mean?' said Adam.

Not being the type to back down, Alice looked him squarely in the eye. 'Every time you start a conversation with me, you seem to ask about him, that's all. I thought, since we're here, we might avoid talking about my brother so much, and concentrate a little more on me.'

'Of course, I didn't realise I was being so selfish,' said Adam.

Alice blushed. 'Oh god, I'm sorry,' she laughed. 'It's me who's being selfish, isn't it?'

Adam's reply dripped with sarcasm. 'Not at all, but you're not going to be able to avoid talking about him *all* weekend. He had a lot of friends here. There's even a portrait of him in Solaris.'

'I know,' said Alice. 'Tamara told me about it once. Anyone would think he was a superstar or something, the way they acted. It's a shame they couldn't have done that for the Hathaway boy too. I know I would have felt more comfortable about it.'

'That was different.' said Adam looking embarrassed. 'I was the one who found him. Look, I'm not supposed to talk about this, but Craig Hathaway was murdered, in a manner of speaking. He was tied up and put in a boat that sank. Not that he drowned. He died as a result of exposure.'

'I'm sorry,' said Alice, 'I didn't know.'

'That's not the worst of it, Alice.' He searched her face as if looking for some prompt to cease his confession, but there was none. 'The people who did it … they were after your brother.'

'What for? Who would want to kill Michael?' Alice

gasped.

'I couldn't say,' said Adam. Alice tried to cut across him, but he put a finger to her lips. 'Just promise me that whatever you hear this weekend, you'll reserve judgement on me for a while, until you know the whole story.'

'Of course I'll promise,' Alice responded feeling more confused than she'd been when Adam had suddenly taken an interest in her.

'Thanks, you won't regret it,' said Adam.

Alice didn't hear him. She let her mind wander as she followed the golf trolley down along the path with her eyes.

Theirs had been a strange meeting. Alice had noticed Adam on her very first day at the college. His swarthy good looks and kind eyes had set her heart aflutter almost immediately. Although she certainly wasn't unattractive, Alice had never considered herself to be pretty, at least not pretty enough to grab the attention of someone like Adam, who had never seemed to notice her.

They'd been at the same bar for most of the evening when she'd overheard Adam and his friends talking. The rest was a bit of a blur. They had talked into the small hours of the morning about everything and nothing. Though it wasn't until they had talked about the academy that things had really taken off. It was as if Alice had no choice but to talk about Michael and what had happened, as far she was able.

Now they were here, where she had once dreamed of being, but it wasn't the same. Visiting a place and belonging to a place were two different things for Alice. She hadn't been able to turn Adam down when he had asked her to visit the academy with him. After all, she had wanted to study there for so long. Now she was standing and looking at it for the first time, knowing that she could never be a part of its wonder, it felt almost cruel.

'Hey. Wakey, wakey,' said Adam touching her hand. 'Everything's loaded on the trolley. I thought we might start with a quick trip to the main house. I know you've been itching to see it.'

'Sure,' Alice replied, giving in to the feeling that there was more to this trip than the visit she'd hoped for.

As the electric trolley whined its way back the way it came, she put her anxiety out of her mind and found herself humming along to the tune that Adam was quietly singing next to her.

'London's Burning one of your favourites, is it?' asked Alice, nudging him in the ribs. 'Or are you into nursery rhymes in general?'

Adam grimaced. 'Sorry, it's been in my head since we arrived. You know, it's a wonder London survived at all, between civil wars, plagues and fires. Now there's talk of rioting on the streets of Liverpool, and that bookstore burning down. I'm starting to think the whole country's going to hell.'

'Like school dinners,' Alice said giggling.

'Er …' said Adam clearly not following.

'History,' said Alice. 'A teacher of mine used to say that history was like a school dinner – doomed to repeat. I guess you had to be there.'

Adam laughed. 'I can't really say that I've experienced that. The dinners here were always exceptional, apart from once when the Solaris chef was sick. The substitute they got in to cover him decided tripe and onions in a spicy tomato sauce would be a good idea. Now that …'

'You're missing the point,' said Alice. 'What I was trying to say was, that history seems to be repeating itself, doesn't it? The fires, the rioting - how long will it be before we have another civil war do you think?'

'Oh, not long now,' replied Adam. 'Besides, one bookstore isn't really the same as the Great Fire of London.'

Alice sighed and shrugged her shoulders. 'I suppose not. It's probably me seeing conspiracies where there aren't any.'

Adam hopped down from the trolley before it had a chance to come to a rest.

'C'mon, lots to see,' he said over his shoulder before jogging to a door and holding it open.

As Alice got out of the buggy, the driver eyed her with an air of suspicion, like he was trying to decide something about her. The dark brown of his irises seemed to darken further still as he examined the newcomer. His crushed squint gave him the look one might expect of a constipated owl and gave Alice the heebie-jeebies. Trying her best to ignore him, she stood under the archway that opened into the quad and took in the view.

'I had no idea it was this beautiful,' she said and beamed a smile at Adam.

'You should see it when the flowers are in bloom and the fountains are running. '

'No,' said Alice shaking her head. 'This is far better.

Even cemeteries have flowers to make them pretty. You only see the true face of a building when there's nothing else to distract you.'

'Has anyone told you that you think too much?' Adam joked.

'Frequently, but look at it. I thought some of the buildings at Oxford were impressive. This feels like …' her voice trailed off to nothing. She spied a familiar face flashing in and out of view through the windows of what she thought must be a corridor. 'Um … Adam?'

'Yes?'

'Is there a man here with a long scar on his face and one white eye?'

'Yes,' said Adam. 'Mr Catchpole was here when I was at the academy. I wondered if we might see him. He was your brother's mentor during … his exams.'

'He was the one who did my entrance test when I was a girl. It nearly crushed me when I found out that I hadn't been accepted,' said Alice. Even the memory of it gave her pangs of longing for a better life.

'He did a lot of them, I think. He's a very important man in the Inq … academy,' said Adam as her leaned against the door.

Alice frowned. 'Why do you always do that?'

'Do what?' Adam covered.

'Change what it is you're trying to say, half way through saying it.'

'Just nervous,' he mumbled, a light flush burnishing his cheeks.

'Rubbish,' Catchpole intoned behind him. 'I've never

known you to be nervous in your life, Mr Dakin.'

Adam's flush deepened. 'Thank you, sir,' he managed, appearing more like a schoolboy than Alice had ever seen him.

'And a little advice, if I may? Even attractive young ladies like Miss Ware need to eat. May I suggest that you take her to lunch at Solaris? After all, I have taken the liberty of procuring suites for you both there, rather than at the guest quarters. I believe Alice would enjoy the *full* Braxton Academy experience while she's here, not just the penny tour.'

Alice realised that Catchpole hadn't taken his eyes off of her throughout his entire monologue. They seemed to be fixated on her face, and they were searching for something. It made her feel weak, and a wave of light-headedness swept over her.

'Yes, I am feeling a little peculiar,' she said. 'I'm sure some food would help.'

'Right,' said Adam. 'That's a great idea. Thank you, sir, I should have thought. It's been a long trip.'

'Enjoy your visit, Miss Ware,' said Catchpole. But there was something insincere about it. 'I'm sure our paths will cross again before you leave.' His eyes left Alice's face to glare at Adam. 'In fact, Mr Dakin, why don't you make sure of it, there's a good chap.' Nodding curtly and not waiting for a response, he took his leave.

Alice watched him until he was nothing more than a speck in the distance before speaking.

'He's cheerful.'

'Don't be too hard on the poor chap,' said Adam. 'He's

not always like that. He must have a lot on his mind at the moment. Besides, he seems to have saved us a trip to reception, you ought to be grateful.'

Alice's face brightened. 'So … are you going to take me to lunch, or do you want to spend the rest of the weekend keeping company with a skeleton?'

'When you put it so nicely, how could I refuse?' said Adam offering her his arm.

The trolley trip to Solaris lifted Alice's mood considerably. Evergreens laden with snow waved heavily in the breeze. Despite the cold, the lake around Solaris Island hadn't frozen. Swans idly trawled for fish in its crystal clear depths. Alice thought it tranquil and magical all at once.

When the trolley pulled up outside the open outer doors of Solaris, Alice leapt down from the trolley and bustled inside, leaving Adam floundering behind her. When he caught up to her, she was standing in front of the visitors' lounge fireplace looking at the plaque dedicated to her brother.

'I'd almost forgotten what he looked like,' she said.

'You must miss him,' said Adam.

'I used to feel guilty for being jealous of him, but not anymore,' said Alice trying not to give herself away.

The aromas from Solaris's kitchens wafted through the corridors to tempt them, making her stomach rumble like a freight train in the quiet lounge. In some strange way, the smells reminded her of home. The kitchen had been the sacred domain of her mother until Michael had left them. The scent of sweet apple pie floated on the breeze, followed by tempting odours of slowly roasted vegetables, exotic spices and garden herbs. Rosemary, thyme and mint pervaded her nostrils, such that Alice thought they might lift her and carry her to the dining room like a leaf on the wind.

'If that tastes half as good as it smells, we're in for a treat,' said Adam smiling at her.

There was a cough behind them that made them both turn. Adam bowed low.

'Usually, lunch is served at the main dining hall for students, and only the house staff eats here,' said Tamara. She beamed a smile at Alice and extended a hand. 'Hello, Alice, it's good to see you again.' She nodded her head to the still bowing Dakin. 'Adam.'

Alice looked at him, uncertain whether it was usual for people to bow to each other here, or whether there was something more to it.

'I'm sorry,' she said. 'I didn't mean to be discourteous.' She inclined her head, allowing her shoulders to follow, mimicking Adam's movements.

Tamara let out a small giggle. 'It's okay, Alice, you don't have to do that. I was hoping that Adam had told you at least a little before you came here.' Looping her arms through theirs, she set off for the dining hall. 'Come on, let's get some lunch, I'm starving.'

Most of the walk was taken up with Tamara's conversation with Adam. Uninterested in their general chit-chat, Alice took the opportunity to really look at the house where she assumed her brother had spent most of his time. She noticed that unlike most stately residences, the opulence of Solaris wasn't hiding any sort of self-conscious shabbiness. It really was a peacock of a house, ready, willing and extremely able to show itself off to the full. At first glance, Alice had found the whole academy luxurious beyond compare. Now that she was really looking at it, it had the sickening extravagance that only ridiculous amounts of money could buy.

Some of the senior staff members of the house were seated and eating by the time the three of them arrived, waited upon by the juniors of their various departments. Still arm in arm, Tamara led her guests to a table, where Emily and Rupert were waiting for them with puzzled looks on their faces. Then it dawned on Alice that something had caught Tamara's eye, and it seemed to fascinate her entirely.

Coughing with purpose until she had Rupert's attention, Tamara nodded in the direction of the waiting staff, where the occasional spoon was hovering as though waiting to be noticed. Rupert's cheeks reddened. Suddenly the clatter of metal on metal filled the air, along with angry shouts, followed by the sounds of shattering china from the kitchens beyond. Seconds later, a portly, ruddy-faced man in a white jacket and chequered trousers burst into the dining room.

'Who's the bloody comedian …' he blustered, searching the room for the culprit. As soon as his eyes met Tamara's, his mouth clamped shut and he bowed, hastily backing out of the room as he did so.

'You know,' Alice managed after a few tense seconds, 'I could have sworn I saw a spoon floating in mid-air. Did anyone else see that … a spoon, floating in mid-air?'

Adam giggled, sounding like a choking horse as it forced its way between strained lips. 'Now I know you're hungry. You said you were feeling light headed earlier. Are you sure you're okay?'

'I really don't know,' said Alice. 'Low blood sugar can do strange things to you, can't it?' She hesitated, not really believing herself. 'And another thing, why do people keep bowing to Tamara like she's the queen?' she managed at last, flopping heavily onto a chair and rubbing at her eyes.

'Do they?' said a straight-faced Tamara.

'Enough,' said Emily looking serious. She lowered her voice to a whisper, 'I'm sorry Alice, we'll bring you up to speed soon, I promise. For now, try to relax, okay?'

'She looks so pale,' said Rupert. 'Did something happen on the way here?'

'Catchpole,' said Adam. 'I think he read her. But I don't think he got much because he wasn't at it for long.'

'Alice,' said Tamara resting a hand on her arm, 'did Adam tell you why I wanted to see you?'

Alice looked affronted and glared at her. 'Why *you* wanted to see me? No. I thought he invited me because he wanted to spend some time with me.'

'I did,' said Adam. 'I mean, I do.'

'Good,' Tamara sighed. 'Then Catchpole will think that as well. I thought we might have been finished before we'd even started there for a minute.'

'Oh,' Alice breathed as she put two and two together at last. 'I should have known from all the questions.' She turned to look Adam in the eye. 'This was never about me

213

was it?'

Not able to meet her gaze, Adam stared down at the table.

'No, it wasn't. I'm sorry, Alice. I really like you, I do, but the visit is about something else. If you let us explain, you'll understand.'

'I think I can already guess,' said Alice. 'You needn't have dragged me all the way down here to talk to me. I would have told you the same thing anywhere. I'm not going to talk about Michael, end of discussion.'

'So you do know,' Tamara whispered.

Alice cradled her face in her hands. It was the first true test of her resolve to keep Michael's secret, and she had failed. 'I thought I was the only one.'

'Don't feel bad,' said Emily. 'We didn't find out until a few weeks ago. If it makes you feel any better, Tamara asked Adam to bring you here because he said that you were both on good terms already. I don't think he'd mind me telling you that he thinks a great deal of you.'

'Hmm,' Alice groaned. 'I still think it was a rotten thing to do. How did Michael manage to get a message to you anyway?'

'He didn't,' said Emily. 'I found out from Catchpole by accident. They must have been forcing him to help them because ...'

Tamara held up a hand to cut in. 'Hang on a minute, Em. Just how much do you know about us, and about what happened to Michael?'

Alice took a few seconds to think before answering. 'I only know that he was here. Then that poor Hathaway boy died, and a little while later he was on the run. When he came home, he said he was in big trouble, and that I had to keep it a secret. He said that if I didn't, whoever was after him might come after us too.'

'He came home?' Tamara sputtered. 'When?'

'A few nights after he supposedly died,' Alice replied. 'It was the strangest thing, but ...' she shook her head, not quite sure whether she should say it aloud. 'You're not going to believe it, but I swear it's the truth. He ... disappeared through the mirror, and I haven't seen him since.'

'Through a mirror?' said Adam, his eyes like saucers.

'But it's true!'

'I believe you,' said Tamara. 'We all believe you.'

'We do,' Adam confirmed. 'So where is he now?'

'Last I heard, he was in some abandoned Masonic temple in London,' said Alice. 'Honestly, though, it's been weeks since I heard from him last.' She stared at Tamara's look of horror, which was reflected in the faces of the others. 'Did I say something wrong?'

'No,' said Adam looking around the table. 'However, I think it would be best if we filled you in on a few details if Tamara doesn't mind?'

Adam did his best to tell the story of the war without too much detail or bias. He confirmed that she had indeed seen floating spoons, and why. He also made sure he differentiated between the powers of the Inquisition and those of the Elder Council. And although several plates of food had arrived at the table, nobody had eaten a thing.

Eventually, Adam spoke about the trials and Michael's

part in them. He told her about the final duel, and about Lady Shaw using Emily and Rupert. He talked about how Tamara couldn't possibly have avoided defending herself the way she had because Michael had been drugged.

'So all of this is because of something that happened centuries ago?' Alice quizzed.

'It's more than that,' said Adam. 'Look at it from the Inquisition's point of view. We've been influencing governments for so long, the world practically owes us a favour. Capitalism, education, democracy, it's all because of us.'

'Great, so it's your fault that the rich are rich enough to end up making decisions for all of us, is it?' Alice snapped.

'They're just trying to do the best they can,' said Tamara. 'If it was up to the Elder Council, the world would be a much harder place to live in. They believe that we should live under their guidance like children, being told what we can and can't do, and only knowing what they want us to know.'

'How is it any different from what we have now?' said Alice. 'It sounds to me like you've both lost sight of the message along the way. Now all you've got left is the fear you both have of each other, but you can't remember why. Have you considered that we might not want to be told what's good for us anymore, or that maybe we can decide for ourselves?'

'It happens,' said Adam. 'Some of our worst wars have been because normals have tried to decide what's best.'

'But your whole lives have been based on the idea that magic is wrong,' said Alice. 'Michael's in this mess because of it. Because you're no different from each other really. I think if the world knew about it, they'd want you both gone. So if you're done being all powerful, why don't you tell me why you need a *normal* like me to help you find him?'

'Because someone's going to try to kill him,' said Tamara sounding panicked. 'And this time it is my fault. We were hoping that if we brought you here, you might be able to tell us where he is.'

Alice shook her head. 'It's like I said. He used to send me messages every now and again, but it's been weeks.'

Rupert, who hadn't said a word throughout the conversation, finally held up a hand to silence them, and spoke.

'Exactly how did he get his messages to you?'

'They just appeared on my desk,' said Alice. 'Most of the time, I'd wake up and they'd be there. I had the devil's own job trying to hide them from our parents. I always thought it was strange that they started appearing at the college too.'

'Under the mirror?' Rupert pressed.

'Every time,' said Alice.

'Catchpole's been obsessed with mirrors ever since the trials,' said Tamara. 'Now that you've told us about the night he came to the house, it makes perfect sense that he'd use them to get messages to you. There's no way the Inquisition could have tracked them.'

'Now the only thing that doesn't make sense is what Michael's doing with the Council,' said Adam pushing peas around his plate with his fork.

'I think I can help you with that,' said Alice looking straight into Tamara's eyes. 'He said they were going to kill you after the trials if he'd won. I didn't know what that meant until today. He said that our aunt, Anna, had figured out a way to save you both. He also said that I shouldn't tell you that because you'd go looking for him.'

'He was right,' said Tamara. 'And when I find him, I'm going to give him a piece of my mind!'

'Why would the Inquisition want to kill Tamara?' said Adam looking confused. 'She's our most valuable asset. If Michael knew what was going on, why didn't he get a message to one of us, to warn us?'

'I don't know; *I'm not* psychic!' said Alice.

'Oh, god,' Tamara gasped. 'Just before we went into the final trial, Michael tried to tell me that we needed to get out of here, but he didn't have time to say why.'

'You think he knew?' Emily asked.

'If his aunt has anything to do with the Elder Council, I'm betting he did,' said Tamara.

Alice rubbed at her temples in frustration. 'But he had no reason to trust her. It's a long story. Look, we could speculate on the details all day. The only person who knows the truth is Michael. So how do we get a message to him? Do you think your Mr Catchpole could help?'

There was a resounding chorus of "no" from the others, drawing odd looks from the remnants of the staff that were still in the dining room.

'Don't you people have spies?' said Alice.

Rupert shrugged his shoulders. 'Yeah, 'course we do. But since the raid on the temple went wrong, the Council's

gone deeper underground, and we haven't heard from ...
what?' Alice was staring at him, mouth agape. 'How were
we supposed to know?' he managed.

'Honestly,' said Alice. 'You say you can't trust us
normals to do anything for ourselves. It sounds to me like
you couldn't organise a trolley dash in a supermarket.'

'Go on then, smart ass, show us halfwits how the
normals would do it!' said Adam crossing his arms and
smirking at her.

'It seems to me like you need a target. Someone the
Elder Council would be happy to pick up and take in.'

'A decoy duck?' said Rupert.

'Exactly,' said Alice.

'But how would we get our decoy noticed in the first
place?' Emily pressed. 'It's not like we even know where we
could find some of their goons, let alone just waltz up to
one of them and say: "Hi, I'm with the Inquisition. Take
me to your leader," is it?'

'Followers,' said Tamara, her face brightening. 'I know
where we can find just what we're looking for. The
question now is: who's going to be our duck?'

*** 

In the trophy room of the practice hall beneath Solaris,
Catchpole sat with steepled fingers, eyes closed. His face
was set in a mask of smug amusement. It wasn't often that
he was able to utilise his talent for seeing. Limited though it
was, he could manage forty or even fifty feet sometimes. At
first he'd thought it useless. But at times like this, even forty

or fifty feet could be useful because people often forgot that they lived in three dimensions.

Behind his eyelids, he could see the dining room as though he were looking down on it from the ceiling. There were four obvious figures visible, and the fuzzy static of a blank where the fifth should have been sitting. It had always been Catchpole's firmly held belief, that the powerful are most careless where they are most comfortable. It was the reason the Council had managed to rescue Edward Lucas from under their noses during the trials.

*So, you're going to send Alice to the Council. What then Miss Bloodgood, do you think he'll come back? Or will you join him there?* he thought.

He sighed and opened his eyes.

*As much as I loathe the idea, I'm going to need her before the end. Perhaps if something unfortunate were to happen to Michael, she'd go back to being the miserable, angry girl I could count on. What a prize he would make, dead or alive! Better still, if something were to happen to Alice, our illustrious leader would never be able to face him again. On the other hand, if I play this correctly, I may even come away with both of them!*

*Poor Alice, that's the trouble with Wonderland. Once you fall down the rabbit hole, it's so damned hard to get out again without losing your head.*

He tugged on the red silk bell-pull by his side, making the gold tassel shake violently. After a few minutes, there was a knock on the polished oak door.

'Enter.'

'You rang, sir?' said a red-faced duty valet appearing in

the doorway.

'Yes, I did,' said Catchpole, and he smiled his toothiest smile.

## Chapter Ten:
# Guess Who's Coming to Dinner

Katja's eyelids fluttered as she stirred from a fitful slumber. She hadn't meant for the car to hit her, it had just sort of happened. One minute she was in complete control over it, the way she had been over a hundred other objects before, the next she wasn't. She sat up and blinked the dust of sleep from her eyes, disoriented by her surroundings. She examined her hands carefully for signs. Then she examined her face in the small mirror by the door frame and sighed with relief when she couldn't find what she'd had been looking for.

Pleased that the aging serum was still holding, she pulled a rough white dressing gown from a hook behind the door and stepped out into the corridor. She was surprised to find that there was nobody about. The librarian had made it sound as though the compound was like an ant's nest, full of bustle and the comings and goings of people with jobs to do.

Making her way down through the corridors, she was eventually met by a stern looking woman in a black dress, with a white, ruffle collared blouse. Her silver hair was set in a severe looking bun, and she was carrying strips of material and cotton wadding. The woman smiled thinly as Katja approached her.

'What are you doing out of bed, young lady?' Mrs Davis called. Her voice was stern, but not unkind.

It took Katja a fraction of a second to realise that the

woman was addressing her.

'Um ... I was feeling better,' she lied. 'I thought I might get something to drink.'

'Good,' said Mrs Davis. Striding like a commandant to her patient, she took her chin gently but firmly in hand, glaring into her eyes. 'Pupils look good. Colour in your cheeks. No sign of a temperature. It seems to me that you're doing well. How's your head?'

'A little fuzzy,' Katja confessed.

'I'm not surprised. You took quite a bump,' Mrs Davis huffed.

'The vehicle came out of nowhere,' said Katja. 'I tried to stop it, but it was moving too quickly.'

Mrs Davis patted her arm. 'There, there. Don't you fret about that now. It wasn't your fault, I'm sure.'

'But if I'd been stronger ...' Katja snuffled. 'That poor man. He's dead, isn't he?'

'Yes. Yes, he is.' Mrs Davis replied. 'What on earth were you doing out on the road all by yourself?'

'We were attacked by these horrible creatures,' said Katja wiping her cheeks with the back of her hand. 'I came out at a boarded up house a few miles from here, but my conductor didn't make it.'

'Your conductor?' Mrs Davis quizzed. 'You mean your sponsor. You were on the Railroad?'

Katja nodded. 'We came from the library.'

'And your sponsor? Do you know their name?'

Katja sniffed again. 'She said her name was Sher, I think.'

Mrs Davis gawped. 'Pretty girl, black hair?'

'Yes,' said Katja. 'Did you know her?'

'By reputation only. But she's not a sponsor on the Railroad, she's a librarian. Or she was at least before they burned the place to the ground. How long have you been out there?'

'A few weeks I think, I'm not sure. I've been wandering in circles trying to find you. Every day, I would go a little further from the house looking for signs, but the snow's made everything so hard.'

They wandered back through the corridors until they came to the main hall. Mrs Davis put the girl to sit near the kitchen hatch and made tea for them both from a stand nearby, heaping spoons full of sugar into one of the mugs.

'Careful, it's hot,' she said placing the sweet tea in front of Katja. 'It'll taste pretty foul too, but you look like you could do with the sugar.'

'Thank you,' said Katja as Mrs Davis helped herself to a chair beside her.

'Well then, Katie. Now that we know you're alright, perhaps we can go from the beginning? There are going to be some tough questions, but you need to answer them as honestly as you can for me, okay? If I'm going to make a case for you to stay with us, I need to be certain that the others will trust you.'

Katja looked worried. 'Do you do that with everyone who comes here?'

'No,' said Mrs Davis shaking her head. 'Usually, the sponsor who travels with the passenger has all the information we need. But seeing as your sponsor is missing, perhaps even dead, we're going to start again.'

'What happens if I fail?' Katja asked.

'The Elders will drop you off close to an Inquisition compound somewhere, so they know you'll be safe. Try not to think of it as a test. Try to think of it as a friendly chat. Honest people have nothing to be afraid of here.'

'What do you want to know?' Katja asked picking at the edge of the table with her thumbnail.

'Let's start with your name, and where you're from,' said Mrs Davis.

In spite of the smile, under the old woman's steely gaze, Katja could feel her brain itching. She struggled to remember the story that she had given herself before venturing anywhere near the barracks. Whenever she opened her mouth to speak, she could feel her tongue trying to betray her.

'My name,' she mouthed. 'My name is Katja Pfeffer and I come from Brunswick, Germany.'

'Why were you on the Railroad, Katja Pfeffer?' Mrs Davis pressed.

Katja's mind raced. The words in her head seemed to twist and turn until, by the time they reached her mouth, they were nothing like she had originally thought them. Her father had warned her that this might happen though it took her a little by surprise. It wasn't just that she wanted to tell the truth, but her mouth kept trying to add words that her brain wasn't comfortable with. Quickly she thought of a plan. Perhaps she couldn't lie outright, but what would happen if she could bend the truth a little?

'I don't like the Inquisition. What they want frightens me. The nice woman at the library helped me to come here,' she said and was relieved when it passed between her lips. It was sort of true.

'I would have accepted it without question if you had told me that Grimm had helped you. The girl's another story. What did you have over her?' said Mrs Davis.

Katja fought hard to keep her expression passive. Her hands quaked with effort beneath the table.

'I know why the Inquisition burned the Paris Archives. I refused to tell her unless she helped me find you.'

'That fits. She's a sucker for a good yarn,' said Mrs Davis, seeming satisfied with her explanation. She leaned closer, her eyes unblinking in their intensity. 'Why don't you tell *me* what they were looking for?'

The feeling of pressure in Katja's head was almost unbearable, as though her mind was unravelling. She knew that she was powerless to resist the truth. However, this time the truth was her greatest weapon.

'The casket of Grand Inquisitor Grace,' she blurted.

The revelation broke Mrs Davis's concentration on her entirely. Every child knew the story of Snow White. It had been told and retold in different forms to every generation since it had happened. But somehow, it was never the version as told by both the Council and the Inquisition alike.

In her early twenties, Elspeth (later known as Queen Elspeth the Damned), had been powerful enough to be elected to the role of Elder of the Council, unaware that it would have serious repercussions for her future. Had she known then what she later discovered, it is doubtful that she would have married into the King's family at all. But

226

she did. And in so doing, Elspeth became stepmother to the King's daughter, Grace - a pale girl, with raven hair and lips the colour of ruby.

In those days, princesses (being what they were), were usually educated differently from their brothers. Grace's father, however, thought that as she was his only child, she should be treated as a son. Sending word throughout the country, the king invited the most learned scholars to educate Grace, so that one day she would be fit to rule his kingdom. By the time Elspeth and the king were married, Grace was not only well trained in the sciences, mathematics and philosophy, but had an exceptional aptitude for mental control as well.

It was one of the rare occasions that a Slinger and a Psych had lived peacefully under the same roof, and it wasn't until the king died under dubious circumstances, that things came to a head. Sadly, as time went by, one thing led to another. Grace discovered Queen Elspeth using her mirror one night to converse with the Council. She overheard her stepmother's discussion regarding Grace's mental abilities, and her accusations that she was somehow a threat to the kingdom's safety.

The Council, realising that Grace would ascend the throne on her eighteenth birthday, ordered Elspeth to have her stepdaughter executed. Horrified by their request, Elspeth instead concocted an elaborate plan to have the girl kidnapped and exiled from the kingdom, fearing that the Council would act against her if they knew the truth.

During her absence, Grace, with the help of her tutors, opened the first Inquisitorial academy. In time, she earned the title of "Master of the Talents" – an honour later bestowed as Grand Inquisitor.

Skip forward a few years.

Having gained the support of the academy's staff and students, Grace returned to her father's kingdom. Overwhelmed by the strength of their opposition, the normals of the castle's militia were powerless to stop the advance. Grace swiftly beat a path to Queen Elspeth's chamber door, only to find the room empty.

She tracked the Queen through the wilderness for days, only to be trapped by her stepmother in a narrow valley between two cliffs. All that was recorded of the battle was that it was violent enough to shatter the rock face of the ravine, raining boulders down upon them both.

It was said that Elspeth (disguised as an old woman), brought the broken body of her stepdaughter, half dead and barely breathing, back to the college. There, Elspeth helped the scholars to engineer a machine of copper and crystal to keep her alive. But the price was high, requiring the energy of donors to work its complicated magic.

Truly heartbroken by what had happened, Elspeth spent weeks at the college donating her life to her stepdaughter, until she could give no more. With her last breath, she asked that a bowl of apples from the palace orchard be placed at Grace's side every day until she woke so that she would know how much Elspeth had loved her, and how she had regretted sending her away.

Nearly all of the modern accounts of the tale say that Snow White was woken by true love's kiss, which wasn't far from the truth. It was love that woke her, but it was the love a mother for her daughter.

Once Grace learned what had happened, she ordered the casket to be dismantled and the pieces scattered – or so the story went – so that no one should have to bear the same burden ever again.

'I thought it was just a legend,' said Mrs Davis in disbelief. 'I mean a proper legend. Not one that's been cooked up to keep the normals happy.'

'You know, you really didn't have to use your talents on me. I would have told you anything you'd wanted to know,' Katja scolded her, feeling as though she'd been violated.

'I'm sorry,' Mrs Davis replied. 'It's just that I had my orders. When you said your name was Katie, I knew that you were hiding something right away. The Elders wanted to be certain that you weren't here to burn the place to ground, or worse.'

'Really, what on earth could a sixteen-year-old girl do that would worry you all so much?' said Katja.

'I take it you haven't met the Grand Inquisitor. She's a shade younger than you, but I dread to think what she's capable of now,' said Mrs Davis.

'So, what will you do with me?'

'Oh, don't fret. The Elders will have a great deal more to worry about than you when I tell them about Grace's casket, I'm sure,' said Mrs Davis.

'I saw it once when I was travelling with my father,' said Katja.

'How did you? I mean, where?'

'The Paris archives,' said Katja.

'Damn,' the housekeeper cursed. 'Then they've

probably got it by now. Didn't you know? They set the archives ablaze a while back, the same as they did with Grimm's library. You were lucky to get to the Railroad in time. There's nothing but rubble left. We knew they were looking for something, of course, but until today we hadn't a clue what.'

'Well, it's obvious that you think you know who did it,' said Katja with more conceit than she'd intended. 'But I happen to know it wasn't the Inquisition. And unless they dug down into the lower vault and burned that too, I think the casket's still safe.'

'What makes you think it wasn't the Inquisition to blame?' asked Mrs Davis.

'Because they were still using the archives for research at the time,' said Katja. She smiled at the old woman's reaction. 'Sher told me, that according to the logs, ten, sometimes fifteen Inquisitors at a time would go to the archives each day to research the casket. My guess would be that they were either coordinating search teams, or they were part of a group that was looking for it themselves. The Inquisition's been collecting relics for years, trying to find anything that might help them finish the war. Rumour has it that they even beat the Council to the lamp - you know, *The Lamp*.'

'They didn't beat the Council to the lamp,' Mrs Davis snapped. 'They murdered two couriers and looted their corpses for it.'

'It doesn't matter anyway. Father says you stole it back from them,' said Katja, dismissing the woman's fury.

'That's right, we did,' said Mrs Davis.

230

'Then you'd better not let them get their hands on that casket before you, or who knows what they could do with it.'

'Imagine,' said Mrs Davis with an expression of distant horror. 'They'd resurrect their fallen time and again. And what if they learned to make more of them?'

'They'd be unstoppable,' said Katja.

'Then we'll just have to make sure they don't, won't we?' said Mrs Davis.

'Don't what?' said Harriet joining them.

'Never you mind, young lady,' said Mrs Davis, returning somewhat to her usual self. 'What are you doing out of class?'

'I came to see how our patient was doing,' said Harriet.

'Our patient? I don't remember seeing you there while I was dressing her wounds and mopping her brow, my girl.'

Harriet blushed and extended a hand to Katja. 'Harriet King. I'm the one who found you and went for help.

'Katie ... I mean Katja,' said Katja. 'I'm very grateful.'

Turning to Mrs Davis again, Harriet said, 'Will Katja be staying with us?'

'I don't see any reason why she shouldn't,' Mrs Davis shrugged. 'She's been very helpful.' She rose from her seat before nodding her head to Harriet and giving a Katja cheeky wink. 'I'll let you two get better acquainted. Harriet, make sure that Katja has company at meal times, at least until she decides for herself whether she can put up with that runaway tongue of yours.'

'Yes, Margret,' said Harriet. Once Mrs Davis was out of sight she turned back to her new companion.

231

'You called her by her first name,' Katja gawped.

'She's sort of like my foster mum,' said Harriet. 'Since I was on the Railroad with her and Davis, they decided that I needed parents more than protection. I suppose they just felt sorry for me.'

Katja squinted at her in an effort to measure the strength of her talents. To her surprise, there was nothing. She didn't even have the latent power of an average person.

'Normal,' said Harriet giving a brief smile. 'It's a long story. I was surprised when I found out how many of us there were here. It probably sounds silly to you, but I always thought that I'd be the only one.'

'Are all the people on the Railroad unwanted?' asked Katja.

Harriet balked a little at her frankness and looked offended. 'What a strange question. Of course they want us here. They wouldn't have allowed us to stay if they didn't. Be warned, you do have to pull your weight here, same as everyone else. It's how we pay our way. Usually, they'll ask if you have a particular skill, or something you enjoy doing and see if they can fit you in somewhere. Take me for example, I was a spoilt brat who couldn't do much of anything before the Railroad, but Margaret taught me how to sew and mend clothes. What are you good at?'

'I can play the flute quite well,' said Katja. 'I can also dress wounds, cook, clean, engineer new machine parts, smelt and smith metal ...'

'You play the flute?' Harriet cut in. 'Did you bring it with you? New things are devilishly hard to come by here.'

'I did, but I left it at the house I was staying at. I hope

232

nobody's stolen it,' said Katja. 'Do you think they'll let me go and get it today?'

'Not likely,' said Harriet. 'It's going to take a while before they let you out of the compound. If you tell me how to get there, I'll bring your things back for you if you'd like?'

'You'd do that for me?' Katja beamed, unable to fathom why this girl she had just met was trying to be so kind.

'Of course, silly,' said Harriet. 'They're just being cautious with you for now. You're not the first passenger to arrive without a sponsor, and I'm sure you won't be the last. Tell you what, I'll ask Mrs Davis if Sam and I can be excused from class this afternoon, so we can be back before dark.'

'Thank you, you're very kind,' said Katja trying to brim with girlish enthusiasm. 'I really do miss my flute.'

'It's nothing, really. To be honest, it's been so long since we had any music here, I can't wait to hear you play.'

'You will,' said Katja. 'I promise.'

\*\*\*

After lunch, and much persuasion, Harriet and Sam had donned their heavy winter coats and wandered out into the wilderness. Much to her disappointment, they left without Michael, who was always busy with one thing or another these days. It had only been because she nagged Mrs Davis that Sam had been allowed to go with her and that they had been allowed to go at all.

The two friends passed an hour of trudging through snow-covered fields in relative silence, tripping over hidden rocks and falling into covered rabbit holes, their energy sapped by the rugged terrain. Finally, the stone chimney of the house that Katja had marked on the map came into view above the crest of a hill.

'Thank you!' Sam cried to the world at large and fell to his knees in the snow.

'Wimp,' Harriet joked, panting beside him.

'It wouldn't have been half as bad without the snow,' said Sam.

'Stop moaning and get up, would you? The sooner we get there, the sooner we can get back,' said Harriet.

Helping Sam to his feet, Harriet picked up her pace, buoyed by the sight of the house in the distance. When they reached the top of the hill, they both stood stock still, taking in the view of the valley. A vast reservoir stretched almost the length of the basin below them, its water an icy, menacing grey. It was as though a giant eye was looking up at eternity. The black water of the pupil was stark against the white of the snow on its banks and the vibrant green eyelashes of the Conifers that surrounded them.

'Wow,' Sam breathed. 'I'd never have thought this place could be so beautiful.'

'Definitely worth the trek,' said Harriet.

After a few minutes of appreciative silence, she cast her eyes down to the cottage below. Rough stone steps, half covered with snow, led down the steep embankment to the back door.

'C'mon, let's go get Katja's things,' she sighed.

234

The wooden back door with its missing window creaked as it swung gently in the breeze. Wary that they might not be alone, Sam pushed it gently inwards and stepped inside. Despite the awe-inspiring view, it wasn't difficult to see why the cottage stood empty. Ravaged by time and battered by the weather, almost the whole of the front slope of the roof had collapsed. Harriet stared up through the hole into the blank canvas of the sky above.

'I can't believe Katja survived in this place for as long as she did,' said Sam. 'It's freezing in here.'

Picking over the mounds of slate and stone rubble, Harriet shifted her attention to the chimney breast set into the left-hand wall and prodded at the ashes in the grate with a stick. 'It looks like she had a fire to keep her warm at least.'

'Hey,' Sam called from the remnants of the kitchen. 'I've found her stuff. It's in an old cupboard.'

'Good,' Harriet called back. 'Make sure her flute's there will you? She was really worried that someone might have taken it.'

Sam unstrapped the canvas backpack and rummaged inside, stepping back into what used to be the living room.

'I don't know who she thinks would be up here to steal it,' he said pulling out what looked like a piece of hollow ivory tube. 'I don't remember seeing any other houses between here and the farm. Besides, I really can't see who'd want to steal this thing, it's nasty.'

Harriet joined him on the far side of the room and took the pipe from Sam's hands.

'I bet this is worth a fortune,' she gasped. 'My father's

wife used to collect this stuff. She was always spending his money on it. It looks really old too.'

There was a crack on the path at the front of the house and a sound like stone shifting on stone. Sam took the flute back and stuffed it into the bag. Acting on instinct, Harriet scooted to a broken window frame and, with her back to the wall, peered out into the overgrown remains of the front garden.

'Nothing,' she sighed, releasing her breath. 'It must have been a tile falling off the roof, but I think we should go all the same.'

***

In the catacombs beneath Koppelberg Hill, Nahar was elated. Before she had left for the Council, Katja had brought him a present. He stared at it greedily as it lay on the table, her jet black hair, with hints of plum in the right light, tousled across her youthful, beautiful face. The wool of her sweater had been torn at her spine, leaving only the collar and hem intact. In place of the soft threads, cannulae protruded and vented fluid into the distilling machine. Sher shuddered, waking her from one nightmare and plunging her back into another.

'Good, you're awake again,' Nahar rasped. 'Perhaps we can get back to our conversation?'

Sher sucked on her tongue and smacked her lips, in an attempt to moisten their dryness and said, 'I don't remember a conversation.'

'I was asking why it was that you don't appear to be

dying the way the others have. Do you remember?' said Nahar.

'I hate to be picky,' Sher retorted, 'but it's only a conversation if I answer back. You'll get nothing out of me!'

'Point taken.' Nahar laughed, insofar as he could with his ancient lungs. 'Very well, if you're not going to speak to me, how about we play a game instead? I'll ask you a question and you can wiggle one foot for yes, or both for no. That way you can still tell people that you were uncooperative, provided you survive this of course.'

'Tell you what,' said Sher as she struggled against the straps at her wrists and ankles, 'why don't you unstrap me and I'll ram my foot up your …'

'Don't be so coarse!' Nahar snapped, prodding the back of her head with one of his canes. 'If you knew who I was, you would show me a little more respect.'

'Respect …? I know who you are, and you don't deserve my respect,' Sher spat. 'So go blow your pipe to someone who gives a damn, child snatcher.'

'Wonderful! Your little outburst gives me another clue to the answer to my question,' Nahar wheezed as his death-rattle laugh echoed through the chamber.

'What?' said Sher. 'How was that a clue, you psycho?'

'That you know who I am is a clue in itself,' Nahar chuckled behind her. 'Let's review the facts together, shall we? You're no sorcerer, or you wouldn't have let the girl take you without a fight. Your feeble attempt to struggle at your bonds suggests that you're no psychic either.' Thumping the crook of the cane down onto Sher's wrist,

237

he tugged at her sleeve to bare her forearm. 'I noticed an interesting if somewhat crudely inked tattoo on the inside of your arm. At first it reminded me of the ones they branded prisoners with at the concentration camps, but your face is far too young for that. Unless …'

'Unless what?' said Sher.

Nahar was quite for a few moments, fiddling with a tube beside him. Eventually, some of the blue liquid that had collected in the distillation jar began to drip from the end. Quickly, he connected one end of a copper syringe to the tube and pushed the sharp needle into his arm.

'Unless what?' Sher repeated with definite urgency.

Nahar's reply was gentle, making him seem almost human for the first time. 'Tell me a story.'

'I don't do that anymore,' said Sher.

'You were famous for it at one time, as I recall,' said Nahar.

'That was a long time ago. These days I prefer to write other people's stories, not tell my own. I find it makes more of a difference.' She was beginning to sound drowsy again. 'What are you doing to me anyway? I feel strange like I'm floating away.'

'I'm taking all the years of life left in you,' Nahar said, trying not to lose his patience with her. 'I'll need them if I'm going to face the genie.'

'Jerrick? He's dead.'

'No,' said Nahar. 'No, he isn't; trust me. Now, why don't you close your eyes, and let me tell *you* a story for a change?'

'I'd like that.' said Sher.

238

Nahar could see her giving in to the wave of exhaustion he knew was sweeping over her. As his story began to lull her to sleep, Nahar could see her eyes drift to the unfamiliar grey creeping slowly through a lock of her obsidian hair. In the dim light, the expression of horror that twisted her lips delighted him.

## Chapter Eleven:
# Vanity

The hush of midwinter had descended on the Beacons. Thick, damp fog blanketed the mountaintops enough to deter the most ardent travellers, and all but the ubiquitous bleating of the sheep had fallen silent.

In the musty warmth of the compound beneath the grove, people bustled here and there, hanging decorations and preparing for the feast. Rainbow coloured paper chains hung in swags from the walls. Evergreen branches had been woven into garlands that brought a refreshing scent of the outdoors to the usually bland halls of the barracks.

In the spirit of the season, the Council had shared the bounty of their garden with the farm and had received all sorts of meats in return. The air was sweet with the aromas of roasting and baking, stewing and pickling, candies and spices. It made Michael smile. It wasn't that he didn't feel at home with the Council, it was just that most of the time its people were more like his colleagues than his friends, Lefrick and Anna in particular. In spite of his apprehension about the week to come, he leaned against a square pillar and watched the activities. Sam joined him a few minutes later, concern written on his face like a neon sign.

'How can you look so calm at a time like this?'

'Easy,' said Michael without taking his eyes from the scene. 'It's the only thing keeping me from losing the plot right now. I think I'm gonna go mental If I have to think about the hit anymore today.'

'They're really going to make you go through with it, aren't they?' said Sam. When Michael nodded, he sighed. 'When did it get so real?'

'When the inmates took over the nuthouse,' Michael replied. 'People like Maya and Catchpole can't see that they're exactly alike in every way, and neither is willing to back down until it's all gone.'

'But we're just kids doing their dirty work for them. It's not fair.'

Michael's smile was gentle and understanding. 'There's a reason Maya's got me going after Tam. She's hoping that at least one or the other of us will end up dead. Better for her if it was the both of us, I'd guess.'

'Maya's afraid of you, isn't she?'

'Anna thinks she might be,' said Michael. 'It's got something to do with Renfrew's inheritance, and how Tam and I might be connected. Lefrick told her that the other Elders are scared that I'm becoming a threat to them since I've been learning the Council's craft as well.'

'Isn't that what Lefrick wanted all along, to take a Grand Inquisitor and show them the life of the Council?' said Sam. 'It's what Jerrick wanted. He wanted to repair the divide between the Inquisition and the Council, for the good of the people.'

Michael thought about it for a moment as he watched the toing and froing of the other inmates going about their business. 'I think Jerrick spent his life trying to undo a mistake he made a long time ago. Have you ever really compared the Inquisition to the Council?'

'I s'pose not,' said Sam. 'After what they did to Dad, I

guess I hate them as much as everyone else.'

'I have,' said Michael. 'And it makes even less sense than it did before. They both want the same thing, and they'll do anything to get it. They claim that they want to guide the normals, to stop them from destroying themselves. I don't see how the normals could do any worse than we have, do you?' When he saw the confusion in Sam's eyes, Michael continued. 'What have we ever really done for them? The Council's been on the run for centuries, and the Inquisition has been at their backs for just as long. Everything the Inquisition has done in government has been to position itself for another war.'

'How do you mean?' asked Sam.

'I think,' Michael replied, choosing his words with care. 'I think the normal's attacks on the Council, the ones that forced the other branches to come here, were driven by the Inquisition. It sounds like an old-fashioned witch hunt, like in the dark ages.'

The look on Sam's face changed from confusion to sympathy. 'Come on, Mike, it's always been that way. Nothing's changed, honest.'

'Yes it has,' said Michael. 'Don't you see?'

'See what?'

'The Inquisition's set the normals against us,' said Michael. 'And when they're done, there won't be anywhere left to hide. It doesn't matter who finds us first, Sam. When they do, everyone you see here will die.' The calm returned to Michael's voice in spite of the pounding of his heart. 'There is no bridge between the Inquisition and the Council because there's no divide. They're ... *We* ... are one and the same.'

'Okay, so what do we do about it?' Sam pressed. 'Maya's expecting you to go after Tam soon. And if you don't, I dread to think what'll happen.'

'And not just to me,' said Michael, 'but to anyone who goes with me. Including you.'

'What do you need?' said Sam.

'Time ... I just need time.'

'Well, sorry to be the bearer of bad news, mate,' said Sam puffing out a deep breath. 'I don't think you're going to get it. Here comes your aunt and she's got a face like thunder. I'd better scoot.'

Michael nodded and smiled as he watched his friend disappear into the busy crowd, before turning his gaze to Anna. 'What is it this time?'

'This,' said Anna producing the book that Grimm had given them for safe keeping. 'Did you know that the Piper was Jerrick's fault?'

'Yes,' said Michael.

'Neither did I ... What do you mean, yes? He told you?'

'Back when he went up in smoke, he sort of showed me,' said Michael.

'And did Jerrick happen to mention where the Piper might be hiding out?' said Anna.

'Nope.'

She cursed loud enough for the whole room to stop what they were doing to stare at her. 'What,' she snarled. 'Oh, come on, you've heard worse come out of this mouth!' The crowd seemed to consider this for a moment before returning to their business.

'Look, if the Inquisition had gotten to the Piper first, don't you think we'd have known about it by now?' Michael tried to reassure her.

'I think we already do,' said Anna. 'How do you think they're getting the normals to attack the other Council branches?'

Michael scrunched his eyes and said, 'With the flute. You can't be serious?'

'As a High Court judge,' said Anna. 'What's more, I think he's using the homeless to start the riots.'

'But if he's using them, why do the reports say that they've disappeared? Surely someone must have seen that many homeless people in one place,' said Michael.

'I couldn't say for certain. I have my suspicions, but I still have some reading to do,' said Anna. 'Our last few sources brave enough to stay inside the academy haven't reported seeing anything out of the ordinary. Which I suppose means that the homeless aren't going there. All we have to go on is what we get from the media.'

'What do they have to say about it?'

'See for yourself,' said Anna handing him a newspaper.

Michael read the headline aloud: 'New terror as homeless taken for Council army.'

'I'll save you the bother of reading the rest of that drivel,' said Anna. 'It's propaganda. They're trying to make the normals believe that whoever's burning the haven sites is building an army to overthrow the government.'

'Let me guess. It's us?' Michael closed his eyes and sighed deeply.

'Bingo,' Anna crowed. 'You know, you've really come a

long way, Michael. When I first met you, you'd have believed just about anything. Now you're thinking for yourself.'

'And doing what everyone else tells me to,' Michael replied with as much sarcasm as he thought he could get away with. 'Let me get this straight. You think the Piper is working with the Inquisition, to press the normals into attacking us. Why on earth would he do that?'

'To get to Jerrick,' said Anna. 'Don't misunderstand me, I don't think the Piper is another Inquisition puppet, but I definitely think his intention is to drive us all into one place. Shepherding us like lambs to the slaughter if you will.'

Understanding dawned in Michael's eyes. He grimaced and said, 'Because he knows that Jerrick would have to come here too, eventually.'

'That's right,' said Anna. 'I'm guessing he tracked the lamp back to the academy, and the Inquisition told him that it had been stolen back. That's how he knew the locations of the other safe-houses. Since he couldn't have found him at any of the other branches, I'm betting he's on his way here. And once he's got what he wants, he'll leave the rest of us for the Inquisitors to deal with.'

'Who's on his way here?' said Katja in a sweet, girlish voice that cut across their conversation.

'Santa,' Anna snapped. 'And I just hope he hasn't got his elves with him!'

'Sorry I asked,' said Katja.

'I'll talk to you about it later,' said Anna, rolling her eyes to indicate that what she had to say wasn't for Katja's ears.

Michael understood her meaning instantly. 'Yeah, sure,' he sighed, not relishing the extra weight his aunt had just put on his mind.

'That wasn't very nice,' said Katja as she watched Anna go. She handed Michael a steaming cup that smelled of cinnamon, cloves and orange, with the acrid aroma of evaporated alcohol.

'Try not to take it personally,' said Michael. He could feel his skin crawling and did his best to ignore it. 'She's not always like that.'

'I just wanted to thank you. Harriet told me what you did for me,' said Katja.

'You're welcome. You're looking much better,' said Michael sipping from the cup, unable to shake the uneasy feeling he felt around her.

'Thank you, I feel it,' Katja sang. 'I haven't known Harriet for very long, but I get the impression that she likes you very much.'

'We're just friends,' said Michael nearly choked on his mulled wine.

'She's very pretty.'

'Yes, she is,' Michael grinned.

'Then perhaps you should accompany her to the concert this evening?'

'There's a concert this evening?' said Michael.

'Yes,' said Katja. 'It's Christmas. There should be music and laughter. Harriet is looking for people to play as we speak. She thought it might help to lighten the mood. Mrs Davis thought it was a good idea.'

'It has been a while since we had a party,' Michael admitted. 'Perhaps it's what we need.'

'It's settled then. You'll ask Harriet to the concert?' Katja pressed.

A suspicious chill ran through Michael's spine like an electric shock. 'You've only just met her. Why are you so interested?'

'She told me all about you,' said Katja. 'She said that you can't be with the girl you love, and she can't be with Max. I thought it would make sense for you both to go together.'

As gentle and well meaning as Katja's words seemed, they caused something to well in Michael that he had been trying to bury.

'I'll think about it,' he managed in what he hoped was a polite tone of voice. 'Excuse me, would you?'

'Of course,' said Katja.

Michael thanked her again for the cup of mulled wine and took his leave, Katja's words still ringing in his ears. As he hurried away through the corridors, he could feel Jerrick interfering with his thoughts, and quickly shut him out. He was barely able to understand his own mind and certainly didn't want a stray jibe from his hitchhiker to distract him.

It had been fine when Harriet had talked about Tamara. But it was like someone had shaken a can of fizzy lemonade and pulled the ripcord inside him to hear Katja speak of her in that sing-song voice. Because of his indecision, Tamara was stuck with the Inquisition. Because of his thoughtlessness, he had left her to the whims of a psychotic madman, while he'd escaped to the relative safety of the Council. And because of his connection to her, it would be his fault that she would soon die. At that moment, the only sane idea about how to deal with Maya's request had hit him and hit him hard.

Reaching his bunk room, he shut the door behind him and locked it. Taking his mirror from the grey, metal shelf and propping it against a book on his desk, he peered into it intently, muttering the incantation Anna had taught him. The glass began to shimmer and shadows flitted hazily across its surface. Michael tried to calm his mind, to ease the flow of his will, mindful that he might need to drop his spell in a hurry or risk being caught. After a few deep exhalations it seemed to work.

Slowly, an image came into focus of another room, with a bed neatly clothed in pale peach, opposite a plain, wooden wardrobe. The bottom of the image was partly obscured by the black plastic cab of a familiar television set. The cheap, toffee coloured curtains were open and, most importantly, the vanity case and hairbrush he'd expected to see were missing.

'Idiot,' Michael muttered to himself. 'She must have gone home for the holidays by now.'

He waved his hand vaguely over the surface of the mirror and cleared his mind. Then, refocussing his effort, he stretched out his will again. This time, the room that came into focus was far more familiar and sent pangs of longing through him. It was Alice's bedroom at his parents' house, the last room he had visited before leaving with Anna for the Council. He searched around the room for any sign that Alice might be at home, but the vanity case wasn't there either.

'Where are you when I need you?' he bristled before letting his spell drop in case anyone had heard him.

He was angry that his plan might be scuppered before he could even get it off the ground while Maya's was still moving on unhindered. In his desperation, he clung to the last fond memory he had of his time with Tamara – their candlelit dinner on the balcony of her room arranged for them by Miss Cunningham just before the duel. Michael knew that the academy would be nearly empty at this time of year, with all but a few students and staff lingering in its corridors or various common rooms because they had nowhere better to be. Still with the care of a hunter approaching a bear trap, he brought Tamara's old room at Solaris into focus.

From the seclusion of his vantage point, Michael had a perfect view of the opulent study, with its plush golden furniture and French doors that opened onto the balcony overlooking the lake. Indeed, his own room had been on almost the exact opposite side of the building, but he couldn't help feeling that it wouldn't have had the same effect on him as this one did. Tamara wasn't there of course. The first floor was home to first years only. Now it was two years on, and she was the Grand Inquisitor to boot. It occurred to Michael that he had no idea where the Inquisition would house someone as important as their leader. It left him feeling as though it was something he probably ought to know if he were going to follow through with Maya's plan. He pushed the thought to the back of his mind, hoping that Anna would take care of it with the help of her sources on the inside.

His instincts told him that he had lingered perhaps a little too long and that it was time to go. Sighing, he took one last look around the study and through the door into the bedroom where she had slept. Then his heart leapt as he caught sight of a purple coloured, metal box trimmed with chrome. It had the letters "A.W." embossed in silver on its side, and was half covered with a familiar looking overcoat, as though its owner had been in a hurry to be somewhere else.

The shock of it broke Michael's concentration, and he sat staring into space for what felt like an eternity, his blank expression reflected back at him. Suddenly, and without any thought, he fiddled hastily with the lock on his door and flung it wide. Pushing past a bewildered Sam, he hurtled back through the corridor, almost colliding with Harriet and Katja in the process. Swinging himself bodily around a sharp bend and barrelling through the doors to the hall, he searched the room with wild eyes. Unable to find Anna, he sought the next best option. Spotting Andy and Lefrick in the corner, he was sure that they would know where to find his aunt.

'... and I'm having second thoughts about including Maya,' said Lefrick.

'It might help her understand how valuable his contribution is,' Andy replied.

Michael came to a halt in front of them, breathing hard. 'Have either of you seen Anna?' he panted.

'Just a second, Michael,' Lefrick dismissed. Turning back to the huge former doorman he said, 'I agree, but will it seem contrived?'

'I don't know. Maybe,' said Andy.

'Guys, this is really important,' Michael insisted. 'They've got ...'

Lefrick rounded on him with a look of frustration. 'I said just a second, Michael.' Again he turned back to Andy. 'It seems to me that the Elders are using this as an excuse to quell any opposition to their grand plan.'

'Do you think they'll try to cut us off? An ambush perhaps?' said Andy, a rare note of concern in his voice.

'GUYS!' Michael shouted, but Andy simply raised his humongous palm to halt him before he could go on. Incensed, Michael instinctively diverted his rage from his stomach to his shoulders and pushed it down to the very tips of his fingers. There was little resistance, even from the massive bulk of the doorman. Michael lifted both men, turned them through ninety degrees and tilted them until they were at eye level with him.

'Where is Anna?' he whispered, his voice quiet and threatening through his gritted teeth.

'In the training room,' said Lefrick.

'Good,' Michael snarled. 'Both of you suit up, you're coming with me. If you're right about Maya, it'll be better for all of us.'

He lowered them to the floor again, turned on his heel and jogged away, leaving Andy and Lefrick trailing wordlessly behind him.

\*\*\*

In the small warehouse that was now their home, Grimm and Eunice were busy cataloguing the boxes that had been salvaged from the library. Being what it was, the library held more than books. Over the centuries, the Grimm family had amassed a number of interesting little trinkets - the odd glass slipper, poisoned needle from a spinning wheel — that kind of thing. But among the collection was a much larger item. It was one of a kind, incredibly old and, until recently, had been abroad for study. The large wooden crate that housed it was more than six feet long and four feet wide. But for all of its bulk, it stood only three feet high.

'Shall I do the honours, sir?' said Eunice, crowbar in hand.

Grimm looked up from his ledger to see what she was referring to. 'Thank you Eunice, but I think we'll keep that as it is for now. You never know when we'll have to pack up and go again.'

'Are you going to contact the Council to tell them?' said Eunice moving on to the next, very much smaller crate.

'Huh, and tell them what?' Grimm chuckled. 'That I torched my own library to keep these things safe from them and Inquisition? Good heavens no. Events are gathering pace now. It's time we took a hand in things for ourselves.'

'What do you mean?' asked Eunice.

'Tell me what you see, Eunice,' said Grimm gesturing around the room.

'Inventory,' the librarian replied. 'And significantly less

of it now than the last time we catalogued it. I'm just glad we managed to salvage most of the papyrus.'

'As am I,' said Grimm. 'But that's not what I see. I see weapons. I see weapons that both factions would give their eye teeth to get their hands on if they could.' He pointed to the large crate with his fountain pen. 'Reports are coming in almost every other day now about haven sites around the world being desecrated. The Inquisition is calling it some sort of plot to destabilise the government, to confuse the ignorant among us. Normals are attacking Council safe houses. Under whose direction, I have no idea. The whole world seems to be going mad.'

The fear in Eunice's eyes was obvious, but she kept her voice steady as though she were only waiting for confirmation of something she already knew. 'But what can we do about it? We're just a handful of academics. Even if you rallied all of the curators from every haven site on every continent, there's nothing we could do.'

'If there's one thing my long years have taught me, my dear, it is not to underestimate the significance of a well-organised resistance.'

'What are we resisting? Neither side has moved against the normals. They're only interested in fighting one another,' said Eunice dragging a crate to her friend's side so that she could sit down next to him.

'For the moment,' said Grimm. 'It's happened before, so many times. Two factions tooth and nail, neither able to gain a clear advantage over the other. They will turn to propaganda like children in the playground until they gather the support of people who will do the fighting for them. Like generals, they will set their battlefield until everything is rubble and ash.'

'Surely you're being melodramatic?' said Eunice.

Grimm raised his eyes to look into hers and said, 'We'll see. The cull is almost upon us. If history is anything to go by, it'll all start small. Then, like a snowball gathering momentum on a hill, there'll be curfews and registrations and segregation. Eventually, they'll force people into specially policed zones, and from there ... I dread to think.'

'But what can we *do* about it?' Eunice repeated.

'I don't rightly know,' Grimm admitted. 'But we can start by building a memorial to reason, and invite the whole country to see it. Something snazzy, with a fitting centrepiece ...'

'And where are you going to build that now?' said Eunice.

'I hear there's a vacant shop with rather a roomy basement just come up on Jermyn Street,' said Grimm.

\*\*\*

The little daylight that was left had given way to night by the time that Michael and a select few of the Guardians were ready to leave. The group consisted of ten including Michael. Knowing the academy best, he would take the lead. Anna and Lefrick would naturally be on hand to ensure that he didn't get sidetracked. Two Guardians Michael hadn't worked with closely before would act as sentries – Jack Goodbody, a lively, furtive man who reminded Michael of a dishevelled weasel, and Daniel Joy, a rugged mousy haired youth who was still in his trial period as a Guardian. He was a few years older than Michael but had come highly recommended by another staple member of their team, Andy. Somehow, every situation felt easier to handle with Andy around.

Not being one to rush in where angels feared to tread, Anna had insisted on at least a little time to plan their incursion into the academy, and to brief the others. Now she was adjusting the straps on Michael's ill-fitting leather armour.

'I wish you'd told me that you'd almost grown out of it,' she said. 'We could have had a new one made for you.'

'There's no time for that now,' said Michael as he squirmed to be free of her. 'Stop fussing, will you? I don't see why you're making me wear it at all. I'll be quicker without it.'

'Look around you,' Anna snapped. 'Everyone else is in armour, including me. Now stop wriggling and let me get this last one.'

'He's missing something,' Andy boomed, looming over her shoulder.

Anna regarded at her nephew with a critical eye, and said, 'I don't see it. What's missing?'

'One of these,' said Andy producing a metal badge with a wolf howling at the moon behind it.

'I suppose he's earned it,' she tutted.

'Thanks,' was all Michael could muster as he stuffed it into his pocket with embarrassment. It wasn't that he didn't want the badge. It was a great honour in the Council to be awarded one. It was that he already had his uncle's.

Michael had found it years ago amongst a few other treasured memories. Now it was safe in his bedside drawer, and he made a mental note to swap it for the new one when they got back so he could have a little of his uncle with him for good luck.

'I guess that makes you a proper Guardian,' said Andy. 'Must be an all-time record, so many wolves in one family, eh, Anna?'

'Yeah,' Anna replied. 'They'll be calling us "Wares Wolves" before long.'

'Got a nice ring to it,' said Andy, and he laughed like a sonic boom.

Wrapping her fingers around the top and bottom of Michael's breastplate, Anna tugged hard on it, causing Michael to shake like a rag doll. She slapped her palms on his shoulder guards and nodded, indicating that she was happy.

'Come on, they're waiting for you,' she said.

Michael marched back to the great mirror with the Guardians following in pairs behind. In the hall, the other Council members, young and old, were gathering for the evening's entertainment. In spite of her attempts to ask why they were leaving before the concert, Harriet couldn't get Michael's attention. Even Sam, who tried to insist on going with them, was dismissed out of hand as they trooped through the glass and out into the dusk beyond.

As they followed the dim light of the path to the portal, Michael ignored the baying of the Flayers in the distance, doubtless drawn by the potential feast that was crossing their domain. But there was no time to worry about them.

His guts churned with thoughts that his sister was being used to get to him, the way Anna had said she would be if she knew he was still alive. What bothered him more was the thought that you didn't ask someone to pack before kidnapping them, did you? Michael had gone over it repeatedly in his mind but still couldn't find an answer that satisfied him.

Then there was Tamara herself. Now that they were on their way, he felt lost. There hadn't been time to talk about it in any detail. Anna hadn't been much help in any case. All she'd said on the subject was: "Concentrate on Alice. She's your target now. If Tamara gets in the way we'll deal with it."

He'd wanted to tell her that he didn't want Tamara dealt with. He wanted to tell her that Maya could shove her request where the sun doesn't shine. He had thought he'd have more time than this to reach a solution. But as usual, time had passed him by. And in amongst all of his fears, the poisonous seed of an idea began to germinate, that Tamara might even have planned this. There was no doubt that Catchpole had known him at the library that day. Now, with Tamara as his superior, he would be obliged to tell her, wouldn't he? Michael wondered if the news could cause her to hate him so much that she would hurt his family to get to him. His lips moved silently as he tried to reason his questions out in his head.

'Now's not the time to get hormonal, Michael. We're just going to have to take it one step at a time,' said Anna glancing over at her nephew.

'Not getting hormonal,' Michael grunted. 'I'm trying to

find the reasons behind it all.'

'The most important thing right now, is to get your sister and as many of us out alive as possible. The rest is gravy. Now get your head in the game,' said Anna.

'But what if I do come face to face with Tamara?' Michael blurted.

'Like I said, we'll deal with it,' said Anna.

'Don't worry, Mike, we've got your back. Whatever you decide, we're with you,' said Andy placing a giant paw on his shoulder.

'Thanks, Andy,' said Michael.

Their pace quickened as the portal began to flash like a beacon in the middle distance. Anna had mentioned before that there were only a few Council spies left at the academy. As such, it had taken everything in Lefrick's persuasive arsenal to secure an entry. There had been many objections from their contact. The strongest of which was that their incursion would almost certainly put pressure on the Railroad now that the library was gone. But Lefrick had managed to persuade the man that it was really no different from their original plan, and now the results of his hard work were evident.

Two by two they emerged into a small, neatly decorated room, and had to leap down from the table below the mirror, except for Andy. The giant seemed to stride out of the mirror directly onto the floor below, before clapping their host gratefully on the shoulder. But there was no time for pleasantries as they were ushered through a small parlour, out through a wooden back door, across a patch of ground and into the woods beyond.

Thankfully, a dank mist obscured the party from view as they crept swift and silent through the undergrowth to a clearing, away from prying eyes.

'I know this place,' Michael whispered. 'We're in the wood that separates House Ignis from Solaris Lake.'

'That's right,' said Lefrick beside him. 'Sorry I couldn't get us any closer, but since the Davises retired, we don't have anyone left in Solaris that we can trust.'

'I don't understand what Tamara's still doing here in the first place,' said Anna. 'Doesn't she have a home to go to?'

'Knowing Catchpole, he's got her on lockdown with the Piper around,' Michael huffed in a curious kind of sympathy.

'I'm surprised they're not out looking for his flute,' said Anna. 'They seem to be after everything else these days.'

'Too close to the cull,' said Michael. There was a gasp behind him. 'We all know it's coming.'

'I don't blame them for being scared,' said Andy. 'We've all read about the cull, but there's hardly anyone left who actually remembers the last one.'

Lefrick raised his palms to quiet his companions. 'We can discuss Pipers and flutes, and culls later. Right now, we have a girl to find. Michael, as planned, you and Anna will lead us out. Everyone else: it's by the numbers. With any luck, this mist will provide some cover.'

Michael nodded and began to move through the trees, Anna close behind. A short time later he could see the glow of the ornate street lamps lighting the path to Solaris on his right. It reminded him of the time Tamara had used her new found talent to strip Max Bennett of his belt and beat him with it for bullying Rupert and Emily. It amused him so much that he almost forgot himself and had to stifle his laughter. All of this had been little more than a game to him then, something wondrous and fantastic that should never have led to this moment.

A few minutes later, following the murky light from the lamps, they came to halt at the shore of the lake. Once upon a time, there had been an old leaky boat where Michael was standing. It had played a very important part in the accidental death of a friend. Michael tried to remind himself that it wasn't really Harriet's fault. Fate had been as cruel a mistress then as she was now. There were footsteps in the bracken as the others joined them. In the distance, as the light played havoc with the fog, Michael could just make out the bent, distorted shadow of a guard circling on the path around Solaris.

'Why didn't we just portal inside Solaris again?' Michael whispered.

'When you can navigate the portals by yourself, you'll understand,' Anna sighed. 'There are far too many mirrors close together here. We might have ended up in the wrong room if our calculations were off by a fraction of a degree. A building like Solaris is built on more than one level, but the portals only work on one plane. It would have taken days for us to figure out which was the right room without someone like Jackson on the other side.'

'But I found Tamara's old room really easily when I was looking,' Michael replied.

'That's because spying on a mirror is different. It

requires less geometry,' Lefrick hissed behind them. 'I'll explain it when we get back, I promise. Let's cross this bridge first. Any ideas how, Anna?'

'Yeah, I have an idea,' she said looking at Michael with a grin. 'What is it that schools have lots of that people don't notice, even during the holidays?'

'Oh no,' Michael protested. 'I know what you want. Even in this fog, do you think they won't realise?'

But his aunt didn't reply, she just gave him one of her insistent "do as I say" looks. So, with the others trailing behind at a fair distance, Michael crossed the bridge. His foot hadn't even crunched on the gravel path around the house before he was being challenged.

'Whadda you want?' said a gruff voice from beneath the cowl of the guard.

'Going to see a friend in Solaris,' Michael responded in an effort to stay calm. 'I'm from Aqua, and I'm staying on over the holidays.'

'Bit late to be out visiting on a night like this, ain't it?' said the guard.

The bell in the clock tower of the main building tolled seven. Michael waited for it to finish before saying, 'Er ... no, not really.'

'This friend of yours got a name?' the guard pressed, taking a step closer.

'Yes,' said Michael, 'of course he's got a name. It's Omar.'

The guard took another few steps. 'You yankin' my chain, son? What's his last name?'

'Goolies,' Michael announced trying to keep a straight

face.

'Omar Goolies,' the guard repeated. A heartbeat later the penny dropped. He lunged forwards and grabbed Michael by the hair. 'You little sod, I'll give you ...'

He yelped as Michael's boot connected with his groin and didn't fall to the floor so much as crumple into a groaning heap. Michael gathered his will and flung the prone guard into the gloom. There was a rustling sound and some muffled cries. Then all was quiet again, except for the lapping of the water against the bank.

'That was subtle,' Anna reproached her nephew as she emerged from the fog. 'Couldn't you have come up with anything better?'

'It got us a robe didn't it?' said Michael. 'Come on, let's get going.'

Leaving one of their members, Daniel, behind to pose as the guard, Michael led the others around beneath his old window to the back of the house. Normally he could have seen the gardens on a clear day, but now he could barely see to the end of the wall. They came to a stop on the far side, beneath the room where he had seen Alice's case in the mirror. He tried the drainpipe, but it was far too slippery. Holding up a finger to ask the others to wait, Michael slipped quietly around the house to where he was sure another guard would be keeping vigil over the bridge that led to the trade entrance. He was gratified and relieved to see a figure leaning against one of the lamps there. Letting his eyes un-focus, he watched for the change in the guard's aura, but the reflection of the lights in the fog was making its colour too difficult to discern. Choosing to risk being caught, Michael closed his eyes tightly and tried again. This time, he could make out the clear, bright orange glow that he'd been hoping for and began drawing upon it until a stream began to flow between him and his target. The energy squirmed inside him, twisting and writhing like an eel in a net, unwilling to be bound to a new host. It had been a long time since Michael had felt anything like it, and it made him feel giddy and uncomfortable. Careful not to take too much, he broke off his invisible assault and tiptoed back to the group.

'What was all that about?' Anna whispered.

'I needed more power,' replied Michael. 'The pipe's too slippery to climb and someone needs to get up there to open the door.'

'Why didn't you just draw it out of the ground, or one of us?' said Anna.

'Because I didn't want to have to give back what I don't use,' said Michael. 'And in a few minutes we're going to need everything we can get. Now stop grumbling and let me do this my way, would you?' The look on his aunt's face was enough to dissuade him from waiting for an answer. Instead, he turned, pushing his will to his palms and motioned to the balcony as though he was grasping its rail with both hands.

Slowly, Michael rose into the air and pulled himself on unseen threads until he was level with the bars. Lifting one leg then the other over, he stood looking at his reflection in the glass of the French doors. As he peered into the gloom, he caught the glint of light on a small key on the other side of the lock. Reaching out with his mind, he felt for it and turned it until there was a muffled click. Pressing the handle, he pushed the door inwards, waiting with bated breath for an attack. When it didn't come, Michael turned back to the rail and waved the all clear to the others.

Once the Guardians had regrouped in the study, Anna slipped into the sumptuous bedroom and flicked the switch on one of the bedside lamps. Except for the usual furniture and a few of Alice's things, the room was empty.

'I don't get it,' said Anna. 'If they've taken her hostage, why are her things still here? That's her suitcase over there.'

'They're trying to use her to get to me,' Michael answered.

'Why would they do that, Michael?' said Lefrick. 'Unless she knows that you're ...'

'I told her,' Michael blurted, cutting across him. 'I've been writing to her every now and again to tell her that I'm alright and to get news from home.'

'You risked all our lives for news from home?' Anna rounded on him. 'You told me they had her, Michael! You told me she was in trouble and needed our help! Now you've dragged us into what, a friendly visit?'

'I'm sorry,' Michael mumbled. 'But why else would she be here? I swear to you that Catchpole knows I'm alive since that day at the library. He's going to use her to get to me ... us. Her being here puts us all in danger.'

'We might not like it,' said Andy as quietly as he could. 'But the boy's got a point. If she knows about Michael, then so do they by now.'

'Alright, alright what's done is done,' said Anna. She glared at her nephew. 'Let's find her and get her out. You

... get to the door and see who's about. We'll deal with this later, mark my words.'

## Chapter Twelve:
# The Long Night

Sher looked up from the table not knowing how long she had been unconscious, but her eyes felt gluey, as though she had been asleep for a very long time. Raising a hand to rub them, she was surprised to find that it was free from her bonds. She felt stiff, and ached, and struggled to think of the last thing she could remember. Nahar had been talking about Jerrick, and how he was going to be free of something, but she couldn't remember what.

Once her eyes were clear of dust, she pulled herself upright and dangled her legs over the edge of the metal slab. Her back felt sore, but the constant tugging pinching of the cannulae had gone. Her cheeks flushed with the embarrassment of her immodesty, as her woollen pullover gaped from where it had been torn to reveal her spine.

Lowering herself to the floor, Sher almost collapsed with the effort of standing after so long. In the dim blue light of the glass flasks, she could just make out the walls of the cathedral cavern for the first time. Turning to look at the table, she inspected the intricate machine that had been connected to her.

'Good, right on cue,' said Nahar from the mouth of a corridor. The intonation of his voice was the same, but he somehow sounded different.

'What does it do?' Sher asked.

'Oh, the explanation is long and complicated, and I'm afraid we don't have time,' said Nahar crossing the floor between them.

When he reached her, Sher could barely contain herself. Nahar was so very different from the man who had goaded and threatened her. He was handsome, with neatly cropped blonde hair, a strong stubbly chin and, despite the lack of illumination, his eyes sparkled like sapphires. His shoulders were broad, and he stood proud and tall, not at all like the ancient, withered old man, crippled by arthritis and time that she had seen before.

'What have you done?' she gasped, staggering backwards until her back struck the table.

She tried to steady herself, but her arm gave out and she came face to face with her hand. She stared at it as though it didn't belong to her, breaking into a sob as Nahar strode past her with confidence and vigour.

'What have you done?' she repeated.

'In a few minutes it won't matter,' said Nahar as he skipped between the vats and beds, before disappearing out of sight into another corridor.

Sher dragged herself to her feet, stumbling after him. Tired and distressed, her shoulders scraped as she bounced from wall to wall along the path. Eventually, she fell to her knees in the prison room, where Nahar was busy unlocking the cages.

'If you want to leave this place, follow me,' he shouted above the clamour of the unwanted as they shoved at one another to reach the rear of the cages. 'Come on, I'm giving you your freedom.'

The unwanted were nervous of him and wouldn't budge. Finally, he lost his patience with them. Extending his arms, he began a low, mumbled chant. It was slow at first but soon gathered pace and volume as his arms began to flail. One by one, bodies began to erupt from the cages like detritus from a volcano, landing in the atrium one on top of another.

'Stop it!' Sher yelled, horrified by the scene. 'Can't you see they're terrified by you?'

But Nahar didn't break his rhythm. His chanting became violent as more and more captives were hauled on invisible rope from the cages. When they were empty at last, the cage doors slammed shut with a deafening clank of metal. Spinning on his heel, Nahar marched to where Sher was kneeling and lifted her to her feet as though she weighed nothing.

'Where are you taking us?' she pleaded.

'You still don't understand, do you? For all your time, and after all you've seen, you're still as ignorant as they are.' He pressed his face closer to hers, his breath foul. 'This place is my prison, *my* cage. Tonight I am leaving it behind for good. So, unless you want to stay buried here until you rot, you should come with me.'

Sher tried to harden herself against the stench of him, almost gagging as she took a breath to retaliate. 'Let me take them. I can navigate the portals. Let me get them away from here.'

'And go where?' Nahar asked through his laughter. 'Back to the streets to live like the rats they've become? Look at them, Scheherazade. There is nothing about them that is human anymore. They are unwanted, discarded by society and left to live out their days like animals. They're better off coming with me, truly. As for the portal, I doubt that you would have the skill or the power operate it. Fashioned from the guilt money of greedy Hameliners, it's far too dull for the average Slinger to use. Not even the strongest of the Council could activate it, for all their conjuring.'

'You really are soulless, Agnar Bjornson,' Sher snarled before spitting in his face. 'Let me take them to the Council. You know the lore as well as I. It's forbidden to leave them there.'

'Forbidden by whom? No, my mind's made up. Now move, or none of you will see daylight again.'

He smiled as Sher's saliva dribbled down his cheek and rested on his lip. Still gripping her arm like a vice, he turned them both to face their cowering audience and dragged her kicking and screaming in protest back into the main cavern.

The homeless followed him like sheep, too scared to disobey and too weak to fight. Nahar was already at the top of the roughly hewn steps before the last of his captives had joined them. Placing his free palm against the centre coin, he watched as it melted away until it merged with those adjacent to it. In next to no time, the golden portal shimmered like sunset on water against the stark face of the rock.

'Through there,' he commanded.

The homeless looked at one another in their uncertainty. Finally, one brave soul, a youngish looking woman, shuffled closer and put one cautious hand into the world beyond. Looking back at the others, the woman nodded and stepped through the portal. After a few breaths of anxious silence, she reappeared.

'Come on,' she shouted. 'You'll never believe this.'

At once the others surged forward, ignoring every protest from Sher. Any that slipped or fell on the steps were half trampled by those behind as they fled, their faces filled with relief to be leaving the darkness of the mountain behind them. When the last of them was away, Nahar gave a quiet laugh and dragged Sher through the portal after them. Unsure of what to do next, or which direction to strike out in, the homeless huddled together in a group to wait for further instructions.

Nahar pointed his finger and said, 'That way until you reach the horizon. Now go, before I change my mind.'

Sher watched the homeless run until they were little more than specks moving against a grey horizon. Then the baying began.

'You've murdered them,' she mumbled.

'You could call it self-defence,' Nahar replied. 'It was them or us. I can't travel here without a few assurances of safety after all these centuries.'

'The Flayers are your fault, aren't they?' said Sher as he dragged her in the opposite direction. 'You used them for the same reasons you needed me. Then you abandoned them here.'

'Why do you think the lore forbids willfully trapping people in this place?' Nahar gloated. 'It's because of my discovery. Living things that remain here for too long become a part of the landscape, not quite dead but certainly not living. When I left the first here, I genuinely thought that she would die of starvation. But after a time I realised what had happened.'

'I don't believe you. You must have known. There are thousands of them,' said Sher.

'Yes, quite,' said Nahar. 'The only way to truly kill a Flayer is to force them to leave this place. But it seems they've learned from the mistakes of their predecessors. They'd rather camp outside the portals now, than risk following their prey into our world by mistake.'

In spite of her loathing for the Flayers, Sher risked a glance behind them and saw nothing but stars against the dusky backdrop.

'It won't be long before they're done with those people and come after us,' she said.

'Then perhaps we should move faster. We have quite a way to go to our destination,' said Nahar.

'Why don't you just leave me here? You'd be so much quicker on your own.'

'Nice try,' Nahar huffed. 'But you've already told me that you can navigate the portals on your own. Even in your rather spoiled condition, I'm afraid you're far more valuable to me alive ... for now.'

***

At the academy, Michael was ahead of the group as they crept through the first-floor corridor. It had been decided that, in all likelihood, Alice was being held in the interrogation rooms beneath the training hall. Under normal circumstances, hardly anyone knew of their

271

existence, and there were very few who were allowed to enter. Michael, on the other hand, had discovered them by accident while at the academy, when Sam's father had been taken by the Inquisition. They had been interrogating Mr Lucas for information on the Council, and it had taken a considerable amount of time for him to recover afterwards. The suggestion that the same thing was happening to Alice was enough to make Michael's stomach lurch.

At the corner of the first-floor corridor, before the plush, red carpeted staircase, Michael risked a peek and was relieved to find that there was nobody around. Usually, at this time of the evening, the housemaids would have been turning down the beds. Because of the time of year, however, Anna had assumed that most of the staff would be on leave themselves.

The last time Michael had descended the staircase it had been lined on both sides by well-wishers. They had formed an imposing, human path to the training hall for the final duel of the trials. Now that he had the opportunity to look at it again, it didn't seem nearly as bad. Neither did the rest of the house really, in spite of the fact that it was devoid of decorations, where there should have been sumptuous garlands of holly leaves and expensive glass baubles.

Tiptoeing to the banister that overlooked the communal meeting area below, Michael was surprised to see that it too was empty. He listened carefully for the sounds of an evening meal being served in the dining room, but there were none. His nose tingled with the memories of fragrant spices and fresh herbs, but he couldn't smell those either. Concluding that the kitchen was most probably closed, he waved for the others to follow him and swung his legs over the rail of the banister, dropping to the floor on a cushion of energy. Checking that the coast was clear, he scooted across to the mouth of the servants' corridor, where the Davises had once lived. The others took the stairs down in pairs, hugging the wall beneath the balcony in case anyone still on the floors above would notice. Bringing up the rear, Anna was the last to arrive.

'I see they've got your mugshot above the fireplace,' she joked.

'Huh?' said Michael, not really paying attention.

'There's a plaque in your memory and everything.'

'Great,' Michael sighed. 'Perhaps I should have worn a mask. Now anyone we come across is going to know right away who I am.'

'Could work to our advantage,' said Lefrick. 'Perhaps you can pretend to be your own ghost haunting the house you died in.'

'Alright, that's enough,' said Michael rolling his eyes. 'Jack, wait here as discussed. The rest of you: I'm sure you remember how long the corridor is before we even get to the doors, so let's keep the pace quick and quiet.'

They negotiated the long corridor corner by corner, ducking beneath the level of the windows set into the various doors they passed. Everything was just as Michael remembered it. Not even the decor had changed. It was as though the design was mandatory and could not have been any other way. It only appeared to have been freshened up every so often, to maintain the air of sickening opulence and sensation of entitlement.

'It's just along this corridor,' Michael whispered to the others. 'Anna and I will go and open the door. The rest of you follow in pairs so we can keep it shut as often as possible.'

The others nodded their agreement as Michael and Anna moved towards a patch of green wallpaper with gold stars. It was as innocent looking as the rest of the wall surrounding it, and would have been completely overlooked by any normal intruder. Feeling around for the latch, Michael heard it click and pushed it inwards, ushering Anna inside.

'Is it me, or is it too quiet?' he asked his aunt.

'Something's definitely not right,' Anna replied. 'But we came here to do a job and we're damn well going to finish it.'

'Why would they post guards outside the house if there's nobody home?' said Michael.

'I don't know. I can only guess that your friends are expecting to come back here sometime tonight,' said Anna. She pulled a small compact from her pocket and opened it. Tapping on the glass, she waited. 'All clear,' she said eventually. 'Next two down.'

Michael opened the door in time to receive the next wave of their party, before closing it behind them again. Once all of the group were safely in the hallway between the main house and the training hall, he led them to the impressively carved double doors and risked a look inside. The braziers were cold, but the sconces were lit and the hall appeared empty. Taking a deep breath, Michael readied himself for whatever could be waiting for them and stepped through. Aside from the echo of his footsteps on the stone floor, he was alone. Giving a wave over his shoulder, the others followed him in, taking up their customary formation beside their leader.

Lefrick was the first to break the silence. 'I don't understand. If they're holding her down here, there should be some sort of guard.'

'Catchpole doesn't work that way,' said Michael. 'If he's got her down here, he'd prefer that nobody else knew about it. Isn't that so, Mr Catchpole?'

There was silence.

Michael tried again. 'You may as well come out of the closet, and bring Alice with you. I know you're there.'

The click of a metal latch and the creaking of the door confirmed Michael's suspicions. Catchpole emerged from behind one of the Inquisitor shaped pillars that supported the floor above them. With him was Alice, her eyes vacant but full of tears as though she had been crying for hours. Michael couldn't see any marks on her face or wrists, but he knew that she had been subjected to something terrible. After all, Catchpole had a reputation for being very good at his job.

'Good to see you again, Mr Ware,' said the Magister from the shadow of the pillar. 'It took me quite some time to figure out how you might have pulled off your little stunt. But when I saw you at the library with ... your aunt, is it? I knew you must have had help from some unusual friends.'

'What do you want with Alice? She doesn't know anything,' Michael snapped.

'I know,' Catchpole answered. 'It was an oversight on my part. I'd half expected you to slip up in your communications with her, or for her to have worked out where you were for herself. She really is a very bright young lady. Unfortunately, I had to dig a little deeper than usual.' When he saw Michael start towards him, he pulled Alice closer. 'Oh, don't worry, there's no permanent harm done. I doubt she'll remember a thing once she comes around.'

'Then leave her out of this,' Michael shot back.

Catchpole cocked his head to one side and said, 'In exchange for what? You have nothing I need. Except ... her.' He glowered at Anna as though he was trying to fit the last pieces of a puzzle together. 'Call it an eye for an eye, if you'll pardon my crude humour.'

'Now I remember,' said Anna puffing out a breath. 'He was with Renfrew that night. He's the reason I couldn't save Mike.'

'How precious,' Catchpole giggled. 'They named you for your dead uncle.' Pushing Alice ahead of him, he stepped into the light and turned his attention back to Anna. 'You see this,' he said pointing at the long scar that ran almost the length of his face. 'You gave me this when you threw me through that window. I'd say I owed you for that.'

'I'm here right now,' Anna snarled. 'Give it your best shot.'

Keeping his distance, Catchpole shoved Alice into the

276

centre of the room and put her to stand on the brass plate embedded there. For the first time, Michael realised that his sister was dressed in a sleek black cocktail dress, though her feet were bare, and he breathed a sigh of relief as he put two and two together.

'They're all at the town/academy ball,' he said. 'You took Alice while she was getting ready, hoping that you could have her back before anyone noticed, didn't you?'

'That's very good, Michael, what else?' said Catchpole, his face brightening.

'That would mean that she was invited here to stay for a few days,' Michael continued. 'I doubt that you've told Tamara that I'm alive because you want her under your thumb, the same way you wanted me. But she knows, doesn't she? She wouldn't have asked Alice here otherwise.'

Looking genuinely impressed, Catchpole said, 'Yes, you're right. Our Grand Inquisitor did invite your sister to join us for the ball, with the help of a friend. And yes, she does know that you're alive. But shall I tell you where your assumptions let you down, Mr Ware, for old time's sake?'

'Be my guest,' said Michael.

'She also knows who you're keeping company with these days.'

'Is that so?' Michael sighed, beginning to lose his patience.

'Oh yes,' Catchpole retorted. 'That's why she's made a new friend for her own. Lovely girl; looks about your age. Blonde hair? Her daddy's a bit of a charmer - plays a pipe, so I've been told. Ring any bells?'

Anna and Lefrick gasped at the same time, and Michael stared at them both as it dawned on him who Catchpole was referring to. He shook his head, trying desperately to think of any explanation for Katja's appearance that didn't confirm Catchpole's story.

'You're lying,' was all he could muster. 'If anything, she's there because of Jerrick, and not because you had Tamara send her. You don't even know where the Council is hiding.'

'Quaint little farm, not too far from the reservoir?' said The Magister as he bobbed his head from one shoulder to the other. 'They're a very welcoming family by all accounts. I'm sure the Piper will do his best not to hurt them. I hear there's a concert going on there this evening. I do love a good flute solo, don't you?' Michael took another step towards him, causing him to wrench Alice in front of himself like a shield. 'Now, now, Michael, we wouldn't want any accidents.'

'Step out from behind my sister and you'll have more than an accident,' Michael growled. There was a tapping noise from Anna's pocket, followed by a niggling feeling in the back of his mind.

*They're coming,* Jerrick barked in his head.

Michael looked at Anna as the tapping became more insistent. She nodded at him almost imperceptibly, causing the butterflies in his stomach to take flight once more. He could feel his brow begin to sweat as he panicked. There was no way he could get his sister away from Catchpole and get to Tamara now. It was going to have to be one or the other. Then he noticed it. Alice's eyes twitched once,

278

then twice. Then she blinked, and the light in them returned slowly. She was awake.

Michael reached out with his mind and brushed her cheek. Just as she was about to speak, he clamped an invisible hand over her mouth to stop her. He glanced down to her feet, then back to her face and scratched at his elbow. In that secret code that siblings everywhere develop between them, she seemed to understand what he wanted. Alice blinked twice.

'Well,' said Michael. 'We'd love to stay and chat, but we're expecting company any minute. I'm going to ask you one last time, hand Alice over or I'll ...'

'You'll what?' Catchpole interjected. 'Pardon the pun, but I'm holding all the cards, Mr Ware.'

'Oh, you'd be surprised at what I keep up my sleeve,' said Michael. He lashed out with his will, wrapping it around the brazier at the far end of the room before flinging it at the Magister, spilling its oily contents on the floor. It stopped more than a foot from its target.

'After all this time, that's all you've got?' Catchpole laughed. He brought the brazier around to his side and was just easing it to the ground when Alice took her cue. She stamped hard on her captor's foot, causing him to loosen his grip, then brought her elbow sharply into his ribcage and wriggled free of him.

Taking advantage of the confusion, Michael dropped to one side and rolled. As he came to a crouch, he brought his hands together, sending a shockwave out in Catchpole's direction.

'Get her out,' he yelled to the others. 'I've got you

covered.'

In the nick of time, Catchpole raised his arms and the shockwave dissipated around him. The backs of the retreating group disappeared through the doors, leaving Michael as his only target. Catchpole's face split into a manic grin as he advanced on his opponent.

'You should have left with them,' he sneered. 'But I'll take you over your sister, it's a fair trade. Surrender yourself now and I'll call off the others.'

As if in time with his words, Michael could hear the sounds of fighting from the corridor above, and fired a succession of mental attacks towards his former mentor.

'It's a kind invitation, but I think I'll be going,' he said.

Without breaking stride, Catchpole deflected the attacks, retaliating with some of his own. It was what Michael had been preparing for, only the adversary was different. Unlike his first encounters with Catchpole, it now seemed easy to sense where the energy distorted the air in front of it. Almost by reflex, he raised his hands and willed a barrier in front of himself, feeling the tingling of Catchpole's energy as it reflected away.

***He's only expecting one kind of assault,*** said Jerrick in Michael's head. ***Use it to your advantage. Draw him in.***

Heeding his companion's advice, Michael wrapped his mind around Catchpole's legs, tugging sharply. His target stumbled but seemed to bounce on thin air as he repelled himself skywards, flailing an arm in Michael's direction as he did so. Michael's face stung as his head whipped sideways, spinning his shoulders with it. But he had little time to recover, as Catchpole redirected his energy towards the ceiling and darted towards him at an alarming speed. Dropping to his knees, Michael crossed his arms over his chest to absorb the impact, before punching sharply outwards to throw his opponent away.

Tumbling out of control, Catchpole had few options. With the dexterity of an alley cat, he reached out with one arm. Curling his fingers around a pillar sconce, he swung in a wide arc, ripping the decoration from the stone, before descending to the floor on one knee.

'You've improved since we last fought,' he jeered.

'That was only practice,' Michael answered. 'You'll find that I've learned a lot since then.'

The sounds from the corridor seemed closer now than they had been, as though the others were being pushed back towards the hall. His eyes half closed, he extended his arm and concentrated on the older man's throat in an attempt to close his fingers around it. But Catchpole's will was stronger, filling the space between them, prying them apart before he could get a grip. The backlash caused Michael's arm to jerk violently, wrenching his shoulder in its socket. He yelped with pain and raised his other arm, unleashing a stream of energy that caught the Magister beneath the chin, snapping his head backwards.

Seeing his advantage, Michael swung his aching right arm around in a mock haymaker, connecting his will with Catchpole's cheek. As his left hand came to bear once more, he frantically unleashed a blast of flame.

The fireball sent Catchpole reeling, wreathed in fire across the smooth stone floor. As the heat of the attack ignited the spilled oil from the brazier, he let out a roar of anguish. Michael watched him briefly as he writhed and rolled, before sprinting back to the slipway to join his friends in their battle for freedom. When he reached them, the place was a mess, and Michael found himself staring at the backs of a group of black-robed Inquisitors.

Thankfully, the corridor was wide enough to fit three abreast. Hanging back behind the rear rank was Daniel, the Guardian they had posted to keep watch outside. With as much care as he could muster, Michael edged closer and put a hand on the Guardian's shoulder, making him jump with fright.

'Hey, Dan, what's happening?' he whispered.

'Gees, Michael, you scared the hell out of me!' Daniel breathed. 'They've got us pinned down just before the entrance to the servant's quarters. I overheard someone say the Grand's on her way, so we've got to get moving.'

'Why didn't you do something?' Michael hissed.

'I can't take six of them on my own, can I?' said Daniel.

'Yes, you can. I'll show you,' said Michael.

Sweeping his colleague behind him, he spread his arms wide and curved his hands inwards. Then, with some effort he brought his hands together again, clashing the heads of the two outer Inquisitors into the head of the middle assailant. Collapsing forward, the second rank stumbled into the first, sending them sprawling to the floor where Andy and Lefrick were waiting for them.

'See?' he said, sauntering towards his companions.

'Smart ar ...' said Daniel.

As Michael turned to look at him, his colleague was looking down at the wooden shaft of a javelin protruding from the chest of his leather jerkin. His eyes were filled more with shock than pain. Sagging to his knees, Catchpole came into full view behind him, face burned, robes charred and ruined. Finally, Daniel slumped forward, snapping the jutting pole in two.

Michael looked up from the body and mouthed, 'Why?'

'I was aiming for you,' Catchpole replied.

Michael stared at the blood seeping from Daniel's body. He'd seen death before in his shared memory with Jerrick, but this time it seemed more real. Rage welled inside him, knotting his intestines like rope, squeezing the blood through his veins until a red mist clouded his vision. Tweaking his wrist, he summoned the tipped end of the spear that had broken away to his hand and hurled it in one swift motion. As it flew, he pressed his will behind it to keep it true and give it speed. But Catchpole swatted at the projectile as if it were nothing more than an annoyance, sending it clattering away along the adjoining corridor.

'I wanted to bring you home,' said the Magister. 'I was going to make you great. But you've chosen your side. In a way, I admire you for that.'

Not listening to a word that came from his mouth, Michael launched into a sprint towards his adversary, but his experience was no match for Catchpole's. Suddenly he felt himself being scooped up in a mental net as his enemy began to pound him from floor to ceiling, yelling, 'That's ... for ... burning ... my ... robe!' in time with each stroke.

His tirade done, Catchpole hurled Michael like an

oversized bowling ball at the far wall, missing Lefrick by scant inches. Barely conscious, Michael felt himself slam into the massive bulk of the doorman before slumping to the ground.

Recovering, Lefrick gestured in the air with practiced ease, expanding his arms to fill the corridor with a green semi-bubble of light.

'Andy? Now would be a great time for you to get up!' he yelled over his shoulder as Catchpole bore down on them.

'Hans Lefrick,' the Magister sneered, his hands held in front of him, ethereal blue lightning flashing between his fingers and jumping from palm to blistered palm. 'I know *all* about you. You should have stayed tucked up behind your books.'

'I know enough about you too, Catchpole,' said Lefrick. 'Do you think you're my first Magister?'

Catchpole let loose with a bolt from his hands that crackled and sputtered as it crashed against Lefrick's shield, causing it to waver significantly.

'Almost out of juice?' he crowed.

In his turn, Lefrick's hands wove complex patterns in the air, drawing energy from the mound of Inquisitors that lay prone on the floor of the corridor, and redirecting it to his shield. The shimmering became an emerald glow that was barely transparent enough for Michael to see the faint outline of the Magister behind.

To their right, he could see that Anna and the remaining Guardians were busy with a fight of their own. During Catchpole's battle with her master, a detachment of the household guard had arrived, and space was in short supply. As Inquisitors fell or ran out of energy, they were pulled out of the melee and replaced by fresh faces.

Like a Spartan phalanx, Anna's formation relied on each fighter to protect those to either side and until now it had worked. At seemingly random intervals, they would drop their shields and attack, reducing the front rank of the enemy. Then they would raise their shields again and advance, pushing the next rank backwards. They were only a few more feet from servant's corridor, and safety.

In the face of repeated attacks, Anna and her cohort were beginning to flounder. With no way to attack through their opposition's shields, their opportunities to damage their opponents were limited to small, accurate gestures. But even a fly swatter takes energy to lift, and each spell seemed to be taking its toll on them.

'It's getting serious up here,' his aunt yelled behind her.

'It's pretty serious down here, too!' Lefrick responded.

'I don't know how much longer I can hold them,' said Anna.

'I'll trade your lackeys for my Magister any time you like,' Lefrick cried as he withdrew pace by gruelling pace while Catchpole whittled away at his shield with every hammering stroke.

His vision swimming in and out of focus, Michael could feel oblivion creeping up on him. He blinked a few times, trying to stay awake. But the harder he tried, the more his body seemed to want to give in. With the battle still raging around him, something in the back of his mind came to a decision on his behalf, and he passed out with a groan.

At that moment, Jerrick began to take stock of the situation. The cuts on Michael's face and head weren't severe. However, judging by the tenderness around his eyes, his nose was broken and he'd most likely have one heck of a concussion when he woke up. Nevertheless, lids fluttering, Jerrick forced his eyes open and stared into the face of a bemused Andy.

'Enough!' his voice boomed through Michael, making the floors quake. He eased himself onto feet that were unfamiliar to him and steadied himself against the wall with one hand. Taking a long breath, he pulled at the straps of Michael's ill-fitting hauberk, flinging it to the floor. Relishing the unconfined feeling of a body once more, he gathered his thoughts for a moment, before turning to Lefrick.

'It's not often I regret that Jeshemon's curse will not allow me to kill. But him I could make an exception for.'

'Well, whatever you can do, do it now,' said Lefrick. 'I'm almost out of power.'

'Then let go,' Jerrick replied. 'I am ready.'

As Lefrick let his shield fade, Catchpole began to come into focus, the six fresh guards at his rear feeding energy to him like a tap. Jerrick smiled with Michael's face and wagged an accusatory finger at him.

'I would tell you to pick on somebody your own age, but then I could not justify this!' he cried.

Curling the middle finger of his right hand against his thumb, he flicked it against the last of the shield, bursting it

286

like a soap bubble. The shock of it rippled along the corridor, slamming into the Magister before sweeping the guards with him until the wave broke against the far wall. With Michael's left hand, Jerrick motioned as though he were wrapping his fist around a rope. As he pulled, wisps of power rose like steam from their bodies.

'Just men again,' said Lefrick.

'For the time being,' Jerrick replied.

'It's a shame you can't make it permanent.'

'It is as it must be,' said Jerrick.

'I understand,' said the Elder.

They turned towards Anna and her waning battle with the other household guards, impressed by their progress towards their goal. However, there were still several ranks between them and the servants' corridor. Jerrick eased his way between the shoulders of the rear Guardians to stand next to Anna and assessed the situation. She looked at him, his hair matted with the blood from his wounds.

'I'd tell you that you shouldn't be here looking like that, but I could use the backup. How much have you got left?'

'Enough,' the genie answered. 'I'm going to miss this, Habibi. I always did enjoy your company.'

Anna leaned over and kissed his cheek. 'I'm glad you came. But I need to ask ... How long are you going to be away?'

'Too long. You'll be an old woman before I return. And even then, who knows.'

'I wish,' said Anna.

'No. No, you don't,' Jerrick cut her off. You know what happened the last time. She's still paying for our friendship, now more than ever.'

'Then I hope,' Anna amended.

'I hope so too,' said Jerrick. 'Now, let's get out of here before we both regret it.'

With the confidence of ages, he stepped out ahead of the line and waited. The barrage of Inquisition attacks flared as they rebounded against the waning shields of the intruders. Raising his hands one above the other, he began to trace circles with his palms, muttering an incantation in a language he was certain Anna hadn't heard him speak before. It was soothing to the ears, soft and velvety, warm and disarming. As he conjured specks of sparkling sand into being, their glittering drew the attention of the entire assembly.

The master's incantation gathered pace. In response, the sand formed a dust devil between his hands. As it grew, everything was peaceful, except for the ancient sorcerer's hypnotic song and the restful murmur of the caged tornado. All eyes were on Jerrick as he moved his hands to his lips and blew gently, exploding the swirling twister into shimmering, beautiful stars that fluttered gently over the guards. They watched like children seeing their first snow as the flakes fell into their hair, onto their shoulders and into their eyes, and one by one fell gently asleep. Jerrick turned to find Anna open mouthed in awe beside him.

'Desert magic,' he whispered. 'I have never mastered it until now. It was always too subtle for me.'

'Are they ...?'

'Sleeping,' said Jerrick and gave the most winning smile he could with a face like a panda. 'Even in war we must remember that the soldiers have families too, yes?'

His comment seemed to bring Anna around sharply. 'Would they have thought the same about us?'

'Perhaps now they might. Come, let us leave.' He raised his voice slightly to address the others. 'Try not to rouse them as you go. No doubt they will be dreaming happy dreams, about cuddly sheeps and fluffy teddy bears and such like.'

'Jerrick, it's ... never mind,' Anna giggled.

They filed into the corridor weakest first. Andy, Daniel's body cradled in his arms, led the way, and Alice, pale with shock, slunk behind him. At the butler's apartment, the hulking bouncer took his boot to the handle of the door, shattering the lock and strode into the vacant rooms.

Neatly arranged wooden furniture had been carefully placed to maximise the space in the lounge. Two functional looking, burgundy leather sofas were set at right angles around a hessian rug. In the middle of the rug was a modern looking wood and glass table with books artistically placed on it, giving the illusion that someone actually read them. The overall impression was that the usual resident was a man of taste, but very definitely single, and possibly looking to impress whomever he brought there.

'Mrs Davis would have a fit if she saw this!' said Anna. 'She was very fond of her parlour, so I hear.'

'Never stops going on about it,' said Lefrick. 'I hope the mirror's still there.'

Passing through an impeccable, black and white tiled

kitchen, they made their way into the bedroom-come-study and were relieved to find the standard issue gilt-edged mirror in place above the desk. In truth, the apartment was the same as any of the student rooms at the academy, with a few exceptions. Had they not known better, the study that led to the bedroom and en-suite bathroom could have been anywhere, in any of the other houses on the vast campus. There were even double doors that led out, not onto a balcony, but to a small paved terrace overlooking the lake.

'You first, Andy,' said Lefrick as he held the frame of the mirror and the portal flickered into life.

The doorman looked down at Alice, who had begun to quiver, and said, 'C'mon, love. You take my arm and stay close. We'll have you safe, with a nice hot cup of tea before you know it.'

She looked back at her brother. 'Is Michael ...? I mean, he will be alright, won't he?'

Jerrick nodded. 'Yes, Alice, I promise you that he'll be your brother again soon. He will be a little sore, but no worse for this. I will see to it.'

Alice nodded stiffly as she took Andy's sleeve and followed him through the glass. The other Guardians followed as Anna ushered them out until only she and Jerrick remained.

'You know they'll be waiting for us on the other side?' she said.

'Yes,' said Jerrick. 'I had hoped that Nahar had died along with my body. But alas, it was not to be.'

'Grimm's journal says that his wish was to live to see

you dead,' said Anna.

'A fact that I had overlooked,' Jerrick admitted. 'When you've lived as long as I have, Habibi, the mind plays funny tricks. This is the price I have paid for my arrogance.'

'Overconfidence perhaps, not arrogance,' Anna replied touching his cheek. 'What do you want me to do?'

'What you have always done,' Jerrick smiled. 'Be there for your nephew. We live in troubling times, Anna. He will need you more than he knows, for longer than he thinks. To lead is not an easy burden to carry alone. When we get back to the compound I will distract Nahar. You must make certain that the girl doesn't get between us. As for the others, let them rest in whatever peace the flute brings them for now.'

He watched as Anna disappeared into the world beyond, sighing with a mixture of sorrow and apprehension for what was to come. But as he put his hand to the glass, a sudden feeling of dread pulsed in Michael's veins, as he realised that the face of the glass had remained unchanged. He couldn't follow.

## Chapter Thirteen:
# The Darkest Hour

Gripping the mirror's frame tightly, Jerrick muttered his spell again, but the reflection in the glass remained unchanged. He closed his eyes and checked that place inside Michael where his store of power should have been. The well was almost half full, depleted from his earlier exertions against Catchpole. Not that Jerrick had relied on internal stores of power in aeons.

'Don't bother,' said a young female voice from beyond the door. 'It looks like we got here just in ... Michael!'

The genie turned to look at the group of Inquisitors that had just entered, led by the speaker, who was wearing a black robe with white fur trim. He searched Michael's memory. She was taller than Michael remembered, perhaps a little broader in the shoulders. But the feathers of the raven coloured ponytail sticking out beyond her cowl were definitely the same.

'You are Tamara Bloodgood, the Grand Inquisitor,' he said. It wasn't a question.

'And you're not Michael Ware,' Tamara replied. 'I'm a little confused. You're him, but every fibre of my being tells me that you're not. Even your aura's wrong.'

'This body is his,' said Jerrick. 'I am ... how would you say ... a passenger on a runaway bus.'

'Train ...' Tamara corrected him. 'It's "passenger on a runaway train".'

'Is it?' said Jerrick smiling. 'Thank you. Michael was

injured by one of your Inquisitors and I had to get him to safety. He is here, in his head, but he cannot see you or hear you.'

'You're him, aren't you?' said Rupert beside her. 'You're the genie.'

'I am, Mr McEvity. My name is Jerrick. And you must forgive me but I have to go, or people will not die.'

Miss Cunningham raised an eyebrow. 'People will *not* die? That's got to be the worst excuse I've ever heard.'

'I am serious!' Jerrick snapped. 'The curse you have put upon us is worse than you could possibly imagine. To die would be a blessing compared to what is about to happen to my people. Do you know what a Flayer is, girl?'

'I'm not a girl,' Tamara protested. 'I am the Grand Inquisitor of the British Isles thank you very much. You will address me as "my lady". Do you understand?'

'My apologies, *my lady*,' said Jerrick raising a hand to his chest and bowing. 'I am more than two hundred times your age. It is difficult to remember that you are not a child, and neither is Michael.'

'Whatever,' Tamara huffed. 'You've taken Alice. Why?'

'Michael was concerned for her safety,' said Jerrick.

In the face of his honesty, Tamara paused, looking first to Rupert, then to Adam with questioning eyes. Both shook their heads in reply to her silent question.

'Anybody not on my immediate staff, get out now. Except you Adam. Clarissa, go and see to Catchpole.'

'B ... But,' Miss Cunningham stuttered.

'I'm going to need him when I'm done here. Please see to it that he is in the training room with the seers when I'm finished.'

'As you wish, Grand Inquisitor,' said the school-mistress, her eyes narrow with suspicion.

Once the room was clear and the door was closed, Tamara moved to the closest of the study's sofas and sat, whilst Rupert, knife drawn, took the sofa opposite. Adam took up station behind him, guarding the double doors and Jerrick's only remaining escape route.

'Michael obviously knew that Alice was here,' Tamara reasoned. 'Which means one of two things: either that the stories about magic and mirrors are true, or there is a Council spy at the academy, and I can imagine there are many.' She chewed her lip for a moment. 'Catchpole kept talking about mirrors whenever I mentioned Michael or the duel. But whenever I asked him directly what he was talking about, he always changed the subject.'

'Then if I may be so bold, my lady?' Jerrick ventured. 'He is lying to you by omission of the facts.'

'Yes,' Tamara agreed. 'He is, isn't he?' She shook her head and seemed to come back from whatever faraway place her mind had been occupying. 'But that's none of your concern. What bothers me is that Michael seems to have come with you quite willingly.'

'Why wouldn't he? said Jerrick puzzled by her statement.'

'Because he's ours,' Rupert blurted. 'He was meant to be our Grand Inquisitor, no offence, Tam. He hates the Council. He hates them for what they stand for – all your lies, your lust for control. So why? Why would he come here with you willingly? Unless you've done something to him, or played some twisted trick that your lot seem to rely on like you did to Jeshamon's people?'

'It always comes back to that,' Jerrick sighed. 'I can assure you that we did not trick Michael into coming with us at all. In fact, if you hadn't brought Alice here, he would have come soon enough anyway, to kill ...' He realised what he was saying too late. Turning to the mirror, he was horrified by his reflection. Here he was, destroying Michael's hopes with his own mouth. Then something caught his eye. At the edge of the glass, he could see the older boy, Adam, unscrewing a snooker cue that had been resting against the frame of the French doors. Jerrick closed his eyes and leaned his forehead against the glass in shame.

'Who was he supposed to kill?' asked Tamara, annunciating every venom-pricked word.

When Jerrick didn't answer her, she raised her hand for Rupert's attention. Rupert loosened his control over their intruder enough for Tamara to be able to take a hold of his shoulder and spin him sharply around.

'Look at me. I said LOOK AT ME!' she yelled. 'You were bringing him here to kill someone, and I demand to know who. Was it me? Was it Catchpole? TELL ME!'

'All of you,' Jerrick mumbled as he turned to face her. 'The Grand Inquisitor and her entourage. Those were his targets.' Unable to look Tamara in the eye, he looked to Adam, hoping that the now disassembled cue would take the pain he felt away.

Curiously, however, Adam seemed to be trying to gesture with his eyes between the thicker half of the wooden pole and Rupert. When Jerrick raised an eyebrow to query his intention, Adam simply rolled his eyes and swung, striking Rupert across the back of the neck, knocking him unconscious. Taking advantage of Tamara's confusion, Jerrick waved a hand and clamped the Grand Inquisitor's jaw shut. Quickly applying mental pressure to her shoulders, he pinned her in place. He could feel her summoning all her will to push against the sofa, but the genie's grip was iron.

Jerrick was at her side in a flash, draining her of her energy. Struggling against his attack, Tamara kicked and flailed, sending the small table between the sofas hurtling into the writing desk beneath the mirror.

Jerrick touched a finger gently between her eyes, and muttered, 'Sleep.'

'We have to go,' said Adam.

'We?' said Jerrick.

'I'm coming with you,' Adam insisted. 'I'm requesting sanctuary … on the Railroad!'

The genie glared at him, scrutinising him like an insect under a microscope. 'I cannot sponsor you. Neither can I guarantee your safety with us. Before I give you my answer, just tell me why?'

'Because I'm in love with Alice. I'm going to marry her; I've seen it. That and the fact that the guards are going to burst in here any second. They'll never let me leave here alive … Please!'

'I always was a sucker when it came to love,' said Jerrick. Having rested Tamara's head against a cushion, he clambered up onto the desk again and pressed his hand to the gilt frame. 'You first,' he said as Adam joined him.

At that moment, the door burst open. It was Emily, angry looking guards following in her wake.

'Rupert, look out! Adam's going to ...' she shouted, stopping in her tracks as she took in the scene.

'I'm sorry, Em,' Adam called back as Jerrick shoved him into the void, throwing himself in after.

***

The *whump* of the mirror announced the team's return to the barracks. Even though they had been gone for hours, the concert seemed still to be in full swing. The audience was entranced. They sat in their seats or leaned against the pillars of the hall listening to nothing at all. Anna's watch chimed, breaking the silence.

'What the ...?' Andy spluttered at her side, Daniel's body limp in his arms.

'Nahar,' said Anna. 'He's here. He came for them and we weren't ready.' A tear dribbled from her eye and rolled down her cheek.

'What's going on? Why are all those people so still? Are they ... you know?' said Alice in a small and frightened voice behind them.

Anna turned to her, placing her palm softly against her niece's cheek. 'It's okay, my girl. They're going to be just fine. But I need you to do something for me, alright?'

'B ... b ... but I can't do anything,' Alice stuttered still pale with shock. 'N ... n ... not like you and Michael can.'

'This one's easy,' said Anna. 'I need you to find

somewhere to lie low, okay?' She pointed to the double doors that led to a set of bunkrooms. 'Down there ought to do it. Just pick a room, fast as you can.' Watching Alice run until she was out of sight, Anna dried her cheek and turned back to her team, leading them towards the silent spectators.

'What do we do?' Lefrick croaked as they crossed the floor. 'I can keep going, but I don't know for how much longer. The fight at the academy took a lot out of me. I wasn't expecting this.'

'None of us was,' Anna replied.

'There's nothing you can do,' said Katja, stepping out from amongst the seated audience. 'My father is here now. Soon the Inquisition will demand their evidence that my bargain with them is complete. They're waiting outside in the barn to view your bodies.'

'What have you done to them?' Anna asked, choking back her anger.

'They're under the flute's influence. Don't be afraid, they're not in any pain.'

'How do you know?' Lefrick pressed.

'Because I lulled them to sleep,' said Katja as if the Elder's words had cut her. 'Please understand, I'm not inhumane. They will die, but I won't allow them to feel a thing. No pain, no distress or anxiety, they will simply slip away to whatever they believe awaits them on the other side. Of course, father would rather we drained them and left them in the netherworld between the mirrors, but I have a contract that I must fulfil.'

'Where is Nahar?' Anna demanded.

'Collecting something that belongs to him - a lamp. Perhaps you could help us look,' said Katja raising an eyebrow at her.

'That lamp doesn't belong to Nahar, girl. It belongs to Jerrick,' Lefrick snapped. 'Tell me, has he told you why he wants it? Why he feels it belongs to him?'

Katja smiled. There were no signs of innocence in her eyes. 'I know all about his wish. Oh, and before you begin to tell me of the horrific things he's done - that he's not my father, for example - I am well aware of them all. I forgave him a long time ago for the brutal things that he's done, and for the things that he made me do in his name.'

'Why the hell would you do that?' said Anna.

'Because he is the only father I have known,' said Katja.

'You see?' boomed a voice from the front of the hall as Nahar strode confidently to meet them, the lamp in his hands. 'Her loyalty knows no bounds. She is my daughter in every way. Now tell me, where is your leader?'

'I'm the leader here,' Anna spat. 'What do you want?'

'You have spirit for one so young,' said Nahar looking her up and down with admiration. 'I almost believe you could lead them, but you are not the one I am looking for. Where is the sorcerer?'

'Dead,' Anna replied. 'Go ahead, open the lamp and see for yourself.'

Nahar's eyes narrowed. Without taking them from her, he lifted the copper lid and tipped the lamp away from him, spilling grey-black ash onto the white floor. He looked down at the mound. Letting the copper vessel fall from his grasp, he grinned.

'The librarian was telling the truth. That surprises me.'

'Then you have no more business here,' Lefrick ventured.

'A contract is a contract I'm afraid. The girl has sold you to the Inquisition. There's nothing I can do about that now,' said Nahar.

Reaching into his robes, he produced the flute. It was more ordinary than anything Anna could have imagined. The stories and legends surrounding it had made it so extraordinary in their minds that Anna found herself disappointed by it for a moment. Though the bone was perfectly smooth and reflected the light of the hall, it was no more beautiful or magical looking than a teaspoon or a toilet brush. Anna supposed that it had been created that way by Jerrick for a reason. She braced herself.

'Don't trouble yourselves, it's pointless to resist,' said Nahar.

'When will people learn? Resistance is never pointless or futile,' Lefrick huffed, puffing his cheeks with frustration.

'But what purpose would it serve?' Nahar countered. 'Nobody will hear of it. No songs will be sung about the heroic last stand of the Elder Council. My daughter tells me that you have been declared enemies of the state. Every vigilante looking to make a name for themselves is wishing that they were in my pointy shoes at this moment in time. There is no honour to be won here, and no dishonour in accepting it.'

'Oh, shut up and get on with it already!' Anna scolded

him. 'You attack, we'll resist. That's the way *we* do business.'

'Very well, let's be gracious about this and lay down the rules then,' said Nahar. He scratched his ear with the mouthpiece of the flute for a moment. 'I will take one side of the hall, you the other. For every five minutes you resist, someone in the audience there dies. Agreed?'

'Now hold on a minute,' Lefrick protested. 'Why do you get to dictate the terms?'

'Because I'm the one in charge, *Master Lefrick*. So, will you agree to my terms, or do I start the killing now?'

Anna bowed her head and closed her eyes in an effort to find any other reason to stall the madman. Her shoulders rose and sank as she breathed deeply, trying to control the pounding of her heart.

Andy broke the tense silence. 'Um, can I put Daniel down somewhere safe first? He's seen enough horror today, don't you think?'

'I'm not unkind,' said the Piper nodding his consent. 'He's no longer part of this quarrel. Lay him down and I will ensure the Inquisition treats his body with respect.'

'That's very magnanimous of you,' the doorman replied as he laid Daniel's body down behind the nearest pillar and covered the wound in his chest with his leather jacket. 'There you go son,' he said in a whisper that echoed around the room. 'Rest easy, you've had a busy day.'

Nahar's face softened briefly as he said, 'Your grief is quite touching.' Then his expression hardened again, as though he'd just remembered why he was there. 'Let us begin.'

Pacing to the opposite side of the hall, he turned in front of the great mirror. Placing one pointy, patchwork shoe in front of the other he gave a low theatrical bow, flourishing his arms as though he were presenting himself at a medieval court.

Insulted by the arrogance of the man, Anna's hands moved quickly. Tugging a strand of her own hair from her head, she spun a faintly glowing lariat out of it. With Nahar's head still bowed, and a little effort on her part, she tossed the newly conjured lasso at her target. The strand of hair whipped out like a hemp rope, looping itself around the Piper's neck. As soon as it closed around him, Anna tugged on it sharply, catching Nahar off balance and throwing him to the ground. Clattering against the tiles, the flute slipped from the Piper's grasp and spun away across the floor beneath the seats of the enchanted audience.

Nahar's response was swift and sharp. The rope burst brightly into flame, tinged green by the chemicals from the burning hair dye. The fire raced along its length like fuse wire, scalding Anna's fingers as it reached her. When he raised his head, the look in the Piper's eyes was malicious and vengeful. Snapping his fingers, the floor beneath the feet of the Guardians began to tremble and shake as the tiles cracked and split. The brown roots of old trees wormed their way back into the light by the Piper's command. Creaking with new life, they wrapped themselves around the ankles of the defenders, ensnaring their legs.

'Katja,' Nahar yelled in an insane half laughing squawk, 'kill one of them. It doesn't matter which!'

With their assailant's attention elsewhere, Lefrick went to work, his incantation muffled by the backs of the Guardians. Anna and the others writhed, struggling to breathe as the roots clung to them and threatened to entomb them. Using his massive frame to his advantage, only Andy was free to hurl ball after sapphire ball of electricity at the Piper, who dodged it and rolled with a grace that belied his age. Meanwhile, gasps of relief rang out across the room as the roots began to crumble, turning to dust under Lefrick's counter spell.

Clambering to his feet between the colossal man's attacks, Nahar brought both arms around in an arc that ended above his head. Driving an unseen wind from his fingertips, he swept the Guardians up in a swirling, biting hurricane that flung Lefrick against a pillar. Unable to resist, Anna slammed against the plasterboard wall, smearing it with scarlet as she slid sideways onto the cold ceramic of the floor. Andy, on the other hand, wasn't so lucky. Unable to take his formidable weight, the wall gave way and he landed heavily, collapsing the metal desk of the bedroom beyond, with Jack Goodbody sprawled beside him.

Face bloody and body aching, Anna twisted and brought her knees beneath her, shaking her head to clear it. There was a tingling in her mind as her ears registered a melody that seemed to soothe her rage. Her instincts taking over, she raised her hands to form a shield around herself, but it was too late. Stars began to cloud her vision as Katja stepped around a pillar, the flute at her lips. Trying to fight against the fog, the Elder staggered to her feet and gave a final, desperate lunge towards Nahar. Then something remarkable registered on the edge of her consciousness.

Falling into him, Anna pushed the Piper towards the great mirror as it burst into life. Nahar seemed to disappear as though he'd been sucked backwards through the glass, only to be replaced by a much younger looking man of roughly the same height. There was a look of utter bewilderment on Adam Dakin's face as a silver candlestick emerged from behind him. Spinning past his ear, it struck Katja's head with a hefty thump. The music stopped with an abrupt squawk as the girl slumped to her knees, clutching at her skull while Andy tore the flute from her grasp.

'You stole a candlestick?' Adam called out over his shoulder. 'Wilkins is going to be furious, he ... oh.' Apparently realising that his travelling companion was missing and that he was talking to thin air, he closed his mouth and took in the scene.

'Where's Michael?' Anna panted.

'He was right behind me. There was this howling like a pack of wolves, and he seemed really agitated. When we got to that portal thing, he shouted "no time" and shoved me through. Next thing I know, I'm here, wherever that is.'

Panicking, Anna grabbed the young man's arm and hauled herself to her feet. Running to Lefrick's side, she tapped his face.

'Hans, come on, Michael's still out there!'

Lefrick drew a ragged breath as his eyelids fluttered open.

'Wha ...? Michael's where?'

'Get up!' Anna barked, pulling him upright. 'Michael's out there with Nahar, and the Flayers are coming!'

\*\*\*

Beyond the glass, all hell was trying to break loose. Flayer packs encircled the portal, drawn by the comings and goings of the Council bunker. The only thing keeping them at bay was the wreath of blue flames conjured by Jerrick to form an arena.

When he'd reached the portal with Adam, Jerrick's heart had sunk to Michael's boots to see the Piper there. Thankfully Nahar's hubris had got the better of him. He was toying with them like a cat with a mouse. But he had severely underestimated the survival instincts of the Guardians, and their willingness for self-sacrifice in the face of mortal danger.

It had been sheer luck that the Piper had been in the right place at the right time. It had allowed Jerrick to reach through the portal with the last of Michael's mental stores and pull the intruder backwards into the ether.

'It *is* you!' Nahar crowed. He looked Jerrick up and down. 'You're a little shabbier than I remember. Did the boy go willingly, or did you shanghai him when he wasn't looking?'

'I admit that it wasn't wholly with his consent,' said Jerrick. 'But what's a dead man to do without a body?'

'You expect me to believe that you're dead, when you're standing there in front of me?' the Piper laughed.

'Believe what you like, Agnar. This body is just a vessel. When its owner wakes I will have no more control over it than you have over the seasons. You should celebrate. You have seen me dead and your curse is lifted.'

'That may be,' said Nahar. 'And I can't say that I'm sorry that I didn't drop dead at the sight of you. That's usually how your twisted wishes work, isn't it? But I confess myself to be more than a little disappointed. Where is the ray of light, or the choir heralding my mystical release from bondage?'

Jerrick raised a quizzical eyebrow. 'Was there a clap of thunder when you made your wish? Did an orchestra suddenly appear out of nowhere and play some sombre tune when you cursed yourself? You're caught up in your own legend, Nahar. Tell me, now that you have me here and aside from correcting your mistakes again, what is it that you want from me?'

'I want you to suffer,' Nahar scowled. 'I want to hear you cry with the pain I've felt for centuries. There hasn't been a night that Sigrun's face hasn't haunted my dreams.'

'That wasn't my fault, Agnar,' said the genie. 'I'm as sorry now as I was then for your loss, but I refuse to carry the blame for it. The Inquisition …'

'The Inquisition followed where you led, you arrogant son of a goat!' the Piper yelled. 'They came to us because of you. You had no right to involve us in your war when we had so many troubles of our own!'

The baying of the Flayers redoubled at the sound of his tirade. Looking around them, Jerrick could see freshly torn rags and the traces of fresh blood on ragged flesh. There

306

were still signs of humanity in the faces of the newly reborn. They were angry, sickened, terrified looks, bent on vengeance, and hungry, not for blood, but for power.

Jerrick pointed an accusatory finger, tracing it around the circle of fire. 'Look around you, Nahar. This is your legacy. Your story should have ended in the Weser with those rats, not here between the living and the dead. How will Sigrun ever forgive you?'

'How dare you mention her name?' Nahar exploded. 'It was you that kept me from her, and I swear to you that when I'm done parading your bodies in front of the Inquisition, their shells will join the Council's here in the nether for their part in it!' Without warning, a blast of lightning burst from Nahar's palm, breaking like a wave around his opponent.

'Your grudge is with me, Nahar. Let the rest of them go,' Jerrick called out over the squealing of the electricity against his shield.

'Damn you, and damn the Inquisition,' the Piper cursed. 'I am what I am because of you both. You made me, now deal with the consequences. I wonder, what does the lore say about doing nothing and allowing that boy to die? You must be burning inside!' Twirling his other wrist, a circle of flames burst into life around the genie's feet, engulfing him in a furious inferno.

The Flayers howled, scorching themselves against the barrier, driven by their need to feed. The smell of charring flesh filled the air with a foul stench and the glittering stars of the world's portals were obscured by wisps of smoke from the tattered rags they wore. As Nahar's spell subsided, he could see Michael at its heart, eyes closed and lips moving in silent incantation, untouched by the blaze.

'You're tired, Agnar,' said Jerrick. 'I understand.'

'Understand? How can you understand? You haven't aged a day since the pyramids were new. But I did. If I hadn't gone East, I would have withered and rotted in this body for all eternity. It's *your* fault!' Nahar clenched his fists and the floor shook in sympathy, raising more howls from the hungry pack.

For the first time, Jerrick was aware of the hum of the portal behind him, and he could feel the eyes of the Guardians glaring in. A feeling of relief rushed through him like a waterfall as he whispered, 'Then kill me ... if you can.'

Nahar's lips twisted into a grin, his eyes twinkling with insanity. 'Gladly,' he purred, leaping into the air. As he began to fall he drew a dull, bone handled knife from his boot and quickly clasped the palm of his other hand over the pommel. Eager to plunge it into the chest of his enemy, he yelled, 'To hell with the Council!'

Feeling Michael's heart pounding, Jerrick reached out for the portal behind him and let go of his hold on his vessel. Stepping out from his host's body, there was gentle pop as Michael was pulled back into the compound, accompanied by muted shouts of concern from the other side of the glass.

The smoky remains of Jerrick stood with his arms outstretched at his shoulders, a grin splitting his ethereal face as Piper bore down on him. The ring of flames around the arena dropped, and Jerrick laughed as the Piper plunged his dagger into flesh that didn't exist, burying it in the floor between his feet. The Flayers charged at once. Free of the scorching fire that had been keeping them at bay, and pouring over one another like floodwater, they pounced. Pinning Nahar face down to the ground, they tore into him tooth and claw.

'It is time to repay the Piper,' Jerrick whispered. Turning his back on the feeding frenzy, he stepped into the light.

Their attention drawn by the fresh movement and the bounty of the world beyond the mirror, some of the newborns rushed to feed. Passing over the threshold, they exploded into puffs of insubstantial smoke. On the other side of the glass, Anna and Lefrick coughed and spluttered in the plume, closing the portal on Nahar's terrified screams.

'There's no time to waste,' said Jerrick, his usual composure returning. 'You have to wake the others immediately.'

'I know,' said Anna. 'The Inquisition is on our doorstep.'

'And I'm afraid I'm out of time,' said the genie.

'How many and what kind?' asked Lefrick.

Insofar as he could, Jerrick shrugged. 'Your guess is as good as mine. Quickly now, give me the flute.'

Without hesitation and with Katja still firmly in his custody, Andy tossed the flute in the master's direction. They winced collectively as it passed in quick succession through Jerrick's hand and then his body, before clattering against the great mirror and skittering briefly on the tiles.

Lefrick bent and picked it up.

'Um ... what do you want me to do with it?' he asked.

'Dismantle it and put it somewhere safe,' said Jerrick rolling his eyes as his ghostly form began to swirl like mist. '*Don't* use it. It is not called the flute of shattered dreams for nothing.'

Across the floor, the lamp began to rattle. Turning to look at it, they could see the genie's ashes begin to flow back into it.

'Goodbye, Jerrick,' said Anna.

'Nothing is forever, Habibi.' Jerrick's voice echoed as the lamp righted itself and began drawing him in like the steam from a kettle in reverse. 'I will always be with you.'

They watched as the vapour became a cloud, the way it had when Jerrick's body had died. Only this time, instead of rushing, it drifted and billowed gently until it was all but gone. The last wisp scooped the copper lid from the floor and sucked it into place with a metallic, ringing finality.

\*\*\*

Anna watched as her colleague looked down at the flute, turning it this way and that in his hands.

'Last time it took him nearly three hundred years,' said Lefrick. 'I wasn't there, of course, but he didn't look half as bad this time as he'd described the last. Perhaps a decade or two will see him right, eh?'

'Come on, Hans,' said Anna, her face streaked with tears. 'We've got more work to do.' The soles of her boots thumped as she strode over to Katja. 'How do I wake them?'

'It's like he said,' said Katja. 'If you dismantle the flute, they'll come around.'

'If you're lying to me, so help me I'll ...' said Anna raising a hand.

'I'm not lying, I have no reason to,' Katja replied. 'Without the flute, I'm just as feeble and ordinary as everyone else.'

'She's telling the truth,' said Lefrick. 'Andy, tie her and put her in a seat over there. We'll deal with her later.'

Taking Katja by the arm, the doorman hauled the girl to her feet and marched her to the front of the room. Meanwhile, as Lefrick pulled the flute into sections, a pained murmuring erupted amongst the stricken Councillors. Stepping onto the podium that had been the concert stage, Anna took a deep breath, letting it out raggedly.

'I know you're all in bad shape, but I need your attention.' she shouted, trying not to be too loud.

'Wha's goin' on?' said a bleary voice from the middle of the audience.

'We're under attack,' said Anna. 'If you're able, I need you up and ready.'

Pushing himself to his feet, Davis stood and swayed a little.

'You heard her,' he said, clutching at his brow. 'Let's go, you know the drill. If you can't fight, get to the training hall. There's no time to evacuate.'

'I'm staying!' Sher croaked from a chair at the back of the podium.

'My god Sher, what happened to you?' said Anna. She knelt beside the old woman, shocked to see a face that didn't fit the voice she knew.

'I got old,' Sher replied looking at her wrinkled, liver-spotted hands. 'The Piper ... he did something to me and I got old.'

'We'll figure it out, I promise,' said Anna brushing a lock of silver-grey hair from her friend's face. 'But first I need you to go with the others. You're no good to us like that; you'll end up getting yourself killed.'

'I'm staying put. Is that the girl?' Sher asked nodding in Katja's direction.

'Yes.'

'Then I'm staying with her. We'll have less chance of fixing this if she dies.' She placed a shaking hand onto Anna's shoulder and stood up. 'You haven't got time to argue with me. You'll find me just as stubborn as I used to be, perhaps worse.'

'Alright then, but you sit on her if you have to. Just don't let her out of your sight,' said Anna getting back up. There was a muffled bang from the doors of the barn above them. 'Quickly now, they're coming.'

'There's no time to get there,' said Lefrick joining her. 'They'll pen us in like lambs.'

'Then we'll have to use this place to our advantage. Nahar said that he was supposed to deliver us to them,' said Anna. Jumping down from the podium, she pressed her way through the throng to Katja, lifting the girl's face so that she could look her in the eye. 'How many?'

'I don't know,' said Katja gasping as Anna squeezed

her cheeks tighter.

'You'd better come up with something fast, girly, I'm losing my patience.'

Katja's eyes began to well. 'I don't know. I told them where you were, and I told them that I'd have the doors open before dawn. They've had the farm under surveillance since you took me in. That's all I know.'

Anna let her go, her hands quaking with a mixture anger and fear. 'Okay then, there's our chance. They know something's wrong, but I'm betting there aren't too many of them, and they're not expecting resistance. The deal was to see bodies, yes?' Katja nodded her response. 'Then we'll give them bodies. Lefrick, get these chairs scattered and make it look like there's been a struggle. I want some people in their seats and some lying on the floor. Nobody moves until the Inquisitors are well inside, understand?'

'Got it,' Lefrick confirmed and put the flute pieces aside as he set about his task.

'Andy, go to the kitchens and find anything that looks like blood. Smear it around the place. They'll be expecting to see it most probably, but for heaven's sake, don't make it look like a Hollywood horror movie.'

'Right you are, boss,' said Andy running for the door.

'And you,' Anna spat turning back to Katja as the barn door rang again. 'If you so much as breathe too loud ...'

'I know,' said Katja, 'I'll be the first to go. You're just like my father!'

'Oh no, I'm nothing like Nahar,' said Anna shaking her head. 'When I kill you, you'll be awake and looking at my face. Not the way you planned to cut my family's throats while they were bewitched. I promise you that.'

There was a creaking noise like someone tearing the side off a truck. It heralded the entry of the Inquisitors upstairs. From the sound of it, Anna guessed that there were easily thirty of them moving across the floor of the barn. It wasn't going to take long before they found the entrance to the ramp at the back of the building, but there was no time to panic.

'Places everyone,' she whispered, breaking the hush that had descended over the Councillors. 'Remember to wait until they're right inside. If we give the game away too soon, we're done for.'

As the Councillors positioned themselves, Andy began to distribute the hastily gathered meat juices he'd collected from the kitchen. When he heard the footsteps on the ramp, he threw himself to the ground and Anna silently prayed that they hadn't jinxed any of their friends.

From the chair that she'd chosen, she could see everything through half-closed eyes: the entrance, the other "corpses", the lamp, and the pieces of the flute. Realising too late that there was no way she could retrieve them both without being seen, she gestured quickly towards the lamp and slid it towards Lefrick. Catching it in one hand, he slipped it into the deep pocket of his overcoat. Stifling a sigh, Anna watched as the first of the soldiers appeared through the door of the hall, the black, polished leather armour under his robe gleaming under the strip lights.

'Clear,' the Inquisitor announced over his shoulder as more and more emerged from the corridor. 'Looks like there was some action here.'

314

'Seems Catchpole's insider kept their word at least,' said another.

The leader raised his fist and motioned for the others to enter. 'I thought he was supposed to have the doors open for us?'

'Perhaps the Council took him down before we got here?' said the second. 'I'll be thankful if they've done the job for us to be honest. Would you really wanna go up against someone who could solo this many Slingers and live to tell the tale?'

'Still,' said the first nudging Anna with the toe of his boot, 'there's something not right here. Look at them, what do you see?'

'They died in their seats, sir,' said a young woman's voice from amongst the group.

'No resistance,' said the leader. 'Well done, Simms. Whoever did this took them mostly by surprise.'

Simms stepped forward. 'Is it me, sir, or are there fewer than we were expecting? Perhaps we should go through the compound corridor by corridor.'

'What do you suppose this is?' said the second picking up a piece of the flute.

'Flute,' said Simms. 'I used to play when I was younger. Whatever happened here, it looks like there was a concert going on when it went down.'

The leader held out his hand and willed the flute pieces to him, taking the second by surprise as he pulled the piece he was holding from his grasp.

'Catchpole's orders,' he said. 'Anything else interesting gets logged through me. Let's mop up and get out. Fire crews, do not burn until we're on the way out, I don't want any accidents. Do I make myself clear?'

'Yessir!' the troop chorused as they began to form up into groups.

From her vantage point, Anna could see that at least one Inquisitor in each group was carrying a metal tank with a hose attached to it on their backs. Her heart pounded as she watched the Inquisitors move further into the hall and made a mental note of the leader's face for future reference. Her palms slick with sweat, she hoped the man wasn't smart enough to try playing the flute for himself.

They were almost where Anna needed them to be when the one identified as Simms stopped in her tracks.

'Sir?' she said bending down.

'What is it Simms?' said the leader.

'Isn't this the old Solaris butler, Davis?'

'Boo!' Davis yelled into the curious Inquisitor's face, before flinging her back into the group and knocking some of her company over.

The cacophony of sounds was deafening as both sides began barking orders and screaming signals to their fighters. To the horror and amazement of the interlopers, the Councillors sprang into action from their prone positions. Looking like zombies from some second rate b-movie, Andy's makeshift gore dripped and spattered as they gestured their first attacks. It covered their targets and just about everything else in wet, sticky animal blood. Realising that they were surrounded, the Inquisitors huddled together in groups, trying to repel the onslaught.

'You're outnumbered. Give it up,' Anna yelled above

the din.

Turning his head to look at her, the lead Inquisitor grabbed a hose from the side of one of his subordinates, trying to click the ignition button. To his credit, the subordinate realised what was about to happen and elbowed the man in the nose with as much force as he could muster. Anna was just as quick to respond, scooping the leader up in an incantation that sent him spiralling towards the wall next to Sher.

Taking their cue from him, the battle began in earnest. The Inquisitors let fly with stream after stream of attacks and some found their marks with terrifying precision. But for every Councillor that fell, another stepped into the breach.

## Chapter Fourteen:

# The Battle of Brecon Farm

In one corner of the hall, Katja turned to her guard. 'Do you want to live?' she said as the battle raged around them.

'Of course I want to live,' Sher replied.

'Then get my flute out of that man's coat and untie me!' Katja hissed.

'No way,' Sher snapped back. 'I'm not falling for that. Anna said to sit on you if I had to, so keep your mouth shut, unless you want a lap full of old woman.'

'That's what I'm trying to tell you,' said Katja rolling her eyes. 'You don't have to stay old. But we have to go now, or you'll definitely be that way for the rest of your life.'

'Why?' Sher countered. 'Just tell me why it's so important that we go now.'

'I … I can't,' Katja faltered. 'You need to trust me. Your friends will not understand what needs to be done to change you back. They won't allow it.' She ducked as a stray ball of lightning passed over her head and scorched the wall in front of them.

'I can navigate the portals on my own,' said Sher. 'Tell me what I need to do and I'll take you with me, but we're leaving the flute here.'

Wide-eyed at the proposition, Katja shook her head. 'No deal. The flute goes with us, or we don't go at all.' She flicked her head in the direction of the fight. 'Do you think any of them are responsible enough for such a thing? They would use the flute to kill as much as my father did. Could you allow that?'

'I guess not, but why should you have it? Wasn't all of this your fault?' said Sher.

'Yes,' Katja muttered.

'Sorry, I couldn't hear you over the noise.'

'Yes, I did this,' said Katja. 'But everybody deserves a second chance, don't they? Your Council will not give me that chance.'

'You're right, they won't,' said Sher. 'Did you ever think that maybe you deserve everything that's coming to you?'

'Perhaps I do,' said Katja. 'But you didn't deserve what father did to you. Let me put that right at least.'

'I'm going to regret letting you talk me into this, but alright,' said Sher. 'But if you try anything, I'll leave you in the void like they did to Nahar.'

Once untied, Katja helped Sher to her feet, watching as she took the flute pieces for herself. Together they skirted around the on-going fight to the mirror and slipped through almost unnoticed.

\*\*\*

From the door at the rear of the hall, Michael gawked at the mess and wondered what he had walked in on. He felt strangely empty now that Jerrick had left him, as though the genie had taken a small part of him when he'd returned to the lamp. His head and legs throbbed and ached from Catchpole's attack at the academy, and he was also vaguely aware that he felt scorched but had no real idea why. At the forefront of his mind, however, was the scene he was struggling to take in.

The Council seemed to have been caught off guard mid-evacuation. Having just seen Katja leading an elderly lady he didn't know into the nether, he knew that something had gone terribly wrong. From the number of bodies on the ground and the blood pools all over the place, he assumed that the Councillors had taken some heavy casualties. Nevertheless, it buoyed him to see that they had managed to corral the intruders near the centre of the hall, where the Inquisitors were showing their animal instincts. He was about to join the battle when it occurred to him that he had nothing in reserve. Whilst his two years with the Council had taught him a great deal, in combat he had always relied on what he had learned at the academy.

Then he saw it. Davis's feet left the ground as some invisible attack swept him up and flung him sideways. It caught Michael's attention immediately and flipped that switch inside him that only Catchpole had reached before. A mixture of exhaustion, rage and an urge to lash out with whatever came to hand gripped him. Dismissing the pain of his previous confrontations, Michael clenched and unclenched his fists, striding towards the fray. Part way across the hall, however, he was interrupted. The raiding party's leader, although in need of attention, stepped in front of him.

'I know you,' he said, blood dripping from a split lip. 'You're that Ware kid that supposedly died in the trials.'

'What's your name?' Michael asked as he let his eyes unfocus.

The leader gave an awkward, callous smile, showing off a freshly broken tooth. 'It doesn't matter what my name is. You won't be around long enough to remember it.'

His face burning with anger, Michael flicked his eyes to a nearby chair. With freshly borrowed energy, he brought it crashing down against the leader's back. Unprepared for the assault, the Inquisitor sank to his knees. Again and again Michael hit him, until the leader was face down on the floor, struggling to drag himself away from his opponent's wrath. Dropping the chair, Michael turned his attention to the Inquisitor's ankles, wrapping his attention around them like a boa constrictor. It was something Tamara had done to him at the trials and, for reasons he couldn't fathom, the thought of her made him feel sick to his stomach for the first time.

Just as she had done then, Michael began to swing his captive from side to side. Once he had enough momentum, he spun like a hammer thrower and flung the leader hard in an arc that put his troop in his path. There was an audible thump and cries of pain as the leader collided with some of the other Inquisitors in the closest group. Still seething, Michael marched into the battle lines, pushing his way through the combatants until he reached the front and stood next to Anna.

'What are you doing here?' she said, glancing at him long enough to make her point as she blocked an attack that burst with an orange flash against her shield. 'Get back and start pulling out the wounded.'

'No,' said Michael. 'I'm not going anywhere. I need to be able to see them.'

'You're in no fit state to fight, Michael,' said Anna. 'Don't argue with me right now, I don't have ...'

'Just trust me for once, will you?' Michael insisted. 'I have an idea.'

As soon as he had sent the Inquisitor airborne, a thought had occurred to him about the differences between the Inquisition and the Council. It wasn't just what they believed that put them at odds, it was how they practiced. More specifically, it was the way they had been trained to deal with their enemies. While the Council's sorcery drew upon the streams of energy that surrounded them, the Inquisitors had been trained to store reserves of energy. They relied on them almost exclusively, having to fall back out of prolonged engagements to recharge. It had been one of the most useful lessons the Davises had taught him.

Aware that he was putting himself at risk, Michael closed his eyes, trying to drown out the sounds so he could concentrate. Focussing his attention on the Inquisitors, he could see the glow of power that surrounded each individual fighter. Most Importantly, Michael could see the myriad colours and the dip in the brightness of their auras as they expended energy. He watched entranced for a moment or two, dazzled by the beauty of the spectacle. Remembering himself, he realised that he was seeing something he hadn't seen before. There appeared to be a constant haze over his vision like a glistening mist that flickered from time to time. It distorted what should have been definite blocks of colour surrounding each person, the way shafts of light are confused by heavy fog. He opened his eyes.

'Damn it! Between our defences and theirs, I can't get a clear shot.'

'At what?' Anna panted as she braced against another attack.

'If only there was a hole I could get through, I'm sure it would work.'

'Well, unless you can hang from the ceiling without them spotting you, you're out o' luck,' his aunt responded. 'These guys are good. I'm not sure how much longer we can keep this up.'

'Up,' Michael repeated, his eyes widening. 'You're a genius! They didn't stop him from falling in on them because they didn't see it coming.'

'Huh?' said Anna.

Michael closed his eyes again, centring on the Inquisitor closest to him. Extending his will, he let it wander until it met the warrior's defences, feeling an unpleasant tingling in his brain as he came into contact with the barrier. Tracing the line of the wall upwards until the tingling subsided, Michael pushed his mind over the top until he came into contact with the barrier's caster. The Inquisitor's head snapped upwards immediately. The sickening, renewed tingling broke Michael's concentration.

*Okay,* he thought. *I can't attack, but perhaps I can disarm.*

Just as he had done time and again, Michael began to draw on his target's power. He willed it upwards until the ribbon of energy arched over the Inquisitor's shield and wound towards him. Risking a glance, he was elated to see that his attack had gone unnoticed. He stopped, knowing her suspicions would be raised if she suddenly ran out of power.

*Is it possible to do more than one at a time?* Michael wondered.

Stretching out again, he began with the woman and spread his attention to the next Inquisitor in the circle. As both streamers rose, Michael felt a noticeable difference in the ease of his endeavour, but it was still manageable, so he moved on to a third. The tricolour of energy felt like a sack of wet sand on Michael's mind, and when it reached him, the squirming of it made him blanch. His stomach felt like he'd eaten an eight-course meal, and his head spun from the effort of moving so much weight so far.

*It's just like the trials,* he reassured himself. *If I can move an anvil, I can do this. What did Rupert say: "let's kick some serious booty,"?*

This time, he took a deep breath and let his shoulders drop. Watching through closed eyelids, he drew on the nearest Inquisitor once more, splitting his attentions in both directions. The weight of it was much easier to bear as he directed the ribbons to a space above the centre of the circle and held it there. Extending his will to the next in line, Michael felt a jolt of pressure as he watched the fresh colours mingle with the others.

By the time he had completed the circle, his shoulders were shaking and sweat poured down his face. He groaned with effort, trying to control the ball of energies that hung in the air above the Inquisitors. Unlike the dull, cold iron of the anvil, the ball felt white hot in Michael's head, as though he were trying to lasso the sun. It struggled against him, wriggling and twisting in Michael's mental grasp. At last, he cried out in anguish, shuddering with pain as he let it go.

The ball hung in the air for a moment, invisible to the naked eye. As he clutched at the sides of his head, Michael watched it fall almost in slow motion. Disappearing between the much dimmer auras of its contributors, the sphere struck the floor and burst like a supernova. Carried on the wave of energy, the Inquisitors slammed up against their own shields before collapsing backwards into the circle. The thunder crack that accompanied the explosion shook the hall, kicking up plumes of dust as plaster rained down on them all.

'What have you done?' Anna shouted over the ringing echo, as the combatants stopped to gawp.

'It's fine,' Michael replied, still cradling his head in one hand and dismissing her with the other.

His aunt turned and took him by the shoulders.

'Michael, I think they're dead,' she said, her voice shaking.

'N ... no,' Michael stuttered, his rage turning to uncertainty. 'They're probably unconscious, look ...'

Glancing around the room, Anna watched as the other Inquisitors placed their hands behind their heads and dropped to their knees in submission. Lefrick rushed forward to check the fallen, quickly moving from one to the next, looking for signs of life. Looking back to Anna, his face pale, he shook his head. Michael's mouth opened and closed a few times as the awful news sank in, but he couldn't speak a word.

'It's alright,' said Anna, trying to comfort him. 'They were going to do the same to us, *all of us,* given half a chance.'

Michael's bottom lip shook and tears streamed down his face. 'B ... but I killed them. I murdered ten of them.'

'This is war, son,' said Andy kneeling beside him so that he could look him in the eye. 'This is what they were training you for at the academy. It's what we've all been training you for. I'm sorry it came so early to you, I really am. But we've all had to do some unpleasant things.'

'It's true,' said Anna. 'Your uncle gave his life to protect us from them, so did Daniel.'

'But I'm a murderer,' Michael sobbed again.

'No,' Andy countered. 'They are casualties of war. They were brave men and women who were sent here to do a job, same as you. Honour them by remembering them.'

Laying a hand on the behemoth's shoulder, Anna said, 'Andy, we've got get moving. Find out how long before their backup arrives would you?'

'Go on now,' said Andy getting to his feet. 'Fetch Mrs Davis and the other medics from the training hall. We've our wounded to tend to.'

'I want to bury them,' Michael snuffled, 'Daniel too. They deserve a funeral, don't they?'

'Yes,' Anna replied. 'We'll do our best with the time we've got.'

Nodding, Michael ran as hard as he could for the training room, trying not to look at the bodies of the dead and injured as he passed. When he returned, Lefrick was with Anna, a mask of deep concern on his face.

'How are you, Michael?' Lefrick ventured.

'As you'd expect,' said Anna. 'Look at him, he's shaken. It's going to take a while before he's fit for any duties. Do you think we should ask Margret to …?'

'No,' said Lerfick cutting across her. 'He's going to have to live with what he's done. It'll make him a better person. He'll be more conscious of his actions next time.'

'A better person?' said Anna. 'He's a child, Hans. He shouldn't have been there in the first place!'

'He's a Grand Inquisitor,' said Lefrick raising a hand in protest. 'You saw what he did. If he can do that with less than half the training Tamara's had, imagine what she's capable of. We're going to need him, Anna, but I don't want another Catchpole on our hands. It's better that he learns compassion now, however bitter the pill is to swallow.'

'Why are you talking about me as if I'm not here?' said Michael.

Anna put one arm around his shoulder and pinched the bridge of her nose with her free hand. 'You're right. I'm sorry, Michael. You have as much right to have your say in this as we do. You know, Andy had a good point. The Inquisition was training you for this, and so were we.'

'I know,' said Lefrick. 'We're turning children into soldiers.'

'The very thing we were arguing against at the last Grand Council,' Anna hissed. 'We're going to get them killed, Hans. Maybe Maya can live with that, but I can't!'

'Then I suggest you look at the faces of the people you were fighting,' said Michael. 'Aside from their group leader, I doubt any of them are more than seventeen or eighteen years old.'

'What?' Anna gasped.

Michael drew a deep, ragged breath. 'While you were worried about the safety of our children, you didn't stop to think who you were fighting, did you?'

She didn't reply.

*** 

'What are we doing back here?' said Sher as she looked around the cave.

Katja skipped down the steps towards the bed that had held her companion captive. 'If you want to undo what father did to you, you need to come here.'

'Do you think I'm going to trust you with that?' Sher cocked her head to one side and glared at her.

'Don't worry,' Katja replied. 'You're not going to be on the bed this time. See that glowing liquid in those globes? That's what we came here for. There will not be enough to put you back the way you were, but it's a start. At least *he* won't have enough when we're through.'

'Who?' Sher quizzed. 'Who won't have enough?'

'Father. Now come on, I want to be away from here when he gets back, or he'll drain us both dry.'

Sher crossed the floor and sat where she was told. Motioning for her to roll up the sleeve of her sweater, Katja inserted a needle into her arm and started the clockwork pump. Soon the blue liquid from the large glass jar began to trickle into the tubing, and Sher shivered as she felt the first few drops enter her bloodstream.

'He's not really your father, is he?' she asked.

'No. And to tell you the truth, I wish Jerrick had killed him. But alas, I am not that fortunate,' said Katja.

'But the Flayers would have finished him off, wouldn't they?' said Sher.

'Not if Jerrick isn't dead, no.' Katja let out a giggle. 'He'll certainly be sore when he gets back, but it's no more than he deserves.'

'I don't understand,' said Sher. 'How could Jerrick have been so wrong about the curse being lifted? It's his magic that did it.'

'That isn't so,' Katja replied with authority. 'The lamp is Jerrick's master. It is *his* curse. Not being entirely alive is not the same as being dead. He knew that all along.' She giggled again. 'Don't you see? He played father like a drum, and after the last time they fought, who can blame him?'

'I think I get it,' said Sher nodding. 'Jerrick lured Nahar into fighting so that he would waste most of his energy. Then he let the Flayers finish the job because the lore of the lamp demands that Jerrick can't kill.'

In her excitement, Katja clapped as though she was praising a child for demonstrating a lesson learned. 'That's right! Father and I have spent decades looking for Jerrick. But after their last fight, he went to ground. We had no idea where he was, or who he was with. When we heard about the fire at the museum in Berlin, we began investigating the Inquisition. Eventually, we learned that the lamp was at their academy ...'

'Until it was stolen back by the Council,' Sher finished. 'That's why you made the deal with Catchpole, isn't it? You went to the academy looking for the lamp. When you found it was missing, you needed an excuse to keep them off your backs while you searched for it.'

Katja beamed again as she added more liquid from another jar to the tank. 'You are clever, in spite of what father says. You are also correct about everything, except Catchpole. I didn't make the deal with him ... I ... made it with their Grand Inquisitor.'

'Tamara?' Sher sputtered, nearly choking on her name. 'I never thought she would turn out to be so vicious.'

'Even the most beautiful flower can be deadly in the wrong hands,' said Katja. She took a small mirror from the next bed and handed it to Sher. 'It's working, look.'

'Tell me about this ... machine. How does it work?' Sher asked as she examined herself in the glass.

'I cannot,' said Katja. 'Father built them a long time ago. He refused to teach me any more than I needed to operate them, the way he refused to teach me the art of sorcery. The only reason he taught me to play the flute was so that I would bring the unwanted for him.'

'Would you really have killed all those people at the barracks?' Sher asked.

Katja studied the floor for a moment, as though she was thinking her answer through.

'I don't think so,' she said at last. 'I've never killed anyone before.'

'But all those Flayers were people once. Unwanted

people,' said Sher. 'You brought them here, didn't you?'

'Yes,' Katja whispered.

For the first time, Sher could see the little girl in the young woman before her. 'You must have known it was wrong, so why didn't you run when you had the chance?'

Katja turned and lifted the hem of her shirt, uncovering a criss-cross of scars that covered her back. 'This is what happens when you run from father. Even at his weakest, when he needed me to hunt for him, he was able to give me these.'

'You're his prisoner, aren't you?' said Sher, reaching out a gentle hand to touch her arm.

'I am his daughter,' said Katja. 'Until a few weeks ago, I hadn't known anything else. Whenever I made a friend, father would punish me. If I was gone too long, he would beat me. And every time he did, I blamed Jerrick. I cursed the Council's name with every stroke, for making him the way he was.' Letting her shirt fall back, she crossed her arms over her chest as if she were hugging herself for comfort. 'If only you could have seen the love in his eyes when he talked about his wife, you would understand. He would talk about his unborn child as though he had planned out every detail, always certain that it would have been a boy. Never once has he looked at me that way. When he called me his daughter it was always with a sneer. Until Harriet found me, and Margaret dressed my wounds, I thought family meant loyalty. I thought love meant obedience.'

'That's why you couldn't bring yourself to kill them, isn't it?' said Sher holding Katja's hand. 'You had friends for the first time. They were loyal to you and you were important to them.'

'I know it doesn't excuse what I've done. It should be me out there with the Flayers, not him.'

'Well, I'm not going to judge you,' said Sher. 'Perhaps I would have ten days ago, but not now. What will you do?'

'Die,' Katja replied. 'I'm not fit for anything else. I've been with him for so long that I don't know this world anymore and it frightens me. I feel old inside. I know I don't look it, but I feel it. It's time for me to stop.'

'What about Nahar? Won't he come looking for you this time?'

'I don't plan on being found,' said Katja pulling a tube from one side of the pump and pushing the needle into her own arm. 'Besides, by the time he's free of them, I'll be long gone. With any luck, it might even take a few months for him to get away. His wounds heal almost instantly, which makes him a near inexhaustible meal for the Flayers.'

Sher's expression changed from pity to concern. 'Where will you go?'

When she turned around, Katja was no longer the young woman that she was used to seeing. Crow's feet lined the corners of her eyes and wrinkles indented her brow.

'I have money,' said Katja. 'It will be enough for food and shelter for a while.'

'You could come with me,' Sher offered. 'I could explain to Jacob about you, and he'd understand, I know he would.'

'That is very kind, but I can't go with you,' said Katja.

She ground the floor with her toe, looking nervous for a moment. 'I do have another favour to ask of you if you don't mind?'

Sher watched as another decade or so showed on Katja's face. She swallowed hard as her hair changed from gold to platinum, reminded that this is what it had looked like when Nahar had drained her own life. 'I don't know that I'm in any position to grant it, but ask me anyway.'

'I ... I need to destroy the flute. But before I do, I need it for one last time,' said Katja.

'I can't let you take it,' said Sher shaking her head. 'The flute's caused so much trouble already. You asked me to bring it so that neither the Council nor the Inquisition could have it, not so that you could take it back.'

'The flute is not evil,' Katja protested. 'It's the person who plays it that is responsible for its effect. It used to bring so much joy before Nahar was corrupted by his thirst for revenge.' Her shoulders sagged when she saw how resolute Sher was on the matter. 'It doesn't matter what I say, you still don't trust me.' Sighing, she picked up the mirror and examined herself. Then, without warning, she struck out with a heavy backhand.

When Sher awoke, the light in the cave was much dimmer, and her face ached. She was aware of the sensations of water and debris around her feet. A feeling of dread crept through her and she patted herself down knowing that Katja had taken the flute and left her. Then a second horrific thought crossed her mind. Her eyes darted towards the table and found the mirror. She lifted it, reluctant to turn it over. When she finally plucked up the courage, the face that looked back at her was her own - young, unblemished and glowing. Except for a thin streak of silver hair that ran from her widow's peak and over the crown of her head, she was herself again.

'Well, that's something,' she said putting the mirror back down on the table. A torch crackled in its sconce behind her, making her ears prick and causing her to jump with fright. Standing, she crunched and splashed over to it and carefully eased the torch from its iron cage. The light cast long shadows behind her as she lowered its burning tip to the ground, trying to make sense of what had happened.

There were shards of shattered glass everywhere, mixed with brass cogs and splinters of wood. The precious life essence had been spilt, and most of it had seeped into cracks in the floor. Only puddles of eerie blue remained, dotted here and there, growing fainter with each passing minute.

It occurred to Sher that Katja could almost certainly have killed her had she wanted to. She'd had plenty of time to do it. So why hadn't she? She hadn't saved her after the accident like Harriet King and definitely hadn't nursed her back to health like Margaret Davis.

'Come on Sher,' she told herself aloud, 'it doesn't matter why she did it, does it? Just get out before either of them comes home!'

Scampering across the cave, she climbed the steps to where the portal had been, thought about Grimm's library and put her hand to the centre coin. It wasn't what she was expecting. From their settings in the face of the rock, the coins began to melt and pool but refused to connect with one another. It gave Sher the impression of a fractured stained glass window. Concentrating as hard as she could, she tried again. But the coins refused to give in. Infuriated with their lack of cooperation, she balled a fist and hammered on the wall.

After several long minutes of puzzling, she pulled herself together and smiled. At least Nahar had been wrong about the portal, even if she didn't know the way back to the Council's compound.

'Besides,' she concluded, 'they've probably evacuated by now, assuming that anyone survived the assault.'

Grimm, like herself, had no mirrors in his rooms, in case of unwanted guests or prying eyes. And she didn't know any of the other librarians well enough to portal to. Puffing her cheeks before letting out a long, slow breath, she came to a decision.

'Old faithful it is then,' she said to nobody in particular. 'I just hope Benny still works there!'

Putting her hand to the centre coin once more, she was ecstatic when it began to shimmer. Stepping into the world beyond, it wasn't long before she found herself with one foot in the bowl of a porcelain sink. The other was skidding on the bench top of the ladies powder room, at number one hundred and eighty-one, Piccadilly, London – otherwise known as Fortnum and Mason.

\*\*\*

In the aftermath of the battle, there was an ordered

panic. The evacuation was unexpected but necessary. Lefrick was busy in communication with the Grand Council and, judging by the shouting match that was going on, Mistress Maya was less than pleased.

While Mrs Davis had been tending to the injured and Anna organised the exodus, Michael had taken it upon himself to sort a burial detail. There had been protests from some of the other Councillors, but Michael would not be convinced. His insistence that a funeral should take place was unshakable. So, with Andy's help, they had gone to the grove, and with a little magical assistance dug thirteen graves. Now that the dead of both sides had been laid to rest, Michael stood in the bleak dawn, looking at the mounds of bare earth.

Something inside him had changed. He felt dirty, as though no amount of bathing would ever wash the blood from his skin. For the first time, he understood the madness of Macbeth. It was eating at him to his core.

'I've buried a lot of friends over the years. It never gets any easier,' said Andy.

'I can't get their faces out of my mind. I see them every time I blink or rub my eyes. But the worst part ... The worst part is knowing that each one of them was just like me. They were someone's son or daughter. They had their whole lives ahead of them and I took that away.'

The doorman pursed his lips and nodded.

'I wish I could tell you it isn't true, Michael. I also wish I could tell you that you'll forget their faces one day. But they'll stay with you forever most likely. I know mine do.'

'I never thought ...' Michael muttered.

'What, that I'd killed anyone?' Andy finished for him. 'Good heavens, Michael, I didn't think you were still that naive. This is what war is, son, and they're the enemy.' He sighed and watched as his breath hung in the cold dawn air. 'You really think you hate them, whoever you're fighting until you've seen them dead. Then you realise that each one was just a person, like you.'

'Then why do we keep doing it?'

Andy's brow furrowed with concern when he saw the look in Michael's eyes. 'Because at some point you get fed up of them trying to kill you first,' he said, gesticulating like a lunatic. 'But if you count those graves again you'll still get thirteen - the three they killed defending themselves from us, and the ten you killed defending us from them. And no matter how you look at it, dead is still dead. You're a Guardian now. Did you think it was just about running around saving the day and being a hero? Well, let me tell you, sometimes the hero is the one with the most blood on his hands.'

Michael opened and closed his mouth like a goldfish, unsure of what to say next. He'd never seen Andy so distraught. 'But Jerrick ...'

'Jerrick didn't have a clue,' said Andy. 'He was in that lamp before any of this happened. People have killed *because* of Jerrick, whether it was to protect him or to get to him. But Jerrick's never actually killed anyone himself that I know of because he can't. What do you think we're for? What do think Inquisitors are for, for that matter? You're a soldier at war, Michael, a grunt like the rest of us. Generals like Maya and your girlfriend call the shots, but we're the ones that have to bear the scars.'

'I can still feel them with me,' Michael sniffed, his shoulders beginning to quake. 'Have you ever borrowed energy from someone else?'

'Not the way you do,' Andy admitted.

'It's like a piece of them inside you. It's so personal - like you can almost get an idea of who they are ... or were,' said Michael struggling to hold himself together as he described it.

The doorman waved a massive finger at him saying, 'Now don't you go thinking that you knew those people. They would have been happy to trade places with you I'd wager, every last one of 'em.'

'It's not just that,' Michael croaked. 'It's my fault Daniel's dead, isn't it? If he hadn't come with us ...'

'He wouldn't have been doing his job,' Andy continued. 'I don't mean to be hard on you, but what's done is done and can't be undone, not even by Jerrick. Sooner or later you're going to have to start living with yourself. If you don't, you'll never survive this. I'm not saying I'm proud of what you did. But no-one could blame you for doing it, not even their Grand Inquisitor.'

The events of the previous night welled up in Michael's chest all at once. As he broke down, the horror of seeing Daniel skewered, and his terror over the deaths he had caused spilled out of him.

'She'll never forgive me for what I've done,' he cried, burying his face in Andy's side. 'I don't want to bury Tam! We have to make it stop, Andy ... Please help me!'

'We're trying,' said the doorman as he patted Michael's

back with a giant paw. 'You, me, Anna; we're all trying to make it stop. I can't promise that you won't have to feel this way again. And I'm sure there'll be many more funerals before it's over. But we'll make it stop, I *can* promise you that.'

As daylight began to chase the shadows out of the grove, Andy gestured with his other hand and sang a soft lamentation for the departed. Slowly, the soil on the grave-tops began to shift and stir as shoots of green sprouted and grew, eventually bursting into a riot of colourful meadow flowers.

'Go in peace,' he said at last, bowing his head with respect to the fallen.

# Chapter Fifteen:
# Six of One ...

Tamara put down the phone's receiver and slumped into her office chair, swinging it around so that she could stare out of the window at the post-Christmas gloom. The Council's sortie had caused a great deal of alarm around the academy, especially as Catchpole had ended the night in the infirmary.

Concerned for her safety, Niven had concocted some half-baked story about why she wouldn't be able to go home. He'd also been kind enough to do the same for Emily and Rupert. It rattled Tamara. She felt cheated out of her holidays and guilty for having cheated her friends out of theirs. How dare he call her parents without her permission? She knew who had put him up to it of course. Niven never acted on anything without the approval of the Marshalls.

There was a knock at the office door as Catchpole sloped into the room. His hands were bandaged and he was missing his eyebrows, but he appeared to be genuinely happy for a change.

'Great news,' he said waving a newspaper in front of him. 'Officially, Adam Dakin, last seen with his college girlfriend, has disappeared and is believed to be armed and dangerous!'

Tamara didn't turn to look at him. Instead, she just eyed his reflection in the window with suspicion and said, 'How is that good news, Mr Catchpole? The Wares must be heartbroken.'

'As Dakin is one of their former students,' the Magister read aloud, 'the Braxton Foundation is only too eager to assure the family of the missing woman, Alice Ware, that they will do everything in their power to help return their daughter to them. The public is urged ... and so on and so forth.'

'Again, how is that good news?' said Tamara. 'It only gives the impression that the foundation is feeling guilty about something.'

Catchpole perched himself on the edge of her desk and tutted at her. 'Oh, you're always such a pessimist, Miss Bloodgood. The bright side is that we have a spy deep inside the enemy camp at last.'

'It won't work. I don't think they'll be so trusting again, not after the Piper.'

'You might be right,' Catchpole replied as he neatened up a bit of stray bandage. 'But we can hope, can't we? I mean, this whole situation with Dakin could work in our favour elsewhere. What if the foundation just happened to discover that he and Miss Ware have run away to join the dreaded Council?'

'That's going a bit far,' said Tamara. 'Nobody would believe that either of them would join a terrorist organisation. If that's the angle you're still going for.'

'Yes. I can imagine the soundbites on the news: "But he was always so quiet and polite, and she kept herself to herself". They've never said that about anyone before, have they? A person might be bright enough to think for themselves, Tamara, but people? People are sheep. They'll believe anything you tell them, especially if it's about the corruption of our promising youth.'

Tamara snorted at his animated quotes. For once, his hands really looked like slightly shabby bunny ears.

'Next you'll be telling them that the Council eats their young and sacrifices animals in the buff on moonlit nights,' she said, hoping that he would pick up on the note of sarcasm in her voice.

'Why not? It's worked before.' Catching Tamara's reflection in the glass, Catchpole's eyes narrowed. 'You're opinions of the Council haven't changed since Michael was here, have they?'

'Not one bit, Mr Catchpole. If anything, I'm more determined than ever to bring them down. They sent him to kill me. That thing inside him admitted it.'

'So I've heard,' said Catchpole. 'If it's any consolation, I think he would have succeeded if it hadn't been for me. After all, look what he did.' He held up his hands. 'It should be obvious by now, that if he could do this to me, he could have done it to anyone.'

'I appreciate your candour,' said Tamara turning to face him. 'But I refuse to believe that he was acting on his own judgement.'

The Magister's expression was as blank as fresh canvas. 'If Michael loved you, you'd have known it by now. If he still had any respect for his friends, he would have shown it somehow. I'm afraid that the Michael Ware we knew is gone. He's with *them* now, and they'll use your feelings for him against us if you let them.'

'Is that why you didn't tell me that you saw him at the

342

library?'

'Yes, I thought it best not to upset you.' Catchpole's crocodile smile oozed across his lips. 'I gave him enough opportunity to solicit my help. If he had still been the young man I knew, I'm sure he would have asked for it. But he didn't. I thought it best to let you continue to believe he was dead. If that was wrong of me, I apologise.'

'I suppose not. Not now,' Tamara sighed.

'Good,' said Catchpole. He rose and turned his back on her, pretending to examine a painting. It was a portrait of a man with a pallid complexion, and a fierce nose that beset his steely-grey, sunken eyes. 'The Marshalls have asked me to convey a message. I'm afraid you're not going to like it very much.'

'Oh?' said Tamara.

Buffing the plaque beneath the painting with his sleeve, Catchpole said, 'They feel that your advisors have let you down. They want you to make an example of one of them.'

'What? Which one?' Tamara exclaimed.

'They've left it up to you to decide, and I would do so quickly if I were you. If you refuse, the Marshall's will punish *you* in addition to an advisor of their choosing.'

'But why?' said Tamara. 'We haven't done anything wrong!'

'Ten dead and twenty more unaccounted for,' said Catchpole. 'The Flute of Shattered Dreams has been lost. And don't get me started on the incursion into your own stronghold, where you allowed one potentially valuable asset to be kidnapped and another to defect. I doubt the "I'm only fifteen" act is going to wash with them this time.

They want proof that you're taking your responsibilities seriously.'

'Fine, they can punish me,' Tamara retorted. 'But I won't let them punish my friends!'

'You know, you really are thick sometimes,' said Catchpole pinching the bridge of his nose with apparent despair. 'When I say they're going to punish you, I don't mean detention, girl! The severity of your punishment will fit your rank. Now, as they can't unmake you a Grand Inquisitor, it leaves them two options: either to go after your friends or to go after your family. Which do you think would make you more compliant?'

Tamara's eyes widened with terror. 'They wouldn't dare go after my family, would they?'

'Yes, if they thought it would make you consider your actions more closely. Their patience ran thin with Renfrew here,' said Catchpole tapping the painting. 'They want to see commitment and leadership, a willingness to sacrifice everything for the greater good. They don't want excuses, and they certainly won't tolerate any more mistakes.'

'But why do I have to punish one of my friends?' Tamara pressed.

'It's a gesture,' said Catchpole. 'Your advisors have as much influence over your actions as you do. That is their job. The Marshalls feel it would be an appropriate demonstration that you can both follow orders, and give them when it matters most. Otherwise, you're useless to them.'

'Then I choose you, Mr Catchpole,' said Tamara.

Catchpole bared his clenched teeth and sucked a breath

through them. 'It's not that I wouldn't be honoured to serve,' he said without a trace of humility. 'It's just that I'm not officially one of your advisors. It's a fact that you have pointed out to me on several occasions.'

'So it's Emily, Rupert or Clarissa?' Tamara spat. 'And what punishment would the Marshalls feel appropriate?'

'Death's a bit severe, given that we don't want to lose anyone else ... And as we don't flog people anymore ...'

'What about imprisonment, or exile?' Tamara interjected, her blood beginning to run cold.

'No,' said Catchpole shaking his head. 'Imprisonment's not public enough. And exile would risk losing more talent to the Council. It's got to be something people would remember; something that would cement your authority whilst declaring your obedience.' He paused for a moment, then he smiled and tapped Renfrew's portrait again, this time on its ill-proportioned nose. 'Of course, there's always Renfrew's favourite - the crate. A few minutes in one of those should be sufficient. And I'm sure there wouldn't be any lasting damage.'

'That's horrible!' Tamara gasped, shivering at her own memory of the device, which had been used on her during the trials.

The crate was a large wooden affair the size of a coffin. Sandwiched between its boards were slabs of metal designed to absorb any of the victim's mental or magical efforts. Iron shackles were bolted to its walls and floor, and a heavy iron mask hung on a chain from its ceiling. All of which were clamped into place with heavy bolts. The bindings were connected by thick cables that came together into one at the rear of the box. It was then plugged into a metronome which was connected to a supply of electricity. On every tenth stroke of the pendulum, an electrical pulse would be discharged along the wires and into the metal restraints, shocking the prisoner. The cycle would then begin again, increasing in severity each time until the victim was unconscious, or worse.

Tamara rubbed at her wrists, where the heated metal had burnt her skin years before. 'How long do I have to decide?'

'Within the week,' Catchpole intoned. 'Though I would suggest that the actual punishment should coincide with the arrival of the other Grand Inquisitors, for maximum effect.'

'What other Grand Inquisitors?'

'The ones you're going to call to conclave,' said Catchpole, wincing with pain when he tried to steeple his fingers. 'Nothing says "I can do it" better than ordering a cull of the Elder Council.'

\*\*\*

Michael stared through fog at the unfolding scene, his fists pressed up against the glass of the mirror he was trapped behind. In addition to Jerrick and Tamara, he could see Adam standing next to a window, knife pressed against Rupert's throat. As the room came more sharply into focus, Michael realised that he recognised it. It was Davis's old study at the academy. Looking around, he

346

noticed Emily just inside the doorway, surrounded by Inquisitors. The indistinct faces of her entourage were barely visible beneath their hoods.

'I can assure you that we did not trick Michael into coming with us at all. In fact, if you hadn't brought Alice here, he would still have come soon enough,' said Jerrick.

'Who was he supposed to kill? Was it me? Was it Catchpole? I demand to know. TELL ME!' Tamara yelled.

His eyes glinting, the genie's reply was filled with malice. 'All of you!'

'He'd never try to kill us,' said Tamara. She turned to look into the mirror, her eyes filled with tears. 'You'd never do that to us, would you Michael?'

Michael tried to reply, but the words stuck in the sandpaper of his throat. Jerrick turned and winked at him, as though they were sharing some private joke. Then he turned back to Tamara, tipped his head back and laughed so hard that the whole room shook.

Raising his hand, he gestured towards the door. 'Why don't you ask them?'

Tamara rose from the sofa she'd been sitting on and strode across the room shouting, 'Go on; tell him he's wrong. Tell him!'

In reply, the Inquisitors raised their arms, the blood-damp sleeves of their robes covering accusatory fingers.

With one voice they chanted: 'Murderer.'

'No!' Tamara screamed.

'Murderer! Murderer!'

Michael hammered on the glass again, aware now that Flayers had gathered behind him. Drawn by the shouting and the smell of him, they eyed Michael hungrily. He turned to face them, bracing himself for the attack. But instead of pouncing, they too joined in with the chanting of the Inquisitors.

'I'll never forgive you, Michael Ware,' Tamara whispered over his shoulder. 'I'll never forgive you for killing me.'

'Wait!' Michael shouted over the din and sat bolt upright in his bed, almost causing the metal frame of the cot to collapse beneath him. The fluorescent bulb of the lamp flickered behind its mesh shade as another train rumbled by in the distance.

The evacuation hadn't quite gone to plan after the battle. With nothing more permanent available, Maya had insisted that they fall back to a disused underground station. Now, beneath the streets of London, Michael and his friends felt more like rats than people. It was only temporary, but it wasn't comfortable.

The room that he now occupied was little more than a cell hewn into the wall. In it were a green canvas camp bed and a simple wooden stool with three legs which was stacked with his books. There was barely enough room for much else. All of the other rooms were the same, with a few variations, such as an extra bed instead of the stool for married couples. Anna had described it as a bolt-hole for wayward travellers – a stopover for members of the Council moving from one location to the next. Most cities had them in one form or another, so he was told. They were designed to keep Council members off the streets and away from prying eyes. Michael hated it. It was a musty, airless pit, with no natural light, except at the bottom of the stairwell that led to the outside. Where the walls still stood untouched, they were covered in white ceramic tiles. Though they were clinically unattractive, at least they reflected the illuminations of the strip-lights that hung from metal poles in the arched ceiling.

Thankfully, there were no tracks ever laid at the station. When the original plans had been drawn up, nobody had expected a campaign in favour of the old Victorian sewer system that crossed the end of the tunnel. Unfortunately, this now meant that Michael could hear the squealing of carriage brakes through the wall some twenty meters behind him. All in all, the whole situation had made for a miserable Christmas.

Michael reached for the pocket watch that Alice had given him years before. His fight with Catchpole had left the glass cracked, but it still worked well enough. Groaning at the unreasonable hour, he slumped back onto the hard pillow and closed his eyes. There was a knock on his door, followed by Harriet's voice.

'Come in,' Michael called back.

When the door opened, Harriet was standing there in a black and white chequered onesie and fluffy white rabbit slippers, her blonde hair tied back in a loose ponytail.

'You okay? Only I could hear you shouting through the wall again.'

Michael propped himself up on his elbow and looked at her. 'It was just another nightmare,' he said, trying to sound casual. 'Sorry, I hope I didn't wake you?'

'That's the third time this week,' said Harriet. Closing

the door behind her, she sat on the edge of his bed. 'You're dreaming about them aren't you?'

'Most of the time it's about them, yes,' Michael confessed. 'The rest of the time it's about Tamara, Emily and Rupert. It makes me feel sick to think they might believe I could have hurt them.'

'I don't know what to say,' said Harriet. 'If I were Tamara, I'd probably be wondering whether you could have as well I suppose. You are on opposite sides after all.'

Michael grunted his agreement, and said, 'I've been thinking about that too. Now that they know I'm alive, I wouldn't be surprised if the Marshalls asked her to do the same to me.' He pulled himself up to lean against the wall.

'It's funny, isn't it?' said Harriet.

'Hilarious.'

'Behave,' said Harriet. She poked her tongue out at him and blew a raspberry. 'What I meant was: it's funny that you're both thinking the same thing about each other. You're both stuck in the middle of this bloody war that's not your fault, just because of what day you were born on.'

'It is kind of stupid,' Michael replied.

Harriet shuffled up so that she could lean against the wall next to him.

'It's downright ridiculous.' She paused, looking him in the eye for a moment. 'So why *are* you here?'

'Because they were going to kill her,' said Michael.

'That's just arrogant,' said Harriet. 'Do you think you would have beaten her in a fair fight? From what I heard, she had you pegged, even before Davis slipped you that water.'

'Did he really tell you that?' Michael asked.

'No, Margaret did,' Harriet giggled. 'They always argue about who would have won. Margaret thinks Tamara's the stronger Psych, and the only reason Lefrick pulled you out is because of your aunt.'

'Oh, great,' Michael huffed.

'It's okay,' said Harriet laughing at his dejected expression. 'Roger's on your side. He says that with your other talents, you could have finished it in the first round if you hadn't been soft on her.'

Michael stared at the rough green blanket that still covered his legs. 'Did they tell you that the seers saw the outcome? Did they tell you that I left because I wanted to save her?'

'No,' Harriet admitted. 'And I don't know what would have happened if you'd chosen to stay. But I am sure that Tamara can look after herself.'

'Really,' Michael snapped, but he was hushed by Harriet's finger on his lips.

'The trouble with you, Michael Ware, is that you think we're all damsels in distress and that you have to save us all. That's why you went after Alice and nearly got yourself killed.'

'But ...'

'And that's why you insisted on taking Katja down into the bunker, instead of leaving her at the farmhouse!' Harriet finished.

Michael gently took her hand away from his mouth. 'That was different. I couldn't have left her in the road any more than I could have left you on my balcony that night.'

'That's what I mean,' said Harriet. 'You had no reason to let me stay the night. I didn't need rescuing, and neither did Katja.

'As for Alice,' Michael continued, 'family's family. Alice doesn't have any talents. What good would she have been against someone like Catchpole? He would have used her to draw me out. He practically said so at the academy. He wanted me to go back to the Inquisition.'

'Which brings us back to my original question,' said Harriet. 'Why are you still here? Do you even hate the Inquisition all that much?'

Michael looked down, noticing that he was still holding her hand. 'Yes. No ... I don't know. I should. They killed my uncle. Catchpole was torturing my sister for information on me. They're using the people I care about against us. They even put us through hell at the trials.'

'But they didn't ask you to kill anyone, did they?' said Harriet clasping her other hand over his. 'If you ask me, it's six of one and half a dozen of the other.'

'Well, I'm in it up to my neck now anyway,' Michael replied as he rapped the back of his head on the wall. 'With everything that's happened, I might as well be public enemy number one. I'm just glad that Davis is looking after Alice. I don't think I could explain it all to her right now.'

'Are you worried about what she might think about ... you know.'

'A little,' said Michael. 'I don't know if I can look her in the eye. I don't think she'd understand.'

'You'd be surprised,' said Harriet. 'When I killed Craig Hathaway, I felt the same way.'

'And now?' said Michael.

'I still do. But the Davises helped me to understand that it was an accident,' said Harriet. 'I didn't mean to kill Craig any more than I think you meant to kill those Inquisitors. It just happened. And I don't think people are going to judge you the way that they judged me.'

Michael looked into her eyes and realised why Harriet had needed his forgiveness so badly.

'I'm sorry, Harriet,' he said, meaning it more than he'd ever thought possible.

'You dope,' said Harriet putting her arms around him. 'I didn't mean you.'

When she let go, their cheeks brushed. There was a sharp intake of breath from them both, and for a moment they paused, each unsure of what was passing between them. Harriet leaned forward and put her forehead against his. Suddenly, Sam burst into the room.

'Michael, your aunt left a note. Oh ... Um ... sorry ... I'll come back later,' he said, quickly covering his eyes with the letter.

Her face a bright shade of cerise, Harriet clamped her eyes shut with embarrassment, and said, 'It's okay Sam. We were just um ...'

'Messing around,' said Michael, moving her aside. 'Anna left a note you say?'

Sam glanced between the two of them, finding enough voice to say, 'Yeah. That is ... yes. She says she's running an errand and not to worry. She'll be back by your birthday.'

'Did she say where she was going?' Michael asked.

'Nope, that's all she wrote: gone away, back soon,' said

Sam, who was still looking at Harriet.

'Okay ... thanks, mate,' said Michael trying to catch his attention.

'What?' said Harriet.

'Nothing, honest,' said Sam grinning as he turned to leave. 'I've just never seen anyone in a onesie and bunny slippers before. Very stylish, I'm sure.'

Once he was out of sight, Harriet turned back to her host. 'Michael I ...'

'Got caught up in the moment? Don't worry about it. Nothing happened. There's no need to be embarrassed. Come on, let's get some breakfast.'

Slipping past him, Harriet stopped at the door and said, 'I think I'd better change first.'

'Thanks, H. I'm glad you're here,' said Michael, taking her hand before she was too far out of his reach.


He didn't have a chance to finish his breakfast. Lefrick had come to escort him to the mirror room as demanded by Maya. When they got there, a table and two chairs were already in place in front of the large single pane of glass set into the wall.

Without saying a word, Lefrick drew out a chair and motioned for Michael to sit, before taking a seat beside him and gesturing at the mirror. As usual the glass shimmered and swam, but instead of settling to reveal an image, the mirror turned black.

'What's going on?' Michael asked feeling anxious.

'Just wait,' said Lefrick.

It felt like an age before the blackness rippled and the

cover of the mirror beyond was lifted. On the other side, Michael could see a curved oak desk, lit from behind in an otherwise darkened room, with seven white-robed figures seated at it. Nearly all of them were hooded, and shadows obscured their faces, except for one. Mistress Maya sat at the centre of the group, conspicuous by her lack of disguise.

'Lefrick. Ware,' she said nodding to them.

'Michael,' said Michael.

'Excuse me?' said Maya.

'My name is Michael. Or you can call me *Mister* Ware if you'd prefer. I am a Guardian after all, which means you might as well treat me like an adult.'

There was a muttering from the others and Maya snorted loudly at his insolence. 'It's lucky for you that I am in an amiable mood this morning, Michael. I wouldn't normally tolerate that kind of rudeness. But you have struck a blow for us, and I am willing to be lenient on this occasion.'

'What blow?' said Michael. 'You mean killing ten Inquisitors that weren't much older than I am?'

'Yes, and enabling us to capture twenty more,' said Maya. 'Their information has been quite useful so far.'

Michael had been so caught up in his feelings about the dead that he'd forgotten about the living. Just knowing that they were alive gave him a small measure of comfort.

'Is that why you brought me here, to congratulate me?'

'Not quite,' said Maya, her cheerful demeanour a little more forced. 'We wanted to ask you how you managed it.'

Michael looked at Lefrick, but the master's expression

remained blank. 'I don't know. I was just messing around with something that I learned at the academy.'

Leaning forward on the desk so that her face seemed more sinister in the shade, Maya said, 'Just tell us what happened then. I'm sure we can figure it out together, once we know how it all came about.'

'Well, you know when you borrow energy from someone?' said Michael trying to organise his thoughts. 'I was told by my old mentor at the academy, that you shouldn't use a person's energy against them because it can cause feedback or something.'

The hooded Elders began to mutter again. Maya held up a hand to silence them.

'Go on.'

'The Inquisitors had blocks up around themselves the same as we did, so I couldn't attack over the top of them,' said Michael.

The owner of the hood to Maya's left whispered something in her ear and she nodded.

'But if you couldn't attack over the top of their shields, how did you manage to borrow from them?'

'Because borrowing isn't the same as attacking,' said Michael. 'I'm surprised you didn't know that.'

'There are a great many things that we still don't know about the Inquisition, Michael,' said Maya. She smiled. It wasn't pleasant. 'Even after all these centuries, we're still learning some of the finer details about how they fight.

'It's not a skill we've bothered to learn,' said Lefrick. 'Because we don't need to borrow energy like they do, it just wasn't useful to us.'

'Until now,' said Maya. 'It's a weakness in their defences that could turn the tide of the war in our favour. If we can learn how to exploit it that is. So, you borrowed energy from them. How did you use it against them?'

'First I tried to borrow from more than one person at the same time,' said Michael beginning to feel uncomfortable. 'But the more people I borrowed from, the heavier the energy felt.'

There was a great deal of muttering this time, even from Maya.

'Just how many of them did you borrow from?' asked Lefrick.

'All of them,' said Michael.

'All ten at the same time?' Maya pressed.

'Yes. Is there something strange about that?' Michael asked.

'Michael,' said Lefrick, 'we might not know everything about them, but we do know that even the most skilled Inquisitors can only borrow from two, maybe three at a time. Up to now, it's always been a part of our strategy to separate groups in a fight, so that they can't power each other.'

'I didn't really borrow it exactly,' said Michael as he tried his best to describe what he'd done in detail. 'I sort of bundled their energy up in a ball above their heads. Then it got too heavy for me to hold and I had to let it go. When it hit the floor it exploded and ... killed them.'

'Lefrick tells me that they died almost instantly,' said Maya.

'Could be,' Michael said. 'I don't know. I didn't check

their bodies, I just buried them.'

The farthest hood to the right bowed, and a man's voice said, 'It was very gracious of you.'

'Could you do it again?' said Maya.

'Why would I want to do that?' Michael gasped, taken aback by her request.

'Because it's a weapon we can use,' said Maya in slow, deliberate tones.

'No,' said Michael, his reply as deliberate as his superior's.

There were more mutters from the Grand Councillors, and a brief pause for consideration before the man on the right said, 'We understand your concern, Michael, and we sympathise with your feelings on this. But perhaps you'd be able to teach someone more … willing to accept the responsibility?'

'There isn't anyone else who can,' said Michael. 'Like Master Lefrick said, you've never heard of anyone that can borrow from that many people before. So how could I teach it to someone else, even if I wanted to?'

'There are no other *Inquisitors* that we know of,' said the man. 'But there might be others in the Council who could learn from you.'

'Don't you understand what's at stake?' said Maya rising from her seat. She rounded the table and approached the mirror. 'I won't debate this with you, Michael. You have a duty to do this for us. Now, I suggest you go and speak with Lefrick and get your priorities straight.'

There was a rustling and the mirror darkened once more. Michael was about to speak, but Lefrick held up his hand as a stream of vulgar insults was directed at them both from behind the curtain. Then the glass reflected the room again. Heaving a sigh of relief, the master rubbed at his forehead.

'What has she got against me?' said Michael.

'She doesn't trust you,' said Lefrick. 'They still only see the Inquisitor. They don't see the man you're becoming. But they need you now. You have something they want.'

'Figures,' Michael spat. 'All people seem to want me for is to get what they can out of me.'

'Not everyone's like that,' Lefrick laughed.

'Catchpole was,' said Michael, 'and so is she.'

The Elder opened the door and stared out into the tunnel, watching their little world go by. People were going about their business as usual. Mrs Lucas and Andy were apologising constantly for tripping over one another in the narrow kitchen. The Davises were at breakfast together, which was a rare sight, and children were enjoying the last days of their holidays. As much as nomadic life had changed over the centuries, there was still a lot that was the same. No matter where they were, no matter what was on the horizon, life went on.

Reaching into the pocket of the coat he seemed to live in these days, Lefrick produced the lamp. 'He'd want you to have this.'

'What am I supposed to do with it?' Michael asked.

'Just keep it safe. And for all our sakes, don't let Maya anywhere near it. When Jerrick's ready to come back, he'll let you know. That's if there's anything left for him to come back to of course.'

'What do you mean?' said Michael joining him at the door and taking the lamp. Tilting it this way and that, he watched as the light glinted on its intricately engraved patterns.

'I'll just say that I'm not so sure it's only the Inquisition we need to worry about,' said Lefrick. 'With the cull coming and the Council broken, we'll be lucky to see out the next year.'

*∗∗∗*

Things weren't going so well at the academy either. Tamara and Emily sat opposite Miss Cunningham and Rupert in the Solaris guest lounge. The damage to the West end of the ground floor was considerable, but most of the house remained largely untouched.

'I don't know what to do,' said Tamara as she stared at the photograph of Michael above the fireplace. 'I don't care what Catchpole says, he didn't know that Michael and I were going to run after the trials. I don't believe he would have tried to kill any of us.'

'Then why did he come?' said Rupert.

'For Alice,' replied Tamara. 'I don't know how he knew that she was here, but my guess is that he thought Catchpole was going to try to use her. I should never have brought her here, or Adam.'

'Shouldn't we get a message to Mr and Mrs Ware?' said Emily.

'And say what?' Miss Cunningham frowned. 'No, I think it would be best if we stayed well away. We've caused them enough heartbreak already.'

They sat in awkward silence, unwilling to address the elephant in the room. Rupert and Emily stared at one another across the table, speaking with their eyes. Meanwhile, Tamara went back to staring at the memorial plaque on the wall.

'I still think it should be me,' said Rupert. 'I'm strong, I can take it. Besides, a gentleman wouldn't let you choose Emily or Miss Cunningham.'

Emily tutted and rolled her eyes. 'You're not going to start that again are you? I hate it when you try to be all chivalrous. It makes me feel like you don't care what I think.'

'I appreciate what you're trying to do, really I do. But it's not helping,' said Tamara. 'I have to choose one of the three of you and, to be brutally honest, I think Rupert's right.'

'You do?' the others chorused.

'Yes,' said Tamara. 'It should be someone strong; someone who can take that sort of punishment. I need someone I can count on to not blame me for being forced to choose, and who will keep supporting me afterwards.'

'Great,' said Rupert. 'That's settled then. When do you want me?'

'I don't,' said Tamara looking to her former mentor. 'I want you, Miss Cunningham.'

'But ...' Rupert sputtered.

'My mind's made up,' Tamara interrupted over his protests. 'Clarissa, would you do this for me?'

'It would be my honour,' said Miss Cunningham.

\*\*\*

In the room below Solaris's dining hall, Catchpole opened his eyes and smiled broadly, feeling unusually pleased with himself. Everything seemed to be going according to plan for once. Strictly speaking, the Marshalls hadn't called for anyone to be punished. Catchpole had taken it upon himself to suggest it, as a way of building Tamara's reputation for the coming assembly. After all, if she were seen to be weak it could put everything in jeopardy.

Then there was the matter of Adam and Alice. Catchpole was positively bubbling with excitement that his efforts had been so richly rewarded. The Council had had people inside the academy for so long that he'd been wondering how the Inquisition was still functioning. It was about time the tables were turned. And now, not only did the Inquisition have someone inside the Council, but Catchpole could claim both the credit and control over his source. He sniggered with boyish delight as he imagined the look on Lady Shaw's face when she first heard the news.

Pulling a pile of invitation replies towards him, he began to sort them into groups. First, there were the Grand Inquisitors that he knew would support him. Then there were those he knew would be opposed. Finally, there were those he didn't know and needed to research further. He checked the names in his ledger with glee, making the appropriate marks like some psychotic Santa Clause.

Finishing off his work and settling back into his chair, he considered his last obstacle. He was still unconvinced by Tamara's belief in Michael's motives. It was one of those irritating problems that got under Catchpole's skin. Short of a miracle, Michael wouldn't be returning to the academy again anytime soon. Indeed, now that they had left the farm, it could be months before any reports of their whereabouts came in. Even then, it was possible that his source would be discovered before the information could be sent. Unfortunately, this particular problem required a more immediate solution. He considered it for a moment. Tamara was much more suited to his needs before she'd found out that Michael was alive. She had even turned on her best friend in quite spectacular fashion.

'She really did hate the Council when she thought they had killed him. If only there was a way to bring that back?' he mused as the beginnings of a fresh plan began to hatch.

As a Magister, he was used to being able to extract information from even the most trained mind. But to implant an idea or change a feeling was beyond his abilities. He mulled the problem over in his mind for a moment. There was no way that Michael could be reached before the cull, and killing him was out of the question. So too was any thought of lying to Tamara again. It hadn't worked the first time.

'I need her ice cold and steely, but still able to function,' he said and chewed on his lip a while. 'Clubbing her over the head's too risky, and I'm not guaranteed the result I want. Fake assassination attempt ...? No, Emily would see that coming a mile away. If only I could get those rose tinted spectacles from her eyes and make her see things my way.'

He pushed his chair back and walked into the training hall, crossing the stone floor to the trophy room. Inside, glass cabinets lined the walls, lit from within by small round lamps. On their shelves were artefacts that had been amassed through many centuries of work. Amongst them was a poisoned needle from a spinning wheel, which Catchpole duly dismissed as inappropriate for the time being. In another of the cabinets, there was a pot with a ladle, traces of porridge still stuck to its rim. Though it wasn't exactly a weapon, it had once caused quite a stir when it had been set cooking as a prank in eighteen-hundred and ten. On the shelf beneath it, however, was a small deerskin vessel sealed with wax.

Catchpole grinned. Opening the case, he reached in and took the jar, along with a cardboard tag that read:

**Description:** *Andersen, H.C; Mirror Dust.*
**Date of Origin:** *Unknown.*
**Warning:** *Avoid contact with eyes. Do not inhale.*

When he shook the vessel, the tinkling of sleigh bells filled the quiet of the room. Satisfied that he'd found the right tool for the job, he slipped the jar into his pocket. On the short walk back to his study, he remembered a conversation that he'd had with Renfrew many years before.

The then future Grand Inquisitor had been bragging about breaking into the trophy room at their old school. In his gloating, he had mentioned the deerskin jar that rang when you shook it. But it wasn't the boasting that had caught Catchpole's attention. Renfrew had been prone to blowing his own trumpet ever since they'd met. It was the way that he had seemed to change that puzzled the young Magister. Renfrew grew more callous and driven with each day that followed. He was suspicious of his friends and devoid of his former humour. When the first academies began to open, and their trophy collections were relocated, Renfrew had insisted that the jar was kept in his care. It wasn't until his death that anyone remembered that he'd had it. And in the absence of a will, it was bequeathed to Cheritton Hall.

There was a spring in Catchpole's step now. Not usually given to tuneful humming, he was surprised to find that there was music on his lips. Of course, he was disappointed that the flute was lost and annoyed that some of his Inquisitors had been captured. But not even the casualties of war could subdue his present mood. If his hands had allowed, he'd have patted himself on the back to congratulate himself for his ability to turn straw into gold. Tamara was about to put her most trusted advisor in his care and, with a little ingenuity, his plans would be set in motion once and for all. Throwing his study door wide, he broke into song.

'London's burning, London's burning. Tum-ti tum-ti, tum-ti tum-ti. Fire, fire! Fire, fire ...!'

# Chapter Sixteen:
# Double Bluff

It was New Year's Eve. In the grand main hall of the academy, preparations were underway for those staff and students that had remained to celebrate. In the Solaris training hall, however, preparations of a different kind were taking place.

When the trials had been held, bleachers had been constructed at the copper inlaid edges of the floor to form an arena. On this occasion, three-tiered rows of red leather seats, each with its own oak note table, had been erected in a horseshoe shape inside the metal bounds. At the head of the horseshoe, where all eyes would be firmly fixed, was a platform with an ornately carved table, and three thrones that Tamara was familiar with.

'Is Lady Shaw going to be sitting up there with us?' she said to Catchpole.

'Yes, but She's going to be representing the Marshalls. Don't worry, she's not here to judge you this time.'

'Oh good,' said Tamara, relieved by the news. 'But I thought only Grand Inquisitors were allowed inside the conclave.'

Catchpole gave a perfunctory laugh. 'Lady Shaw, as emissary to the Marshalls, will act as speaker of the house. Her job is to keep everyone in check. And she'll make sure nobody speaks out of turn and behaves and such. I will act as the recorder. My job is to make sure that everything that's said is taken down on paper, for the record. I'm not actually allowed to speak unless instructed to do so.'

'That's convenient,' said Tamara, blanching as she realised she'd said it aloud.

'I don't know what you mean, ma'am,' said Catchpole.

'I mean that, for a Magister, you seem to be able to go wherever you please. Even if it's a closed session for particular ranks only,' she replied sharply. 'I'd almost bet that you could get into the Marshalls' private meetings if you tried.'

'What makes you think I haven't?'

She turned to look at him. 'You can't be serious?'

Crocodiles bare fewer teeth than Catchpole when they smile. He winked at her, causing his scar to wrinkle unpleasantly.

'There are some things that I'm not allowed to discuss, Miss Bloodgood, even with my Grand Inquisitor. What I can tell you, is that sometimes being a Magister has its privileges.'

'I wish I'd had more time to prepare for this. There are some points in this folder you gave me that I really don't agree with,' said Tamara following him up the steps at the edge of the platform and taking her seat in the centre throne.

There were three heavy thumps on the hall's closed doors.

'It's too late to argue them out now,' said Catchpole. 'Here they come.'

He nodded to the two Inquisitorial guards at the entrance, their black armour polished to a high sheen. With great ceremony, they swung the heavy wooden doors

367

inwards. At the head of the procession was Lady Shaw, a red velvet cloak draped from the shoulders of her usual ermine-trimmed robes. Approaching the front of the podium, she bowed her head before climbing the stairs and taking her seat on Tamara's right. Behind her came a steadily snaking stream of Grand Inquisitors from all over the world, each pushing their fur trimmed hoods back to reveal their faces before paying their respects and taking their seats.

As their guests settled in, Tamara motioned to the guards once more. Leaving for a moment, they returned pushing a large trolley between them. Upon it stood the crate and, judging by the sound it made as it crossed the floor, Tamara guessed that it wasn't empty. When they came to a stop and connected the device, the guards pulled the latch on the door, opening it to reveal the already shackled Miss Cunningham. Tamara stood and addressed the assembly.

'Ladies and Gentlemen,' she said with practiced confidence. 'Welcome to Cheritton Hall, and thank you for answering our summons. I'm sure that you have heard about the events of the last few weeks, particularly those involving the failure of my staff. Before we commence with our conference, I will administer a punishment according to the will of the Marshalls.'

From the corner of her eye, Tamara noticed Lady Shaw looking to Catchpole in confusion, apparently unaware that any such order had been given. And the smile on the Magister's face was enough to convince her that he was up to something. Catchpole brushed his index finger across his lips in an effort to mask his amusement.

'Magister Catchpole, you may proceed,' Tamara commanded in an attempt to call his bluff.

Catchpole looked shocked, as though he hadn't a clue what she was asking him to do. 'I'm honoured, ma'am. However, as the offender is a member of your staff, I gladly pass that honour to you.'

'As you wish,' said Tamara.

Descending the steps, she crossed the floor to the crate feeling as though she was being railroaded. Checking to be certain that the shackles had been fastened securely at Miss Cunningham's hands and feet, she turned her attention to the lock at the side of the iron mask.

'Ready?' she whispered.

'As I'll ever be,' Miss Cunningham whispered back. 'Don't worry about me. I'm just glad it's you and not Catchpole down here.'

'There's no need to close the door unless anyone's particularly squeamish?' Tamara called as she moved back.

There was a ripple of laughter from the others. Looking around the stands at their faces, she noted that there were very few in their company that could be considered middle-aged. It wasn't unusual for a Grand Inquisitor to die young, even in the farther, quieter reaches of the world. But until now, she hadn't really appreciated how short her life expectancy truly was. Like vultures waiting to feed, they looked down on her with hunger as she released the metronome's pendulum from its clasp and set the weight onto the scale. The sound of the tick filled the room as it began to sway.

'Five. Four. Three. Two. One ...' Tamara counted under her breath. There was a pause, followed by a gasp from her friend. Then the ticking started again.

At the next pause, she watched as Miss Cunningham's muscles tensed in anticipation of the next shock. When it arrived, the pain in Clarissa's eyes was obvious as she silently pleaded for it to stop. Tamara shook her head almost imperceptibly, trying to reassure herself that it would be over soon enough. The next silence was broken by a juddering wail, and the faint, acrid smell of burning hair wafted from the crate. Again Tamara's wrists ached at the memory of the pain, but she ignored it and kept her gaze fixed on the iron mask.

'Ten. Nine. Eight,' she mouthed, unable to help herself. Her eyes flicked to the apparatus, searching for a way to intervene. 'Seven. Six. Five.'

She let her mind wander around the machine. In spite of the wood, the shell of the box felt as cold and lifeless as the metal that lined it.

'Four. Three. Two.' A sense of unquenchable panic welled in her belly like a swarm of angry butterflies. 'One ... Pause ...'

Even at her distance from it, the crackle of electricity caused the hair on Tamara's arms to stand on end as Miss Cunningham screamed and shook. Fighting to keep her tears at bay, Tamara watched as the skin on her friend's arms and ankles reddened with the heat. And the clacking of the pendulum began again.

*Ten ...*

*Nine ...*

Frantically feeling around the crate again, Tamara's mind came into contact with the cable that connected to the crate. She tugged on it gently, but it refused to give way.

*Eight ...*

*Seven ...*

Following the wire down to the floor, she felt her way along its length until it connected to the metronome.

Six ...

Five ...

She scanned the faces of the audience and was glad to see that their attentions were firmly fixed on the victim of their amusement.

Four ...

Three ...

Tamara knew that her timing would have to be perfect. Anything less would arouse the suspicions of the crowd, especially Lady Shaw. Thankfully, her training with Catchpole and Rupert had prepared her for instances such as this, and her eyes narrowed as she began to divide her attentions between her two targets.

Two ...

One ...

Pause ...

To Tamara, the whole world seemed to slip into slow motion. In her mind's eye, she pulled the plug from the metronome and the tingling of the electricity tickled her consciousness sharply. As it came free, she wrapped her will around Miss Cunningham's torso and shook her back and forth with gusto, causing the chains of her bonds to rattle like an unruly ghost. When Tamara eased her hold on her friend, Clarissa sagged, held awkwardly by the metal clamped around her head. In the nick of time, the plug was reconnected, and the world rushed back to normal in a nauseating, chaotic wave of sounds and smells.

'Enough,' she said putting her hand over the pendulum to halt it.

The jeers and hoots of dissent from the other Grand Inquisitors echoed through the hall. Tamara could see the dissatisfaction in their faces and the bloodlust in their eyes as she raised her hands in a call for silence. Concentrating on her friend's bindings, she flicked at the heavy iron bolts and let them drop to the ground. Wrapping her mind around Miss Cunningham again, Tamara lifted her from the floor of the crate and raised her into the air. Manoeuvring her prostrate form into the open, Tamara raised her up and spread her arms wide to display her victim to the audience. Her head lolling to one side, Clarissa's face was scorched where the mask had touched her and blood trickled from her wrists and ankles, pooling on the cold stone floor.

'Enough,' Tamara repeated. 'After all, I don't want to lose any more of my Inquisitors before the cull.'

There was a titter of general amusement from the benches. Floating Miss Cunningham's body to the entrance, Tamara opened the door and commanded the guards to escort her friend to the infirmary for care. Then, taking a white towel from a shelf beneath the metronome table, she tossed it onto the floor and scrubbed at the blood with her foot. Returning to the stage, Tamara pitched the towel into a brazier, took a match and set it alight before taking her seat.

'Well played,' Catchpole whispered grinning like a Cheshire cat as leaned across to speak to her. 'I don't think anyone noticed your little deception, except me of course.'

'I'm sure you're mistaken,' Tamara replied without batting an eyelid.

'Perhaps,' Catchpole murmured. 'But you forgot to add a few drops of blood on the way out.' The lid of the box snapped closed, causing Tamara to jump nervously. 'Still, it was very clever of you to burn the evidence before anyone could examine it.'

'Very well, let's begin,' said Tamara, her mouth suddenly feeling dry as she tried to swallow.

\*\*\*

New Year's Eve at the bolt-hole station was a very different affair. The nomadic nature of the Council usually came with an overwhelming sense of optimism; something Michael believed had been instilled in them by Jerrick. There was a general hustle and bustle in the tunnel that was beginning to give the place a more homely air.

Every so often, Michael could hear a clock strike above the sound of the traffic in the distance. It made him wonder if they were within reach of the palace of Westminster, or at least somewhere near the Thames. It felt strange to him to be back in London, probably within walking distance of the Masonic temple they'd abandoned. Every time he thought about it, the faces of the homeless that the Council used to care for crowded his mind. They mingled with the faces of the dead Inquisitors and the shocked look in Daniel's eyes. He shivered as he nursed a mug of coffee at a table with the Davises. He'd been there most of the morning, silently watching their ever decreasing world go by while Mr and Mrs Davis chatted about this and that.

'What do you think about that, eh?' said Davis clapping a hand on his shoulder.

'Hmm? Sorry, I was miles away,' Michael blinked, waking from his thoughts.

'Never mind, you'll catch up with the rest of us in your own time, I'm sure,' said the butler.

'Honestly, Roger, you're treating him with kid gloves,' said Mrs Davis. 'You've got to snap out of it, Michael. Come back down to earth will you.'

'I was thinking,' said Michael. 'Without Jerrick, we're as stuffed as a prize turkey, aren't we?'

The Davises' eyes met briefly and Mrs Davis said, 'Why do you say that?'

'Because this whole war is pointless,' Michael replied. 'It's something that's been niggling at the back of my mind since before we found Katja. Every time I thought I had it figured out, something happened and I got distracted. But the last few days have given me time to really think about it.'

'You're not making any sense,' said Davis What's that got to do with Jerrick?'

Michael shuffled his chair around so that he could face them both. 'Ever since he was in my head, I've had this feeling that he knew the whole story. That King, Jeshamon, became so hungry for power that he would have done anything to get his hands on Jerrick's book, right? Well, I have the book now and I can tell you it can't be read. So if it can't be read, this whole war is about something that happened thousands of years ago. And the only one who can actually prove it happened is gone. It all comes down to a bunch of idiots arguing about who's right!'

'It's about an awful lot more than that,' said Mrs Davis. 'Without the Council to concentrate on, the Inquisition could do unspeakable things. The only thing that has stopped them up to now is us. Let me ask you - when we talk about the Inquisition, who is it that you think we're talking about? The people in high places who influence countries and their petty disputes? Or do you think about people like Catchpole and that withered old hag, Lady Shaw?'

'All of them I suppose,' said Michael, taken aback by Mrs Davis's fury. 'They're all a part of the same machine. And to be honest, they haven't really done such a bad job so far.'

'I think,' said Davis, 'that Margret is asking why on earth you would need money when you can do this:'

Gesturing to a metal table a little way along the disused platform, the gentleman's gentleman coaxed it into the air and guided it out over the bare concrete where the tracks should have been laid. Suddenly, the sound of tearing steel rang out through the tunnel like a thousand nails on a chalkboard, causing everyone to stop and stare. The flat tabletop buckled upwards, bunching and balling until it resembled a body, head and arms. Then, setting the newly fashioned mannequin to stand next to the curved far wall, the butler nodded to his wife.

In the three years he had known them, Michael had never seen Mrs Davis exhibit her talents. They were her closely guarded secrets and she treasured them as one might treasure an heirloom. He watched in anticipation as the aging housekeeper's face relaxed into a mask of serenity. After a few moments, Michael was aware of a change in the light and a faint hum behind him. Turning to look at the dummy again, he could see the fruits of her labours. A cylinder of energy encapsulated the twisted table, pulsing with turquoise incandescence.

As the hum became a purr, Michael could feel the throbbing of the air, disturbed by the woman's efforts. There was an intensity to it that made his cheeks warm. Inside the cylinder, the metal man began to change from shining silver to a deep, hot red, as droplets of molten steel dripped from its rigid arms. Within moments, the red became a brilliant white, out-shining the glow of the tube that encased it. Her demonstration done, Mrs Davis let her concentration drop.

'There,' she said, seeming pleased with her work. 'At least it'll warm the place up.' She looked at the stunned expression on Michael's face. 'You see, the cull is a chance for them to make their move. It's not just the most dangerous time for us; it's the most dangerous time for the normals as well. *That's* why it's so important for us to fight.'

'Did you think that we fought because we enjoy it?'

said Davis. 'I thought more of you than that my boy. What has Anna been teaching you?'

'I wasn't sure until now,' said Michael. 'Whatever it was, I don't think I was listening.'

'These are troublesome times,' said Mrs Davis. 'Lefrick has told us a thing or two about your concerns, but you can't go airing them in public, not here.'

'Trouble's brewing in both camps,' said Davis. 'And after that stunt at the academy, I'd say the only reason some of us are still here is because of your new found talent.'

'Some of us are betting heavily on you,' said Mrs Davis. 'When the time is right, we'll be right behind you.'

'Behind me,' said Michael astonished by the admission. 'Why?'

'Why not?' said Mrs Davis. 'Lefrick convinced Jerrick to let him bring you here for a reason. When you find a way to read that book, you'll know what your part is in all of this. Trust in that.'

They passed a few moments in awkward silence as Michael digested the Davises' revelation. If they were right, then a number of people were pinning all of their hopes on him. It wasn't a burden he wanted to bear and it reminded Michael too much of his time at the academy.

'How's Alice?' he asked, eager to change the subject.

'Not doing as well as I'd hoped,' said Mrs Davis. 'Whatever that villain, Catchpole did to her it's taken its toll. She barely responds to anyone except Adam, and I'm none too sure about him.'

'What happens when you read him?'

'The same as when I read Alice,' said Mrs Davis. 'All I get is that stupid nursery rhyme going round and around in their heads.'

'Normally, we would have evicted Dakin by now,' said Davis. 'But Margaret here thinks we stand a better chance of breaking your sister's conditioning with him around.'

'When can I see her?' said Michael.

'Any time you like for now,' said Mrs Davis. 'But I'm going to have to report to *her* soon, and then, who knows?'

'I won't let them take her away again,' Michael snapped. 'If they do, I'll get her back, the way I did at the academy if necessary.'

'It won't come to that,' said Davis. 'Your aunt wouldn't let anything come between her and her niece, the same way that she protects you.'

It was the housekeeper's turn to look uncomfortable. 'There's something else you should know.'

'What?' Michael asked.

'When I read your sister, it wasn't just Catchpole's conditioning keeping me out of her mind. I could actually feel her resisting me of her own free will, what little of it she might have left right now.'

'B ... But ...' Michael stammered, 'how can that be? If she'd had any latent talent of her own, the academy would have taken her before now.'

'I don't know,' Mrs Davis shrugged. 'It's not the first time people have developed talents later in life, especially girls. She could be one of those lucky few.'

'I wonder what else she can do,' said Michael. 'If you'll excuse me, I think I'd like to go and see her.'

378

'Just don't tell her anything. Not even about where we are. Though I'm sure she's probably figured that one out for her herself by now,' said Mrs Davis. 'If she will talk to you, try to find out what Catchpole did to her down in that dungeon of his. The more we know, the more we can do to help her.'

Michael nodded. Turning his back on them, he walked along the platform towards Alice's room, still marvelling at the glowing table-man. It was more orange now, singing as it cooled in the air. It never occurred to him that the housekeeper could be capable of unleashing such a torrent of power.

When he arrived at Alice's room, he was greeted by two guards standing sentry outside. The door was exactly like his, as was the room, he suspected. He rapped on the wood and waited.

'Go away,' Alice shouted from inside. 'I don't want to see anyone.'

'Not even me?' Michael called back.

There was a moment of silence before the bolt slid back and the door opened. Alice looked terrible. The lustre was gone from her usually sparkling emerald eyes and her autumn hair was unkempt. She was even paler than usual and looked worn, as though she hadn't slept in days. Despite her appearance, her lips broadened into a warm smile as she threw her arms around her brother and held him tight.

'I thought I'd dreamt it, but you're here. You're really here!'

'I'm here,' Michael said patting her back. Disentangling

himself from her embrace, he led Alice back inside and sat with her on the edge of her bed. 'Where's Adam?'

'Getting some sleep. He was up with me all night. The noises here are really strange, and someone was screaming again.'

'Yeah,' said Michael feeling sheepish. 'I heard it too. Don't worry; it's not always like that around here. Are they treating you alright?'

'What do you think?' said Alice. 'The door locks from the inside. Adam's been taking care of me, and aside from the guards and this strange old woman who keeps pestering me, I can do what I like.'

Michael smiled at her description. 'Mrs Davis can be quite persistent, but she's only trying to be kind. She says you won't talk to anyone but Adam. I told her you were just being stubborn again. She doesn't know you like I do.'

'I'm not trying to be stubborn on purpose,' Alice defended. 'It's just that since that night at the academy, I haven't been feeling like myself.'

'What happened? Michael asked, his face darkening. 'What did Catchpole do to you?'

Alice's expression became suddenly distant and she stared at the wall as though she were searching it for the right thing to say. The longer she thought about it, the more agitated she seemed to become. Michael watched in horror as the rational, calm young woman she had been just moments before slipped away, and Alice began to rock back and forth. Her fingers twisted into her hair, pulling roughly at it as she clenched and unclenched her fists. As the rocking became more violent, the humming started.

380

Soon after, a little girl's voice that Michael remembered from his childhood began to sing in a quivering half-whisper.

'London's burning, London's burning ...'

Michael froze, feeling helpless. On the edge of his vision, he could see a shadow around her body that chilled him to the bone. It was black, the kind that comes not just from the absence of light, but from the absence of anything, and it writhed under his fleeting attentions. Letting his focus wander, Michael began to search his sister for a thread of power that he could tap. He only knew of one person with an aura that dark, but if he could sample it for himself, he knew that it would confirm his suspicions about its originator.

Closing his eyes, he found a thread and pulled. But the more he tugged at the foreign energy, the harder Alice rocked and the more she pulled at her hair. Sweat began to trickle from his forehead, stinging his eyes as he struggled in vain to dislodge any of the power. Alice's singing intensified.

Suddenly, the door burst open, framing a glaring Adam in the entrance. Without warning, Michael felt his friend's attack strike his chest. The pressure of it pinned him into the corner of the bed, jarring Michael's shoulder against the wall.

'Whatever you're doing to her, you need to stop,' said Adam.

'She's my sister,' Michael groaned. 'I'm trying to help her.'

With Michael's concentration broken, Alice began to

calm down again. Her rocking eased and the rhyme became no more than a pitiful whimper.

'It's alright, sweetheart,' said Adam sitting next to her, cradling her head into his shoulder. 'Hush now, it's going to be alright.'

'Did I do that?' said Michael.

'I don't know,' Adam replied. 'It comes on whenever she tries to remember what happened at the academy. Sometimes she wakes herself up with it. It's as if her brain's been programmed not to think about it.'

'How long does it take her to snap out of it?'

'A few minutes,' said Adam as he stroked Alice's hair. 'When she comes round, she won't even know it's happened. Sorry for pushing you by the way. No hard feelings?'

'None,' said Michael rubbing his shoulder. 'I was trying to borrow from her. But the harder I pulled, the more insane she seemed to get. '

'She's not insane,' Adam barked. 'She's just … broken.'

'And you?' said Michael. 'Mrs Davis says you've got that nursery rhyme going through your head too. What's going on, Adam?'

'It's complicated. It all started when I took Alice to the academy. I didn't even know I was singing it. Since then, every time I try to see, it keeps playing over and over in my mind, as though it's blocking me and I can't get past it.'

'So why is it affecting Alice?'

Adam thought for a moment. 'I suppose it's possible that she could have caught it from me.'

'Like a virus?' Michael pressed. 'I don't know. I've

never heard of it happening to anyone else before. If Jerrick were here, he might have some ideas. Tell me about the others. Rupert and Emily, are they sick?'

'No, Emily saw that I was about to hit Rupert and tried to warn him,' said Adam.

'Then it must have been something that happened while you and Alice were alone together,' said Michael.

'We didn't share the same room if that's what you were thinking,' Adam replied. 'The academy would never have allowed it.'

Michael blushed. 'It never even crossed my mind, but thanks for being honest. How did you two get to the academy?'

'Tamara arranged a car for us,' said Adam. 'Alice was really excited because she'd never been in a limousine before. There was even a bottle of champagne on ice in …' his voice trailed off.

'Catchpole strikes again,' said Michael. 'I'd hoped our fight at the academy would be the last I was going to hear of him, but I should have known. My luck's not that good.'

'A poison that blocks talents makes sense,' Adam reasoned. 'After all, if the oath drug kick-starts talents, it's reasonable to think there might be an antidote. Though, I can't see why it would affect your sister.'

'Why what would affect me?' said Alice bleary eyed.

Michael shifted to the edge of the bed. 'I'll give you some privacy.'

'You don't have to go,' said Alice. 'You've only just got here and I want to hear all about what you've been up to. It's been months since your last letter.'

'Soon, I promise,' said Michael leaning over to kiss the top of her head. 'Get some rest now.'

***

'And you are confident that your new powder will do the job?' said the Spanish Grand Inquisitor.

'I am, sir,' said Tamara. 'I have been assured that the adjusted recipe heavily restricts the use of any talents.'

The French Grand Inquisitor stood, clasping her hands at her waist.

'What about the side effects on the normals?' she said above the muttered concerns of others.

'What about them?' Catchpole retaliated. 'My lords and ladies, the oath doesn't affect anybody without latent talent. The same is true for our new blocker.'

While there were further discussions amongst the others, Tamara leaned across to him and whispered, 'Is that true?'

'No idea,' Catchpole hissed through his triumphant grin. 'We haven't tested it fully.'

A dark skinned lady stood and announced herself as the Grand Inquisitor of Jamaica above the din. The gathering fell silent once more.

'If your claim is true, how is it that we haven't heard of it before now?'

'If I may?' said Lady Shaw. 'Mr Catchpole has only recently perfected the drug. It was the Marshalls' decision to withhold the news of its development until this conclave, to prevent any unnecessary leaks.'

'Before Jamaica approves your plan, we would like proof that the drug exists,' said the lady, her eyes narrowing.

A chorus of agreement spread like a wave around the hall. Catchpole looked to Tamara for her consent. When he received it, he produced the small deerskin jar and a knife from his pocket and cut the wax seal. Pulling at the lid, he was outwardly embarrassed to find that the bone plug wouldn't budge. Apologising to the assembly, he tried again. Tugging roughly at the cap, it came loose with a sharp popping sound, the jolt causing the jar to slip from his grasp.

As it clattered to the table, a plume of glittery dust kicked up in front of Tamara. The tinkling of sleigh bells hung in the air for a moment as she sputtered and rubbed at her eyes. Lady Shaw covered her nose and mouth with her sleeve in panic, scrambling from her chair to put some distance between herself and the cloud.

'What have you done?' Tamara growled between coughs.

'It's alright,' said Catchpole pulling a flask from his pocket and handing it to her. 'Here, drink this quickly, it's the antidote.'

She took a pull on the flask and almost choked.

'Ugh, what the hell is this? It tastes like peppermint.'

'Special formula,' said Catchpole taking the flask from her. 'You're fine, trust me. Try something.'

Cocking an eyebrow at him, Tamara whipped the flask from his hand with her mind and tossed it towards the front row of the conclave. With lightning reflexes, the

German delegate caught it mid-flight, opened it and sniffed at the contents.

'Smells like schnapps,' he said with a thick southern accent.

'Among other things,' said Catchpole. 'It's a safeguard against accidents like this one. As you can see from my demonstration, Lady Bloodgood has suffered no ill effects.'

Again, the world's Grand Inquisitors went into a deep discussion. This time, when Lady Shaw tried to call them back to order, they ignored her. Unused to being so blatantly disregarded, she stood and spread her arms, flexing her will. A hush descended like a blanket over the hall as mouths were forced shut.

Once she was certain that she had their full attention, she said, 'Shall we call a short recess of fifteen minutes?'

'Do I have time to go and check on Miss Cunningham?' Tamara sighed, slumping back into her ornate chair as the delegates began to file out.

'I suppose,' replied Catchpole. 'Give her my regards, won't you? She coped with her punishment rather well considering the circumstances.'

*** 

Once they were alone, Lady Shaw began to giggle quietly. 'I wonder if anyone else noticed how our young leader disconnected the metronome on that last pass.'

'I doubt it,' said Catchpole smiling at her. 'I only just caught it myself. I think we have a tendency to look at the victim and not at the surroundings.'

'She's far too soft of course. If any of my aides had betrayed me like that, they'd have had what was coming to them.'

Catchpole drummed his fingers on the table. 'She may have been soft once upon a time, but I have a feeling that's going to change.'

'Hmmm, I suppose it will,' said Lady Shaw, 'especially since you dosed her with that ice mirror dust.'

'Very observant,' said Catchpole, impressed with his colleague's knowledge.

'It was hardly a great leap of imagination. I had my eye on that jar at the trials. I just couldn't get to it without arousing suspicion.'

'One of the only perks of my position,' said Catchpole.

'And the new anti-oath? Lady Shaw asked.

'I'm testing at present. The outlook is promising, but it seems to have had an unusual side-effect on one of my guinea pigs.'

'Anything worth mentioning?' asked Lady Shaw.

'Hardly,' Catchpole replied. 'It's nothing more than an anomaly. I'll keep an eye on the subject over the next few months to be sure, but I'm certain the finished compound will be ready for delivery by the time we need it.'

'When those halfwits at the Council realise what's happened, it'll be far too late to do anything about it,' said Shaw. 'There's a certain irony about the whole thing, don't you think?'

'Yes, and if it succeeds, I will have surpassed even the great Jeshamon himself,' said Catchpole.

Lady Shaw let out a guffaw, which she quickly

disguised as a coughing fit. 'Of course, Mr Catchpole,' she said with all the innocence of a fox in a hen house. 'You're quite the Pied Piper.'

'Don't talk to me about her,' said Catchpole ignoring Shaw's attempts at sarcasm. 'If she hadn't failed at her task, we wouldn't have to resort to cheap parlour tricks to subdue the general populace. With that flute in the Council's possession, it's more important than ever that we get the compound out on time. '

'You're certain they have it?'

'Not absolutely,' Catchpole admitted. 'But it's a big risk to assume that they don't.'

'I see your point,' Lady Shaw agreed. 'What do you suggest?'

Catchpole scratched his nose as he pondered her question. 'Give it a few months. Let's see how things pan out. If the Council has the flute, you can guarantee they will make use of it as soon as possible. I know I would want to. It won't cost us anything to be prepared and, whether they have the flute or not, we should continue as planned. Who knows how long the effects of that mirror dust will last on our young leader.'

*\*\**

When Tamara reached the infirmary, Miss Cunningham was already sitting up in bed. Her face was pale and there were bandages around her neck, wrists and ankles, but there was a sparkle in her eyes when she saw Tamara enter.

'You look frightened,' she said.

Tamara perched on the edge of the bed examining her aide's bandages. 'It wasn't long ago that I was in your position. I know how much they sting.'

'I never thought I'd say it,' said Miss Cunningham with a laugh, 'but I wish Mrs Davis was here with that foul smelling ointment of hers.'

Her comment brought a smile to the Grand Inquisitor's face.

'Really? If I'd known how long the smell would hang around, I'd have preferred to put up with the pain.'

'It could have been worse,' said Miss Cunningham. 'Thank you for what you did. Do you think we got away with it?'

'I think so. Though you never can tell with Catchpole; or Lady Shaw for that matter. I know I should be letting you rest, but are you interested in some news?'

'Of course,' said Miss Cunningham. 'Have the conclave reached a decision so soon?'

'No, there's an awful lot on the agenda still to discuss, but I think the main point has been decided. Catchpole's got some powder he claims will reduce the risk of the normals being able to fight back. I think he's hoping it will get into the water supply and affect the Council as well.'

'Good grief, he's not still harping on about that, is he?' said Miss Cunningham. 'He's been working on an anti-oath for years, ever since I was in school at least, probably longer.'

'Well he opened a jar of it in the hall and spilled it all over the place,' said Tamara. 'I think I might have got some in my eye. It's a good thing he had the antidote with him.'

Miss Cunningham's brows furrowed. 'I didn't realise he was that close to completing it. The last time we spoke about it, he was having problems making it stable. And that was only a few months ago. Who knows, perhaps he's made a breakthrough since then. How do you feel about his plan?'

'You know, when I first saw it on the agenda it worried me,' Tamara confessed. 'But now, I don't seem too bothered about it. After all, the whole aim is to subdue the Elder Council. The last thing we need is resistance from the normals as well. Since the Foundation only began testing people in earnest a little over ten years ago, there are bound to be many more people with talents out there. I think it's a good thing if we can take them out of the equation before they become a threat.'

'Spoken like a true Grand Inquisitor,' said Miss Cunningham.

'Tell me it doesn't make sense,' Tamara countered. 'We should try to make it as easy as possible. I think Catchpole's plan is sound. Not that I would admit it to him.'

'What happens to the water supply afterwards? Anybody drinking from the contaminated water will have no end of problems,' said Miss Cunningham.

'Not if we have the antidote,' said Tamara. 'With the antidote, it should be easy to get the job done without too much inconvenience to us.'

'And what about the normals? What happens to them?'

'As long as they work with us, there shouldn't be anything to worry about,' said Tamara. 'I'm not anticipating any trouble from them. It's not like they've been trained to use what they've got after all.'

'So you're taking the "what they've never had they'll never miss" approach?'

'Exactly,' Tamara beamed. She glanced at her watch. 'Look at the time. I'd best be getting back before I'm missed. You stay here. I don't want anyone thinking that you got off lightly.' Trying to pull her robe back down over her wrist, it caught on the charm bracelet that she had worn since Michael had given it to her. 'This damned thing,' she spat. 'It's always getting in the way.' Undoing the clasp, she threw it to the floor in a fit of temper. Then, smiling briefly at Miss Cunningham, she turned and left.

## Chapter Seventeen:
# The Beginning

It was bitterly cold on the banks of the Thames. The last of the New Year's revellers were still finding their way home, but there was one last appointment that Katja wanted to keep. Descending the concrete stairs close to a familiar bridge, she pulled the hood of her coat up over her head to keep the wind from nibbling at her ears. As the police cruiser puttered past, she turned her face away to hide it from the light.

Swapping places with Sher had felt good. It felt like she was sticking her middle finger up at her father for all of the things he'd made her do over the centuries. He was going to be so mad when he finally made it back to the cave. She knew that he was going to be too weak from the Flayer attack to fix the machines. And without her to fetch and carry, or to bleed for energy, he was probably going to fade into nothing in no time at all.

*He deserves everything he gets,* she thought, smiling to herself. Looking into the gloom under the bridge, she could make out the faint smouldering of a fire in the distance and reached into the folds of her coat. Drawing nearer, she found Scraps wrapped in the rags of what had once been blankets. He looked up and smiled at her.

'Evenin' miss,' he said and barked a cough like an angry guard dog. 'Spare a bit o' change for an ol' man?'

'I thought we might have a drink,' said Katja pulling out the brown paper bag she'd been clutching under her coat, twisting the cap to open it.

'Aye,' said Scraps, 'that sounds good. If you don't mind me saying, it's a bit of a cold night for a lady likes o' you to be down 'ere.'

'Don't worry, I've stuffed,' Katja laughed.

Scraps leaned closer to get a better view of his companion in the dim light. 'Katie?'

She nodded. 'I should never have left you here on your own, Scraps. I'm so sorry. Can you ever forgive me?'

'Nothin' to forgive,' said Scraps. 'But perhaps you wouldn't mind telling me how it is that you look …'

'Old?' Katja interrupted.

'Mature,' said Scraps. 'I was going to say mature.'

Katja took a long pull on the bottle, her face contorting as she swallowed. 'I still don't know how you can drink that!'

'It's good for the soul,' said Scraps. 'Reminds you that you're still alive.'

'Yes, I can see that.' She looked nervous as she rubbed her hands together to wake her fingers from the deep freeze. 'Can I ask you something?'

'Ask away, missy,' said Scraps smacking his chops.

'The last time I was here, I played you a tune and you saw something in the darkness,' said Katja. 'What would you say if I offered to send you back there?'

Scraps coughed hard, spitting the contents of his mouth into the fire, making it hiss. 'Sorry,' he said. 'I never could stand the taste o' blood.' He wiped his mouth with the back of his hand and began to roll himself a cigarette. 'Will it hurt?'

'Oh, no,' said Katja, 'not one bit. It'll be just like it was before. Only this time … you won't come back.'

Scraps considered her proposal, striking a match and taking a long puff on the impossibly thin cigarette. He coughed violently again, throwing the roll-up into the bin.

'Do yourself a favour,' he said between gasps, 'don't get hooked on them, they're no good for your singing voice.' Once his wheezing had calmed, he said, 'Well, I suppose I'm about ready to go. But if I do, could you do something for me?'

'Sure,' said Katja.

'Leave the rest o' me here, would you?' said Scraps. 'Pretty girl like you shouldn't have to deal with an old man's corpse. And it's only right for the others to get first pick o' anything I got left before the crows get to me.'

Katja nodded and took the flute from around her neck. She put it to her lips and began to play a sweet, sad melody.

'Thank you, missy,' said Scraps, his eyes beginning to close. 'Only kindness anyone's shown me in such a long time. Bless you.'

As Scraps began to nod, his shoulders relaxing, Katja could have sworn that there was a smile on his lips in the dim firelight. And when she was sure that the old man had moved on, she cradled his head and laid him back before covering his face with a blanket.

Instead of replacing the pipe around her neck, she pulled it apart, tucking the mouthpiece into the old man's coat pocket. The middle section she threw into the river and, by the time she reached the road again, the foot had been trodden and ground into a concrete step until the dust was scattered by the wind.

Free of it, Katja's footsteps were lighter and a smile spread across her lips. For the first time in seven hundred years, she had no idea what she was going to do with her time, or the considerable wealth she had squirreled away. As she walked, she found herself wondering what it would be like to start afresh. Perhaps she would change her name permanently to Kate and lose herself anywhere in the world that took her fancy.

Stopping to admire the variety of new fashions in the windows of shops, she noticed the dawn reflected in the glass. Turning to watch the sun peep over the cityscape, she gave a sigh of relief that she could finally get on with the life she wanted.

And as Katja strode into the sunrise, she was blissfully unaware of the haggard, rent face of Nahar behind her, watching her from the window as she went.

*** 

At the bolt-hole, Michael was sitting on the edge of his bed, still reeling from the nightmare he'd just woken from. In his hands, he held the melted remnants of what had once been a beautifully carved candle.

Since Alice's rescue, flashes of memories that weren't necessarily his had been coming back to him. One, in particular, concerned him the most. It was a vague memory of speaking to Tamara and Rupert in a room that looked like Davis's old apartment. He couldn't remember the details of what was said, and it irked him that he might never find out now that Jerrick was gone. When he'd spoken to Adam about it, Adam's eyes had glazed over. Michael worried that he might have the same reaction as Alice to his questions, so he'd backed off.

'Fifteen and no Anna. Alice might as well be on another planet and Tam hates me. Great start, Michael,' he whispered to himself.

He knew that there wouldn't be any fuss over his birthday. It was the same for everybody. When you count your lucky stars that you've survived another day, another year older doesn't seem quite so important. There were morning sounds coming from the kitchen now, and the smell of sausages, bacon and eggs invaded his nostrils, much to the protests of his stomach.

Padding barefoot out onto the platform, he scooted to the mirror room where his meeting with Maya had taken place. Touching his hand on the frame, he thought of home, muttering his incantation in little more than a murmur. The mirror came to life beneath his palms, a familiar looking landing appearing in the glass.

Michael waited, listening for any sounds of movement in the house. The last time he'd ventured home it was a few days following his own death. Now that Alice had disappeared too, he had an inkling that his parents might have gone to pieces. But all was quiet. He stepped through the glass and let the portal close behind him. Tiptoeing across the carpet, he pushed his bedroom door open and stepped inside, careful not to make a sound as he closed it behind himself.

His room hadn't changed at all. Everything was where he had left it on the night that Anna had brought him back. The only thing that had changed was the colour of the candles that were burning out in their glass jars.

*Two years on and they're still lighting them,* he thought.

It made him smile to think that they still remembered him, especially on his birthday. But why shouldn't they? He still remembered them well enough. The familiar smells of home were comforting. The feel of his duvet and the view from his window reminded him of happier times. Still, it was unusual for there not to be any noise at this time of the morning. His parents should have been downstairs by now.

Putting his ear to the wall, Michael listened for his father's snoring, or the sound of voices in the room next door, but he heard neither. Tugging at the door with his mind, he eased it open and risked a glance into the hall. The coast clear, Michael padded to his sister's door and slunk into her room. Until now, he hadn't realised why his feet had taken him to the portal, or why his hands had brought him home. But as he stood in his sister's room his heart reminded him. He'd felt a great sense of comfort from his last visit, if only because he'd taken some keepsakes back with him to the Council. Not that he could compare his own situation to that of his sister. It occurred to him, however, that by taking a few of Alice's favourite possessions back with him, they might help to snap her out of whatever Catchpole had put her through.

He wasn't surprised to find that many of her things were already missing and concluded that Alice must have taken them away with her to university. There were a few things left that Michael recognised, like the stuffed bear she called Steve. There was also a framed photograph of her and Michael with Gamma Laura. Gathering them together, he felt as though he'd be pushing his luck to take any more, or to stay any longer. He was already running the risk of being caught, or worse, being missed back at the station.

Crossing back to the door, he peeked through the crack before slipping out into the hallway. Just as he put his hand to the fame, he felt something clamp around his throat and a sharp pain in the backs of his knees. The clatter of his purloined presents preceded the loud thump as he hit the floor.

'Move and I'll tear you a new one,' said a voice from the bathroom.

'Anna, it's me,' Michael wheezed, his hands at his throat.

His aunt stepped out from behind the bathroom door and glowered at him. 'What the f ... fart in hell are *you* doing here?' she snapped as she let go of her spell.

'I was trying to get some stuff for Alice. I thought it might help her. What are you doing here?' Michael gasped as he struggled to catch his breath.

'Getting a few things for your mum and dad,' Anna replied hauling him to his feet by the collar of his pyjamas. 'Look at the state of you! You're out in public half-dressed. You're not wearing any armour, and you haven't got any backup. What were you thinking?'

'What do you mean, getting stuff for Mum and Dad? What have you done with them?' Michael barked.

Her expression changed from anger to embarrassment in the blink of an eye and she could no longer seem to hold his gaze.

'I've moved them for their own safety,' said Anna.

'But how?' Michael managed, his mouth flapping like a carp.

Anna put a hand on her nephew's shoulder and smiled. 'I think it's best if you come with me.'

Michael nodded without question, stretching out with his mind and gathering up his sister's scattered belongings while Anna opened a portal to destinations unknown. With trepidation, he stepped into the vortex and was soon treated to the sight of a small warehouse stacked with crates. It reminded him a little of that scene in the movies, where the American Secret Service take possession of the Ark of the Covenant. When Anna joined him, she put her hand on his shoulder again and half led, half frog-marched him to a set of steps leading up to an office door.

'Go on,' she said. 'Consider it a birthday present.'

Racing to climb the stairs, Michael put his hand to the handle of the door and turned it, his nerves jangling like a pocket full of loose change. As the door creaked inwards, the pale and tired face of Grimm greeted him with a broad smile. Their backs to Michael, two familiar shapes shifted in their seats to look at him.

'Michael!' his mother shrieked. 'Oh my god, Michael!'

Immediately moved to tears, she threw herself from her chair and ran to him, scooping her son into her arms, squeezing him half to astounded death. He felt like the parcel in a party game as she passed him to his father, who hugged him for all he was worth.

'My son!' wailed Mr Ware. 'Oh, my beautiful, beautiful son!' He kissed the top of Michael's head, breathing in the scent of his hair before pushing him out to arm's length to get a better look at him.

Unsure of what he should be doing, Michael turned to look at his aunt as she leaned against the door jamb, a smile as wide as a continent on her lips. There was nothing else for it. He did the first thing that came to him and burst into tears.

'I'm so sorry ...' he sobbed, dropping Alice's things to the floor again. 'I didn't mean to ...'

His parents closed ranks, squashing him lovingly between them.

'It's okay, Michael,' his mother murmured. 'Anna's told us everything. We know what you had to do.'

'Seems to me that you saved a lot of lives,' Mr Ware whispered. 'It can't have been easy for you.' He sighed deeply. 'If only we'd known what you were going through.'

'Perhaps we should give you a little time alone,' said Grimm rising from his desk and ushering Anna out of the office.

After a few minutes, Michael pulled himself together again and flopped into one of the chairs, feeling as if the weight of the world had been lifted from his shoulders. His parents dragged seats of their own around to be close to him, and they sat in silence for a little while just staring at one another.

'How's Alice?' Mrs Ware ventured, her voice still shaking.

'She's in the best place she could be,' Michael replied. 'Her um ... boyfriend, Adam is looking after her.' Michael could practically smell the elephant in the room. 'You want to ask me about why I'm different, don't you.'

'It might help us to understand what's going on a little better,' said Mr Ware nodding.

'Promise me you won't freak out?' asked Michael raising a hand.

***

'You shouldn't have brought the boy here, Anna,' Grimm chastised her as they crossed the floor of the warehouse.

'Aw, come on, Jacob,' Anna laughed. 'Have a heart. I had to get his parents out of that house. And you know the Railroad's no place for them. It would only put them further into harm's way. That's why I'm relying on you.'

'Yes, but you shouldn't have brought the boy here,' Grimm insisted. 'Couldn't you have taken the Wares to him?'

Anna shook her head. 'No, no, no. That would never have done. The reason they're in your care is because they need to disappear off the grid entirely. Not even I can know where they are, not for the time being at least.' She paused and turned to look at the old man. 'If the observations in that book you lent me are right about the cull, then it's best if they're out of the picture altogether.'

'Mmm, the grapevine is full of rumours on both sides right now,' said Grimm. 'That's why I've had Eunice put a team together.'

'Eunice?' asked Anna. 'What's Eunice got to do with anything?'

'You'd do well not to underestimate her, Anna,' said Grimm. 'She's got more connections in the outside world than the Council and the Inquisition combined. I've a feeling you're going to be asking for her help before long.'

'*Her* help? What about *your* help?'

'You know I can't get involved,' said the librarian raising a hand. 'It's not in my power. I mean, look what happened to Sher. That's what getting involved does to people like us. "It's one of my many curses," as she might say.'

'Fine,' said Anna rolling her eyes. 'Just get the Wares out. I'll deal with the rest as it comes up. Now, what can you tell me about that nursery rhyme?'

'It's a just a kiddies' song,' Grimm shrugged. 'It's about the great fire of London. There's not much else I can tell you about it. I've had a look into the tune, but there's nothing sinister in the music. Quite why it's muddling up your niece's brain, I don't know.'

'It's got to be something to do with Catchpole,' Anna hissed. 'Do you think you might be able to find out what?'

'And risk everything we're trying to rebuild?' Grimm asked quirking his eyebrows at her. 'I'm sorry, Anna. I have my hands full trying to get these relics out to safety.'

Something clicked in Anna's brain. 'That's why you're planning to build a memorial to the haven sites in the ruins of the library, isn't it? You're planning to hide some of your artefacts there, in plain sight.'

'Do yourself a favour and forget about that,' said Grimm.

'Not a word,' Anna reassured him. 'Let me take care of things at my end, and I promise to keep Maya and the Council out of your monument in return.'

'Deal,' said Grimm extending a hand.

Anna shook it, sealing the bond between them. 'Speaking of Sher, where did she get to? I haven't seen her since before the evacuation. I take it she's skipped town with Nahar's daughter?'

'Tried to,' the librarian snorted. 'Seems like whatever plan she was cooking up backfired. That's what I mean about getting involved. It's against the rules for us to interfere.' He sighed again. 'I'm washing my hands of her.'

'Really? I thought she was your mentor?' said Anna.

'Was,' Grimm scoffed. 'Past tense. No, I'm getting too old to run around cleaning up after her. It's about time she got off her high horse and faced up to reality. I'm not going to be bound by her any longer; though it may cost me my life. I'm tired Anna, and my shoes are rubbing. It's about time I retired from all this.'

'Nonsense,' said Anna. 'There's still a few good years left in those old bones yet.' She clapped her hands together and rubbed them with enthusiasm. 'Alright, I hate to break up a family reunion, but it's time I was getting back.'

*\*\*\**

When the office door opened and Anna walked back in, Michael's heart sank. He was holding a freshly minted rose out to his mother, who looked at it as though it was the most wondrous thing she had ever seen.

'Michael, I'm so sorry, but it's time to go.'

Michael nodded, his shoulders sagging as he deflated. 'You're going to be alright,' he told his parents, in that way adults speak to their children when they've scraped their knees. 'It's going to be a while before I can see you again, but think of it like I'm going back to school.'

'We've just got you back,' said his mother.

'And we'll have him back again,' said Mr Ware comforting her. 'He's a man now, love, in spite of his age. Michael's got important things to do.' He looked up into Anna's face. 'You promise me that you'll bring my boy home safe, and his sister too, or so help me ...'

'I promise,' said Anna. She had a look about her that suggested to Michael that she was only just holding her nerve.

'We're so very proud of you, son,' said Mr Ware extending his hand.

Michael looked at it for a moment before throwing his arms around his father's neck. 'Oh, Dad, I'm not too old for a hug you know!'

'I wish I'd known you were coming,' said his mother dabbing at her eyes with a handkerchief. 'I'd have brought you a birthday present.'

Michael moved over and held her tight. 'It's okay, Mum, this is the best birthday present I could have ever wanted.' He pushed the conjured rose into her hand saying, 'Something to remind you that I'm still here.' Then, collecting Alice's belongings, he turned to Anna. 'I'm not allowed to know where they're going, am I?'

'Not even I'm allowed to know where they're going,' said Anna. 'Jacob's going to take care of their travelling arrangements.

'What about Gamma Laura?'

There was silence in the room. Michael's eyebrows furrowed as he looked from Anna to his parents and back.

'What about Gamma Laura?' he insisted.

'Michael, there's something you ought to know,' his father replied. 'When Alice went missing, your grandmother took a bit of a turn. She's been so fragile since we found out that you were dead, that she just couldn't take any more bad news.'

'Gamma's dead?' asked Michael, steadying himself on the arm of the chair.

'No, darling,' said Mrs Ware. 'She's had to go into care for a while. She had a stroke you see. Now, before you get too upset, we're crossing our fingers that she'll be alright. She needs to have help for the time being, so the hospital's the best place for her.'

'We've already discussed it,' said Anna. 'I'm going to be keeping an eye on her until she's well enough to travel, and we'll decide from there. The Inquisition won't be able to use her against us, for now at least. So I think it's best that we let Laura rest and get well.'

'Your aunt took us to see her yesterday,' said Mr Ware. 'I explained the situation to her as best I could and she seemed to understand.'

Michael took a deep breath. Letting it out slowly through pursed lips, he wiped at his eyes with the back of his hand.

'Okay. I think I can deal with that,' he said.

'Well,' said Anna after a long pause, 'I'd best get you back to the bolt-hole. You caught me in the middle of an errand for your parents, so I'm going to need a little more time to collect the last of their things before I join you there.' She crossed the room and put her hand to the frame of Grimm's office mirror. We'll head back to the house first and go our separate ways from there. At least they won't be able to trace the portal back here. I don't want anyone else knowing about this place yet, not even Lefrick, understand?'

'Understood,' Michael agreed.

The Wares stood and his mother kissed him on the cheek.

'Just be careful,' she warned.

'I will, Mum,' Michael answered managing a weak smile.

When he reached the mirror, he turned and took a last look at his parents before willing himself through the glass in case he changed his mind. Then he waited patiently for Anna to arrive, only just able to catch the faint whispers of her conversation with his parents before she appeared.

'What?' she asked as the portal closed and her nephew eyeballed her with suspicion.

'What did you do to my parents?' Michael snapped.

'Nothing, I swear,' said Anna.

'Then how come they swallowed everything I told them without question? They didn't even freak out when I showed them what I could do.'

'I told them the truth,' said Anna. 'Though, they took an awful lot more convincing than you did, I must say. I practically had to tie them both to the sofa before they'd listen to me.'

'You told them everything?'

'Do you think I'm that stupid?' she said rolling her eyes at him. 'I only told them what they needed to know, but every word of it was true. I even told them about the attack on the farm; about how you saved a lot of lives that day and about how you rescued Alice.

Michael blanched and muttered, 'You said that you told them the truth.'

'I did,' said Anna. 'I think you're a trooper, Michael. I know I don't tell you very often, but you deserve to hear it.'

'Thank you,' said Michael. A moment later a grin brightened his face.

'Too much?' said Anna.

'A little, but I don't mind,' said Michael.

Anna let out a chuckle. 'Go on then. I trust you can find your way home without too much trouble?'

'Yeah,' said Michael. Putting his hand on the mirror again, he paused. 'There *is* something you could do for me if you can manage it.'

'What's that?' said Anna raising an eyebrow at him.

'I'd really love a birthday cake.'

*** 

The building that housed the Grand Council's

chambers was huge. But all that could be said about its location was that it was next to a busy intersection of roads. Grand Council members, both past and present, were permitted to enter by no other means than mirror portal. This was deemed essential to preserve the secrecy of the building's location. Needless to say, it was a fortress, and tucked away in its recesses, Mistress Maya was holding court.

The panel that had been assembled for the interview with Michael was seated around a long, oak table. Now that there was no risk of being identified, they wore their hoods about their shoulders. Maya had taken her customary seat at the head of the table and was looking particularly smug.

'The boy's becoming a problem,' said a weasel–faced man seated to her left. His ginger hair was matted with grease and an angry looking boil protruded from his neck like a puss filled golf ball.

'Now, Eric, there's no need for that,' said Maya. 'He's just stubborn and a little short sighted. He probably gets it from his aunt. The question is: now that he knows that we need him, how do we convince him to give up his secret?'

'Why do we need 'im at all?' asked Eric, his whiney voice doing great injustice to his northern drawl. 'Surely we're better shot of him now as later. Reduces the risk o't Inquisition taking him back.'

'Because he's our best bet for ending the stalemate with them,' said the woman opposite. In stark contrast to her colleague, her accent was clipped and quintessentially English. 'You heard what happened at the compound. We were just as ineffective against them as they were against us until Michael came along. This war's been going on for so long that we're just pecking at each other like hens. His secret could turn the tide in our favour now that Jerrick's out of the way.'

'Thank you, Sasha,' said Maya cutting her short. 'It's only unfortunate that Nahar couldn't do what he was told. If he had, we'd have been free of Lefrick and Anna, as well as that meddlesome idealist. Then at least the boy would have been ours to control.'

Sasha looked shocked. 'Y ... you sent Nahar after Jerrick?'

'Who do you think arranged for the assault on the temple? He was supposed to get them all during the evacuation, but the Flayers got in the way. After that, I put the idea in his head about getting the Inquisition to help out,' said Maya rolling her eyes. 'I've known about his little vendetta with Jerrick for years. You all wanted him out of the way. All I did was make it possible. How was I supposed to know that his girl was going to botch the plot?'

'What about the book?' Eric asked. 'With Jerrick gone, Lefrick's going to let the boy keep it, instead of giving it to you.'

'Yes,' said Maya. 'It should be mine. In fact, as leader of the Council it's mine by right.'

'So take it back,' said Sasha.

Maya's smug grin faded and she glared at her colleague, unwilling to be told what to do.

'Stop twirling your hair woman,' she snapped. 'You

know it drives me insane.'

Sasha disentangled her fingers from the mass of tawny curls that brushed the table top and stared back at her leader. Maya's eyes locked with her subordinate's and they glared at each other with venom. Sasha was the older of the two women, but Maya took great pleasure in watching her squirm. She was a great believer that there could only ever be room for one queen. When her opponent looked away first, Maya knew that she had control.

'If we plan this carefully, we can have the Ware boy's secrets *and* the book. Then the only thing standing in our way will be the Inquisition.'

Playing with his boil, a ponderous expression on his face, Eric asked, 'What are you proposing?'

Maya smiled. 'We've spent far too much time out of the field. Leaders should be seen, don't you think?' The group nodded their reply. 'What I'm proposing is a change of scenery.'

\*\*\*

When Michael's feet hit solid ground, he crept to the door of the portal room. To his relief, life was going on seemingly without his absence being noticed. When he'd left, he'd been so determined to go home that he had barely noticed that he was still in his pyjamas, let alone thought enough to put on shoes. Steve's head poked out of the pile of possessions he was carrying, but aside from a few strange glances at the bear, nobody challenged his presence as he padded to his sister's door.

'New recruit?' said one of the guards, a huge grin on his face.

'He's just visiting,' said Michael feeling as though nothing could sway him out of his good mood. He knocked on his sister's door and waited for her invitation before going inside. Huddled into the corner of her bed, she looked dreadful.

'Steve!' she managed, her eyes brightening when she saw the stuffed animal. 'How on Earth did you ...'

'I popped home for a little while,' said Michael sitting down next to her. 'I thought you might be missing some of your things like I was when I first got here.'

Alice smiled, took the bear from him and sniffed it. Then she took its paw and gave herself a wave as though Steve was greeting an old friend.

'Thank you, Michael. Oh, but I'm the one that's supposed to be giving you a gift, happy birthday.'

'Thanks. Actually I've got something to tell you,' he said wondering if he should tell her the whole truth in her state. 'Anna took me to see Mum and Dad. I told them that you were safe with me and not to worry because I'll be looking after you for a while.'

'That's great,' said Alice. She looked exhausted and her speech slurred a little when she spoke.

'Only ... they're going into hiding, just in case the Inquisition tries to use them against me for rescuing you.'

Alice groaned and screwed up her face, obviously in a great deal of pain. Michael put a hand to her forehead.

'Is there anything I can get for you, Moo?'

'You haven't called me that in ages,' she said giving a

weak snort at the name. 'I'm so sorry I was such a cow to you, Spud.' When she blinked her eyes, her lids were slow to come up, as though she'd almost fallen asleep.

Something clicked in Michael's brain that took him back to his brief time with the Inquisition, and his eyes widened with realisation.

'Looks to me like you've got the Braxton Curse,' he said. 'How's the head?'

'Pounding like a jackhammer,' Alice replied. 'But at least I managed to sleep the whole night without Adam having to come and take care of me. What's the Braxton Curse?'

Michael told her about his first day at the academy and about the poison that he'd been fed without his knowledge. He explained about the week following the oath ceremony and the mysterious illness known as the Braxton Curse which had affected almost all of the House Solaris first years. Finally, he told his sister about the mishaps that had befallen his classmates as their talents manifested themselves in the following weeks.

'If I'm right, you're going to be out of action for a few more days, but you should start to feel better after that.'

'That's good,' said Alice sounding drowsy.

Michael rested a hand on her cheek for a moment and smiled. 'You get some rest now. I'll be by to check on you in a few hours.'

Just as he was about to get up, Alice reached out a hand and grabbed his arm lightly.

'I'm so glad you got to see Mum and Dad again, I really am,' she slurred.

'Me too,' said Michael tucking Steve in next to her under the blanket.

Pleased with himself that he'd managed to do something good for his sister, Michael decided that it was about time he dressed and went to find something to eat. After spending so much time barefoot on the cold floor, the feeling of warmth as he slipped his feet into his socks was heavenly. He hummed to himself as he tied his shoelaces, and even used his hairbrush as a microphone while he made himself presentable.

*Rocky start,* he thought. *But this is shaping up to be the best birthday ever!*

Practically dancing his way across the station, Michael snatched up a plate from the rack, spinning it between his palms before loading it with a full English, hoping that Mrs Lucas would let him get away without the grilled tomato, on account of the occasion. He knew that she thought the wrinkled fruit was the only healthy part of a meal like that, but he only ever ate them to please her. She and Andy went to so much effort to prepare the meal once a week that Michael wanted to show his appreciation by tasting every aspect of it. Thankfully, she smiled at him and let him off. Finding a spot away from the general hubbub, Michael sat and watched as the Davises helped to erect a line of trestle tables in preparation for a New Year's Day meal.

'Funny,' he chuckled to himself between mouthfuls of baked beans, 'they don't celebrate birthdays, but they always manage enough feasts.'

Just as he was about to question himself as to why that

413

might be, a commotion kicked up behind him and he saw the Davises begin to run towards the portal room. A piece of sausage halfway to his lips, Michael followed them, turning in his seat to watch as Anna limped through the door. Seeing the state of her, he dropped his fork immediately and ran.

One sleeve of her leather trench coat was torn at the shoulder, revealing a gouge so profuse with blood that Michael knew its severity instantly. Her lips and chin were stained with more blood from her newly crooked nose, and a gash in her trouser leg barely covered yet another deep rent. Ignoring the others, she limp-marched her way to her nephew and thrust an envelope into his chest.

'Bastards were watching the house,' she panted. 'They got me as I was coming back from the shop with your birthday cake.'

'How many?' Michael whispered, anger beginning to bubble inside him as he took the letter.

'Six,' Anna replied shrugging off Mrs Davis's attempts to patch her shoulder. 'There's no point going back, they only wanted to send you a message.'

Michael tore at the envelope and pulled at the note inside.

'What does it say?' asked Anna.

Michael's face reddened. 'It's just a few lines.'

'Well,' said Mrs Davis. 'Don't keep us in suspense; I've got to get Anna to the infirmary.'

'It says,' said Michael as he read the note aloud:

'*Michael,*
*For every one of mine you hurt,*
*I'm going to <u>kill</u> one of yours.*
*I'm coming for you.*
*Tamara Bloodgood,*
*Grand Inquisitor.'*

He knew what it meant. It wasn't intended simply as a threat to his own life. This was an announcement of far greater importance.

'It's the cull ...' said Michael to the assembly. 'They're coming!'

By day, G. J. Reilly is a teacher of (mostly) ICT in the South Wales valleys, where he lives with his long-suffering wife and 2.4 cats.

Having gained his degree, he spent ten years working in industry, before deciding to change career and head into education. In many ways, it is the vibrant young people that he teaches that have shaped the characters in his writing.

With an interest in high fantasy, contemporary fantasy and science fiction from a young age, it comes as no surprise that his first work falls into the young adult contemporary fantasy genre.

# Want to Know More?

Find out more about **Inquisitor – The Book of Jerrick – Part 1** and what happens next at:

## www.gjreilly.co.uk

There you'll find video trailers and news about Part 2 and the rest of the series.

Thank you for reading and see you there.

Printed in Great Britain
by Amazon